Christopher saw them start walking towards the bed slowly, continuing to mock him. He looked at the book, it was now or never. Whatever it was, if it was anything at all, it was all he had left. It was stupid to think that a book could be of use at a time like this, but what could it hurt? He looked at the book again. It had changed now, it said *Dante's Inferno*. Christopher almost laughed.

Filled with a painful mixture of hate and fear, Christopher opened the book.

The words 'THAT WAS A BAD IDEA' were written on the inside.

The words started to blur and shake like he was reading through an earthquake, and then the pain started.

ALSO BY ERIK LYND

NOVELS

Asylum

The Collection

THE HAND OF PERDITION SERIES:

Book and Blade

Eater of Souls

The Demon Collector

Rise of the Soulless

SILAS ROBB SERIES:

Silas Robb: Of Saints and Sinners

Silas Robb: Hell Hath No Fury

SHORTER WORKS

The Hanging Tree

Dark on the Water

His Devil

Dreams

Siege of the Bone Children

In the Pit

THE HAND OF PERDITION

BOOKS 1-3

ERIK LYND

BROKEN GODS PRESS

THE HAND OF PERDITION BOOKS 1-3
by Erik Lynd

Published 2018 by Broken Gods Press
www.brokengodspress.com
Cover design by Damonza Designs
ISBN-978-1-943069-14-9

For my family, both old and new.

BOOK AND BLADE

BOOK ONE OF THE HAND OF PERDITION

1

The Beast struggled to hold his entrails in as he stumbled through the underbrush just outside Hapensbury College. The irony of his recent evisceration was not lost on him.

He was weak. Weaker than he had ever been before. Blood seeped from multiple wounds, wounds that if made by any mortal weapon would have healed instantly. These wounds, however, had not been made with any mortal weapon. How the dark soul had obtained a Relic was a mystery.

Laughter brought him out of his dark reverie. Through the brush he could see a group of students walking down a path on the edge of the campus. The Beast hated the sound of laughter, it grated on him. Laughter was a distinctly human trait, which was all the more reason to kill them when his work allowed. But now, in his weakened state he sank lower into the underbrush. Though he was growing weak, it would be nothing to kill this group of mortal children. But he knew his end here was eminent, and he had little time for sport.

Like a primal instinct, the idea and need to find a successor rose up in him. The need had taken hold of him as soon as the thought entered his mind. He had never thought of having to pass along the gifts, let alone bequeath it to a mortal. Since the First Light on the First Day he had always been the Hunter.

When the group of college students passed, he stepped out onto the walking path. He pulled his long coat tighter about him to hide most of the carnage that was left of his body.

He sniffed the air looking, hunting for something. But all he smelled was youth, coddling, and weakness. He needed strength, viciousness, anger and around him walked kids to and from class, their biggest concerns: Am I ready for that history test? How will I write a whole philosophy paper in one night? Am I going to get laid tonight? Am I pregnant? Their petty thoughts disgusted him. But this town was all he had to work with.

He sat on a bench, trying to look inconspicuous, but suspected his seven-foot, blood splattered frame was anything but. He wove thoughts around him to make it easier for mortal eyes to slide past him. Then he waited. Watching each child as they walked by, smelling the scent of their blood, tracing it, following it back to its origin to the rest of the child's family. Mostly it led back to lawyers, business men, and doctors. Those that could afford to put silver spoons in these children's mouths. They could be ruthless in their own right, but not bloody. Not hunters.

He was beginning to think that he would expire right there on the bench before he could find what he was looking for, when he saw him. A boy, walking across campus, anger infusing him. The Beast searched the boy's bloodline and smiled. Yes, this would work just fine.

2

F*uck Professor Waynscott.* Christopher Sawyer thought. There was no way he deserved a D on that paper.

It was a beautiful early spring day. Sunlight, the first warmth since winter's chill, streamed through the oaks and elms that lined the main campus courtyard, dappling the ground with gray and black shadows. Squirrels scampered about in the trees.

It was all lost on Christopher. He stormed across campus, his sweater hood pulled tight against his face, the offending paper crumpled in his hands. He ignored the annoying squirrels and picturesque campus facade around him.

He had left class early. Once he had seen the grade, he hadn't wanted to stay and listen to the professor drone on and on. Christopher had actually worked hard on that paper. Anthro was the only class that was significantly below his B average, and he had thought this paper would give it a nice lift. Fat chance now with only a few weeks left in the semester. His dad was going to be pissed. His dad, the super crime fighting DA, who had aced college and law school, would never understand. It was all or nothing in his world, and Christopher fought all the time not to be on the nothing side of it.

It didn't help his case that he was in his third year and still hadn't decided on a major. His father had known from high school what he wanted to do with his life and was continually disappointed that Christopher did not share a similar sense of direction and inevitability. But the only thing Christopher feared more than his dad was the idea of being locked into any one choice for the rest of his life.

The exception being Courtney.

In the middle of the courtyard he paused and then abruptly turned. He had been on his way back to his dorm room, but now he decided he needed to see Courtney. She wouldn't have answers, but she'd be there for him, someone to vent to. After all, that is part of a fiancé's job.

He rounded the corner of Babbet Hall and headed up the stairs to the front door to join the flow of students streaming in and out. Hapensbury College was a coed college and recently had made the dorms themselves coed. But old habits die hard, and while the floors were segregated and though he had been here a thousand times, he still received the accusing stare from some of the girls as he walked down the hall. He ignored them, anger and anxiety clouding his thoughts.

He didn't bother knocking on Courtney's door. Normally he would out of deference for her roommate, but he was angry and common courtesy was not in the forefront of his mind.

In retrospect, he should have knocked.

His mouth started speaking, while his mind, uncomprehending, took in the scene.

"Guess what just..." Christopher started, but stopped abruptly.

Courtney was there, but so was another guy and they were both in bed, apparently naked from what exposed flesh Christopher could take in. Her long blond hair slightly messed. Sex hair. It splashed against her creamy white skin.

She spun in the bed towards the door, eyes wide with surprise. Christopher found his voice again.

"What the fuck!"

Anger reared up in him full force. The day had built it up, but this, this stunning, horrible vision ignited it.

"Chris?" Courtney asked. "What are you doing here?"

She was cut off as the other guy in the bed sat up abruptly, the movement pushing her off the double bed. With his face no longer hidden Christopher recognized him immediately. Jeremy. Besides Courtney, Jeremy was the closest thing to a best friend he had here.

"Shit dude," Jeremy said. "You weren't supposed to find out like this."

"No shit?" Christopher asked.

"You were supposed to still be in class," Courtney said, as though that was a good enough reason to be fucking his friend.

He trembled with rage and embarrassment. He wanted to fly at Jeremy, maybe even Courtney, with fists flying. Jeremy, however, was much bigger than Christopher. It wouldn't be much of a fight, and Christopher would end up even more humiliated than he already was. So he did the only thing he could. He turned and left the room.

"Chris!" Courtney called after him.

He could hear her scrambling to get up and try to catch him before he left, but he ignored her. His impotent rage burned through him, and he could already feel the tears welling up. He quickly walked down the hall, shoving past other students. It felt like they were all looking at him. He could feel their pity, maybe even laughter, chasing after him as he moved faster and faster out of the building.

He still couldn't fully get his mind around what happened. He never expected it. He and Courtney were perfect for each other. They even did that annoying thing of finishing each other's sentences.

He was halfway across campus before Courtney caught up with him. She had managed to throw some sweats on, and it tore Christopher's heart that he still thought she looked beautiful.

"Jesus Christ, Chris. You were supposed to be in class. You didn't even knock," Courtney said.

"Really? My fault I interrupted your fuck fest. Next time just hang a sock on the door so I know someone is fucking my fiancé."

"It's not like that..." she drifted off unsure what to say next.

"Sure as hell looked exactly like that to me. What the fuck Courtney? We, we've been together since high school. I've never loved anyone else. Hell, I've never even been with anyone else."

"That's just it Chris. Don't you see? We were high school sweethearts. You were my first kiss. My first, well, everything."

"Well I sure as hell wasn't your last," Christopher said.

She ignored him.

"High school was such a small world. Now we're in the bigger world, and I needed to explore."

"So you explored Jeremy? What the fuck? The least you could have done was find someone I didn't know for your expedition into the great unknown."

"I didn't pick Jeremy on purpose. It just sort of happened. But don't you see? This is your time to spend time with other people and find someone."

"I didn't need to explore," Christopher said. "I had found the one I wanted. I was one of the lucky ones. I found the perfect person right away."

Courtney looked down, tears leaking from her eyes.

"I never meant to hurt you," she whispered.

He wanted to soften, to hold her and say it would be okay, but then he thought of Jeremy with her in that bed and he knew he couldn't.

"Yes you did. You knew damn well how this would turn out, but you chose it anyway," he said.

He turned abruptly from her and headed toward his own dorm. It was across campus and a mirror image of Courtney's. Moments later he stood just inside the front door where he stopped. He suddenly had no desire to head up to his room. He would see too many people he knew, and he was in no mood to deal with smiling faces and good natured shit-talking from the guys on his floor. Tears still threatened to show up at any minute, and that was the last thing he wanted them to see. Besides, at some point Jeremy would be there, and he would have to deal with that.

But not right now. He turned to the stairs and headed down to the basement. He was not sure why, it was just where his feet were taking him. Although it was as good a place as any to be alone, very few people would be down there. It was mostly used for storage. There was a large garage that many of the students used to store bikes and an old laundry room that hadn't been used since washer and dryers were installed on each floor. There was also an old boiler room that was no longer in use which now served as the janitor's office. Christopher had been there on occasion to borrow cleaning supplies for spills in his own room.

This office is where he was now heading, albeit subconsciously. He didn't care where he ended up, he just had to get away from people for a while. The tears were already spilling over as he made his way down the hall to the old boiler room. He just hoped the janitor was not in.

He wasn't. Christopher opened the door carefully just in case.

Once he was satisfied he was alone, he shut the door behind him and fell into the old metal chair behind the desk.

It was an ancient boiler room, probably close to 100 years old. Several large boilers dominated the room with a maze of pipes leading to and from them. There were enough dials and valves to be a steampunk fan's dream. The pipes themselves looked ancient and rusted, some bent and twisted out of shape. Green and brown paint peeled from the wall while scum, and maybe even mold, climbed the walls. It looked like something out of a horror movie.

A part of Christopher's mind sensed there was something wrong with that. The couple of times he had been down here it had looked old, but not abandoned. There shouldn't have been this strong sense of decay and corruption. But mostly he ignored it as he focused on what had just happened. He put his head in his hands and let the tears flow.

"Boy."

The voice startled him, made him jerk in the chair and he had to steady himself with the desk. It was a dark voice full of gravel and melancholy undertones. Christopher didn't know why, but it conjured up images of violence and pain in his mind. It came from the shadows toward the back of the boiler room. Christopher leapt out of the chair and spun around.

"Boy, I need to talk to you," said the voice from the shadows.

It definitely wasn't the old janitor. This voice held too much strength and power. Christopher tried to see into the shadow, to pierce the darkness with his eyesight, but it was murky in the glow of the overhead lights. Christopher subconsciously moved around the desk keeping it between him and the voice. This also kept the door at his back. He inched towards it.

"I know you want to run, but we need to talk. Many lives depend on it," said the voice.

Christopher saw movement then. A shifting of the shadows.

The figure was a man, but low to the ground, like he was crawling or leaning against the wall.

"Do you need help? I can get you help."

Christopher moved to the door. Just before his hand reached the knob, he heard a creak come from the wood, like something had just tightened around it. He tried the handle, but it wouldn't budge—not even a little give, as if it was suddenly made of concrete.

"I can't let you leave just yet, but don't worry. I will not kill you."

The panic that had been growing in Christopher turned to full terror at those last words. He began banging on the door, but it was like banging on concrete, muffled and painful.

"Help! I'm in the boiler room! Please, there is something in here!" He cried, but even as he did, he could hear his pleas bouncing off the door in front of him, muffled like his blows.

"BOY!"

The voice was now a shout, a voice of command. It sent terror like ice up Christopher's spine. He spun around, his back against the unmoving door.

He heard a scratching, followed by rustling and a wet sound like moist pasta spilling out of the bowl. The thing was moving. From the darkness Christopher saw it materializing as it crawled out of the shadows. It was man-shaped, dragging itself out of the dark. It clutched at its stomach, blood dripping from the pieces of entrails that poked out past its hand. The thing looked up out of the dark and stared directly at Christopher.

And Christopher knew he was staring at the Devil.

3

Christopher could not speak, his throat had closed up. He could not scream, although he wanted to. He did not know exactly what this man was, dying on the floor, but he knew it was not normal. This man was not human. It wore a long, black coat and old, slightly anachronistic, clothes. They were stained with the creature's own blood and guts. Its long hair hung loose and greasy across its eyes. Its face was pale and gaunt. Christopher imagined it was the face a corpse wore just before rot set in.

"I need you to deliver a message for me to your father," the Beast said.

His father? This thing knew who he was? The idea that this man had dealings with his father jarred him out of the paralyzing fear he was in.

"How... how do you know my father? Did he put you in prison?"

"No. Any bars around me are of my own making," the Beast said. "I see your father in you, in your past. I have a... gift, so to speak, to see the bloodlines of people, to understand their history and the make-up of their character."

"So you know what my dad does for a living?"

"Yes, that is I know he hunts. That he is relentless and stops at nothing. The details remain fuzzy."

Christopher almost smiled in relief. Almost. There was some mistake, his father was not a hunter.

"My dad is a district attorney. He is dedicated, but he lives in the city, not the forest. I'm pretty sure he's never even held a rifle," Christopher said.

The thing looked at Christopher with those dark, almost dead eyes and for a moment Christopher thought the man was going to smile.

"I did not say what he hunted. He is a hunter of men, and that will be of use to me," the Beast rumbled.

"Look, I think you might have the wrong guy, or the wrong idea about my dad. He goes after criminals and is an ass at the best of times, but he is no 'hunter of men' as you put..."

"Quiet boy!"

Christopher abruptly closed his mouth. The fear was back.

"I need you to listen. I don't have much time left, and you are the only choice I have," the thing said. It pulled itself closer into the light, and for the first time Christopher got a good look at it.

It looked like a man, but Christopher was still reluctant to refer to it as human. It was injured, severely. Many lacerations crisscrossed its body, leaving tears in its clothes and bleeding, rent flesh. Part of its intestines spilled out into his lap. Not only was this thing dying, it should already have been dead.

"How did you do that thing with the door?" Christopher asked when it had settled itself again against the wall.

"No time for that," the thing said, "I need you to listen closely. I don't care if you believe me or not, your belief is of little consequence, but you must listen and you must remember."

It paused and dug through the pockets of its trench coat and pulled out a small book that looked like a journal and a pocket knife. It tossed the objects onto the ground between them. The effort alone seemed to make even more blood seep out of its wounds. It was now surrounded by a red pool of its own blood.

"Hell, amongst other things, is a prison for the dark souls that populate the world. Dark souls like the ones your father condemns to prisons here in your world. And, like here, sometimes those dark souls escape from Hell. It is rare, but it does happen."

Christopher once again tried to push at the door. It was talking about Hell now? Whatever this thing was, it was bat-shit crazy too.

"I do not speak of your average bad guy. The dark souls that escape from the inescapable are powerful and corrupt beings. It is not the Adolf Hitler's of the world that I speak of, it is those who whispered in his ear and guided him in his mission. They are not the mass murderers you hear about on TV, although they have all killed in great numbers. No, it is the truly evil that I am speaking of.

"One of the tasks of the Devil—Satan—whatever you want to call it, is to collect these dark souls when they escape. That is... was my task. I am the hunter aspect of the Devil."

"You are the Devil?" Christopher asked. *Yeah, this guy is nuts.* But the thought didn't lessen the fear washing over him.

"Again, I do not care that you believe me. You are only a tool to carry my message."

It shifted, wincing in pain as it leaned back against the wall.

"I am dying. The last dark soul I was retrieving had a weapon I did not expect. I cannot be killed easily, in fact, I never have been. I have existed since the beginning of humanity's reign on this planet. I have been hurt, slowed, even evaded for a time, but never have I known death. But this dark soul had found a Relic, a weapon, that has done this to me."

He coughed then, blood splattering from his lips.

"It never occurred to me that I would need a successor. I should be forever, but at least this embodiment of me is at an end. Unfortunately, that means I must pass my job on to a mortal. No human is truly equipped to take on this job, but that is not a problem that can be solved.

"You must take this book and this weapon to your father. I see in him the strength to take on this job. When he begins to read the book, the power of this position will be his. Make sure he understands what I am telling you. He may not believe at first, but make sure he understands. Once he reads the book, there is no going back."

"Make him understand? I don't even understand," Christopher said. "What is in that book?"

"It is the Book of Knowledge. It contains all knowledge that exists," the thing said.

"Looks a little small to be so thorough," Christopher said, a little amazed he had the calmness to quip.

"This book, the Weapon, they become what they need to be, when they need to be it. The book opens doors to all knowledge. Most mortals could never begin to fathom its depths."

"So then reading this book will make him like you?"

The thing looked at him sharply. Christopher paled under the scrutiny.

"No, not like me. His is mortal and it will be different. But he will be bound to this job, this purpose. I don't know what will really happen. Like I said, a mortal has never held this office. Your father is the best I could find in the time I have."

The thing seemed to pull itself a little deeper into the shadows —or the shadows moved forward to surround it.

"Take my message and these two objects to your father. Explain the best you can, but he must take this job. If the dark souls are allowed to run free, they will bring hell to earth. Because," it leaned forward again, its soulless eyes holding Christopher's, "humanity's capacity for evil is far greater than anything the Devil could cook up."

A sudden click behind him made Christopher jump. The door to the boiler room opened with a creak. Whatever force had been holding it was gone. Christopher surprised himself by not running out the door immediately. Instead he took a cautious step forward, although every fiber of his body told him to run from this mad thing. He picked up the book and pocket knife. His hands stretched out, keeping as far from the creature as possible, ready to spring back at the slightest movement from the shadow-shape. He couldn't help but ask one last question.

"What happens if he doesn't read the book or want this job?" Christopher was not sure why he asked. He didn't believe this shit for a second, but something weird was going on and he wanted to have all his bases covered.

"Then boy, throw this Book and Weapon as far out into the ocean as you can. And pray it isn't in your lifetime that the world goes to hell."

At that the thing started coughing again, spraying more blood. The sudden noise startled Christopher, and he sprang to the door like a spring releasing its tension. He was halfway through the door when the voice of the thing stopped him.

"Don't tell anyone I am down here. There is no need and it would not go well for anybody else finding me down here. I will be gone soon. And boy, whatever you do, don't read the book. I doubt you'll be tempted, but it is not meant for you. You are too weak for this."

Christopher left the boiler room at a run and didn't stop until he was back in his own room four floors up.

4

Two weeks later Christopher was on a train out of Boston, the meeting with the Beast in the basement all but forgotten. If he had been asked about it, he would have remembered—remembered it clearly in fact. But without a reminder it just seemed to slip into the back of his mind. It was as if some slippery substance sat on the memory and slid it just out of notice beneath his everyday thoughts and growing anxiety of seeing his dad.

For the past weeks he had ignored the attempts by Courtney to get ahold of him. Even to the point of hiding quietly in his room while she banged on the door, demanding that he answer. He hid because he did not have the strength to deal with her. He didn't want it to be over and if he avoided her, he did not have to admit to himself that it was. He did not want to talk to her about her seeing other guys or assuring each other that they could still be friends. He didn't want this new situation, he wanted things back to normal. As long as they didn't 'talk about it, part of him thought it would remain the same. So he hid from her and he hid from just about everyone for those last two weeks before heading home for spring break.

A girl sat across the aisle and a few rows up from him. He had seen her when he came in. She was pretty with dark black hair, a large tattoo across her neck and more piercings than he could count. She glanced back at him once, a look of surprise on her face, or possibly confusion. He thought maybe she had thought he was someone else.

He didn't think too much of it, Courtney was on his mind. He had planned on heading home with Courtney, maybe even taking her to the coast for a couple of days. But now here he sat alone on an almost empty train car, hood pulled over his head, ear buds nestled in his ears pumping out indie rock as he stared out the window at scenery he had seen a thousand times. The music and motion of the car had almost lulled him to sleep.

He did not see the man step into his car. He didn't see the man look around briefly and then, after spotting Christopher, start walking down the aisle, hand sliding into his leather jacket. Christopher did not look up to see the man slip a gun from that jacket. But he did hear the scream.

"Terrorist!" screamed a man, standing up from his seat. "He has a gun!"

Christopher looked up in time to see the man in the aisle hesitate at the screaming business man pointing at him. The other passengers in the car jumped up and after a moment of confusion, chaos erupted as passengers began running and screaming.

Christopher's eyes met the man's, and Christopher knew instantly the man was looking for him. The gun began to rise. Christopher threw himself into the aisle and ran for the back door. He had only gone a few steps and almost reached the door when a gunshot, followed by an explosion of pain in his left shoulder, spun him around violently.

"Freeze, police!" cried another man who had just stepped in, pistol raised, from the forward car.

The gunman ignored him and raised his gun for a second shot, this one aimed at Christopher's head. Numb, Christopher hooked his hand in the door and forced it open. But he was too late. He didn't hear the second gunshot and only felt the searing pain in his head for a brief moment as he fell through the open door and into darkness.

5

Christopher woke slowly, clawing his way out of unconsciousness and dreams. Dreams where he ran down endless library stacks chased by a dark hooded figure. He looked for a book that would save him and banish this demon pursuing him. But now consciousness beckoned and he raced towards it, expecting at any moment to feel the hand of the demon on him, pulling him back.

His eyes opened to a burst of light and dull white ceiling tile. He lay in a hospital bed, various wires connected him to a machine by the side of the bed. The machine made an occasional pinging noise. Thin tubes of oxygen wrapped around his head and uncomfortably into his nose. He looked at the IV line against the back of his hand, trying to piece together what had happened.

Then he remembered the man on the train, the gunshot. He tried to lift his left hand, but a stab of pain in his upper arm and the sling around it stopped him. With his IV hand, he carefully felt around his head and discovered gauze bandages just above his left ear. He remembered getting hit in the arm, he must have gotten shot in the head also. Since he was still alive, it must have just grazed him.

The room was empty. No family or friends. He found the remote control on the bed and pressed the nurse call button. Seconds later a nurse walked in. Behind her, in the doorway, Christopher thought he saw a man in a police uniform.

"Sleeping beauty awakes," she said and immediately began checking all the machines attached to him, "How are you feeling?"

"I'm not sure," Christopher mumbled, his lips unused to moving.

"It's okay to feel confused, that's perfectly normal. The doctor will be in here any second."

"Why is there a cop outside the door?"

He saw her hesitate for a fraction of a second. "I'll let the doctor or police explain that to you. As far as I know you are just a special patient."

Even in his confused state, he could sense that she wasn't telling him everything.

"How long have I been unconscious?"

"Three days."

She put a cuff around his ankle to take his blood pressure. The door opened and an older man, the doctor, came in. Just behind him a man in a slightly rumpled suit came in. He screamed cop.

"Hello, Christopher. I am Dr. Wilson. How are you feeling?" The doctor asked.

"Fine, I think. What happened? How did I end up here?"

"What's the last thing you remember?" the man Christopher thought was a cop asked.

"Excuse me detective," the doctor interrupted, "but I need to ask you to wait until I have finished my exam before you start with the questions."

"Of course Doctor," the detective said and stepped back.

The doctor did his exam, flashing a light in Christopher's eyes and asking him a series of questions obviously designed to gauge his state of mind. He checked the dressing and seem satisfied with everything. He told the nurse to take Christopher off the oxygen and prescribed more medication. Christopher hoped it was pain medication, now that he was awake his shoulder was starting to ache.

"Well Christopher, you are a lucky guy. Both gunshots wounds were fairly superficial and should heal nicely. The head shot was the only thing that was really worrying us, but now that you're awake, I think recovery should be fairly quick."

He turned to the detective.

"We'll need to keep him for at least a week, probably two to keep an eye on the wounds in his shoulder and head." To Christopher he said, "Everything looks great and the nurse here will make sure you get some painkillers. The detective here would like to ask you a few questions, but it's totally up to you." He gave the detective a meaningful glance. "The moment you're too tired let him know and he'll leave."

"I hear you doctor. I'm here to help the kid, not hurt him," the detective said.

The doctor gave him one more meaningful look and then nodded to the nurse. They left with one last smile at Christopher.

"Christopher, I'm Detective Hamlin with the NYPD. I need to ask you a few questions about what happened on the train."

"I have some questions too, like what happened? Why did someone try to kill me? Why is there a cop outside my door?"

"And I will try to answer some of your questions, but first I have some for you. Before the incident on the train, did you have any unusual confrontations with any strangers? Did you think you were being watched or maybe even followed?"

Now the conversation with the thing in the basement jumped

forward from the back of his mind. But Christopher didn't think the detective was referring to that. Something told him this wasn't the time to bring it up.

"No, nothing that I noticed."

"Did your father speak to you about anything? Anything unusual? Did he call or try to get a message to you?"

"No, I haven't talked to him for a while. The other day I sent an email with the train number I was taking so he could pick me up. Where is he by the way? Or my mom? I would think that at least one of them would have come around while I was here." He and his father had their problems, but he would like to think that somebody from the family would have stayed with him. It didn't make sense. Unless they were being kept out in the lobby while the detective was here.

"What was the last thing you remember?" Hamlin asked.

"I was on the train. I heard somebody scream and I looked up. This guy was standing there with a gun and he was pointing it at me. I tried to run, but he shot me in the arm and then the head. Then everything went dark. I have no idea who the dude was or why he was shooting at me. Must have been a nut."

"He wasn't a nut, at least not in the way you mean. He was looking for you. His name is Karl Abeln. He is a suspected hitman in the employ of Ambros Falk. He's a bigwig in organized crime here in the city."

This shocked Christopher, "Why was he after me? I'm just a college kid..." He trailed off. His father.

"It's because of my dad, isn't it? It has to be. They went after me to get to him."

The detective sighed and looked down.

"Yeah, it was because of your father, but not because they were trying to get to him. They already had."

It took a second for it to sink in, but the look in the detective's eyes made the meaning clear. It suddenly made horrible sense. Why his dad wasn't here by his side.

"He's...my...he's dead? My father is dead?"

The detective nodded. "Your father, Mathew Sawyer, was murdered the same day you were attacked. They were trying to kill you to set an example."

Christopher could barely hear him. The world he had just woken up to moments ago was closing in on him. It was surreal. The idea that his father was dead couldn't really register. It had no meaning for him, the concept was too foreign for his mind to wrap itself around. It took a moment for him to realize Hamlin was still talking.

"...wanted the authorities to know that you don't go after him. If he can get to a DA's family, imagine how easy it would be for him to kill a beat cop or detective's family. He's trying to make some of us cops think twice."

"His family? Does that mean my mother also? My sister?" Christopher asked.

Hamlin nodded his head slowly.

"Yes Christopher, they came to your family's home and got everybody. I am sorry, but your mother and sister are also dead."

There was a rushing sound in his ears that throbbed to his heartbeat. He leaned back and stared up at the ceiling. None of this seemed real. How could it? Everything gone—no, taken. It was hard for him to think, to anchor his thoughts. It seemed like the world was spinning out of control.

"Christopher, I have something else to tell you. I don't want to, but you will hear about it in the news anyway, and I guess it is best to come now. There was evidence that both your mother and sister were sexually assaulted before they were murdered."

It was too much for him. He couldn't listen anymore, his mind snapped. It was as though he couldn't quite grasp what Hamlin was saying. Darkness surged up around him and he felt himself sliding back into unconsciousness. Faintly he heard Hamlin calling out over the suddenly frantic beeping of the machines around him.

"Oh shit. Doc! Doc! We're losing him again. We need..."

The rest was lost to the darkness.

6

Just one week later the doctor proclaimed Christopher sufficiently recovered to be released the next day. For Christopher those days had passed slowly as he sunk into a dark malaise. His father's attorney had come to visit him several days after he had awakened. He told Christopher that he was the only surviving heir and the entire estate would go to him. Probate would be straight forward and simple, but it would still take a couple of months. Until then he could stay in the family home. After, he could sell or keep it as he desired.

His father hadn't always been a DA. For a while he had been a high-priced defense attorney, and even after finding his calling to go after the criminals rather than protect them, he had invested wisely. So the estate was not trivial. In fact, Christopher never had to work again if he chose, nor did he have to continue school for that matter. But he thought of none of that now. He nodded his understanding to the attorney more to get him to leave than to indicate he was paying any attention.

He had been in shock for most of the past week, numb to most things. Still ignoring calls from Courtney. He couldn't talk to her. Mostly because he couldn't bear it if the only reason was to tell him how sorry she was for what happened to his parents. He knew she wouldn't be calling to ask him to come back.

Detective Hamlin had stopped by to let him know that they would station someone outside his home for protection. Nobody knew for sure how long he might be in danger, but eventually they would capture this Ambros Falk. Either that, or he might decide that getting to Christopher was more trouble than it was worth and let it go.

"Yeah he already killed everyone else in the family. I think that sent a message pretty clearly. Is one last kid worth troubling over?" Christopher said to Hamlin the night before he was to be released.

Hamlin looked down, not knowing how to respond. "Well it has made getting the evidence harder. We had some leads, but they dried up quick. It appears to us that he is consolidating his power all of a sudden, taking over more things outside his territory. But we have no proof of anything. Everyone is just holding back info."

"So what you're telling me is that everybody is running scared of him? Even you cops?" Christopher tried to keep the anger out of his voice, but he couldn't. He had changed, he realized. A part of him had changed over this last week. Every time he thought about how he wouldn't hug his mother again or get the occasional smile out of his father or laugh out loud with his sister when they stayed up late at night to watch a stupid movie another piece of him seemed to die a little. Bitter emptiness was all that was left.

Hamlin stiffened but nodded. "Yes Ambros has a lot of power right now, but you might want to change the attitude. We're the best chance you've got of getting justice for your family."

Justice? Did he want justice? This need growing deep down

inside of Christopher might be called justice, but he suspected it had another name.

"I'll be going now. But Officer Cooper is stationed right outside your door, and we have several other officers throughout the floor. Actually, I think Cooper's a little disappointed you're out tomorrow. He's new and these hospital assignments are pretty cake."

Hamlin left, and Christopher stood up and looked out the window. He had a private room, one of the benefits of having a psychopath trying to kill you. He stood by the window a long time watching the lights of the traffic through the dark and the streaks of rain on the glass.

Over time he became aware of a sound. It was very subtle, almost as though it was subconscious. But once he became aware of it, he realized he had been hearing it for a while. It was a droning that became a buzzing. At first Christopher thought it might be a hospital machine, but most of those had been removed from his room and if it was coming from next door, it had to be one damn big machine. No, it wasn't a machine. He tried to ignore it, but now that he'd heard, it seemed to be more instant, pulling at his attention. After a moment he noticed something strange about the noise. It didn't seem to be a noise at all, it started to sound more like a voice. Like something trying to talk to him.

As he focused on it, words began to take form. Quietly at first, but then at a level he could almost start to make them out. It was like people talking in another room. You knew they were talking and could hear voices, but it was just muffled enough that you couldn't make out the words. Christopher strained to hear the voices. It was like trying to hear the last whisper of a dying man. Something told Christopher that this was important, that his life depended on understanding the words.

He heard a noise by the door. He spun, his nerves suddenly frayed, to see the officer standing in the doorway.

"Everything okay?" Officer Cooper asked.

Don't trust him!

The voice suddenly screamed in Christopher's head. Christopher stumbled forward, startled at the loud voice. Cooper moved forward to catch him. Christopher threw up his hands.

"No! No, I'm just fine. Just got dizzy for a second."

"You should lie down and rest," Officer Cooper said.

"Yeah, you're probably right," Christopher said, but made no move to the bed.

"Don't worry, I'll be just outside the door," Cooper said and left the room.

Christopher could feel tension in the air, adrenaline was roaring through him. He wanted to run. His legs vibrated, but he had nowhere to go. Part of him thought he should question the voice. He still heard it, or rather, felt it at the back of his head. It was faint, like mumbling.

Why should he not trust a cop? Was this Cooper in on it? Was he working with this Ambros? Hamlin had said he was new. Perhaps he's just waiting until late tonight when the place clears out. Christopher could feel it, not just the voice in his head. He could feel the wrongness of this cop outside his door. It was like this voice had just pointed out something obvious that for some reason Christopher had been unable to see. But now what was he going to do about it?

He looked out the window. The roof of the adjacent building was about one story below him. *Really*? Was he actually thinking about jumping out of a window? His eyes caught the phone on the table by the bed. He could call the police, but then who could he trust? If there was something going on with the guy outside his door—and he could not shake that cold certainty that there was—then he couldn't trust any cop. Maybe Hamlin? There was no bad vibe from him, but he wasn't here and Christopher wasn't sure how to get ahold of him without calling the police. Besides the only evidence he had was the voice in his head, and he did not think that would go over very well with the police.

He went to his closet and found his pants and shirt. His shirt still had the hole from the gunshot in it. He slipped on his pants and shoes on as quickly as he could, which was tricky with one arm in a sling. There was no way he could get his shirt on, so he settled for wearing his sweatshirt stretched over his sling, but it worked when he zipped it up. He pulled the hood up out of habit. Now all he had to do was jump out of the window.

He pushed open the window and leaned out for a look. It was a standard rooftop. He saw what looked like a rooftop access shack a hundred feet away. He could only guess an access door was on the other side. But of course there was no reason for it to be open. This wasn't a movie. How the hell was he going to get off the roof? He was beginning to think this was a bad idea when the door opened again behind him.

Cooper was standing there. He looked surprised for a moment, but quickly recovered and reached for his gun. Christopher jumped.

He landed hard and stumbled to the ground twisting so he fell on his good shoulder. He bounced up as quickly as he could, but his bad shoulder screamed in protest. He sprinted to the shack not taking the time to look up at this room. Cooper would be at the window in seconds. He felt exposed and expected at any moment to feel a bullet in his back. Just a few feet away from the wall he heard the report of the pistol. A piece of roof nicked his leg as a bullet hit inches from his foot. Christopher threw himself around the corner putting the rooftop shack between him and Cooper, but not before he looked back. Cooper was climbing out of the window.

He didn't wait to see if Cooper made it to the ground. There was a door on this side. It looked like it hadn't closed all the way, like the last person to use it hadn't been paying attention. It opened easily and Christopher ran through it, making sure it shut and locked behind him.

He was shivering with fear as he made his way down the stairs. Halfway down the second flight he heard Cooper banging at the door, trying to open it. He took the last few steps jumping three at a time.

He lurched out the door at the bottom of the stairs and into the hallway, surprising an orderly. Behind him he heard a muffled bang and knew that Cooper had found a way through the door. Might have even shot it open. Christopher didn't miss a beat as he ran down the hall looking for a way out. His shoulder ached, but he didn't have time to think about that now. He shoved passed a family gathered around a boy in a wheelchair to get to the elevator, mumbling "Sorry," as he dove into the elevator car and pushed the ground floor button repeatedly. As the doors to the elevator closed Cooper came through the door. Christopher saw him looking around. Christopher crouched lower behind the family, ignoring their odd stares, until then the doors closed and the elevator started going down.

Christopher knew he had only bought himself moments. Cooper would figure out where he had gone and take the stairs. As soon the elevator's doors opened he shoved past the family and out into the lobby. He had banged his shoulder a couple of times and it was on fire. It felt like a hammer pounded inside his skull. He was running scared, but he knew he had to keep moving. He ran through the lobby doors and into the night beyond.

Twenty feet away from the hospital entrance he paused. He realized he had no idea where he was headed. Getting out of the building had been his only plan. After a moment's thought he realized his decision was made for him. He had nothing, so he had to make his way home. His wallet, phone, everything was there. Hamlin had told him they had taken his bags from the train to his family's... his house while he was in a coma. Of course that's also where the guy trying to kill him will expect him to go. Either way he couldn't stay standing in the middle of the hospital driveway. He ran off through the exit and under the Broadway Bridge trying his best not to jostle his shoulder too badly.

He decided he needed to get ahold of Hamlin. Let him know that he was heading home. It was a risk, but he had to trust somebody. This was not the kind of situation you can handle by yourself. And it wasn't like he didn't have proof now.

He walked a block down the street to a diner. He looked back a couple of times, but didn't see Cooper following him. Inside, despite the way he looked and the odd looks he got, they let him use their phone for a local call. In a few moments he was connected to Hamlin.

"This is Detective Hamlin."

"Your boy Cooper just tried to kill me," Christopher said.

"Christopher! Is that you? What the hell happened? I just got a call saying shots were fired at the hospital."

"Like I said, Cooper just tried to kill me. I had to jump out of the window and run over the roof."

"Where are you? Are you safe? I can send a car to pick you up," Hamlin said.

"Fuck that, I barely trust you at this point let alone random patrolmen. Did someone get Cooper?"

"Not yet, there is still a lot of confusion on what happened and nobody can find him. Look, we need to talk."

"Yeah," said Christopher, "but I can't stay here. And I have to at least stop by my house, I don't have any money or ID. I'll grab a cab. You be waiting outside my place so you can pay the driver."

Christopher hung up the phone and then asked the counter

girl for the number to a cab company. Five minutes later he was in the back of a cab heading to his parents' house—his house now. His shoulder hurt, he was freezing in the cool night air and he was heading into what might be a trap. He was scared as hell. What the hell had happened to him? How did this happen? It was like something out of a bad movie.

It all started the day he had met that thing in the basement of the school dorm. The memory suddenly became clear to him, like it had just been waiting for the right moment. He remembered everything. The crazy story, the book, the pocket knife. The memory made him shudder. Looks like he wouldn't be able to help whatever was in that basement, his father was dead now. But that thought gave him no relief. He felt as if the thing's mission still lay heavily on him.

7

Christopher had the cab drive slowly past the house. He saw a parked car out front, but he could also see Hamlin in the front waiting. Nothing else seemed off or out of place. Still, Christopher crouched behind the cab door and took a long moment to see if anything was amiss. After he had satisfied himself that everything seemed normal, he had the cab pull over. Hamlin paid the driver and they went into the house.

Hamlin went in first with gun drawn. He told Christopher he needed to clear the house and make sure there were no surprises waiting for them. Christopher waited inside the foyer as Hamlin cleared the home. The detective went slowly and meticulously through each room, finally arriving back at the entrance to tell him it was all clear. In the living room with the shades drawn Christopher quickly told him everything about that night.

"Just to be clear," Hamlin said, "Cooper was new to me, and I had no idea he was on Ambros' payroll, but you got to understand not all cops are corrupt like that, not even most cops. You got to trust us to make this right."

"I'm talking to you aren't I? I can't survive this on my own, so I knew I had to trust somebody."

"I can get a couple of guys stationed out here to protect you," Hamlin said and held up his hands before Christopher could protest. "These are guys I have known for years. I'll talk to some captains and get them reassigned. If you trust me, then you can trust them."

Christopher leaned back in his chair and rubbed his eyes.

"While you make your calls I need to go find some ibuprofen."

Christopher went to the upstairs bathroom. Whoever had brought his bags had left them in the entrance way. He grabbed them as he headed up. The brownstone was a nice home with rich wood accents and dark hardwood floors. High ceilings and crown molding highlighted every room. His father had always wanted everything to be in tip top shape and maintained the house as he did everything in life, impeccably. His family had died here. No, had been murdered here. Walking through the house now he felt like a stranger, like he was disturbing something. He imagined it might be what one felt like walking through a mausoleum by themselves. He did not think he would be able to stay here for very long.

He dropped his bags in his bedroom then hunted for painkillers in the bathroom. After lucking out and finding some Vicodin left over from his mother's dental surgery, he went back into his room and dumped the backpack on his bed.

Amongst the half-complete school papers that may now never be complete, gum and an unopened Red Bull can, the book and pocket knife fell out onto the bed. As soon as he saw them the fear he had felt in the boiler room came back, the memory of the intense stare, the blood seeping out of the creature's stomach between its fingers. Why hadn't he told anybody? He couldn't think of a good reason, just like he couldn't think of a reason why he had ignored it for the past couple of weeks. Nobody found that dying thing in the boiler room. Maybe it didn't die? Maybe it would come for the book and knife now that his father was dead? The thought of that creature coming to this house to collect his things scared him more than having another one of Ambros' hitman come after him.

He picked up the knife. It was a simple Swiss Army knife, with a bottle opener and screwdriver as well as many other features. Nothing remarkable. He pulled the blade out, and somehow accidentally cut himself. It was a shallow cut. He had lost his grip and it twisted in his hand and like a snake biting, it cut him. It was a shallow cut, but it was enough for him to yelp and drop the knife onto the bed. He examined the wound. Blood welled up in it, but only a little. He stuck his thumb in his mouth.

As he sucked on the wound he became aware once again of the voice in the back of his head. The background mumbling became more insistent. He looked down at the book and realized that although the voice was in the back of his head, he felt a sudden certainty that the voice was coming from that book. Without even realizing he had picked it up, it was in his hands. He rubbed the cover gently, it seemed like his senses were stronger, and the feel of the book more intense—as if the book was more real than everything else around him, the only important thing left.

He remembered the warning the thing had given him, to not read the book, that doing so would do something to him, something that he was not meant for. He was too weak, it had told him. But there was a need inside of him and it was growing. He couldn't describe it, just something said he should do it. Something in him that needed this tool to make things right.

But nothing could be made right again. His mother was dead, his father, everyone that was important to him was lost, even Courtney. No, no book can make things like that right. It was just a stupid book and pocket knife given to him by a crazy, albeit creepy, man.

Still his fingers gently scratched at the edge of the cover as though they might open it of their own accord. Perhaps just a quick look? Maybe just check the table of contents? What could that hurt?

"Christopher?" Hamlin called from downstairs.

Christopher jumped and drop the book back onto the bed. He shook his head as though to dislodge the cloud that had formed inside his skull. It left quickly, and with it the voice receded back to the dark corner of his mind where it belonged.

"Yeah?" He called back.

"I got it all arranged, they'll be here in an hour or so. I'll stay here until then. Also I went ahead and ordered a pizza. Don't know about you, but I'm fucking hungry."

"Yeah, sure. That sounds good to me," Christopher called down.

To help clear his head he looked out the window. Below on the street a lone street lamp left a pool of light on the ground. Somehow this made him feel even lonelier. Then he caught movement from the edge of the light. He ducked back behind the wall, cursing his stupidity.

They could have been waiting for him to just stick his head out and then shoot him with some sort of sniper rifle. But something about what he had seen made him peek around the edge. After a moment he could make out the shape in the shadows. That was what had caught his attention. It was a slight shape, a feminine one. Not the image of a thug.

It was a girl, maybe his own age, hard to tell in the shadows. She had dark hair and was dressed in dark clothes. From his window it looked like part of her neck and chin were obscured by something. It could have been shadow, or possibly a tattoo.

He was almost positive he had seen her before. Then in clicked. On the train. She had been on the train when he left Boston. He had glanced at her briefly. She was pretty and the tattoo on her neck had been striking, even if he hadn't been able to make it out. But Courtney was on his mind and besides, she had not struck him as his type, so he had mostly ignored her. Was she following him? Why? Coincidence?

But what bothered him the most was that she was looking directly up at his window. He jumped back and closed the curtain. Probably just a homeless girl. She didn't look like a threat, but he would let Hamlin know just in case.

He took one last look at the book and then headed downstairs. He just hoped nobody would try to kill him for the rest of tonight.

8

Two hours later Hamlin was gone, replaced by two officers by the names of Gillard and Lee. Lee positioned himself outside in an unmarked car so he could keep an eye on the approach. Gillard took up position in the front room where he had a view of the hallway and the stairs. Christopher eyed them carefully, he didn't want to trust them, but he also didn't have much choice. Hamlin vouched for them and their replacements, who would be coming in the morning.

After introductions they kept to themselves and Christopher had nothing to do with himself. He walked the upstairs hall of his home, moving from one photo frame to another. He saw his mother laughing at a BBQ with friends. He remembered the BBQ. His dad had burnt the burgers, and coming far short of perfection had almost ruined the day for his dad. As hard as he was on Christopher, he was harder on himself. There was a photo of Christopher and his sister standing on the beach, he was holding her hand. She was five years younger than him, so she must have been about four when the photo was taken.

There were other photos, all of a family lost to him. Taken, rather, by this Ambros fuck. Until now—this moment of walking through his family's sanctuary—he had been sort of numb. He had spent the last week in a subconscious state of denial. Now, looking at these pictures, he could feel it, like scabs ripped from a wound. The pain seemed fresh and everything that had happened over the last week came rushing at him. Waves of grief pounded at him.

The strength gone from his legs, he sunk to the floor at the end of the hall and curled up into a ball as the tears streamed down his cheeks. He was a man, but at that moment he felt like a child again, living in a world so out of control that everything could be taken from you in an instant. He wanted to hate everything, to lash out at everything, especially this Ambros that had destroyed his life. But he was also afraid.

It was this fear, more than anything, that alerted him to the sudden change from below. A noise had brought him out of his despair by grating on his frayed nerves.

It was a loud plink sound followed by a loud grunt, another plink sound and then what sounded like a chair falling over.

With cold certainty, Christopher knew they had come after him. Why was he so valuable dead? A simple college kid. In the end, his death wouldn't be much of a statement.

He had no time to think. He jumped up and ran to his room. Once there, he looked around futilely. There was nowhere to run, no escape out the window here. It was too far of a drop and nothing for him to land on but concrete. Down on the street he could see Lee's car with him asleep behind the wheel, but Christopher knew he was not asleep.

Noise from the hallway spurred Christopher into action. He could hear them coming up the stairs, loudly. They were laughing, all pretense of stealth gone. They were just outside his door.

He dove under the bed. He wasn't a small guy, but his mom had liked big, grand furniture so the bed was fairly high off the ground. Enough for him to fully squeeze under just as the door opened. Christopher froze.

Boots clicked as two men entered the room slowly. Christopher couldn't see above their ankles. On the floor on the other side of the bed was the book and pocket knife. Somehow he had knocked them off the bed.

"Listen Chris, don't make this hard. Just come and we'll make it quick," one of them said. He had a low voice with a slight German accent.

"Yeah don't make it so hard on yourself," the other one said. He had a higher voice.

"Your mother, your sister, they made it hard on themselves," Low Voice said.

High Voice chuckled.

"Hard is the operative word there," High Voice said and laughed harder.

Low Voice joined in laughing. "Yeah, we had some real fun with those two. I tell you if the boss hadn't told me to fuck'um I still would've."

A mixture of rage and fear shook Christopher's body. Every part of this body screamed at him to do something, run or fight, anything, just do something other than listen to these two men. But that same fear kept him from moving. Once again he saw the book and knife and his body let him move, just a little, enough to reach out quietly and pull the book and pocket knife toward him.

"Maybe the closet?" Low Voice asked.

Christopher heard his closet door slam open.

"Nope, college boy is out of the closet," Low Voice said and they both burst into laughter.

"Guess that narrows down our choices doesn't it?" High Voice asked.

"Yep, guess there's only one place left," Low Voice answered.

Christopher saw them start walking towards the bed slowly, continuing to mock him. He looked at the book, it was now or never. Whatever it was, if it was anything at all, it was all he had left. It was stupid to think that a book could be of use at a time like this, but what could it hurt? He looked at the book again. It had changed now, it said *Dante's Inferno*. Christopher almost laughed.

Filled with a painful mixture of hate and fear, Christopher opened the book.

The words 'THAT WAS A BAD IDEA' were written on the inside.

The words started to blur and shake like he was reading through an earthquake, and then the pain started.

9

The words pulsed on the page and then seemed to leap forward into his eyes, burning into his skull. The searing pain was worse than any gunshot wound. It felt like his whole body had exploded into a giant fireball. Organized thought was impossible. Every thought, each piece of knowledge, anything that was once him was scattered instantly into chaos. He was formless and void. There was some vestige of self-awareness, he was able to understand that this was happening to him, although he no longer remembered who 'he" was.

In moments he was everywhere, somehow he engulfed the universe. He was everywhere, he knew everything. Countless civilizations and wonders throughout the universe were his to experience, without any judgment or bias of his mortality. Like a god, everything was open to him, but it was useless. With no purpose, no sense of self, he did not know what to do with it. He was an observer, an experiencer, and he could not act, could not direct any action. For a moment he was the Watcher Over All, and then he began to shrink. He collapsed in on himself, his awareness and sense of self came flooding back. And so did the pain.

The fire flared up, burning through him, this time in reverse. Every nerve ending in his body woke with that touch of intense pain. He longed like a mad man for the nothingness he just was to free him from this purifying fire. He imagined his body a burnt out shell. Gone were the billions of worlds and cold stretches of space and time. He was the left with the charred remains of his soul.

It took him a few minutes to realize the pain was gone, even if the memory of it was only just now starting to fade. He was lying face down on a cool stone floor. He didn't want to move. He didn't care what happened to the two guys about to kill him, or how he ended up on a stone floor even though his room had a wooden floor. He just wanted to enjoy the cool stone against his face as he waited for the memory of the pain to recede.

His mind tried to grasp what had just happened, but understanding slipped away from him like a dream only vaguely remembered in the morning. He felt different, his thoughts refused to hold together for more than a second.

As the memory of pain became more distant, it felt like a gap was left behind, a hollowness that almost ached. But slowly he realized it wasn't hollow. There was a seed, a little spark of something that was starting to grow in the empty space left behind. At first he did not know what it was that grew there, then he understood. What started to fill him back up slowly, but surely, was anger and purpose.

"Well... yes, I suppose it would be a rough trip for a mortal," said a voice from above him.

It took Christopher a moment to realize he was being spoken too. Slowly, he tried to push himself to his knees. Every joint ached and his muscles vibrated with exhaustion. His whole body felt bruised and battered. After a moment he found he could sit back on his knees and look at the person addressing him.

He was impossibly tall, maybe eight feet, dressed head to toe in a hooded robe. His arms were held low in front, but his hands were lost in the sleeves. His face, if he had one at all, was hidden in the darkness of the hood which held blackness so complete and deep it seemed to stretch back farther than his hood would suggest. The blackness of its robes shifted about in different shades, giving it varying depths and textures. To Christopher it looked like a gathering of shadows draping themselves over a very tall man.

"Who... where, where am I?" Christopher asked.

"You are in the Library and I am the Librarian," it said.

Christopher was in a cavernous room, surrounded by shelves overflowing with books and stretching up to the ceiling several stories above. Row after row of shelves stretched off into the distance. It did indeed look like a monstrous library, though very unorganized and unkempt. Books and stacks of papers piled on the shelves and the stone floor in messy stacks. The walls, at least the ones Christopher could see, were of old stone, making the library look like a medieval castle. Light came from lanterns in sconces along the wall and a strange glow emanated from the ceiling, like the moon was shining through.

"What is this place?" Christopher asked.

"This is the place of all knowledge. All thoughts, ideas. Every answer to every question that has been or ever will be. To know this place is to know the mind of God. No, even more, it is to know the mind of gods and men."

"Where are we? I mean like what city or... or country are we in?"

"This place is nowhere really. It is a concept. What you see around you is just your interpretation of the idea of this place. For someone else it would look different, it would *be* different. But you are the Master of the Book and Weapon now, so it becomes what it needs to be for you."

Christopher tried to stand, but he was still a little weak and settled for leaning back against a shelf. He could not quite grasp what this thing said. They had to be somewhere.

"No. I mean, what is outside the door if I were to leave?"

"A door to an outside?"

"Yes, if I stepped outside where would I be?" Christopher asked again, his confusion making him impatient.

"There isn't one," the Librarian answered.

"There's no door?"

"There's no outside," the Librarian answered again. "Honestly, if I have to repeat myself every step of the way, this is going to go very slowly. I have all the time in the world, but I was led to believe mortals were more impatient."

Christopher paused and tried to collect himself to ask the right question.

"Okay, let's start at the beginning. What the hell happened to me?" Christopher asked.

"Well that is hardly the beginning, but I will answer you the best I can. Understand that some of this is new to me also. There has only ever been one Master of the Book and Weapon.

"You opened and started to read the Book given to you by The Beast, The Hunter of Lost Souls. He has other names, the Devil, Satan. He was an aspect of the Devil, the part of Satan allowed to roam free on the earth so that he could collect escaped souls and perform other services for Hell."

Christopher was feeling a little stronger, so he stood up on shaky legs and tried to make sense of what the Librarian was telling him. As soon as Christopher was on his feet, the Librarian turned and started walking off into the stacks.

"Hey, wait..." Christopher started, but the Librarian ignored him and kept walking. Although it seemed more like gliding than walking, like he was floating a little off the ground. He was still talking, so Christopher had no choice but to follow him.

"For whatever reason the Beast chose you as his successor," The Librarian said.

"Well actually, it was my father he chose, but he's dead," Christopher paused for a moment. It was the first time he had said the words out loud. "The same guy that killed him sent some guys to kill me. They were just about to grab me, I had no choice, I had to try the book. I had no idea..."

Christopher trailed off when he realized the Librarian had stopped in front of him, he almost bumped into his back.

"The Beast did not choose you?" The Librarian asked. He spoke quietly, and Christopher thought he detected a hint of concern.

"No," Christopher said and then remembering, continued reluctantly, "in fact he specifically told me not to open the book. He said I was too weak."

"Oh?" said the Librarian. "That could be a problem."

The Librarian continued moving. He turned at the end of an aisle and it opened up into a large space with several desks scattered about. They were large ornate wood desks. Pictures and symbols were carved along the side and legs of each desk. There was a rug, a large fireplace (the chimney of which stretched off into the invisible ceiling), and several very comfortable looking chairs. Christopher could imagine himself surrounded by 19th century businessmen smoking cigars and drinking their after-dinner brandy, while their women folk were gathered in the drawing room.

"I have a question before we move on. It's been bugging me for a while."

When the Librarian made no response, he continued.

"I heard voices warning me that I was in danger. Were you that voice?"

"No. At least, not exactly. It was the book, and I am part of the book, but I was not consciously part of its communication."

"What exactly is it that you do here anyway?" Christopher asked.

"I am here to assist you in learning what you need to learn and knowing all that it is you would know. I am your assistant, so to speak."

Christopher sat on one of the chairs. He was still weak from his journey to the Library.

"So you think I'm supposed to take over for this Beast thing? I'm supposed to hunt down evil souls and somehow take them back to Hell?" Christopher asked.

"I do not *think* this is the case. I know."

"But what if I don't want to? I mean, nobody asked me. I'll just turn it down and go back to my normal life. I'll just give the Book and Swiss Army... I mean Weapon back to you, and you can give it to somebody else."

The Librarian stepped closer, looming over him as he sat on the comfy chair and suddenly he wasn't so comfortable. The room seemed to grow darker, more oppressive. Christopher had the distinct feeling that the Librarian was angry.

"When you chose to open that book, for good or ill, worthy or not, you inherited the seed of Hell into your being," the Librarian said. "You are damnation on earth with all the power of Hell at your beck and call. You are a reaper of souls, judge of eternity. Knowledge of all things in one hand and a power that can unravel the very fabric of the universe in the other. You don't get to just pick and choose these things, Mortal."

As the Librarian spoke, growing louder and louder, Christopher buried himself deeper and deeper into the chair.

"The Beast was right, I am not the right guy for this," Christopher said, wishing it had sounded less like a squeak.

The Librarian stepped back.

"You will have to do."

"So what am I supposed to do? I mean this Library is impressive and all, but that pocket knife is hardly going to 'unravel the fabric of the universe'. I mean where do I start?"

"That pocket knife, the Weapon, will become whatever you need when you need it. Trust it, it is your most potent power."

"Power?"

"Yes. When you opened the book and read it you accepted the gifts of damnation, certain abilities. You don't feel any different now, but you will. In time you will learn what you are now capable of."

"You mean like Superman? Flying and shit?" Christopher asked.

"No, not like Superman. Flying maybe, we will have to see. As I said, no mortal has ever held this office. As for where to get started, that I can help with. I will assist in getting you information on the souls you are required to hunt and return to Hell."

"And how do I do that? Return them to Hell, I mean?"

"Use the Weapon. Anything killed with the Weapon is condemned to Hell, even innocent souls, so be careful."

Christopher was confused. He was not even sure he believed any of this. How could any of this be real?

"Too fast, this is all coming too fast," Christopher said quietly.

"Maybe, but there is one last thing you need to do. You need to leave and kill those men about to kill you. Killing is the final part of the initiation. You need to understand what it is you are and what your world has become."

"Kill them? I thought they would eventually be gone and I could just go back and find Hamlin..."

"You misunderstand your predicament. While your consciousness is here in the Library, your body is back there at the mercy of your world."

"What?" Christopher jumped up out of the chair. "You mean this is all happening in my head?"

"No, your head is way too small and simple to hold this vastness. But your consciousness has left your body to come here. Your body is..." the Librarian paused and lifted his head as though listening to something and looking off into the stacks, "Currently tied to a chair and they are starting to torture you. Seems they want to leave a statement with your death."

"So if I go back, I am going to wake up tied to a chair about to be tortured?"

"Yes," the Librarian said.

"Then why would I go back? Sounds like a good reason to stay put for a while."

"Again, you misunderstand. When they tire of torturing you, and I would believe torturing an unconscious person loses its appeal rather quickly, they will kill you. I can't say for sure what would happen to you if they kill your body before you take your first soul, but I doubt it would be a good thing for you. You have no choice. But as I said, you are not going back the same man you were. You will have new strengths. You just need to learn how to use them fairly quickly."

Behind the Librarian, a door appeared on a wall behind a row of stacks. Christopher did not remember it being there a moment ago. It opened revealing nothing but darkness beyond.

Christopher looked at the door, but didn't move.

"I don't think I can go through whatever it was I went through coming here. Whatever it was, I fear it even more than death," Christopher said.

"That was a onetime thing on the trip here. It was part of your transformation. It will not be the same going back."

Christopher nodded and walked towards the door. He didn't want to go through it. Despite what the Librarian said, he feared what lay beyond. And what was he going to do against two killers while tied to a chair? But he couldn't stay here, that was obvious. A part of him still felt he had gone insane and this was all a delusion. Either way, he had to go back to the real world sometime. He stepped through the door. As he departed the Library, he heard one last thing from the Librarian. It was hard to make out, but he could have sworn the Librarian had said, *It will be worse*.

10

Christopher drifted in darkness only a moment before the pain came again. This time however, it came from that seed left buried in the empty place inside him and it swept through him like a raging fire. It wasn't purifying this time, it was liberating and it stoked his rage. The pain was intense, but it was more than physical.

He remembered his mother and father again and his kid sister. The pain awakened the sadness and memories he had been trying to bury for the last week.

The pain showed him what he had hoped never to see again. That all shreds of his former life were gone. Courtney's betrayal, his entire family raped and murdered without him even being able to say goodbye, all of this stoked the fire inside him. He never considered that it was corrupting him, changing him, killing who he used to be, making something more or something less. Instead he embraced it. He welcomed the pain as part of him and the anger as the purest of pleasures.

No, everything that had been him was gone, but the pain

showed him something else to replace all of that. It showed him the need for revenge.

Christopher opened his eyes.

He sat in a chair, his wrists tied to the wooden armrests. He did not need to look to know that the left two fingers of his left hand were broken. Nor did he need a mirror to know that his face was black and blue, his lips swollen, and his cheeks lined with cuts. They had been working him over it seemed. He felt the pain, but it was nothing compared to the pain he held within himself.

"Well, it looks like Mr. Sleepyhead is awake. What bad timing for you."

This came from Low Voice. He was a short man, but stocky. The t-shirt and black jacket he wore seemed too small for him. His knuckles look skinned and a little bloody. He must have been the one doing the most damage. The guy standing by the door must have been High Voice. He was much bigger than Low Voice, well over six feet tall. He flexed his gloved hands like he was just waiting for his turn.

Both of them had an aura about them, gray with little swirls of darkness. Without being told, Christopher knew he was seeing the weight of their souls.

"We were hoping you would wake up. It makes this stuff much more fun. I was just about to kill you, but maybe we can take some more time."

Low Voice pulled back as if to swing, but then he caught Christopher's eye and hesitated at the fire he saw.

"What the hell?" Low Voice said.

"Exactly," Christopher said.

Christopher pulled his arms away from the arms of the chair. The ropes held but the wood splintered and fell apart as though it was made of balsa wood. He stood up and the ropes and broken wood fell away from him. The anger burned through him, and he could feel the power begging to be set free. They had torn off his shirt and when he looked down at his body, he could see power emanating from him as though he burned with mystical fire. He decided that this would not do. He couldn't be running around half naked.

Not knowing exactly how, he reached out to the shadows in the far corner of the room and pulled them to him. The shadows swarmed him instantly and coalesced into clothes of black and gray and a hooded jacket covering his head. Like the Librarian's robes, the jacket swirled with shades of black.

Low Voice stepped back, eyes wide with panic. High Voice recovered faster and pulled out his gun.

Christopher felt the impact of the bullet in his stomach. He was knocked back and stumbled. But unlike his other gunshot wound, which he noticed no longer seemed to matter, he could feel his body repairing the hole almost instantly. Again, the pain was nothing compared to the pain he carried within.

He felt something calling out for him, and he saw the pocket knife on the ground by the bed. On instinct he snatched it up. It almost leaped into his hand, eager and, he could tell, thirsty.

It shifted in his hand, lengthening and erupting in a mixture of black and red flames. The flames did not harm Christopher, in fact, they seemed to give off almost no heat. The knife had become a sword in his hand. He had hoped it would be something more modern, maybe a gun, but it was what he had to work with.

Two more rounds hit him in the shoulder and thigh, spinning him slightly.

He realized the bullets would not kill him, at least not quickly, but they could fire at him faster than he could heal and that would slow him. So whatever these new gifts were, he was not exactly bulletproof. He had to act.

Low Voice had his gun out despite the terror on his face.

Before he could fire, however, Christopher swept the Weapon up, slicing through the man's thick forearm without resistance.

Low Voice screamed a very high pitched scream. Christopher reversed the direction of the sword and sliced Low Voice through the torso diagonally.

Again there was no resistance, and the Weapon's flames spread over his entire body. His scream ended in a gurgle as both parts of his body hit the ground. But then there was a new sound. A weak, pitiful warbling scream.

Low Voice's aura now strung from the sword to his body like cheese from a hot slice of pizza. This was where the sound was coming from. The sound of a soul being pulled out of its body.

With a sickening wet sound, Low Voice's soul pulled away from his body and was absorbed into the Weapon.

High Voice had realized his gun was of little use and ran out the bedroom door. Christopher looked around quickly and found the Book on the floor next to the bed. He slipped it into the interior pocket of his shadow jacket.

With a short run he jumped through the window, shattering glass and wooden frame all around him. He wasn't sure he could fly, but something told him that the thirty-foot drop would no longer hurt him.

He had more strength than he had thought, and the momentum of his jump carried him well past the sidewalk. He landed on his feet in the center of the street. He was alone on the street for the moment. No cars were around. For now, the neighbors were inside, but that would change soon. Bursting out of a third story window made a lot of noise.

Christopher sniffed the air. He could smell something, something rancid yet sweet. He realized he had smelled it up in his room. Yes, it had been the scent coming off of High Voice. It was the smell of his soul.

He sniffed again, it was coming from behind one of the cars parked next to the house. Christopher started toward it. High Voice jumped up from behind the car and ran down the street. He got in the passenger side of a large black sedan. As soon as he was in, it pulled away from the curb with a squeal of tires.

Doors were opening and neighbors were stepping out on their porches. He didn't have time to see their reaction to a man cloaked in shadows wielding a large flaming sword.

Again acting almost on instinct he crouched down and leaped. He landed with a loud thud and dented the top of the sedan.

Before he could be thrown from the car roof, he held the sword in both hands and thrust down into the passenger side. The Weapon cut through metal and flesh easily, he felt it sink home in High Voice's soul and heard the same faint warbling scream as High Voice's soul was ripped from his body and sucked into the ever-thirsty Weapon.

Before he could pull the Weapon free and strike at the driver, the driver screamed in terror and made a sharp right turn. Christopher was thrown from the roof of the car, but he managed to hold onto the Weapon.

He landed on a parked car, smashing through the windshield. He kicked open the passenger door and stepped out onto the sidewalk, the cuts and scrapes from the fall and glass slowly fading.

At the end of the street the sedan turned north and disappeared. He could go after it, but he was suddenly tired. He staggered slightly as the realization of what he had just done started sinking in.

He had been running on adrenalin and instinct since the moment he came back from the Library. Now it was all leaving him. The anger, the hate. He felt himself calming down.

Around him more neighbors were coming out of their homes and looking around. In the distance he heard sirens. In New York you heard sirens all the time, but this time he thought these might be for him. He had to get out of here.

He ran into the alley nearby. Without knowing how, he dismissed the shadows that formed his clothes and the sword once again become a Swiss army knife that easily slipped into his front pocket. The Book became a small book of some sort in his back pocket. Now clad only in jeans he ran through the alley that became a garden area for the nearby homes and then across the street to the courtyard area at the rear of his home.

Once there he took only a few steps before the shock of what had just happened fully hit him. He sank down into an over-sized living room chair and tried to understand what he had just done. He had killed, had almost been killed.

He had been... possessed by some sort of power that he now understood came straight from Hell. His hands shook, his whole body shook. He heard a noise and it took him a moment to realize it was his sobs.

11

Ambros Falk was not in a good place. There was blood on his shoes and maybe a piece of flesh. He did not really like this part. It was necessary, but he did not enjoy it the way Rath did. That man seemed to revel in the smell and feel of blood. To Ambros, it was just good business.

Ambros turned back to the chair where the half-alive body of what had been a former business partner slowly bled to death. Rath stood above him, blood dripping from his red, wet hands. His tall, gaunt body showed no signs of exertion, although he had just spent the last ten minutes progressing from simple beating to ripping out the man's intestines and playing with them in front of him. His mouth, too wide for his face, was split into a maniacal grin.

Ambros had the horrible idea the Rath was using everything he had to hold back from diving in to the man's gut with that large mouth. A part of him believed that if he left, Rath would just dive right in.

He was wearing that stupid black wide brim hat. Ambros

thought it looked ridiculous on top of his head, especially with Rath being so tall. It made him look like a clean shaven, demonic Abraham Lincoln. Why couldn't he just wear a nice suit like Ambros, look more professional?

"I don't think he has any more to say," Rath said.

Rath's voiced carried, but it seemed little more than a whisper. Ambros was not sure how he performed that acoustic trick. But then again, Ambros was not sure about a lot of things regarding Rath. But he had become Ambros right hand man, no matter how much the man creeped him out. Rath also didn't appear to speak German or have an accent, which made him rare among Ambros' lieutenants.

"It's okay, we knew his answer already, but an example had to be made. Leave him where his people can find him. I think they will be much more willing to work on my terms when they see this."

Ambros took out a handkerchief from his inner pocket and wiped off the top of his shoe, no use ruining a nice pair of Jimmy Choo's just to make a statement. They were in an abandoned warehouse in Yonkers. The walls were covered with graffiti, and layers of muck covered the floor of the dilapidated building. He hated these kinds of places, but it seemed he did quite a lot of business meetings in places like this. He was eager to leave and get back to his penthouse. Maybe take a shower.

Rath thrived in decaying places like this. He almost seemed at home here. Ambros made an involuntary shudder.

There was a slight commotion from outside the warehouse door. Ambros was not concerned, he had his men scattered all over the grounds. They would not be disturbed without quite a bit of warning.

The door banged open and Karsten came through.

"Sir, Ich kam so schnell, wie ich konnte. Wir haben ein problem," Karsten said.

"English please," Ambros said calmly with a glance towards Rath.

Karsten look disheveled and had a light sheen of sweat like he had been running quickly. The right side of his jacket and part of his shirt were stained dark, as though splattered with blood.

Karsten slowed down as he approached his boss. He shot a quick glance at Rath and hesitated. Most of his people were nervous around Rath. Ambros didn't blame them. One reason Rath's interrogation techniques were so effective was his aura of savagery. Like he would rip your head off without a thought.

"Of course sir, I didn't see... um, him standing there in the shadow."

Ambros didn't believe that, you don't miss a figure like Rath, shadow or no. More than likely, whatever had him so shaken up had distracted him.

"We have a problem," Karsten began again.

"The Sawyer boy? I assume he is finally dead?"

"No sir. Something went wrong, both Jon and Malden were killed."

"What exactly went wrong?"

Karsten swallowed audibly and flicked his eyes to Rath and back to Ambros.

"Jon and Malden went in as planned. They took out the cop outside, and I am pretty sure they took care of the one inside."

"You're pretty sure?" Ambros asked. This didn't sound good.

"Yeah, it was my turn to wait in the car. So I didn't see what happened in the house, but then about fifteen minutes later the upstairs window exploded out onto the street. A guy had jumped through the window and was standing in the middle of the street."

"That had to be thirty feet below the window," Rath said in his unnaturally loud whisper. "He didn't break anything?"

"No, he just stood there like he had just taken the stairs. And he had a flaming sword in his hand..."

"A flaming sword?" Rath suddenly interrupted. He stepped closer, his eyes seeming to burrow into Karsten. "Are you sure it was a sword? And flaming?"

"Well, it looked like a sword and it was lit up with this strange looking fire. But that's not the craziest part. Malden came running out of the building. He ran straight for the car, and I started it. He got in and I pulled out. I floored it because I have never seen Malden so scared before. Anyway, this guy jumps like fifty feet and lands on the roof of the car. Yeah, I know that sounds crazy, but it's what happened."

He looked at Rath as though daring him to contradict his story. Ambros didn't for a minute believe that a man had jumped from a window thirty feet up and landed on a moving car, but he did believe Karsten thought he had seen what he said he saw. Ambros didn't interrupt because Rath was listening with such intensity that he thought he might be missing something. Rath usually showed dispassionate apathy around most people.

"Then the fucker shoves this flaming sword through the roof of the car right into Malden."

"So he killed Malden?" Ambros asked.

"You could say that, but it was more like the sword tore him apart. Splattered blood everywhere."

"How did you make it here? Did you lose him? Were you followed?" Rath asked and suddenly he was looking around.

Rath's sudden change in behavior was making Ambros nervous.

"No, he didn't follow me. I took a sharp corner, and he flew off the car. I got out of there as fast as I could."

"Rath, don't tell me you are believing this stuff. Something happened, yes, but a flaming sword? Jumping thirty feet?" Ambros asked.

"But sir, I swear..." sputtered Karsten.

"Karsten, I don't think you are truly lying, but you have to agree that this is a little unbelievable."

"Don't be so quick to dismiss him Ambros," Rath said as he stepped closer to the other two. He towered over them. He seemed to grow, his mouth wider, his top hat taller. "There might be more truth behind this man's words than you think."

"Do you know this man?" Ambros asked.

Rath didn't answer right away, but before Ambros could asked again he said. "No, I don't know him. But I have a feeling, a feeling that this is no trivial matter."

Ambros knew Rath's feelings. The last time he had one, Ambros had found out that one of his chief soldiers was going to betray him and sell him out to a competitor. It had taken some doing with no small help from Rath to turn the tables and kill both the soldier and his rival. Rath's feelings were like that—vague—but they uncovered significant truths. He turned back to Karsten.

"But you don't know for sure if the boy was killed or not?" Ambros asked.

Karsten shook his head. "No, I just saw Malden and that flaming sword guy come out of the house. I don't know what happened to the kid."

Ambros just nodded. "We will have to assume he's not dead. And the man cloaked in black seems to be a new player. Killing a simple college kid is proving much harder than I thought it would be. Rath, maybe it's time you take a hand in this personally."

"But enough for the moment," Ambros clapped his hands and rubbed them together as though they were cold. "Let's get out of this shithole and back to my place. I need a drink and this place stinks."

As Ambros walked away, Rath's powerful and ominous presence fell in behind him. Rath didn't completely dismiss the story his man had told and this gave Ambros some pause. Rath seemed to grasp things that were beyond others' senses and had talents that Ambros would not describe as normal. Talents that had proved very useful in the past.

He left the building and got into the backseat of his car. His people would take care of the grisly scene behind him. Take care of it and make sure the right people see the corpse and understand its message.

12

"Let me get this straight. Two highly decorated dead police officers, a third story window shattered from the inside out, and three witnesses that said they saw a man waving a burning torch running from the front of this house down the street and jumping onto a moving car and you didn't see a thing?" Hamlin asked.

"I was scared, I told you." Christopher said. "I was taking a piss. I heard the commotion downstairs so I hid in the bathroom, hoping they would look and then leave."

"So you don't know who this guy is? Or how your window got blown out?"

"No."

"How convenient," Hamlin said.

They were in his bedroom. Technicians from the forensic unit were looking through his room, spraying chemicals all over the window and half the room.

Christopher knew he couldn't tell Hamlin the truth. As soon as he walked in Christopher could see his soul, it was a dingy white, with spikes of gray, but he intuitively knew that meant Hamlin was a fairly decent guy. He also knew that Hamlin wouldn't believe him. He didn't even believe it. One moment he was about to be killed by low life thugs, the next he visited an interdimensional library operated by a ghost-like creature, then he was chasing bad guys down the street with a flaming sword. Yeah, that made lots of sense.

"The question is, what are you going to do with me? You guys have two strikes, hospital and now here. Great job protecting me so far."

Hamlin grunted. "We don't have the resources to leave enough guys here. Technically, you aren't a witness so we can't put you in any of those programs. Maybe a safe house... I know we're afraid of leaks in the department, but they can't all be bad. Maybe we can keep this to just a few of us? Do you know anyone out of town?"

"No," Christopher said. "I don't think I should run this time."

"Run? Son, I don't think you understand who you are dealing with here. At first you were just icing on the cake, but I think after this it's gonna be personal. He can't let you get away. Too much has happened. You won't be running away, you'll just be making a smart move."

But Christopher wasn't fully listening to him.

"I've always run, from home, from my father, that's why I went out of the city for school, to get away from him. From my classes, even from my girlfriend. Did you know she was cheating on me? I didn't even confront her, didn't even talk it out. I just stopped talking to her. I ran."

The more he spoke, the more he knew it was true. He had always run rather than fight. Maybe it was the seed of power sitting in his chest, but he didn't think he could run anymore. At some point you reach the end of the runway. At some point running is harder than staying and fighting. He did not think he would be running anymore, ever.

Hamlin sighed, resigned. "So, are you just going to stay here? Right where they just tried to kill you? You'll be a sitting duck."

"I don't think they'll be too quick to come back here. Not after what happened."

Their eyes met and something passed between them. Christopher knew that Hamlin knew he wasn't telling the detective everything, but they had no choice but to trust each other.

"What about this girl you saw?" Hamlin asked. "Do you think she could be involved? You sure you never saw her before the train and then your window?"

"No. I have no idea who she is."

"And no better description than dark hair and a tattoo on neck? Goth, or do they call it Emo now?"

Christopher just shook his head. *Old people.*

"I don't know. She was dressed in dark clothes. It was night, I couldn't see much."

"No problem. I'll put out and an APB, she should be easy to find in New York," Hamlin said. "She'll stand out like a sore thumb."

They looked at each other and neither could hold a straight face. They both started laughing.

It felt good, Christopher thought. He needed that.

"You gonna be okay with tomorrow? I mean the funeral?" Hamlin asked. "I'll be there with some guys of course. Just to watch out. I don't think he will make a move at something so public, but we'll be watching."

"Yeah, I'll be fine. It won't be a long service. Burying all three at once, side by side at the family plot and all that."

"Do you want me to pick you up?"

"I'm supposed to take a limo. My dad's assistant set it up. But I think I'll cancel. I'd rather ride with someone I know."

"Okay, watch your back. I'll pick you up in the morning."

And with that he was gone and Christopher was alone.

13

The day of the funeral was overcast, but no rain. Christopher thought that maybe the rain part only happened in movies. He wished it would rain to fit his mood.

More people attended the funeral than he had expected. His father had been a crime fighter in a way and beloved by many people. The lanes of the cemetery were packed with cars. Co-workers, city officials, family friends that Christopher had only met in passing stood in a loose semicircle around three neatly dug holes in the ground with the coffins hovering above them. They all waited patiently for the priest to start.

His family was not particularly religious, but tradition was important. It would be a proper affair. Christopher stood uncomfortably in a suit, trying to pretend his shoulder still hurt from the bullet wound. He even kept it in a sling.

It was hard to focus, Christopher thought. He shook hands with many people, accepted their condolences and kind words, but he forgot who they were or what they said moments after they left. He saw their auras, the ongoing ability the only thing that kept him from thinking the night before was only a dream, but he didn't pay too much attention. He didn't know what all the different colors meant, and he didn't have the strength at the moment to try and figure it out.

It was surreal, he thought. Like he wasn't really there. That none of this, not the deaths of his family, not the weird library, and certainly not last night, had really happened. He felt like he wanted to lie down and fall into a deep sleep. Maybe not even awaken.

Detective Hamlin was there, as were ten more of New York's finest. Christopher was grateful for the detective's presence, he was the closest thing Christopher had to a friend. At the very least, Christopher knew he could trust him. Hamlin stood next to him while the others were scattered about the area in what Christopher assumed were strategic locations. They were looking sharp of course, because their boss was in attendance. The chief of police stood only a few feet away from Christopher. It would be crazy for anybody to try and get to him here. That made him relax a little.

That is when he began to smell it.

Like smelling salts, the harsh stench woke him up and made him look around for the source. It was horrible, and for a moment Christopher thought maybe a body was exposed and rotting nearby. This was a cemetery, after all, and that was the only explanation for the stench. It fell over him like a wave. He grew slightly dizzy, and for a moment he thought he might fall over.

God, now it smells more like a pile of rotting bodies.

Hamlin noticed him teeter and steadied him.

"Everything okay?" Hamlin asked in a whisper.

"You don't smell that?" Christopher asked and immediately regretted opening his mouth. Now he could taste the horrible smell.

"What smell? Just grass and trees."

"No that smell like rotting bodies."

"What? No, I don't smell anything like that and I have smelled my fair share of old corpses."

"God, it's awful! I can't believe you don't smell it."

"Well, you must be super sensitive to something. Maybe a dead animal in the bushes? Don't know what to tell ya," Hamlin said.

Nobody else seemed to notice the smell either. Christopher felt like he was going to throw up, but nobody around him seemed to be affected. It was more than just a smell Christopher realized. It was like an itching in his brain, as though something was misfiring inside his head and making him smell something that wasn't there. It took him only a moment longer to realize it was coming from the same place inside him where his aura sight came from.

Suddenly alert, all vestiges of the fog that had held sway over him were gone instantly. He looked around desperately as the priest continued the service. He needed to find where the stench was coming from.

"What? You went from being half asleep to alert as a guard dog. What happened?" Hamlin asked.

"I'm not sure, but something..." Christopher let what he was saying drift away. A man was walking over the hill directly across from the service. He was wearing a dark suit and jacket, but what really stood out was the black, wide brim hat on top of his head. He was tall and rail thin even with the coat on.

But what really made him forget what he was saying and suddenly turned his stomach was the pitch black aura around the man. It writhed around him as though the darkness was fighting with itself to stay contained. There was no other color to temper the blackness. This was the source of the smell, the stench of corruption. His aura brushed headstones as he passed, leaving behind withered moss and dead flowers rotting in their stand. He was a walking abomination, an affront to the reality around him and Christopher could almost imagine the world screaming in pain at each step he took.

Christopher slumped, suddenly weak, and Hamlin caught his arm to help him stay up.

"Whoa, you okay Christopher? You look like you ate some bad fish."

The man had stopped some distance away and stood watching. Christopher suddenly had the feeling he wasn't there for the funeral. His eyes were on Christopher.

"Yeah, I think I'm fine."

He straightened up and pulled his arm away from Hamlin.

"Think?" Hamlin asked.

"Yeah. Hey do you see that guy over there? The tall guy with the hat?" Christopher asked.

Hamlin looked to where he nodded.

"Yeah, tall son of a bitch, ain't he? Do you recognize him? A friend of your father's perhaps?"

"No."

Christopher felt like he was going to throw up. People around him were looking at him curiously. Most nodded sympathetically, thinking it was the grief affecting him. A few hands fell on his shoulder for comfort. He wanted to walk away, get away from the ominous presence of the thing watching over them. But he stood there and listened to the priest drone on and on.

He noticed that he was feeling better. Strength, subtle at first, was seeping into him from that seed of hatred, that gift from hell that dwelt deep inside him. He welcomed the comfort and warmth it brought. As though his acknowledgement gave it strength, the seed of anger flared to life and burned any nausea out of him.

He no longer wanted to leave. He wanted to charge up that hill and tear apart the flesh of the man on the hill and drag him down to hell. He had no idea why, but he needed to destroy this one. His hand itched to hold the weapon, but he had left that at home. He had even taken a step towards the thing when Hamlin's arm on his shoulder brought him back to himself. He pushed the feeling back down. It was his father's funeral, he could do nothing at the moment.

"I think that man had something to do with my father's murder," Christopher said through clenched teeth.

"How do you know? Did you see him last night?"

"No, but I'm positive it's connected."

"It?" Hamlin asked, but Christopher ignored him.

The ceremony was soon over and the caskets were lowered into the ground at the same time. The crowd began to disperse. Christopher stood at the edge of the grave site as the mourners slowly made their way back to the cars. Many stopped to give him their condolences one last time. Christopher shook their hands and said all the words they expected him to say. But his attention never left the lone figure on the hill. It never left, it waited for him.

He waited for everyone to leave, expressing his need to be near his family one last time alone.

"I'll stay here with you," Hamlin said. "Maybe I should go introduce myself to that man up there."

"I don't think that's such a good idea," Christopher said. "I think he's waiting for me."

"I know. That's why I should go have a chat."

Christopher new instinctively that if Hamlin went up that hill, there was a good chance he wouldn't come back.

"No, detective, I'm the one he wants to talk to."

"Maybe, but if you think he is involved with all this, there is no way I'm letting you go over there alone."

"Hamlin," Christopher said and focused all his attention on the detective, "If you go up there you will die."

"Look Christopher, I don't know what you are thinking but..."

He must have seen something in Christopher's eyes, maybe a little bit of the hell fury seeping through, because he stopped. Christopher could see the shock and concern on his face. Then he sighed.

"Okay. You seem to know something about what is going on you just don't want to let me in on," Hamlin said.

"It's not that..." Christopher began.

"Yes it is. But don't worry, I'll back down a little. Tell you what. I'll watch from the car. I'll be able to see you, but far out of earshot."

"Thanks, Hamlin."

"Yeah, no problem kid, but just remember I'm on your side, and you need all the friends you can get right now. So be very careful about what secrets you decide to keep."

With that Hamlin turned and walked back to the car. Christopher was tempted to call after him. He was right, Christopher needed friends, but there was no time for that. He had a meeting to keep. After the last mourner had left, he made his way up the hill to speak with the dark thing that stank of death.

14

"Ah, the new hunter of lost souls approaches," the tall man said as Christopher drew closer.

The man's mouth was wide and lined with teeth. Teeth that looked like they had been filed to points. When he smiled, tiny needle-like teeth shined wetly. The stench grew stronger as Christopher neared the thing and the desire to attack him reached a fever pitch, as though the seed of Hell inside of him was screaming for him to lash out and claim this being's soul. It took all of his strength to hold it together.

"Who are you?" Christopher asked.

"I am your purpose," it said and laughed. "I am called Rath for the moment."

"Why are you here, at my family's funeral? Did you have something to do with it?"

"I came to meet the new Adversary. The successor to the Beast."

He couldn't stand the rage inside him any longer. He stepped closer and looked up at Rath.

"Look fucker, did you have anything to do with my family's murder or not?"

"Hmm, your concern for the mundane tells me you really have no idea what you are. You have no idea of the power you wield. Dealing with you will be easy. You are not the bloodhound the Beast was. You are but a puppy dog."

Rath leaned his head back and laughed. Christopher took a step forward, rage sweeping him away. He didn't know what he was going to do, but he wouldn't stand here and do nothing.

Suddenly a large knife appeared in Rath's hands. It gleamed hotly. Something about it made Christopher hesitate, some hellish instinct made him pull back.

"Relax puppy. To tell you the truth, I did not do anything to your parents."

Rath brought his other hand up slowly and with the edge of the knife sliced deeply into his palm. Blood welled up instantly and began to drip from his hand. He held the hand over the grave next to him and blood dripped onto the earth with a sound that hissed as though his blood burned the very ground.

"But I know the man who did. Ambros gave the order."

He held his hand above another grave and again the blood fell to the ground as though molten.

"And I could deliver him to you."

He turned and walked through the graves, letting his blood drip on them as he went. Christopher followed behind him.

"What do you mean deliver?" Christopher asked.

"It's vengeance you want right? The police's hands are tied, they all know he was the one that ordered the execution, but they can't do anything about it. They can't even find him. I could tell you where he is. You have a certain... freedom that the police lack. You could accomplish what they can't."

They seemed to be walking in a large circle, Rath fertilizing the ground with his blood. But he didn't seem to weaken despite the blood loss. In fact, he seemed to grow stronger with each step. Once again, as much as he feared it, he wished he had the Weapon with him.

"What's in it for you?" Christopher asked.

Rath paused for a moment as though considering.

"I have worked with him for a while, but he has outlived his usefulness. It is time he and I parted ways."

"And you want me to do the dirty work? Why? It can't be that simple. I mean, I get the feeling you could deal with him yourself if you had to," Christopher said.

Despite whatever he was now, a part of him was very afraid. He wanted nothing more than to turn and run back to Hamlin. He looked around and realized they had come full circle. He could still see Hamlin by the car, but strangely everybody had disappeared. The last stragglers from the service had left, and even the cops Hamlin had stationed around the cemetery were suddenly gone.

Rath stopped and turned to face him.

"Well yes, I could. But no, I offer him as a gift to you, and all I ask in return is that you let me go. Just turn the other cheek and hunt others down."

Christopher was only a little aware of what Rath was talking about, from talking with the Librarian, but he didn't want Rath to know how ignorant he truly was.

"I thought I was just a puppy? Why are you worried about a puppy?" Christopher asked, amazed at his own bravery. Just a week ago he wouldn't have even considered speaking to this thing like he was. Being blessed by hell has a way of changing a guy, he guessed.

"Even puppies can nip at your heels. Even puppies can annoy

and pester. I have plans, and the last thing I need is you running around trying to interfere."

"How do I know you aren't just going to lead me into a trap? Have Ambros and all his men just waiting for me?"

"Oh, Ambros and all his men will be there," Rath laughed. "I said I would tell you how to find him, not that it would be easy. But remember, you have new special skills. For you it is possible to take him out."

"Where is he?" Christopher asked.

Rath stared at him as if judging him.

"He has a house, under another name, just outside of town. This is the address," Rath said and slipped a piece of paper out of his coat, offering it to Christopher.

He took it, careful not to touch Rath's skin. Even the thought of it made his flesh crawl. He slipped the paper into his pocket.

"So, do we have a deal?" Rath asked.

"I can't guarantee anything, not now," Christopher said. He just didn't know enough about what he had signed on for. He didn't really know who he was yet, and until he understood more that was the best he could do. There was a beast raging inside of him that wanted to destroy Rath, and Christopher had no idea if he could control it or if he even wanted to. Of course he could say none of this to this creature before him.

"Tsk, tsk, puppy. You have more mettle than I had thought. Unfortunately, I now have to kill you."

Rath's hand flew up before Christopher could move, spraying stinging blood into his face. Christopher's vision blurred and the ground tilted under his feet. He heard Hamlin cry out behind him as he pawed at this face trying to get the blood off of himself. He blinked rapidly, trying to wash the blood from his eyes.

The earth under him rumbled. As his vision cleared, he could see what was causing the earth to vibrate. Rath was gone, but he had left something behind. The ground above the graves he had bled on was erupting, and creatures were clawing their way out. Corpses, Christopher realized, as the first arms and heads poked out of the holes.

Half rotting bodies, desiccated leathery mummies, and insectile looking skeletons climbed out of the earth. They were all around him in the pattern that Rath had walked him just moments before.

"What the fuck?" cried Hamlin from just over Christopher's shoulder. "What the fuck? How the fuck..."

Hamlin was right, they were surrounded by them. Once again Christopher wished he had the Book and Weapon with him. Hamlin had his gun out, he shot two in the chest. The bullets knocked them back, but just like in the movies, they got right back up.

Christopher let the anger and rage flow through his body. He did not have the weapon, but he was no longer defenseless. He could see the flow of power surround him like it had in his room the night before. It crackled across his body like lighting ready to strike.

The nearest corpse grabbed his arm, its claw-like finger digging into his flesh with far more strength than its body suggested. Christopher grabbed it by its neck and leg and picked it up over his head. He threw it into three others that were moving towards him, they all went down in a jumble of bones and rotting flesh.

Hamlin was in trouble. He was shooting into the mass of creatures, but he couldn't shoot in all directions at once effectively. Behind Hamlin a corpse was almost on him. Christopher leaped into the air, subconsciously pulling the shadows from the corners of the cemetery around him, forming the black coat and hood as he landed in the midst of the zombies behind Hamlin.

With rage and hellfire almost blinding him, Christopher tore into the mass. Fingers clawed at him, teeth chomped, and he could only hope that zombieness didn't spread like it did in the movies. He ripped off heads and other limbs, it seemed the only way to stop them was to literally tear them apart.

Fingernails, like long claws, ripped open his skin across his chest and back. It healed quickly, but the pain was the same.

He might have been able to deal with them quickly, but his movements were hampered by Hamlin. He had to keep an eye on him. He had already gone through one magazine and Christopher was not sure how many he had left.

Luckily it was only the handful of graves that Rath's blood had touched and they weren't dealing with a cemetery full of these monsters. He estimated there were twelve or so of these things.

Corpses latched on to both his arms, their preternatural strength enough to slow him down.

Hamlin screamed in pain as a mouth clamped down on his shoulder. Christopher's own cry joined in when one of the zombies on his arms bit into his bicep.

There were too many of them. No way could they kill them all. Their only choice was to run.

Suddenly, Hamlin went down under a pile of the corpses. Throwing the body of a dead old lady off of his back, Christopher dove into the pile.

He could feel teeth and nails cutting into him as he made his way through the mountain of bodies. Hamlin did not look good. Blood streamed from dozens of cut and bite marks. He was out of ammo and was using the butt of his pistol as a club. Christopher could tell he was weakening, feeling the drain of so many of his own wounds even though they did heal fast.

They wouldn't last much longer. With a final lunge Christopher threw back the closest corpses. He grabbed Hamlin and held him.

The creatures swarmed in when he bent over to pick Hamlin's limp form off the ground. Gathering his power around him he jumped, sending rotting corpses flying everywhere. He landed twenty feet away and started running for the car. He was still carrying the detective.

Behind them the zombies chased after, not at all slow like the movies.

Fast zombies suck, thought Christopher.

"Can you drive?" Christopher asked Hamlin.

"I can fucking drive out of here," Hamlin said.

Hamlin was covered in blood, most of it his own, but Christopher did think he could drive. He could see it in his aura. Hamlin was pretty beat up, but he would survive. If you asked him, Christopher couldn't tell you for sure how he knew that, he just did.

Christopher set him down by the car.

"Get going, I will slow them down," Christopher said.

Hamlin ran to the driver's side. "I'm not leaving you here, kid."

"Go! Now!" Christopher said. A part of the power inside of him crept into the command. Hamlin blanched.

"Okay, but I'm waiting at the end of the street," he said and got in the car.

Christopher turned to face the creatures barreling toward him. He charged straight at the first two. He slammed into one, sending it careening into the other. Before they could get their footing back he grabbed and tossed them into the mass that came charging up.

The front rows fell back, but the ones behind just trampled over them as though they weren't there.

Hamlin had turned the car around and was racing down the cemetery street. It was now or never. He jumped just as the zombies swarmed the spot he had been standing moments before. He was not sure of the limits of this new power or that he could make that jump.

He found the limit. He landed almost directly in front of the car.

Hamlin slammed on the brakes and the car screeched as it slammed into him. He flew up and over the hood. His ribs shattered and his arm broke. He cried out in pain as he tumbled off the car onto the hard pavement.

Hamlin was out of the car but not moving too fast himself.

"Holy shit, kid! I didn't mean to hit you. You okay?"

Christopher looked behind them. The creatures were still chasing after them. He struggled to get to his feet. His bones already started to knit together, but not fast enough. Hamlin tried to help, but winced at his own injuries. Christopher waved him off.

"Just get in the car, we don't have time," Christopher said and ran to the passenger side.

The power was weakening inside of him already, he guessed it had decided he was in the clear. He let the shadows go and was once again in his suit, now torn and bloody. Hamlin had seen everything, no point in hiding his identity now.

They hurtled down the road, exiting the cemetery as fast as possible. Behind them Christopher could see the zombies starting to slow and fall to the ground. Their purpose complete, they were returning to their natural state.

"What the fuck just happened?"

"I wish I knew," Christopher said.

"That guy from last night? That was you wasn't it?"

"Yeah, it was me."

"And you killed those two guys that came to kill you?"

"Yes," Christopher said.

"You know my mother said I needed to quit this job. Why the hell didn't I listen?"

"Look, I'll tell you everything. But I just need to think for a minute."

Christopher looked over at Hamlin. "And we need to get you to the hospital ASAP."

Hamlin nodded. "Yeah, yeah. But you're going to tell me everything, kid. I mean everything."

Christopher nodded. But he knew he would not tell Hamlin everything. He couldn't. Hamlin would never believe him, and in the end there were some things you had to bear alone. In this case, the less Hamlin knew the safer he would be.

15

Christopher dropped Hamlin off at the emergency room before heading home. At first Hamlin had protested saying that Christopher needed even more help than he did, but by the time they reached the hospital, Christopher's wounds had mostly healed, leaving him with bruises and a body that ached like he had just completed a triathlon.

When he saw Christopher moving with a lot less pain, his eyes had narrowed.

"Yeah kid, we need to talk. There is a lot we need to discuss. Like how you should be half dead by now."

"Yeah, I know. Call me when you're patched up and we'll talk," Christopher said as they wheeled Hamlin down the sterile white hallway of the hospital.

On the car ride to the hospital, Hamlin had called in to find out why the patrol officers that had been stationed at the funeral had left.

Dispatch said they had no idea, in fact, it looked as though they had just disappeared. None had checked in yet.

Christopher knew what happened to them. Rath had happened.

Hamlin didn't mention the zombies, he was no idiot. He would be the laughing stock of the department if he had. He would wait until they both had a better understanding of what was going on.

Back at his parent's house. My *house now*, Christopher thought, *I have to start getting used to that*. He wanted nothing more than to take a nap. Just a moment to crawl under the sheets and pretend none of this had happened.

He felt cheated. In just over a week his life had fallen apart. He hadn't even had a chance to mourn his family's death. His body had been beaten, broken and even shot at. In one week he had gone from a world of academic bliss, to shady underworld hitmen, to fighting creatures straight out of a horror movie. He needed a moment to catch his breath, to try and figure things out.

But he couldn't, he had too many questions. Questions that could mean life or death for him and who knew who else. And there was only one place where he thought he might get the answers.

The Book and Weapon were right where he had left them on his bed. He stood there in the room staring at them. The first time he had used the book it had been out of desperation. He had no idea what it truly was, what it meant, or how it could change his life.

If he opened it now, he did so knowing full well what was going to happen. He knew what doors it unlocked. He might already be too late, but he felt that opening that book knowing what would happen was a final acknowledgment. Whatever power watched over it would know that he was on board. But in the end, Christopher was not even sure what "on board" meant. The nightmare had already started and he had no choice but to see it through.

He made himself comfortable in a chair, he wasn't sure how long he would be. Then, with a sigh, he picked up the book and opened it to a random page and read.

The words 'WELCOME BACK' were written on the on the page.

When the words began to blur and shake, Christopher was ready for it.

16

The Librarian had been right. The second trip was a lot less traumatic, which was good. The memory of the first time was burned into his mind. He did not need a reminder.

As the world came into focus, he found himself once again standing in the Library. The gloomy castle-like setting, combined with the dark mahogany woodwork in the shelving and chairs, seemed somehow comforting after the day he had just had in the real world.

The Librarian appear from behind the stacks and approached Christopher.

"Welcome back. It looks like you survived your little altercation," he said.

"Well that is one way to put it. I think of it as two homicidal maniacs who tried to torture and kill me, but 'little altercation' works also."

"I see you have been bloodied. That is good, that means we can get to work," the Librarian said.

"Wait a minute dude. A lot has happened since I was last here."

"Ah, I see. Then let's talk," the Librarian said.

He gestured towards the study area they had talked in before. Christopher could have sworn it hadn't been there a moment ago.

Christopher sat while the Librarian continued to stand, and Christopher told him everything since he last left. He wasn't sure he could trust this Librarian, he wasn't even sure the guy was human, but he had little choice. It was one thing to have mortal hitmen trying to kill him and quite another when zombies start attacking.

When he was done, the Librarian turned and started walking off into the stacks.

"Follow me. It is time for you to see something," the Librarian said.

"Um. Okay," Christopher said and got to his feet a little slowly. Apparently his subconscious took his injuries with him when he came here, though by now he was mostly healed. Fast healing was the only good thing about what had happened to him.

The Librarian took him through a door and into a hallway that stretched off into the distance. Doors lined the hallway and passageways led off in different directions. The Librarian was right, this place was vast. Even the hallway, in between the doors and passages, had books and papers stacked on shelves.

The Librarian took a series of passages, twisting and turning several times before stopping at a large door.

It was several times bigger than the other doors they had come across in the hallway, and it was solid black. No designs, wood grains, or even paint could be seen on it. The door just seemed to absorb the light around it, like it was an endless black hole. Christopher felt vertigo just looking at it.

The Librarian stopped and stepped aside. He gestured to the door with one robe-cloaked arm.

"I cannot open this door, only the Master of the Book and Weapon can open it," he said.

Christopher stepped up to the door and took a closer look at it. That was a mistake. He felt dizzy, and for a moment he thought he might fall into it. He reached out a hand to steady himself and accidentally pushed on the door. It swung open effortlessly and he stumbled through the doorway.

It opened into a large room, not as large as the one with the stacks of books or with the study area in it, but large none the less. It was a round room surrounded on all sides by tall, curving bookshelves.

Thousands of identical black leather-bound books, each about two inches thick, lined the shelves. It looked like the world's largest encyclopedia collection. In the center of the room stood a large stone pedestal, a single volume lying open on it.

"This is the assignment room. This is where you will find a list of the current Black Souls that have escaped hell and need to be retrieved. Your prey, so to speak."

Christopher slowly walked around the room, running his fingers across the spines of each book he could reach, purposefully avoiding the open book in the middle of the room. He could feel the emanations of fear that radiated from it.

"The books along the walls reflect all of the souls retrieved since the beginning of time. Well, since the establishment of hell that is," the Librarian said.

"So many," Christopher said in wonder.

"Yes. Remember, hell has been around for a long time."

"And that book on the pedestal?"

"That is the current book. A hunter's journal, so to speak. It lists the names that you are meant to track down. When you have retrieved all of the souls, a new book will appear and that one will join the others on the shelves.

Christopher pulled a book off a shelf and flipped it open. It looked like each name was a chapter. It started with the soul's name and a fairly detailed drawing of what the person looked like in life, followed by a much less detailed drawing of what they looked like now. Most of the time the two drawings looked nothing alike.

"When the soul escapes, it has little time to be picky," the Librarian said as though he had been reading Christopher's mind. "Sometimes they can possess a person similar, but very different, to a demon. Sometimes they have to use what stolen power they managed to bring with them to form their own bodies. Often they have spent so much time in hell they have forgotten what they looked like."

"Demons? They exist?" Christopher asked.

"Yes. Although they can be dangerous, they are far less so than the dark souls you are charged with retrieving. They have their own agenda, and pure evil is not necessarily on it."

The rest of the chapter on the dark soul seemed to be filled with some details about them, their past, and how they had been hunted down and retrieved.

Christopher realized why the Librarian had brought him here.

"And you think that Rath's name is on that book on the pedestal don't you?" Christopher asked.

The Librarian appeared to nod, although the hooded cloak made it hard to tell for sure.

Christopher put the book back on the shelf and went to the volume on the pedestal. It was open to the beginning of a chapter. Rath's name was listed above a drawing of a tall man. The picture was vague and blurred, but there was no mistake it was the tall man from the cemetery.

"Why is there no detail about his past or the picture of when he was alive?" Christopher asked.

"That is odd," the Librarian said and looked over his shoulder. "I have never seen that before."

"What does it mean?"

"I have no idea."

Christopher flipped the page. There was a narrative of his encounter with the hitmen and of his first meeting with Rath.

"Did you write this?"

"No, the words will appear as you experience them. But I am puzzled as to why there is nothing about his past in the book. That has never happened. I will do some research."

"So I'm supposed to kill him right? That's my first job?"

"Yes. However, you don't need to hunt them down in order. You can simply flip to another chapter in the book if you like, but eventually you will have to go after this Rath."

"Was this the soul my predecessor was hunting when he was killed?" Christopher asked.

"I am not sure, but since the book was open to this page I assume it is."

"When I talked to him, this Beast, he mentioned that the soul he was hunting had something called a Relic? Does that mean anything?" Christopher asked.

"Perhaps. I have come across mention of items called Relics. Although I do not have the details, they were weapons and other devices that had particular effect on supernatural foes, particularly those from heaven and hell. I will do some research."

"Great, I have an academic for a sidekick. How does that help me now?"

"It doesn't," the Librarian said calmly.

Christopher wished he could see his face. He wanted to see if there was a smug smile under that hood.

"Really? All these books in this library and you don't have anything useful for me?"

"I apologize. I seem to have misplaced the card catalog for all the knowledge in the universe," the Librarian said and this time Christopher didn't need to see his face to hear the sarcasm.

"I have enough to think about trying to stop Ambros. I'll get no peace if he keeps trying to kill me. I'll have to worry about Rath later."

"Ah, Ambros I can help you with," the Librarian said. He pulled a small note book from his sleeve.

"I took the liberty of doing some light research on this man. I thought it might help."

Christopher took the small book.

"What is this?"

"Layout of his house, number of men that he has for security, what they are armed with, what times he will be home. That sort of thing."

"Where the hell did you get this info?" Christopher asked, flipping through the book.

The Librarian sighed. "Do I really have to mention how this is a storehouse of all the knowledge in the universe again? Because it is becoming tiresome."

"Yeah, yeah. Can I take it with me?"

"No, nothing can leave this library. It is just a concept remember? A way for you to understand this place."

"Okay, got it. We'll have to work on it though because this is a great resource to have, especially if I can take it with me out there," Christopher said.

He studied the book more closely, making note of how many men he should expect. Mostly they were armed with pistols, but quite a few had assault rifles. He tried to memorize the layout of the house, looking for an entry point, but he was no military man. He was a college student, technically a dropout at this point. Frankly, he didn't have a clue what he was doing. He would have to do this like he'd done everything else. He'd have to wing it.

"A word of advice?" inquired the Librarian.

"Of course. I need all the help I can get."

"So far, your experience with your new abilities has been out of desperation and accidents. I suggest you do some specific analysis to explore your capabilities."

"What do you mean by specific analysis?"

"I mean practice," said the Librarian. "While you are charged with hunting down powerful escaped souls from Hell, there is nothing to stop you from hunting down or stopping other mortals, as you are doing with Ambros."

"Stop other bad people? What, like a superhero? I thought you didn't like my Superman analogy." Christopher said with a chuckle.

"I was merely suggesting that you start with someone a little easier than an underworld kingpin and his supernatural henchman."

Chris had to admit, the idea made sense. A thought occurred to him.

"You said all the information in the universe right?"

"Yes," the Librarian said warily.

"So you could give me stock tips? Maybe a lotto number or two?"

"You are hell on earth, about to do battle with beings most humans don't even know exist, beings that could destroy you very painfully, and you are worried about money?"

"Good point," Christopher said, suddenly less sure of himself.

17

The Librarian was right about one thing—he didn't know the extent of his newfound abilities, and he could use some practice. But he wasn't even sure he wanted to use them anyway. He had to stop Ambros, the desire for revenge burned inside him too strongly not to. But the rest of it? Hunting down these black souls? Christ, he was almost killed by a bunch of zombies.

He was lying on his bed staring at the ceiling and trying to think this through, his iPhone playing a mix of alternative and classic rock through his stereo.

The seed of hell deep down inside of him burned with an angry warmth and whispered hatred into his ear. He could feel it compelling him to hunt, to rip souls apart.

The anger over his parent's and sister's stupid deaths, his anger over his girlfriend dumping him, the frustration of almost being killed several times, all added fuel to the fire that was burning.

It flared up and before he knew it, he was standing by his window. It was repaired, but unfinished—just a plain wooden frame, drywall edges exposed. An ugly mark on what was otherwise a beautiful home.

He had made that mark, true, but only because of that bastard Ambros. The seed inside him craved blood, and Christopher wanted to give it some.

In seconds he pulled the shadows to him, forming his hood and coat. He slipped the Book into a shadow pocket and the Weapon, still a pocket knife, although now vibrating with power, into his other pocket.

But he couldn't just walk down the street like this. He could feel the dark tendrils of force emanating from his body. One good look and he would have the people on the streets running in fear and eventually calling the cops. A swat team trying to take him out was the last thing he needed.

He looked at the buildings across the street. The people in those houses and tall towers looked down on people. Literally, not figuratively. He, himself, had done it a thousand times from this window. Looking down at other people as they moved through their lives, wondering what was going on in their heads, what lives did they live and was it a better one than he had?

These people rarely looked up.

Besides, this would be a good time to work on accuracy, he thought, as he climbed out onto the tiny ledge outside his window. He couldn't stay long on the ledge, he didn't need some neighbor reporting a suicide attempt the night after somebody died in the streets.

Gathering the energy from inside, he leapt, aiming for the top edge of the building across from him.

He missed.

He cleared the edge and overshot it by a lot. He managed to land on the roof with a thud, almost barreling over the other side, and caught himself on the wall. A few more feet and he would have missed the building entirely.

He paused for a moment to see if an alarm was raised. He heard no one yelling or raised voices calling for the cops.

Across the street the next row of house roofs were the same level as this one. He jumped again, this time aiming for dead center.

Almost. He crashed into a large air conditioner. The metal squealed and groaned under him as he pulled himself out of the twisted metal.

Now that made a lot of noise, he thought, *time to get out of here.* He brushed himself off and jumped to the next one with slightly better accuracy.

He moved through the city like this, silently for the most part. Although he did hear the occasional exclamation, mostly from vagrants, he moved on immediately. He never stopped long enough to gather any attention.

He found he could move fairly quickly. His running speed was enhanced with his power, and the jumps covered great distances. He found he moved faster than any car or train could in the city since he could travel in straight lines.

And it felt good.

The power flowed through him easily. It burned in a good way and the more he embraced it, the better it made him feel. It burned away his fears and concerns and left him feeling strong and powerful.

He was fucking flying through the city! Well almost. But it was at least as cool as Spiderman.

Christopher smelled the man long before he saw him. It was a smell he was only now beginning to understand. It stole his attention and drew his focus like a wolf who smells the kill. It was the smell of evil.

He had stopped on a building in the Bronx to take a break and get his bearings. Flying through the city at that speed can be disorienting.

A car drove down the street. It was a restored 70's-style car. Christopher was not a car buff and didn't know the make and model. But he could smell the man driving.

It was not an escaped dark soul like Rath, his was a distinct overpowering stench. No, this man was mortal, but evil nonetheless. The desire that leapt up from the pit of hell inside him was almost overpowering.

The car rolled slowly down the street as if waiting for something. A shadow detached from an alleyway and moved towards it. The driver stopped the car and rolled down the window. A quick verbal exchange, then they passed each other something.

A drug deal, Christopher guessed. As the car drove off, he followed. It was easy to keep up with it, jumping from rooftop to rooftop. Eventually it pulled into a garage. It looked like a body shop.

Others entered the shop and the smell seeping out of the place reeked. If only the police had this ability to smell evil.

It was a gang meeting of some sort, Christopher thought. From the auras he could see that not all of them were on the extreme side of bad as the driver in that car was, but all of them had black marks on their souls, and not just petty theft. Christopher was not sure how he could tell, but it seemed with the combination of his nose and the auras he could get a vague idea of what had put that mark of evil on their souls.

The power inside of him didn't care. It wanted to harvest. And before he could think, Christopher found himself jumping to the street below and walking towards the building.

He could almost taste their souls, and he wanted to grin at this reaping. It was like a blood lust, only nothing so banal. Souls were the only sustenance that would sate his desire.

The garage door was closed, but a man stood nearby. When he saw Christopher approaching, he opened the side door and yelled inside.

"Yo. Some fool out here. He's steppin'."

Then he walked towards Christopher.

"Mothafuka better get the fuck out of here," the gang member said.

Christopher knew the man couldn't see his face, at least not clearly, not in the shifting darkness of the shadows draped about him. But it didn't matter, Christopher was looking at the man's aura. Then to his surprise, as much as the man's, he started sniffing him.

"What the fuck?" The man said and pulled out a gun.

"You have killed," Christopher said.

"Damn straight, mothafuka and I'm gonna kill your ass too."

"You have raped." It was a rhetorical statement, Christopher could see it plainly on his soul. "You have killed the innocent for your own gain, your own pride."

"The fuck you talkin' 'bout?" The man said.

Others had come out of the garage, about four guys surrounded him.

"You in the wrong place little bitch," one of them said.

"We gonna fuck you up little bitch," another said.

Christopher felt no fear. That alone should have caused him to be afraid. But the fury and hatred powered him and confrontation made him stronger. He couldn't hold it back any longer.

A powerful energy seeped out of him, electrical crackling radiated from his body.

"Holy shit," the first gang member said and pulled the trigger.

The Weapon, somehow already in Christopher's hand, made

an upward slice, cutting the gang member's body neatly in half. His gooey soul ripped out of its shell and was slurped up by the Weapon in Christopher's hand.

It was chaos now. The gang started firing weapons and Christopher danced. He danced because he had no choice, the fever of hell was on him. He spun in a circle cutting, severing, dicing into their flesh. They were all corrupt souls and the Weapon drank freely.

He jumped across the street to carve into one and then sprang back thirty feet to catch another by the neck, where he held him up as he gutted him. Bullets slammed into his body, but he was quick enough to avoid being hit too many times and when he was, his body healed itself.

He reveled in the death, in the slicing and dicing. It was over in seconds, body parts lay scattered about. Christopher had claimed their souls, but the piece of hell inside him was not satisfied. He could smell others inside the building.

He grabbed the large garage door and wrenched it up, breaking the internal locking mechanism. He was greeted by screams and more gunfire.

Despite the slaughter outside, he had caught them by surprise when he broke open the door. He used this to his advantage. He had been shot several times and despite his accelerated healing and the driving force of the rage inside him, the gunshots were taking their toll.

He moved fast, avoiding the gunfire as best he could.

Two men and three women were in the garage. In a blur he saw that all of them had dark stains on their souls, but much less than those outside.

The power inside of him did not care. It drove him forward, fiery blade flashing out, power crackling down its length.

At first they tried to defend themselves. The two men ran

forward, guns blazing. Christopher dove behind a car, using it as a shield.

One of the men ran around the trunk of the car and the Weapon flashed, slicing his head off and taking his soul.

Christopher leapt again, almost hitting the steel beams across the ceiling, but he managed to duck in time.

He crashed down on top of the other man, driving his fist into his face. He was unused to his own strength and the man's head was torn open by his fist, killing him.

Before he could stand the women charged at him, desperation in their eyes and auras.

The Weapon, angry at being denied the soul of the man at his feet, almost jumped in his hands at the women's approach.

Christopher knew that this might be wrong, knew it in some distant way, as though some part of his consciousness was watching what was happening on a TV somewhere.

But here and now Christopher wielded his Weapon like a harvest scythe, reaping this gang of thugs.

The last girl tried to escape. In one last desperate attempt, she tried to run for the back door.

Christopher could feel the Weapon twisting in his hand. It had become a javelin. He threw it without hesitation.

It streaked through the air, leaving a trail of ethereal fire and pierced the woman through the heart, then struck the door. The woman died instantly and hung there pinned.

Blood was everywhere. Bodies, mostly in severed pieces, lay strewn about the inside and outside of the garage. The smell of blood overwhelmed Christopher's senses.

The adrenaline was dissipating, the overwhelming power that had been there moments before retreated. He was left feeling hollow, empty.

He saw the broken garage door and the dead all around him as though for the first time. *Such power*, he thought. This was practice? Was it practice for the men and women who had just died? Maybe they were evil, maybe it was true what he smelled on them, but was he the one to judge? Was it even him doing the judging? Or was it the power inside him, the Weapon in his hand? He looked at the javelin embedded in the door and the body hanging off of it. He shivered.

This was not practice, this was slaughter.

The sound of sirens in the distance brought back his focus. He pulled the Weapon from the wall and instantly it transformed back into a pocket knife. He didn't want to touch it, but he had too, he couldn't leave it for the police.

Speaking of which, he thought.

He went out onto the street, pulling the shadows tighter around him, making his hood darker. Whether out of protection or shame he did not know. Other people were out now, mostly looking through their windows, but one or two were coming out their front doors.

It was time to leave. He leapt to the top of the building he had arrived on. As quickly as he could, before the shock of what he had really done hit him, he ran home. But by the time he made it back to his neighborhood, he was shaking uncontrollably.

18

Christopher woke to the sound of his doorbell ringing repeatedly and rapid banging on the front door. He sat up slowly, his head was pounding. On the floor was an empty bottle of scotch, left over from his father. His stomach turned at the faint smell of spilled liquor.

The Book and Weapon were in the far corner of the room where he had thrown them last night after he got home. After that it got fuzzy. He could remember stumbling around the house, looking for something, anything to dull the pain. He found the scotch, he had hoped for weed, but beggars can't be choosers.

He had wandered the house with no real purpose, just sipping on the bottle and trying not to think. He wanted his mind empty, because when it wasn't empty, it was filled with horror. It was filled with blood and severed body parts. It was filled with looks of terror on faces. It was filled with screams and running.

At first he tried to tell himself it hadn't been him. It was the seed of hell inside him that took over, but that wasn't the complete truth either. His own anger and frustration fueled it until it was out of his control.

To think he had been comparing himself to Spiderman when he was jumping from rooftop to rooftop. No, he was more the super villain than the hero.

The loud knocking brought him back from his memories. He threw on a robe and moaned as he made his way downstairs.

Why can't the power heal my hangover like it does my body, he thought.

It was Hamlin at the door. One arm was in a sling and bandages were on his neck and forearm.

"Please tell me you aren't here to eat my brains," Christopher said.

"Was it you?" Hamlin asked. "Was it fucking you?"

Hamlin shoved past him and into the living room. Christopher closed the door and followed him in. He could guess what Hamlin was talking about.

"You found out? About the garage?"

"Garage? You mean the butcher shop where over a half dozen gang bangers were killed?"

Hamlin was pacing.

"I fucking knew it was you. The witnesses all said they saw a man with a huge sword lit up like it was the Fourth of July. They said you moved so fast it was a blur and then jumped from the street to the top of the building. I don't know what the fuck happened, but why the fuck did you kill those guys?"

"Calm down Hamlin, I'll try to explain what I can," Christopher said.

"Yes, you will kid, and you tell me everything. I should be arresting you right now, if I had any real evidence, I would. But if you don't tell me everything, and I mean fucking everything, I'll have a team over here with a search warrant and we'll find your costume and sword."

Christopher fell into a chair nodding his head. Hamlin sat across from him.

"You look like shit kid."

"Drinking most of a bottle of scotch will do that to you," Christopher said.

"Why the hell did you do that?"

"Contrary to what you might think, last night's activities weren't exactly my idea. Not really my idea of a good time."

"Talk. And tell me everything, including what was going on with those zombies yesterday."

Christopher hesitated. What could he tell him? The truth was unbelievable. Maybe just some bits and pieces? But Hamlin was a trained interrogator. If Christopher tried to piece meal this story together the detective would see right through it, and he would lose what little trust he still had. Besides, his brain was in no condition to try and outthink the detective. In the end he went with this gut, he told Hamlin everything.

It was a little cathartic. He started off slowly, not really sure where to begin, but soon it was pouring out of him. Everything from the day he lost his girlfriend and met the Beast to last night when he killed nine people that didn't do shit to him.

Hamlin didn't say a single word the entire time. To his credit he sat and listened to every word Christopher said. By the time he was done, Christopher actually had some hope that Hamlin would believe him. He was a fool, a desperate fool.

Hamlin sat quietly for a moment before speaking.

"That's it? That's what you're going with?"

"It's the truth detective," Christopher said.

"That you're Satan here on earth, and it is your job to hunt down bad guys and send them back to Hell?"

"Well, I'm not Satan or Lucifer or any other name for him, but it was described to me as though I was a part of him on earth."

Hamlin stood up.

"Look, I know you have some sort of skill, you'd have to in order to do what you did. I don't know how you did it, but you can't expect me to believe all the magic power bullshit."

He started walking to the front door. All of a sudden Christopher didn't want to be alone. For all his reluctance, he needed Hamlin to believe.

Faster than any normal person could move Christopher was in front of Hamlin, blocking him from the door. He reached out and pulled shadows around him, forming his now-standard coat and hood. No Weapon though, he was not ready to touch that thing again. Not now and maybe not ever again. Besides, it was in his room.

Hamlin cried out and stumbled back, eyes wide with shock. Power crackled over Christopher's now shadowy form. He started walking towards Hamlin.

"Is this what I have to do? Is this what I have to show you to make you believe?"

Hamlin fell over a table and tried to scramble back up. He moved slowly, his injuries hindering him. Christopher felt bad, he did not want to hurt him.

He reached out and picked Hamlin up easily with one hand. He held him against a wall and leaned into him.

"I am hell on earth Hamlin, Taker of Souls, the Final Punishment," Christopher said, quite pleased with himself for coming up with such cool sounding titles. He let power into his words and the pure force of the seed of Hell inside of him washed over Hamlin so the detective could have no doubt. "And I don't want it."

He let all the power slip away. The shadows, the power, all left him in an instant and he was just Christopher again.

"And I don't want it," he repeated.

He stepped back from Hamlin, letting him recover.

"Did I hurt you Hamlin? I didn't mean to. I just needed you to believe, and I thought this might do it."

Hamlin slowly tried to recover. He pulled himself up straight and took a moment to gather his wits. His eyes darted back and forth like he expected demons to pop out at any moment. Recalling how hard it had been for him to believe all this at first, Christopher understood what Hamlin was going through.

"Well it fucking worked kid, I sure as fuck believe you now. Or at least that something not normal is going on here. I guess I'll have to trust you with the details."

"Last night... I won't try to say I didn't have anything to do with it, but it wasn't just me," Christopher said as he returned to his chair. The hangover had been burned out of him when he embraced the power. "That desire to kill was part of the power inside me."

Hamlin shakily returned to his chair also. From his body language he could see the detective was trying to keep his distance.

Great. I got him to believe a little, but at the cost of trust, Christopher thought.

"So you are saying this... power you inherited has a mind of its own? Some sort of blood lust?" Hamlin asked.

"More like a soul lust. It's like its only instinct is to take dark souls, and if it can't get a dark soul that has escaped hell, it will settle for regular people that have done wrong."

"Well at least it only goes for bad guys," Hamlin offered.

"Yeah, but it doesn't see shades of gray. It overwhelmed me yesterday." At least Christopher hoped it had overwhelmed him. There was a part of him that was worried he had let it have its way. "Any mark of evil, even what you and I would consider fairly minor, is enough for it to give the ultimate sentence. No second chances for the power of hell."

"Is it a numbers game?" Hamlin asked. "Does the Devil win if there is a greater number of souls in hell than in heaven?"

"I don't think so, but I don't know much about afterlife politics," Christopher said.

"Probably not. If it was, I'm pretty sure hell would have won that game many times over by now."

"The question is, what do I do now? I mean, it has come in useful a few times, but I never know exactly what is going to happen."

"Can you quit?" Hamlin asked.

Christopher shook his head. "I asked that when I first got to the Library. I have no choice. I can feel the power in me grow, making me stronger. But also making me crave to take up the Weapon. The only time it relaxes is after the kill."

"Maybe you can control it? Learn to contain it and not let it run loose?"

"I don't know. Maybe. It kind of snuck up on me last night. It felt good though, like a drug, like an all-powerful drug."

Hamlin sat back in his chair. "Don't become an addict on me now kid. I don't want to, but if I have to stop you I will. We can't have another episode like last night," Hamlin said.

"You don't understand. It is my nature now, it is a need that is now a part of me. I might be able to control it, force it into a different direction, but I won't be able to stop it. It's too strong."

"Well we're at an impasse then. I can't let you run around killing random criminals, just because you thought they were bad guys."

They were quiet for a moment, both trying to figure out what to do. Hamlin was probably trying to figure out how to arrest him. Christopher just wanted help to control this raging power inside of him. Christopher decided logic and truth might be the only answer.

"Why not?" Christopher asked.

"What? What do you mean why not?"

"I get it. You're a cop, and there's a process. Regular people can't make those decisions, it has to go through the judicial system. But your own ideology is based on the idea that the judicial system is the right one."

"It's all we got, kid, to separate us from the animals."

"Not anymore," Christopher said. "I see the evil in people. I can judge them more truthfully than any. It is the very nature of the power I have been given. Everybody talks about the final judge being God or some otherworldly being that decides if you go to heaven or hell. I can't open the gates of heaven, but I do have the ability to drag souls to hell. I am the ultimate judge."

"Sounds like you are the ultimate arrogant bastard. What makes you this all powerful judge?"

"Because I can see. I see the truth inside every soul. And every time I use it I get better at reading it."

Christopher searched through Hamlin's aura. He knew he was invading personal space, but he had a point to prove.

"I can see that you killed that man."

"What man? What the fuck are you talking about?" Hamlin stood up.

"The man, the one who molested those children, killed two of them. I see how the evidence was light, but you had no doubt. When the prosecutors wouldn't charge him, you took it into your own hands. You were smart, nobody ever knew it was you. You killed him. You decided to be his judge."

"Enough, you fucking bastard." Hamlin stood up. "What else do you see kid? Did you see how they found out it was another guy? Did you see how I had dropped the case because I thought it was over, but the prosecutors wouldn't drop it? Another detective found evidence and DNA that all pointed to a different guy. Did you see that I killed the wrong guy kid, and that I almost let the real pervert get away? Does your magic power tell you that?"

"Yes Hamlin, I did tell you that it was evil I saw. What you did was wrong, but because murdering an innocent was wrong. In a way you had the right intentions."

"Look kid if this is your way to get me to help..."

"You judge people every day in your work. It's your job. Do I arrest this guy? What is this guy's threat level? Do I need to draw my gun on this guy? Sometimes you make good judgments, sometimes you're off. But what if you had the power to truly see people, truly understand their motivations? I am offering you redemption. I need your help, I can't take this weight on by myself."

"So you want me to be Commissioner Gordon to your Batman? I don't know kid, this doesn't make a lot of sense."

"Yeah, maybe, I don't know. I don't even know for sure half the things I just said. I'm running on instinct here, and I have no idea where the instinct is coming from."

"I need to go kid. I need to think. Please don't kill anyone until you hear back from me."

"I can't promise you that. I still have Ambros to take care of," Christopher said.

"Jesus Christ, did you have to tell me? Look just hold off. I need to sort this out, think it through. Please don't do anything stupid."

"Nothing has changed my need for vengeance."

Hamlin left and Christopher found himself once more in his room staring at the Book and Weapon. It occurred to him that in his conversation with Hamlin he had somehow, without thinking it through, made the decision that he would once again take up the Weapon.

19

The bar was a clean one, if not really upscale. It smelled of beer and liquor, but in a slight and pleasing sort of way. The bar and stools were dark wood. Masculine yet homey. The scent of bar food almost overpowered the scent of sin in the air.

Almost.

Christopher had needed another drink, and that need had led him to this place. You need a strong drink when you are contemplating the revenge-killing of the most feared crime bosses in the city. Or when you just slaughtered a not so innocent group of gang members. Frankly, after what had happened to him, Christopher had any number of reasons to get drunk.

Most importantly it helped him forget about the burning seed of power that burned deep down inside. He would stay drunk for the rest of his life if he had to.

Besides, a public place like this is probably safer than waiting at home for the next round of killers, both natural and supernatural, to show up at his house.

Shifting auras of lights and grays swarmed over the patrons.

He could smell the evil and the good. He was becoming better at using his new senses, and for the most part he found his fellow humans to be a mix. Many stood out as evil, auras almost as black as the thugs that had tried to kill him. Some radiated a preponderance of good.

He didn't look too hard at the dark ones, the last thing he needed was to see the evil in random souls. He could already feel a slight stirring from the Weapon. He pushed it down, there was not going to be a repeat of the other night. More and more he felt it was like a dangerous pet that needed feeding. Only it was hard to keep this pet on a leash.

He sat at the bar and pulled out his wallet and license. He was young enough looking that he always got carded.

But not tonight. The bar tender didn't even glance at his ID. He was large, bald and covered with tattoos. Even so, he seemed to have a reluctance to get too close to the skinny kid that had just sat down at the bar.

"What do you need?" He asked.

"Beer. Surprise me, something on tap."

Soon Christopher had a cold lager in front of him. He scanned the room using the mirror behind the bar, cultivating his paranoia. Interestingly and thankfully he noted that he could not see auras in the mirror, but he could still smell the sickening, rotting stench of evil. It made him hungry.

An image in the mirror caught his attention. Just a quick flash as someone darted out of eyesight behind a pillar. A flash of black hair and pale skin, a glimpse of a tattoo.

He spun around trying to catch her. She was gone, but the pillar was there, across the room. The pillar was not that thick and he could see her arm. He made his way toward it, pushing through the small crowd. When he was almost there, she made a break for it and shot from behind the pillar. Tired of this game, he altered his route to intercept her. She had fewer people in her way, however, and could move faster.

He noticed something odd about her. Her aura was split down the middle almost exactly. One side was light gray with darker clouds swirling through, the other was a much darker gray, almost black, with lighter clouds swirling through. It was unusual enough that it made him pause.

She ran down the back hallway, presumably to a back exit or perhaps the women's bathroom. He chased her down the hallway. She had almost reached the back door when he caught up to her.

Christopher caught her arm. She cried out when he snagged her. He pulled her back from the door and pushed her up against the wall.

"Who are you and why are you following me?" Christopher asked.

She looked up at him through the hair that had fallen across her face. For the first time he saw her up close. She had pale skin and silver-blue eyes. She did indeed have a tattoo that came up from her collar and spilled across her neck. It was a demon or a dragon, something like that. She was beautiful and afraid. He could see it in her timid gaze.

But that didn't matter, she was following him and he needed to know why. Still for a moment, while he looked at her, he had forgotten why he was holding her or what he needed to say.

Then the strong stench of evil wafted up from her and his thoughts cleared.

"Hey! What the fuck you doing with her?"

A large man and a couple of his equally large friends had come around the corner quickly. They had obviously seen the chase and were eager the help a damsel in distress. Especially if that damsel was as beautiful as this girl.

"You okay?" the large leader asked the girl.

Suddenly the fear and timidity left the girl and she smirked.

"Actually this asshole won't take no for an answer," she said. "I told him I won't go home with him, and I guess he thinks he can just drag me out of here."

Christopher released the girl more out of shock than anything.

"That's not true, she's been following me..." Christopher started.

"Sure. That hottie has been following a skinny little pussy like you all night. Did you slip any drugs into her drink?

"What? No..."

The three men moved forward making sure to cut off any escape.

"You one of those bastards that thinks they can just force a woman. Just take what he wants?"

The girl was laughing now as she slipped away from him. He could see the evil glint in her eyes. Mischievous more than evil really.

Christopher looked at the men and he could see inside their souls. The leader had a dark taint, some horrible crime. Given a moment Christopher might be able to decipher what it was exactly. He could feel the power inside of him rising up, he struggled to control it.

"Perhaps we should take you outside and show you what it's like to just take what you want."

"No, that is not a good idea," Christopher said. The power was taking hold, the best he could do was try to channel it.

The leader grinned back at this buddies.

"Oh yeah? And why is that bitch?"

"Because I do not want to kill you."

That made the leader pause. Maybe because it was so unexpected, maybe the man heard something else in Christopher's voice. Either way, he only paused for a moment.

"Oh yeah motherfucker," the leader said as he grabbed Christopher and pushed him up against the wall.

Over his shoulder he saw the girl open the back door with a smirk on her face, like she was enjoying his predicament. Halfway through the door though, she paused and looked back. She shuddered, but more importantly her aura shuddered, and suddenly she looked scared and worried. Her eyes widened in what only could be described as shock.

She said something, he couldn't hear her, but he was pretty sure it was *I'm sorry*.

It confused Christopher enough that he missed the fist flying at his face. It connected with a bone crunching sound and an explosion of pain. Two more rapid punches landed in his gut, bending him over. It seemed the other two wanted to join in on the fun. Caught by surprise Christopher doubled over.

Then the power of hell surged through him. He caught the foot that had kicked out at his stomach, an easy target now that he was bent over. The leader's foot stopped instantly in his vice grip.

Christopher pushed back on the man's leg and sent him sailing into one of his buddies. With the infusion of hell-power the man flew down the length of the hall.

The leader's friend came in, fists swinging. Christopher caught one of his fists and squeezed. It cracked like a walnut. The man screamed.

This man's aura and scent was more clean than dirty. Normal sins, normal mistakes. Christopher fought against the hunger inside, and this time one he pushed it down. He let the screaming man fall to the side clutching his fist, now limp and lumpy like a sack of marbles.

"You have a chance at redemption," Christopher said to the screaming man, although Christopher did not believe he was heard.

The leader of the three had regained his footing and after steadying himself, charged at Christopher.

Christopher easily evaded his slow punches and caught him up by the throat. That was when he saw it.

The scent and sight hit him at once. This man had murdered. He was a cop, a dirty one, Christopher could see. Taking bribes, looking the other way. But it was the true crime that had damned this man.

He saw him pulling over the girl. He saw him pulling her from the car, forcing her to do horrible things. Knowing all the time that he was above the law. He was the law. She would be broken and scared, nobody to believe her. And then when he was done using her body, he upped the ante. Knowing he was untouchable, he strangled her to death. And it was the greatest pleasure he had ever felt. Christopher felt the man's pleasure and it sickened him.

No remorse, no guilt. Christopher knew he would do it again.

He threw the man through the back door, splintering the heavy wood. The man lay sprawled across the alley.

Christopher leaped on top of him. The Weapon, now a small dagger, in his hands. The man looked up at him, unable to breath from his broken ribs, one of which protruded from his chest.

"I condemn you to hell," Christopher said and slipped the dagger into the man's heart.

He felt the dagger tremble in his hands and Christopher knew he was drawing his soul out and sending it down to hell.

Christopher stood up and looked around. While it felt like time had slowed, the whole fight had lasted seconds. He had only moments before people responded to the crashing door at the back of the club.

He sniffed the air. He could smell her. The curious mix of heavy sin and innocence. He knew he could track her, it's what he was made for.

He shot off down the street. She was only seconds ahead of him.

Out on the main street he slowed down. He hadn't pulled shadows around him and wanted to remain inconspicuous.

He sniffed the air again to determine where she went. She headed south. There! Down the street he saw her. She was on the other side of the street running down the sidewalk.

It was a busy this time of night, so Christopher had to carefully navigate the street. Throwing up his hands to stop cars, he was greeted by honks and yelling, but they stopped.

It also alerted the girl that he was behind her. She glanced back and for a moment she hesitated as though torn between turning around and continuing on. Then she made a decision and kept running.

"Wait," Christopher called, but was ignored.

Hearing him call out, she ran faster, much faster. Too fast for a human.

Great, Christopher thought, *another supernatural being*.

He could chase after her via rooftops, but currently he had a several people looking at him and the last thing he needed was to draw more attention.

He watched as she turned the corner and disappeared. He tracked her scent through the streets for several blocks, but it was soon apparent he was far behind her.

He decided to give up for now. He had other problems to deal with at the moment.

Was she somehow part of all this? Probably. Was she on Rath's side? Ambros? Some other player in this game? Whoever she was he was pretty confident that was not the last time he was going to see her.

20

Rath stood on the dark rooftop trying not to inhale the stench around him. It was not the pleasant smell of rotting flesh and blood that he enjoyed, it was the stench of living mortals. It was a waste of flesh. He hated it. He hated them.

He wouldn't be here at all if this wasn't the only place the Other would meet him. The Other preferred dark, hidden places for their meetings. And this deserted rooftop was above the concerns of humans.

He heard a noise and then sensed the approach of one of his brethren.

Across the rooftop the door to the stairs opened and a blob of a man stepped out. Not all fat, at least not entirely, but large and round. He walked with a ponderous gait and for a moment Rath was concerned the roof would not support him.

He stopped about ten feet away from Rath. He was as tall as Rath but maybe five times as wide. Despite being thousands of years old, he wore a dark, modern suit, impeccably tailored. His eyes were deep set and shadowed.

"Rath, why must we meet? This alliance between our kind is unheard of and fragile at best. Why must you test it?"

His voice was like boulders falling downhill.

"I have unfortunate news, Golyat. The Beast is dead, but a new one awakens."

"You had assured us that the Beast was slain and we were free."

"The true Hunter is dead, I saw to that. This new one is nothing but a babe. A child pretending to be something he has no idea about," Rath said.

"Yet here we are, and this new Hunter is not dead."

"For now. He will be dealt with shortly."

"Then you will take care of this problem also?"

"Of course. I promised the Alliance of my brethren that I would kill the Beast, and I will kill his successor."

"Then why are we meeting? You don't need my permission," Golyat said.

"I need the Relic back," Rath said.

Golyat chuckled.

"That is impossible. It was loaned to you for one job, the Alliance will not loan it so easily again. It is one of our greatest treasures. You know this."

"I know Golyat. With it I was able to slay the great Beast, and with it I can easily strike down this new pretender."

"If, as you say, this new Hunter is but a child with no understanding of what he truly is, then it should be easy for you to dispatch him without the aid of our most powerful weapon," Golyat said.

Rath tried to keep the fury out of his voice.

"It is the only sure way to destroy this child. I need it."

"No, Rath. You do not need it."

"Then I demand a meeting of the Alliance to address them directly."

Again Golyat chuckled. Rath wanted to rip his throat out. And he would have if it wouldn't have turned the others against him. The Alliance was powerful, and unity gave them strength, but it often got in the way of his personal agenda.

"Feel free, Rath, to bring it up at the next meeting. But that is a long way off and I think it would be better for you to deal with this little problem long before then. The Alliance will not be happy with your failure."

At that Rath did take a step forward. He raised his hands as if to strike Golyat. But he held himself back.

Golyat's smile grew bigger.

"It seems we have reached a mutually agreeable solution. You will dispatch this new Hunter as soon as you can, and the Alliance will not tear you apart for incompetence."

With that said, Golyat turned and walked back to the rooftop door and the stairs down.

Rath watched him go, seething. Years of cultivating hatred in the bowels of hell blossomed inside him.

First the boy, but next is you Golyat, Rath thought and then he too left the rooftop.

21

Christopher opened the door to see a gun aimed at his head. Fortunately, the man holding the gun was detective Hamlin.

"He was a cop Chris. This time you killed a cop."

He aimed between his eyes only inches away. Hamlin's hands never shook. There was a coldness in Hamlin's eyes that Christopher had never seen before.

"I know it was you. Eye witnesses say it was a young, college age kid wearing a hoodie. The video was conveniently blurry, but when I saw the recording and heard that he was killed with a knife I knew it could only be you. I looked the other way after what you told me and what we experienced, but if you don't think I will pull this trigger... I'll empty the whole magazine in you if I need to."

"He was a cop, but he was also a monster."

Hamlin stepped forward, forcing Christopher back into his house. Hamlin's eyes never left his.

"All cops can fuck up. I fucked up," Hamlin said.

"No Hamlin, not like this guy. He had killed, used his badge to rape and kill, and he had no intention of stopping."

"How do I know this is true?"

"You don't, only my word. I was trying to talk to that girl, the one outside my window. I saw her again at that bar and he decided to be a hero. But I could see his soul. He was no hero."

"What murder? What rape?"

Christopher tried to remember the details. His reading of the man's soul was sickening, and part of him had been trying to forget it. Then he remembered one thing.

"License plate LDA4035. Something like that. That was one of his victim's license plate number."

Hamlin's gun didn't waver, but for a moment Christopher thought he saw a flicker of doubt. So he pressed on.

"I could see it all, Hamlin, like it was all laid out for me. How he did it. How it made him feel. There was no investigation, no one ever found a body. He got away with it, but worse, he wanted to do it again. Whatever gifts I may have, the worst is to see the truth of a man's soul. It horrified me."

Now the gun did waver, slowly he lowered it.

"If I had done nothing. He would be walking free, ready to hurt and kill again."

Hamlin turned abruptly. "I need to check this out. I'm going to my car for a moment. You stay here. If you disappear then the next time I won't talk, I'll just squeeze the trigger."

Hamlin was back ten minutes later. This time his gun was holstered.

"The license plate belonged to a missing person. An unsolved case, but the car had been discovered by Patrolman Grey. Same guy you killed yesterday."

Christopher nodded absentmindedly.

"Christ, kid. I don't know what the hell is going on anymore. Zombies, flaming swords, you being able to read people's minds."

"Not minds, souls."

"Souls, minds, whatever. Look kid, I've been thinking ever since we talked the other day. I don't know what help I can be, but I'm up for it. Especially if it means we get to Ambros."

And Christopher had never been more thankful. It was time. It was time to go straight for Ambros.

22

Ambros' home looked like a castle, or rather something out of a Batman movie. Christopher stood well outside the gate, deep in the shadows, Hamlin next to him.

"I'm not so sure not having a plan is a good plan kid," Hamlin grumbled.

"But we do have a plan. I go in first, soften them up. Once the chaos is well underway, you come through as clean up. We know the basic layout and armament."

"Yeah, and if it gets too crazy I call in for back up, and then we try to explain why we are invading a man's house with no evidence or reason to be doing so."

"Right, which is why it is a last-resort call."

Christopher looked at Hamlin crouched in the bushes. A week ago Christopher would have thought of him as the tough guy, the seasoned cop, and Christopher would have been the cowardly kid, but now Hamlin looked fragile.

"When you kill these guys with the sword, you said it sort of damns them to Hell, no matter what?" Hamlin asked.

"Yes, even if I hit an innocent soul."

"These guys, his soldiers, are bad guys no doubt, but it makes me feel weird that we're condemning them to hell. I mean as bad as they are, that seems a little harsh."

"I know. I have to deal with that. Don't worry, I'm the decider, your conscience is clean."

"Thanks kid, but it will take a lot more than your assurance to appease my guilt."

Christopher turned to him and said, "I will do my best not to use the Weapon, but even if I could get by them unharmed, I can't leave them for you."

Hamlin nodded, but Christopher could see he was not convinced.

"This is the only way to take Ambros down. You said it yourself, you cops can't touch him. His shit don't stink apparently," said Christopher. "This is our chance to take out the man who killed and raped my family, who's committed countless other horrible crimes. Hamlin, I'm doing this with or without you.

And Christopher meant it. He could feel the rage building up, stoked by the seed of hell inside him. His body almost shook with fury. He wanted to feel the weight of Ambros' body as he sunk the Weapon into his chest.

Hamlin was staring at him, a slight glimmer of fear in his eyes, but then he nodded.

"I'm with you Christopher, I just wish we had a better plan."

Christopher reached out to the shadows and pulled on them to drape himself once again in his shifting black and gray coat and hood.

"The plan is simple. We bring hell to them."

With that, he emerged from the shadows and stalked toward the gate. Ten feet away he leapt into the air and sailed over the large iron wrought gate.

He landed in the middle of the courtyard, Weapon out, bands of power leaping from his body to the large sword and to the ground. He vibrated with energy and waited for the first gun shots to know in what direction to take the battle.

But there were none.

He scanned the courtyard and front of the house. Nothing. It was as if it was deserted. No group of goon soldiers came storming out of the shadows. The light was on in the small gate house, but there were no guards.

Something was not right.

He sniffed the air. He detected a slight tinge to it, something vaguely familiar.

Sword ready, he investigated the guard house. He recognized the smell before he reached the small room. It was the smell of fresh blood, of death.

He knew what he would find even before he looked in the large window. Two bodies lay on the floor of the room. They looked as if they had been killed by some sort of large animal. Chests torn open by what looked like claws, throats ripped open by powerful jaws. Blood splattered the walls, sending thick, viscous streaks down the sides of the room.

Whatever had killed these men had enjoyed it.

The monitors in the room showed nothing but static. He opened the door and hit the switch that he hoped would open the gate. He was rewarded by a grinding sound as the metal gate opened. Christopher turned away from the small security room. The house was quiet, lights were on, but no movement. Christopher couldn't smell a soul.

Hamlin came through, gun drawn.

"What the fuck happened here?" Hamlin asked.

"No idea," Christopher said. "I thought we'd need to come in guns blazing."

"What now?"

"Same plan. We have no idea what's inside. I go first."

The power of hell still throbbing through, him he approached the front door. One of the large double doors was slightly ajar.

Suddenly tired of the quiet, itching to reap souls, he kicked open the double doors. With a great wrenching sound, they tore from their hinges and crashed against the walls before falling to the floor.

If anything was in the house, that noise should have woken it up.

But again there was nothing. No alarm, no people crying out, no sound of henchmen running towards him. Nothing.

In the hallway were two more bodies, also torn apart as if by some large creature or creatures. Here too, blood splattered the walls.

Trying to remember the crude map the Librarian had shown him, Christopher made his way through the house. He found more bodies in other rooms. Henchmen or guards slaughtered by some unknown creature or creatures.

Some had body parts gnawed off, others looked as though they had been skidded across the room, their entrails spilling out in large shiny streaks on the marble floor.

Eventually Christopher came to a final set of double doors. If he remembered the map correctly, this would be the large dining room or ballroom. If anything awaited him in this abattoir, it would most likely be in here.

Again impatience won and he kicked the doors, the power in him craving blood so far denied him. But no longer it seemed.

At the other end of the room in a large chair sat Ambros. He sat calmly, his feet flat on the floor, his hands firmly gripping the ends of the armrests. He looked up when the door burst open, but did not move in any other way, except for his eyes widening in surprise. His face was cut and bruised, blood seeping out of several of his orifices.

He looked right at Christopher, but seemed to only half notice him. It was easy to see who had done this too him. Rath stood just behind him, smiling.

"Welcome boy, to Ambros' mausoleum and, I suppose, yours as well," Rath said.

He stepped from behind Ambros, and Christopher could see his arms glistened with wet blood past the elbows. His mouth was also covered in blood, trails of it ran down his face.

This was the creature that had killed the guards. Rath had slaughtered his own men.

"I have come to claim Ambros and to drag you back to Hell," Christopher said, the seed of power inside of him giving his words a confidence he didn't feel.

Rath chuckled. "Big talk for a boy who a few days ago was more worried about his final exams than collecting stray souls for hell."

As he talked. Rath seemed to grow taller, his already lanky arms grew longer and his fingers were more claw like. It was as though he was becoming more bestial as he talked.

"You are not your predecessor, boy. You are just a baby trying to pick up where he left off. No clue as to your true potential, your true strength. Tell me, have you grown fond of the taste of dammed souls Hunter?"

Christopher stepped forward, the Weapon in his hands compelling him onward. Its thirst for Rath overpowering his reluctance.

"You are a fool, boy. A slave to that thing in your hands. I will free you soon, but first let me take care of a little business and deny you the pleasure."

Rath reached out with one clawed hand towards Ambros.

"No!" Christopher cried out. "He is mine."

Christopher had no idea where it came from, but he knew that the whole purpose of his being, amplified by the seed of Hell inside of him, cried out for him to be the one to end Ambros.

Rath hesitated with a smile.

"Ah yes, the seed of hell is alive in you. Stoking the fire of hatred. You are truly just a puppet."

He reached once more for Ambros as though to twist his head off like a beer cap.

"No!" Christopher cried again and acting purely from instinct threw the bladed Weapon in his hand at Rath. It spun like a great fiery wheel.

Rath turned from Ambros and snatched the fire sword out of the air. Instantly the great flaming sword of hell transformed back into its unassuming pocket knife configuration. Rath casually slipped it into the pocket of his waistcoat.

"Well that was almost too easy," Rath said. "The Weapon is mighty, but by itself, useless. Its needs your will to act. A trick like that might work against many dark souls, but not me."

Christopher was stunned. Rath had removed the one Weapon he had. Easily. Christopher suddenly felt like he was a child playing with toys too big for him. And maybe he was. He was just a college kid given the keys to hell. No wonder he fell so easily into what was obviously a trap.

Christopher heard a noise from the hallway. A shuffling noise. At first he thought it was Hamlin, but it was too unsteady, then a moan. Christopher knew what it was.

Fucking zombies.

From the doors leading into the room, guards appeared. Well, former guards. Now they were dead things made to work for the dark soul gloating at him from across the room.

They were still streaming in when the first one reached Christopher. It reached for his shadow coat, teeth chomping.

Unsure what to do Christopher slammed his fist into the creature's gut. He felt bone snapping and organs rupturing as his fist slammed into it. The force of the blow doubled it over and sent it flying to the group of zombies behind it. They went over like bowling pins.

But more kept streaming in. Christopher guessed that Rath must have killed every soldier in Ambros' employ, and now he had an army of the dead to deal with.

At the other end of the room Rath had grabbed the chair Ambros was stuck in and dragged it behind him as he left through the French doors onto the pool patio beyond.

Christopher didn't have time to watch; a hoard of zombies was on top of him, clawing at his shadow coat, their fingers raking his skin.

He threw his shoulder into the nearest group, slamming them back into one another. Some fell, but others surged forward. He began striking out at random as they came at him from all directions.

Christopher struck one in the jaw hard enough to smash its face in, but it just ignored the move as though its head wasn't even needed. He grabbed the body of another and spun it in a circle to knock back the closest. It worked for a moment, but he knew he couldn't keep this up all night. Despite his strength and healing ability they would soon overwhelm him, and he doubted he could heal fast enough when they were feasting on his entrails.

"Kid, jump!" cried a voice from behind him.

Christopher turned around and saw Hamlin standing there. He had a grenade in his hand and a belt of them across his chest. Hamlin hadn't arrived at the house with them, of that Christopher was sure, but somehow the detective had managed to collect some party favors along the way.

Some of the undead looked his way when he yelled. They had only moments before a group would split up from the pack and the grenades became less effective. Christopher gathered his strength and jumped.

Thank god for cathedral ceilings. He landed near where Rath had exited. At the other end of the room Hamlin let the grenade fly, landing it in the middle of the zombies. Christopher left through the French doors just as the grenade went off.

The explosion shook the house, shattering the windows outward as Christopher exited. Little shards of glass cut across his skin, causing pinpricks of pain, healing instantly.

More explosions sounded from the house. Christopher took that as a good sign that Hamlin was still alive. If anything could stop those zombies, grenades could. He had to focus on Rath, who seemed to have disappeared.

Ambros still sat in his chair, locked in place by some force next to the pool as though forgotten. But Rath was nowhere to be seen.

"Fuck!" Christopher exclaimed. He can't get away again, Christopher was tired of this. It needed to end.

Ambros grunted. He wiggled in his chair as though trying to break his invisible bonds. He appeared to be staring at Christopher as his eyes widened. It occurred to Christopher that Ambros was less staring at him and more over Christopher's shoulder.

"Fuck," Christopher said again and tried to spin around.

Halfway into his turn, claws sank into him, slicing neatly past his shadow garments and earthly ones, cutting deep into his sides and ribs in a steel like grip.

Rath had him. He cried out at the intense pain as the dark soul's needle-like fingers split bone and tore muscle. Through the haze of pain Christopher felt himself being lifted up, and then the claws were gone. He was plunged into water and gasped in shock as pool water streamed into his nose and throat.

Human instinct took over and he kicked up towards the surface. He surfaced, coughing and spitting. Rath stood at the pool's edge. Blood dripped from exposed wounds in his hands and splashed into the pool. Where the blood landed, the water began to roll and bubble as though boiling.

"The Beast was a little more difficult, I have to say," Rath said. "I guess it's because you are human as I once was and just a child. This makes you predictable and easy to manipulate."

More and more of the pool began to churn. Christopher tried to swim to the edge, but the violent water pushed him back towards the center. He had never been a strong swimmer.

"I already have the Weapon, once you are dead I will take the Book. I assume you have it on you? Not that it matters. Nobody will inherit your position when you pass. I and my kind will be free to reclaim this world."

Something wrapped around Christopher's leg and pulled his head under. As he reached for whatever it was, something else grabbed at his arm and wrenched it back. The water had turned dark, but he could see what had him. Large tentacles had wrapped around his arm and leg. As he watched, more stretched out from the dark and enveloped his other appendages.

He couldn't move. Briefly he was lifted out of the water. He saw Rath leaving, walking out through the gardens and towards the beach.

Fucker thinks his job is done, thought Christopher as he was pulled under again. *And perhaps it was.*

The tentacles dragged him down and down as though the bottom of the pool had ceased to exist. They pulled at him in different directions, trying to yank his arms and legs off like a captured spider all the while pulling him deeper into the dark.

He struggled at the grip of the tentacles, but he had no leverage. Even though he had the strength to pull against the slimy ropes that entrapped, him he had nowhere to go with it.

Perhaps Rath was right. What was he thinking? He was just a college kid. What the hell was he thinking going after supernatural creatures and trying to avenge his family's murder?

The water around him was growing darker, his chest was hurting. It occurred to him that if he just let go, just let the water in, it would all be over. He could just float away into the dark before he met whatever was at the other end of these tentacles.

It was then that the seed of hell flared up. Like a bright spot in an otherwise dark world the seed became a guiding light. It became of all things, a beacon of hope.

He felt it burn through him, its purifying anger and rage coursed through him. Ambros was still alive. Rath was still alive. That he could not stand. They had to die.

He did the only thing he could do, he was running out of oxygen and time. He grabbed hold of the tentacle and tried to climb towards its owner. Time to meet this beast head on.

A giant head loomed out of the dark. It looked like an octopus, but its beak was set just below the eyes rather than at the center of its tentacles. The beak was lined with small sharp teeth, making it look like a saw blade.

It pulled him towards its mouth, beak gaping. Christopher did the only thing he could think of. He jammed his left fist into the creature's gullet. At first the creature pulled back in surprise, but then in clamped its beak down on his arm. He could feel teeth sawing through his flesh as he reached around inside of its mouth or stomach or whatever the hell he had his arm in.

His hand found a chunk of some flesh inside and grabbed on, wrenching it and pulling himself closer. The creature's beak stopped its sawing motion into his arm as it reacted to his direct assault on its internal organs.

Christopher didn't wait for it to recover. With his other hand he struck directly at its huge, single eye. He felt his hand hit the jelly-like substance of its eye and he pressed inward, puncturing it.

The creature was reacting, now trying its damnedest to get away from him. The tentacles were no longer encircling his arms, they beat against him to try and drive him away.

But he had the devil in him and even with his lungs screaming at him, he fought on. He squeezed with all the might he could pull from the power of Hell and slowly caused his hands to meet. One through the mouth and one through the eye.

He felt flesh tearing as his hands strained for each other. The tentacles beat at him in panic, but the creature was too crazed to effectively pull him away. It struggled to get away as fast as possible.

By the time his hands met, tearing through the organs, the beak had loosened and fallen open, the tentacles drifted, occasionally twitching in final death throes.

Christopher pulled his arms free and immediately swam for the surface, but he knew it was too late. His lungs couldn't hold anymore. His vision was dimming, turning from red to black at the edges.

He could taste salt water rather than chlorine and knew somehow he had gone from the pool to the open sea. Just as his lungs gave out and he opened his mouth to pull in water and end it all, he burst through the surface.

He must have slid into unconsciousness briefly because the next thing he knew he was on the beach, washed up like some sort of flotsam. He stared at the sky and stars as he coughed up water. His arm ached and failed to respond when he tried to move it. The beak had cut through muscle and tendon and sawed at the bone.

It wouldn't move. It would take a while to heal even at his accelerated rate.

"Well you are a tough one, I'll give you that," said Rath from somewhere up the beach.

Christopher turned over, trying to stand using his one good arm for leverage. He managed to make it to his knees when he saw him.

Rath loomed over Christopher with claws extended, mouth full of teeth open wide in a feral grin.

"I just fucked up Cthulhu, you're next," Christopher said as he slowly and painfully rose to his feet. He hoped Rath didn't see the true pain he was in. But it seemed he had.

Rath smiled, "Well you've got spunk and I like that. Unfortunately, this has to be over. I have a war to plan."

Rath stepped forward and plunged his claws into Christopher's side, digging, ripping into him. He pulled Christopher in an obscene parody of a hug. The reek of his evil soul turned Christopher's stomach.

"Time to tear you apart," Rath said with a hunger that said he relished the idea.

"You first," Christopher said and slipped his good hand into Rath's small waistcoat pocket until he felt the cold hardness of the Weapon.

It sprang to life instantly, erupting into a large spear. Its transformation taking it right through Rath's body.

The Dark Soul's eyes widened in surprise and pain then shifted quickly to fear.

He released Christopher and stepped back, spear still impaling him. But Christopher held on to the end and thrust it forward the best he could with his one good arm.

The spear roared with power and Christopher could see the

soul of Rath pull from his body. It tore away slowly and was sucked into the Weapon. But still he resisted.

"I... I... don't... this can't happen," Rath said.

"Oh but it is happening, you insane fucker," Christopher said.

Rath stumbled to his knees, and in an act of defiance he stopped himself from falling all the way down.

"I will come back. I will come back for you, boy. I escaped once, I can do it again. I will return and I will destroy everything you hold dear."

"You and Ambros already did," Christopher said and then pulled the spear out only to slam it back into the Dark Soul's chest, forcing him to the ground.

Rath began to scream as the Weapon finally claimed its soul. The body that had been Rath fell to the ground lifeless. Gone were the claws and other signs of inhumanity. It was just the body of the poor man Rath had used.

The weapon once more became a pocket knife, and Christopher slipped it into his coat next to the book. The beach was deserted in this area, nobody had seen what had happened.

He turned and made his way back to the house, limping and wincing in pain. He would have to ask the Librarian if there was a way to speed up the healing process.

He found Ambros where he had left him, sitting in the chair. Hamlin stood next to him gun in hand.

"The zombies?" Christopher asked.

"Got most of them with the grenades, the last couple just dropped a minute ago for no reason that I could see."

Christopher nodded. "It was because I killed Rath. Their strings were cut."

Hamlin nodded.

"The cops will be here any minute because of the grenades. We need to move," he said.

Again, Christopher nodded.

"What do we do with this one?" Hamlin asked.

Christopher could see that Ambros' arms and legs were broken and useless, his eyes rolled in his head in pain. Christopher reached for the Weapon, but hesitated.

He could feel the need of the Weapon. It seized hold of him, it ached, and therefore made him ache, to carve into this man. But he held back, and with effort he left the Weapon in its pocket.

"I think I'll let God sort this one out," Christopher said and pushed the chair into the deep end of the pool.

23

"I don't think there will ever be whiskey strong enough for what we have seen," Hamlin said as he raised his glass and took a long sip.

They were sitting in Christopher's living room. Christopher had his arm in a sling, but he could feel it was close to being healed. He took a long pull of his drink also.

"You know, I don't feel any different," Christopher said. "I was expecting, I don't know, some sort of closure maybe, some sense of accomplishment with my family, but I'm not sure I feel that."

"There is never closure with death. Vengeance seems like enough, but it never is in the end," Hamlin said. "But that doesn't mean it doesn't need to be done."

Christopher had to admit the house seemed a little less dark, little less final. Maybe he would stay for a while.

"What do you make of what Rath said? That stuff about his brethren? About some sort of war?" Hamlin asked.

Christopher just shook his head.

"I'm not sure, but I think we will know soon. It can't be good."

"Well, I hope it will be a while. I don't know about you but I need a break after all this shit."

Christopher smiled. It made him feel a little bit better that he wouldn't be doing this alone.

"Yeah, Hamlin, a break is just what we need."

A knock at the door startled them both. It was late, only trouble would be on his doorstep this late.

Christopher got up slowly and cautiously approached the door. Behind him Hamlin drew his weapon. He looked through the peephole, but could barely make out the figure in the doorway she was so small.

"It's the girl," Christopher whispered.

Hamlin nodded, but didn't put away his gun. Christopher opened the door.

She looked up at him nervously. She moved from foot to foot as though she would run at any moment. Despite the fear in her eyes, Christopher thought she was quite pretty.

"Um, I ah... I need your help," she said almost too quiet to hear.

Remembering how she had a tendency to run from him Christopher asked, "Are you sure?"

Suddenly her demeanor changed. Her face grew fierce, and she no longer looked like she wanted to run.

"Bitch said she needed your help, didn't she? Damn I need a drink,"

And with that she shoved past him and into the house like he wasn't even there. And just like that Christopher realized there was no vacation in his immediate future.

24

The four members of the Alliance of dark souls sat around the large conference table meant to seat thirty or more. The dim light obscuring their faces and the distance between them gave them some sense of comfort. They remained quiet while waiting.

When the room was full, tension lay thick in the air, arguments erupted and violence was often the norm. Although many are part of this thing they called an alliance, it is always better to work with just a few at a time.

And that was why Golyat had arranged this small gathering with only four of the most influential members. Although, what influence any of them had over such a fiercely independent group was questionable.

They were all different. They all had different ideals, different goals, different fetishes. They also all had different strengths, different weaknesses and different gifts. Each had learned different lessons both in mortal life and then in the afterlife.

But they all had one thing in common. They had all had their trial by fire. All had been condemned to hell, all of them had shed their mortal coil and been re-forged in that hottest of furnaces. They had each made it through their own personal hell and escaped.

In each had grown the seed of hatred. The hatred might have been different in each of them. Some hated mortals most of all, some just hated everything, some just hated the concept of life. But it was hatred pure and simple that formed the tenuous bond between each of them. Even those that secretly hated what they had become.

And this bond, this hatred, is what Golyat sought to exploit as he stepped into the room. He did not sit.

"Ladies, gentlemen, we have a problem. Rath has failed. There is a new Hunter," Golyat said.

There was a sudden intake of breath around the room.

"What do you mean Rath has failed? He killed the ancient one," hissed a voice from the back of the room.

Despite the dark lighting Golyat knew it came from Andre Lavolier. He was actually thankful the dim light kept him from seeing Andre's scale-covered skin. The Alligator King he had once been called.

"He did indeed kill our old nemesis, but the Beast was able to pass on his task and abilities to a successor. A mortal child."

"And he was unable to kill a simple child?"

This came from Anabelle, or as she was called behind her back, the dragon lady. She did lean forward into the light, and it was all Golyat could do not to dwell on her beauty.

"Worse, dear Anabelle. The boy was able to defeat him. Rath has been confined once again to Hell's dominion."

The silence was complete as though they had all stopped breathing. It was their kind's greatest fear, the thing rarely spoken of, to return to that eternal damnation.

"So this boy is not so much a child if he was able to defeat Rath," Anabelle said. "He has come into his full power?"

"No, I do not believe so. A mortal has never held this position, it has always been the aspect of Lucifer that hunted our kind. I think the boy was able to defeat Rath with a combination of dumb luck and our colleague's own arrogance. I think this boy is only scratching the surface with no idea what he really is."

"Then what do you suggest?"

"Spread the word to the others, we must make plans," Golyat said. "We must destroy the boy before he masters the Book and Weapon and sends us all back to hell."

EATER OF SOULS

BOOK TWO OF THE HAND OF PERDITION

1

Pain.

It went on forever. It always had been pain and always would be.

Suffering. It too went on forever.

Then it was dark and cool. The pain was gone.

The thing staggered from the shadows of the alley. Just suddenly there, from nowhere, at least, he did not know where he came from. He just knew that a moment ago he suffered and there was such pain. Now he was here. Not there. Something like doubtful relief passed through him. But where had he been?

He was outside, he knew that much. He was cold, so cold, but still warmer than where he had been. Moisture fell on him, dampening his fur. Fur?

One massive, clawed hand grasped the brick building keeping him upright when every part of his body just wanted to sit down and go to sleep.

No. No sleep. The thing needed to understand. Who was he? Where had he been? Where was he now?

A claw carved into the brick in frustration, sending red masonry dust falling to the concrete of the alley. He straightened up, stretching like it was the first time he had ever stretched. Bones popped and muscles cried with relief as he stretched to his full height of eight feet, before he pulled back into a more comfortable, hunched-over posture.

He could smell the odor of rot and spoilage that came from the metal containers throughout the alley. Foul smelling liquid leaked from them, forming sludge streams that flowed into the center of the alley and mixed with the rain water to form dark puddles of filth. He could hear noise, people, walking, living beyond the alley, just on the other side of the brick wall in front of him. His stomach growled at the thought. Other, harsher noises came to him. Mortals speaking, horns honking, a million other sounds. Despite being overwhelmed, all of this was somehow comforting to the creature.

He looked over himself, a mixture of fur and leathery hide, his arms and chest thick with muscle. His legs and torso thinner but no less powerful. He could feel the strength of his form. The fingers of his hand ended in two inch claws, strong as... as... he was not sure, though he thought he should know.

His mouth was a muzzle, elongated and full of sharp teeth. Thick, viscous saliva dripped from his mouth, mixing with the puddles of rain water at his feet. Above him the old brick buildings stretched to the sky, the walls lined with stairs and ladders.

He smelled something. Something that made him hungry.

He took a few tentative steps down the alley, testing his new legs. Powerful though they were, he was unpracticed with them. He heard a deep rumble, like the approach of an earthquake, and realized he was making it. A growl, deep from within his chest. It was the smell.

It smelled of food, but more importantly of nourishment. He

could feel strength and power flowing throughout his body, but the power needed to be fed. It needed fresh meat.

But not just meat, something more. Then he saw it, in the middle of the alley.

A large *man*. The creature did not know how, but he knew that this thing was called *man*. The man sat against the wall of the alley and smelled of urine and stale body odor mixed with the harsh scent of alcohol. But that did not bother the creature. He smelled fresh meat and that other, even more demanding scent.

More saliva dripped from its maw. The hunger grew, becoming unreasonable. That scent, he needed it. He needed it now.

The man, old with wrinkled, sagging flesh, opened his eyes at the thing's approach. They widened in fear as it loomed over him. He sputtered, "wha...wha...wha..." as though his mouth was moving faster than his pickled brain could formulate thought.

"Jesus Christ, what are you?" he finally managed to say.

The thing thought he should answer. A growl came out, low and menacing.

“I don't know," he said, finding a way to speak through his wolf-like muzzle, "But I know what you are. Food."

The old man cried out and raised his arms as though that would somehow fend off the attack. The creature grabbed his arm and lifted the old man, wrenching his arm into the air.

The old man screamed and the creature heard the crunch as the man's shoulder separated from the abrupt violence in the movement. The man dangled, still screaming a rough, confused scream.

"Help me! What are you? Please, please why?" the man begged.

The thing could smell the warm blood, could almost taste the meaty flesh. Drool oozed out of its mouth. With a roar, he bit into the neck.

Sweet blood exploded into his mouth like nectar. He could feel his teeth sinking into the old man's soft flesh, then he was tearing, ripping the flesh off. Though he couldn't remember anything about himself before the past few minutes, he knew that he could never have a pleasure greater than this.

Then the creature sensed it.

As the piece of flesh slid down his throat and the man uttered his last gurgle, the thing felt the object of his real desire, of his real hunger. He could smell it leaking out of the man. Suddenly panicking, he knew he couldn't lose whatever it was and took another bite out of the man's shoulder. This time, however, he wasn't looking for the taste of meat, but something else.

As his teeth sunk in he felt it, tasted it. He tasted the man's soul. Now he frenzied, ripping the man to shreds physically to get at the soul that lay in the center. Before the soul could depart, the creature tore into it, gulping down bite after bite and savoring each taste of the man's essence, feeling the power flow into him as he consumed it. Strength like he had never felt imbued him. Soon the body was no more than a wet, red mess of tissue and bone, the Creature had consumed everything. But it was the soul of this man that provided the real nourishment. It was the true food he needed.

And he must have more.

The creature would gorge himself on this new delicacy. But, he was still weak, he needed to gather strength. The creature reached down and picked up the man's blood-splattered coat. It had been long and several sizes too large for the man. The creature threw it across his shoulders and found it was a little small, but it would do for now.

"I think I'll call you Ammit," said a light voice from the mouth of the alley.

The creature spun with a snarl, lips pulled back to bare his teeth. He was alarmed someone could sneak up on him so easily.

At the mouth of the alley stood a woman, a girl really, she barely came to his waist. He could tear her to shreds in an instant. But she showed no fear, she just looked at him with dispassionate eyes. Somehow this made the creature more concerned than if she had been his match. Her dark black hair hung loosely across her shoulders, and her eyes burned fiercely green with power. She wore a little black dress. Even though the creature knew so little, he knew he looked on great beauty. If he had ever been a man, he would have chased her forever.

Behind her another girl, younger even than the first, knelt on the ground, slumped forward as though exhausted. She seemed even slighter than the woman who spoke. It could have just been her defeated posture, but she seemed to be sinking into herself. She might have been beautiful once, but her brown hair hung in greasy, knotted clumps across her face, a face covered in bruises and cuts. An iron collar encircled her neck, a chain stretching from it to the speaking woman's hand. A pet of some sort?

"It is a girl's name, ancient Egyptian really, but appropriate I think," she said and walked closer to him as though he was harmless, not the deadly creature he knew himself to be.

He sniffed at her and he could smell it. That same human soul smell, but this time putrid and rotten, as though corrupted beyond all recognition. It sat in her ill-fitting body as though it strained to get out. He knew instinctively that she was like him. His soul, if he had one, would have that same corruption, if he were able to smell it. He did not get the same vile scent from the broken girl on the ground. She was an innocent.

"You are a big one. Congratulations on your escape," she said. He did not know what she meant, but she seemed to know something about him. Perhaps she had answers to his questions.

"Who are you?" he asked.

She said nothing until she stood directly in front of him,

showing she did not fear him at all. "My name is Anabelle. Some time ago I came from the same place you have just escaped."

"Where was that?" he growled. "Where am I now? What am I?"

"What you are and where you are now, you will come to understand in time. As for where you came from?"

She reached up to his face, just within her reach as he hunched over. He flinched back, but then held himself still. She was so beautiful, she meant him no harm. Gently she touched his cheek, a caress and he knew he would be her creature forever.

"You will help me make sure that we, all of us, never have to return to that place ever again."

"How?"

"We kill the one that would send us back to Hell."

The creature smiled, showing teeth still covered in the old man's blood. He liked that. He was good at killing.

2

Christopher looked up when he heard a knock on the door. He was in his father's study, although it was his now, he did not believe he would ever be able to think of it any other way. It was his father's style from top to bottom. Dark wood bookshelves lined the walls, complementing the wood paneling. A dark leather couch hunkered near the fireplace. Christopher sat behind a large executive desk in a very comfortable chair.

It occurred to him that it was very much like the study in the Library, which theoretically was created from his subconscious, so perhaps it was his style too. Or maybe it formed from his childhood memories of this room.

A second knock on the door brought him back to the present.

"Come in," Christopher said. No need to ask who it was, there was only one other person in the house besides him.

Two weeks ago Eris had showed up on his doorstep. She was possessed by a demon she said, but not in the Linda-Blair-vomiting-pea-green-soup sort of way. This one was much less messy and something neither of them wanted. After agreeing to help and finding out she had no place to go, he offered to let her stay with him.

He wasn't sure why he agreed to let a demon sleep under his roof. Maybe it was because he had found somebody that might understand him and who he was now. And it would be nice to have someone in the house he could turn to that wouldn't think he was crazy. Or maybe it was because she was pretty.

The door opened and Eris walked in. He studied her carefully, watching her movements. She smiled when she came in, gently closing the door behind her. As usual, her bright blue eyes caught his attention first. She had dark hair that hung not quite to her shoulders. She was dressed in jeans and a black Misfits tank top, slightly torn. Full sleeve tattoos adorned both her arms and another tattoo decorated part of her chest and neck. Christopher thought he didn't care for tattoos, but for some reason they looked great on her. Even attractive. She moved calmly, even shyly as she came into the room and sat on the couch facing the desk.

For the moment he thought he might be dealing with Eris. He almost let out a sigh of relief, although that relief could change at any moment. Dark Eris, as he referred to her possessed version, could be a handful at times.

"Eris, what's up?" He asked. But he knew.

"It's been two weeks since we first came to you for help. I need her, it, gone from inside me. And you seem to be spending all your time in here in this study, working on God knows what."

Thank God she hadn't come in a few minutes later. He was just about to play some video games.

"I know, I know. But I told both of you that I had no idea what to do. I have gone to the Library and even asked the Librarian for answers. He says he's looking into it, but it might take a while."

The Library was a sort of pocket dimension that only Christopher, since he had inherited the power of the Hunter, could enter. Theoretically it contained all the knowledge in the universe. In practice, it was hard to access information amid such vastness. Everything you looked for was like trying to find a needle in a haystack the size of the Earth. The Librarian told Christopher that it adapted to him in a way that he could understand, he just wished it could be computerized. At least some sort of data base would have been better than an impossibly large Library with books, scrolls and even tablets sitting on shelves as far as the eye could see. The idea of researching anything had him in tears before he even began.

"She doesn't even know her true name, she is just as confused about how she got in my body as I am," Eris said. She put her face in her hands. He could tell she was frustrated.

"Right. So without that, it's going to take a while to figure out what to do," Christopher said.

He got up and walked over to the couch and sat next to her.

"Look I've told you my story. You know how new I am to all this, I barely understand what I have become, let alone how to help you guys with your problem," he said. He had opened the Book and received his new skills only a few weeks before. Somehow he had been granted great power to hunt down and retrieve souls that had escaped from Hell, along with access to a library of knowledge that was more complicated than Ikea furniture assembly instructions.

"I know. We tried to get to the Beast, but it was too late. He had already ended. But when she saw you on the train and realized you carried the Book and Weapon, she thought you or whoever claimed that power would be able to help us. I guess it's just not that easy."

"We will solve this. I have to spend time with my family's estate matters, but all my other time is spent researching how to exorcise demons. It's just not really my purpose."

He had inherited the power of Hell needed to hunt down escaped souls and send them back to Hell, but he had none of the knowledge that you would expect from a warden of Hell. Perhaps he *could* send Dark Eris back to Hell, but he had no idea how to do it.

"Tell me once again how it happened? This time with as much detail as you can remember," Christopher asked.

"I've told you several times. It just happened. I fell asleep and the next thing I knew I woke up with her inside. And she was just as surprised."

"Please just tell me again. Where did it happen?" He asked.

"I was spending the night at a friend's. We had been drinking, and I fell asleep on the floor at some point..."

She began to shudder slightly. Her eyes closed tightly and when she opened them they were black as night. Dark Eris.

"She is not telling you the whole truth, you know," Dark Eris said.

Gone was any trace of shyness. It was as though all traces of innocent beauty had disappeared and was replaced with seductive desire. She was no less beautiful, but an animalistic, sexual aura emanated from her. Her lips turned up on one side in a smirk.

She got up and walked around the room looking at various items on the shelves as though they held real interest for her. Christopher was instantly on guard. He had spoken little to the demoness in the few days since Eris had turned up on his doorstep. All he really knew was that she wanted out just as badly as Eris wanted her gone.

"Oh? Then would you like to explain?" Christopher asked.

She looked back at him with the same expression she always seemed to have. It was somewhere between judging and amusement. She seemed to be deciding something.

"We came here looking for the Beast. I don't remember much about how I came to possess this body, but I do know of the Beast. He was an aspect of Lucifer, Lord of Hell, and his job was to track down those that escaped. If anybody in the mortal world could help us it was him."

Christopher said nothing. He knew this, he lived it. He would give it all back if he could.

"Now I find he has died. He was not supposed to be able to die. He was immortal, just like Lucifer himself. And not only did this impossibility happen, but he passed his immense power on to a mortal. So now Christopher, if anybody can help us it is you."

She had worked her way around the room as she talked and once again sat next to him. He was suddenly aware of how close she was and the heat that was coming off her body. He found himself leaning in for... for what? He didn't know.

With another smirk she pulled back and Christopher did the same, but couldn't help feel a pang of disappointment.

"She wasn't staying at a friends that night. We woke together on the floor of some dirty flophouse. She has no memory of the time before waking up. She was confused of course and deliciously scared. And once she realized I was inside her, her mind almost broke."

"Why would she lie to me? What reason could she possibly have?" Christopher asked.

It was hard to trust Dark Eris, she was a demon after all and took no small joy in teasing him. When he shifted his senses to see and smell Eris' soul—one of the gifts of his new powers—he could see the dark spot on it, the spot that was the demoness. Or rather the sickly shade of gray, not as dark as the ones he had sent back to Hell.

Dark Eris rolled her eyes at his question. "She is scared Christopher. She is incredibly weak. She has no memory of her life, just that she had one. Whether she admits it or not, she is afraid she has lost herself forever, and it appears she may be right.

And here I am, a demon, and I have some memories, but they are dulled and blurry, just out of reach. As for how I got summoned and forced into this pathetic shell, that memory is a complete blank.

"Lucky for her she has me for protection. She had almost no money and wouldn't have lasted three days on the streets. Don't let the tattoos fool you, she is not as tough as she thinks. Got anything to drink in this place?"

She caught him off guard with the question.

"Sure, my father kept a well-stocked bar in here. Bourbon?"

"Yes please," she said.

Christopher poured both of them a drink, bourbon, neat because there was no ice in the bowl and he didn't feel like going to the kitchen. Besides, she was a demon trapped in a mortal body, he doubted she would mind. After getting her drink she went on.

"She had enough money on her to stay in the scummy flophouse that first night and after that she would just have to figure it out. The yelling, the smells, the dirt that was everywhere, she hated that place. I felt right at home."

"How do you know all this? Her lack of memory? Did she tell you?" Christopher asked.

"We share the same mind. It's not really mind reading, but I see so much about her and remember so little about me."

She looked at Christopher and for a moment the smirk was gone and the seductiveness left her eyes. "It may have just been Hell, but they are still my memories, my essence. I would like them back." Then the attitude returned. "The only sure memory I have is waking up in the middle of the night together. That and my name, Eris is mine, not hers."

"And you, a demon, have no memories other than your victims?"

"As I said I have memories, more than just my *victims*. Just not of how I got inside of her. I am the *victim* here also."

Christopher was not entirely convinced of that. But this was the first time they had really talked. Eris had been almost a ghost since storming into his life. He found himself leaning close to her again. Something about her pulled him in, her beauty, maybe, but something else too. Unfortunately, their conversation was cut short. The phone rang and Christopher almost jumped out of his seat.

"Jesus Christ," he said and went to the phone. "Who the Hell could be calling this late at night?"

But he had a good idea who it was.

"Hello Hamlin," Christopher said into the phone.

"Kid, It's... how did you know it was me? Are you using some of that Hell magic on me?" asked Detective Hamlin on the other end.

Christopher sighed. "No, I just don't have many friends who would call me at midnight. Come to think of it, I don't have many friends at all."

"Don't get all sappy on me now kid. I need your help. There's been a murder, I think."

"You think? In your line of work shouldn't you be more certain of things like that?" Christopher asked.

"Yeah well, in my line of work we don't usually work with emissaries of Hell and super villains, but I feel I adapted fairly well all things considered."

"You think the murder was related to an escaped dark soul?" Christopher asked.

"Since you started flying from rooftop to rooftop and swinging a flaming sword, I don't know what to think about a lot of things, but this one is weird and I just want to rule out one of yours. I'll text you the address."

"I'll try to help the best I can, but remember, this stuff is all just as new to me as you," Christopher said. It felt like Christopher was doing a lot of trying to help lately, and not really succeeding. First Eris and now Hamlin need him.

"Got it, just get down here as fast as you can," Hamlin said and hung up.

"Eris, I have to cut this conversation short. Hamlin needs my help with something," Christopher said as he put away his phone and straightened up the papers on his desk. "But let's not say anything to... her... about what we talked about. You know how fragile she is."

Eris came over to him and he looked up, right into her bright blue eyes. Eyes that were filling with tears. Shit. "I'm not as fragile as you, and her, think."

"I'm sorry Eris, I didn't mean that. We can talk about this when I get back and I'll make another trip to the Library and see what I can dig up about demon possessions."

"Great," she said wiping the tears from her checks. "Where are we going?"

"We?"

"Yes both... I mean, all three of us I guess," she said.

"I'm going to a crime scene to help Hamlin out. It might have something to do with my, you know... anyway, it's not safe."

"I don't care. Like I said, I'm not that fragile. I can take care of myself. I am not letting you out of my sight. Besides, I... she has some... talents that might be of use."

Christopher knew very, very little about women, having had only one girlfriend his entire twenty-one years of life on this planet, but the tone in her voice, the set of her feet, her crossed arms, even he could tell there was no way he was going to talk her out of it.

"Okay, but you stay in the car," Christopher said.

Eris just raised an eyebrow.

3

"What is she doing here?" Hamlin asked.

He was standing on the sidewalk in front of a building with police caution tape stretched across the door and broken windows. He was dressed as usual in his perpetually rumpled gray suit, and his hair, never quite right, stuck up with a cowlick on his right side. And for some reason he never seemed to manage to shave closer than three days' scruff. He would be the picture next to the definition of detective in the dictionary. He held a manila folder in his hand.

"She wouldn't stay in the car," Christopher said.

"Great. Last thing I need is two of you," Hamlin said.

"Two of us?"

"You know a demon, whatever you are, magic people or something."

"I'm not a demon, I am a human with a squatter problem," Eris said.

"Sure, whatever."

"This the place?" Christopher asked nodding to the building.

They were in a less than upper class neighborhood. Neon signs covered the windows, graffiti covered the brick walls in between and the corrugated security doors on the stores that were closed. There was a city smell here, like in any part of the city, the smell of steel, oil and gas, the stale odor of dust, but in this neighborhood there was more, the smell of rot, the stink of nearby dumpsters, stale beer from the broken bottles shattered in the alleyways.

Christopher did not like it here, it was too close to where he had massacred a group of gang members when the power inside of him raged out of his control.

"Yeah, let's talk inside," Hamlin said and they followed him to the crime scene.

A patrolman stood outside by the door with a clipboard in hand. He watched their approach with what looked like an amused expression on his face.

Christopher hesitated. "Are there still cops or forensics looking over the place? They're not going to let a couple of civilians just walk on in are they?"

"Most of that is done. The patrolmen are here until the decontamination team arrives to clean the place up. And normally no, we wouldn't let civilians on the scene. But then again you're not civilians."

"What are we?"

"Psychics."

"Psychics?"

"Hello sir. I just need your um... specialists to sign the log before they go in," the patrolman said, handing Christopher a clipboard. He looked like he was fighting a smile.

After Eris had signed—he had no idea what name she used—Christopher handed the clipboard back to him.

"Getting any vibes yet? Figure out who the killer is yet?" the patrolman snickered.

"That'll be enough Williams," Hamlin said with a growl.

"Yes sir," he said and turned away but not without giving them one last amused glance.

"Psychics? You told them we were psychics? Do you guys even do that? I thought it was a myth," Christopher asked.

"It was all I could think of to get you in there. And yes, sometimes we do use psychics though not as much as we did in the nineties. Back then I think some people in the department thought the X-Files was a documentary."

"Says the detective to the 'magic people'," said Christopher.

Hamlin glared at him.

The inside of the store was an eclectic blend of cheap crap you'd find at most convenience stores, smoking paraphernalia, lighters, incense, candies, and the cheap stuff one might find at a flea market, like knives, katanas, and Asian religious items up against anime prop reproductions. In essence, it was a junk store.

Dust covered many of the items, and Christopher's shoes stuck to the floor in spots. Despite the clutter and weapons, it felt like an empty and desperate place. A musty, metallic scent hung in the air, growing stronger the further they entered the place.

"Phew, the smell," Eris said.

Hamlin made his way over to the counter, and Christopher could see the source of the disturbing scent.

The glass counter was shattered and covered in blood, making it impossible to see through. The walls and ceiling behind it were so drenched in red it looked as though that had been the original color and someone had just dappled with spots of white. The trinkets and shelves surrounding the counter were splattered with the same blood. To Christopher it looked as though somebody behind the counter had exploded.

"Ohmygod," Eris said and turned away from the scene.

"What the Hell happened here?" Christopher asked, involuntarily covering his nose with his hand. The smell had suddenly become unbearable.

"That's what we're trying to figure out," Hamlin said. "You think it's bad now, you should have seen it when we arrived. Poor fucker was in pieces all over the place. Had to use multiple bags to get his remains to the morgue. Looked like a pack of wild dogs got to him."

"A pack of wild dogs in the city?" Eris asked.

"No, that's just it. Strays sure, but nothing that could do what we saw here. Besides, the medical examiner said that after a preliminary review of the wounds, it look like a pack of grizzlies were running with those dogs. Obviously, we don't have bears in the city."

Hamlin handed Christopher the manila folder. "Careful, these are crime scene photos, pretty high on the gruesome meter."

"I've cut people in half, unfortunately, so I'm not sure there's much that can shock me," Christopher said. He was wrong.

He opened the folder and his stomach did a somersault. The photos were a mess, he could barely make out the victim had been human. The only clue was the occasional toe or finger. This man had been torn apart and his guts dug through.

"Whatever or whoever it was, the medical examiner said it ate a lot of the guy, but also dug into him as though looking for something."

"Maybe it was looking for a particular organ it wanted?" Christopher couldn't believe they were having this conversation.

"M.E. said he would have to do a more extensive examination, but it appeared that nothing was missing. He said that there was at least part of every major organ left." Even Hamlin turned a little green at that. "Basically, it tore him to pieces with tooth and claw."

Christopher saw Eris shudder out of the corner of his eyes.

"Give me that," she said and snatched the folder from him. He could see the black eyes of Dark Eris looking over the photos without a trace of discomfort.

"The really disturbing thing is that this guy might not be the only victim," Hamlin said.

"There are more bodies?" Christopher asked.

"Yeah. Last night a homeless guy, or at least what was left of him, was found in an alley close to here. His wounds were similar to this. When they found him it was written up to a stray dog. He was just a homeless guy, so nobody wanted to look any deeper," Hamlin said. "Same would have happened with this guy too, but two big attacks like that in the same area and after what I experienced a couple of weeks ago...let's just say I wanted to look a little deeper."

Christopher nodded. He knew what Hamlin wanted. Why he had asked him here. He wanted Christopher to use the power he had to see if there was any residual evil left by a dark soul. But Christopher didn't want to do it. He had been spending the last couple weeks doing everything he could to ignore the power inside him. It was a horrible, horrible power and every day the desire, the aching need, to pick up the Book and Weapon grew. He had avoided the Weapon all together and had stayed away from the Library, despite what he had told Eris.

The burden was immense, and he needed time to figure it all out, time the Book and Weapon did not want to give him.

"Hellhound," Dark Eris said.

"Excuse me," said Hamlin.

"It sort of looks like what a hellhound does to its victims," she said.

Hamlin looked at him. "Is she good girl or bad girl right now?"

"Bad...for the moment anyway," Christopher said.

She leaned over and took a big whiff of the blood on the counter.

For a horrifying moment Christopher thought she was going to lick it. Hamlin must have thought the same because he said, "Be careful to not touch anything, it's still a crime scene. So, is a hellhound some kind of large dog?"

She seemed to ignore him as she hovered over the blood, but she didn't lick it. "No, not a dog. Hellhounds aren't really hounds, they are a concept. Few things in Hell are recognizable as anything you would see on earth. They are entities that can track and consume a mortal's soul."

"But this was obviously done by some sort of animal-like creature—a dog or bear. What would a hellhound look like here?"

Dark Eris shrugged, "They have no form unless given one. But this is what they do, tear flesh apart to get to the soul."

"Seems inefficient and messy," Christopher said.

"Well, Hell likes to be messy sometimes," she said, a smirk returning to her face.

"So you think a hellhound, some sort of evil entity, did this?" Hamlin asked.

"Well it is a possibility, but there hasn't been one on earth in over a thousand years. They have their place in Hell, but here, well, the days of magic and miracles are long gone."

"Says the magic girl to the detective," Hamlin said.

"Perhaps we should ask the hunter here," she said running her finger up Christopher's arm. "It was the Beast that controlled these hellhounds. It was said they were his creation."

He pulled his arm away. "Maybe my predecessor knew something about all this, but that died with him."

"Well, maybe you can ask that Librarian friend of yours," Hamlin said.

"Why does everybody want me to ask that guy everything? In

my experience he knows very little about the stuff I ask him. But sure I'll ask," Christopher said.

"Meanwhile can you, you know, sniff around and see if we can eliminate the theory that this was done by a dark soul?"

Christopher nodded reluctantly. He supposed he had to do it. Even that damn Librarian had told him he had no choice but to learn and embrace his power. By not using it, he would go mad. He thought he could already feel his sanity on edge, if he did welcome it he would go mad simply from all the death and destruction he would cause.

"We're here to help kid, you know that right?" Hamlin said.

Christopher nodded, somehow that was reassuring. Tentatively he reached out with his will and touched the seed of Hell inside of him.

Instantly, the shadows from the corners of the room darkened and wrapped around him, forming his now familiar long jacket and hood. It cloaked his identity although there was no one in the room he had to hide from, it had become habit.

"That still freaks the shit out of me." He heard Hamlin say. Followed by Dark Eris saying, "I think it's kind of sexy."

He shifted his senses and the souls of his two friends were visible. The dirty gray, but mostly good one of Hamlin, and the much purer soul of Eris sharing the same space as the black, oozing soul of Dark Eris. Instantly, the power sprung up inside of him eager, hungry to claim souls. He could feel it rage through him, and he squeezed his eyes shut to focus on containing it.

His hands itched to take the weapon, currently in its pocketknife form, from his pocket and run through the city scything through people, casting them down to Hell. And a part of him that wasn't the power, he could admit that, wanted to as well. Destroying people, sending them to eternal punishment? How like a god. It was a heady feeling, a drug that was slowly building to an addiction.

But not at the moment. He held it in check. He wondered if his friends knew how close they were to a time bomb.

He walked around the room, but stuck close to the counter where real violence had happened. He reached out with his new sense. He was a little excited, this was the first time he was really using his abilities in the capacity as a hunter, their intended purpose.

At first he felt nothing except the subtly shifting smell and vibrancy of his friend's souls. Then slowly he began to detect a different feeling, a different scent. The faint, putrid scent of a dark soul. When he identified it, the scent became clearer. It congregated around the scene of the massacre like the lingering scent of a woman wearing too much perfume after she leaves a room.

It wasn't until he walked behind the counter that he made a discovery.

"There were two of them," he said.

"Two dark souls?" Hamlin asked.

"Yes, I think so."

Christopher moved his hands through the oily residue left floating through the air. There were two distinct souls. Both evil, both leaving a rancid touch on him and a sour taste in his mouth, but each distinct.

"One was here killing the man, but the other... the other stood apart as though watching," Christopher said and then looked at Hamlin, "Or supervising."

"Two working together? That can't be good," Hamlin said.

"No, it's hard enough trying to figure out how to track them down one by one. If they did start to team up..." Christopher left the rest unsaid. He was still too new to understand how bad it could be, but he was certain it couldn't be a good thing.

"Okay, that settles it. I am going to back away from this case, let it get filed as a wild dog attack or some nonsense. This is no longer the department's problem, it's ours," Hamlin said.

Christopher nodded reluctantly.

"Wait, just like that? Wouldn't the police be a great resource in something like this? You're just going to walk away?" Eris asked. Christopher could see the darkness was gone from her eyes. She was just Eris again.

"No girl, *I am* the police, and *I'm* not just going to walk away. But we have found that the general force is ill equipped to deal with this sort of... of..."

"Supernatural," Christopher helped.

"Supernatural threat. I can't risk their lives on something they can't really understand. Hell, I have no idea what I'm doing here either, but at least my eyes are wide open. I can still borrow police resources as needed, but this case is going to needs some...special resources as well."

"There is also the question of trust. We've had bad experiences with members of the force that are less than trustworthy. These dark souls can obtain positions of power, and some can wield a lot of influence. It's best to just keep this to ourselves," Christopher said.

"Okay, got it. But just for the record you guys have only stopped one before right? You guys are talking like you're experts," Eris said.

"She has a point, we really are noobs to all this," Christopher said.

Hamlin nodded, "Yeah, maybe. But still no cops except for me."

"Great, we'll wing it. I'm glad that's all settled," Christopher said as they made their way outside. "I can visit the Library, I suppose, and can get some information on these guys. Maybe we'll get lucky and it turns out they're next on my hunting list."

"Um, guys? Where did that cop go?" Eris asked.

"Which cop?" Hamlin asked.

"The one that is supposed to be guarding the crime scene. Williams, I think,"

They looked up and down the sidewalk, the patrolman was gone. In fact, the whole street was deserted. Something was not right.

With a sickening thump, a body landed right in front of them. It was an almost unrecognizable mass of dark blue and crimson red. But the name tag was still visible. It was the patrolman Williams, or what was left of him.

"Ah, fuck me," said Christopher just before a large hand from above sunk its claws into his chest and yanked him into the air.

4

Christopher felt the claws sinking into his skin as he was wrenched off the ground. The sudden pain stunned him. It felt as if a series of hooks had just been threaded through the skin on his chest. He thought the skin might tear away, but the barbed claws had dug into the muscle, he had no choice but to go where they lifted him.

A creature covered in a mixture of black fur and leathery skin clung to the wall of the building just above the door they had exited. It was huge, maybe half again Christopher's size. Its mouth was a muzzle, lips pulled back to reveal two inch teeth. It pulled him close, its claw twisting into Christopher as it pulled them together. So close, he could see the slick saliva mixed with fresh blood dripping from its massive mouth. A deep, rumbling growl emerged from the creature as it brought them almost nose to nose.

"This is the great Hunter? The one they fear so much?" the creature said. "Ha! I smell *your* fear."

Christopher was frantically trying to get at the Weapon in his pocket, but being held in the air at such an awkward angle was making it difficult.

Below him he could make out both Hamlin and Eris yelling. Hamlin had his gun out and was moving, Christopher thought, to find a good angle to shoot the thing without hitting him. Not that the bullets would have hurt him for long, but Christopher supposed that old habits die hard.

His hand found the pocket knife. Success!

Then the creature heaved, and Christopher was flying backwards through the air. For a moment he was weightless, then he slammed into the building across the street, sending brick and mortar raining to the ground. Pain exploded throughout his whole body. He felt his ribs and other bones break at the impact. The power inside of him raged through his body, repairing the damage, but not fast enough.

As Christopher slid down the building, he saw the creature leap directly at him from the wall across the street, ignoring the gun fire from Hamlin.

Christopher hit the ground with a painful thud, his head smacking the concrete, and for a moment he blacked out.

When he came to, the creature loomed over him, clawed hands extended at his side, flexing in anticipation. Red, bestial eyes, looked down at him. He looked, Christopher thought, like a werewolf. But instead of a man, he was half wolf and half gorilla.

"I will consume your soul," it growled.

Christopher knew it was now or never. Grimacing at the pain, he rolled to his feet and staggered a little, pain flooding through him as his injuries cried out in protest at the movement. He ignored it and pulled the Weapon from his pocket. Instantly, almost with glee, it sprang to life as a sword, engulfed in red and black flames of power.

The creature, now wary, stepped back at the flare of power

from the Weapon. Christopher struck out with the sword. The creature moved fast, faster than Christopher with his Hell power-enhanced speed. But the blade nicked it on its arm, not enough to take its soul, but enough to get a taste.

The creature roared in pain and the weapon grew brighter in joy. Christopher could feel the power radiating through his whole body, making him thrum like the tight strings of a guitar. He could feel it crawling through every cell in his body, and he loved it. His injuries healed quickly, broken bones mended, knitting back together. It made him feel like the most powerful being in the world. And perhaps he was.

He attacked the creature once again swinging the sword in front of him, letting it guide his hand. He wanted to surrender to it completely, but the knowledge of what had happened last time kept him from fully embracing its chaos. He chose instead to channel the power, driving into the monster.

The creature dodged back, but then moved forward again with sudden speed. It was a blur as Christopher swung again. It caught his arm. For a moment they both froze, Christopher in disbelief and the creature in triumph. Then it threw him down the street.

He spun through the air before crashing into a parked car, shattering the windshield and leaving a man sized dent in the hood. The Weapon flew from his hands at the impact and skidded across the asphalt, transforming back to its simple pocket knife form.

Images swam in front of Christopher as his vision tried to focus. He was stunned, unable to think straight. This thing was fast and powerful, nothing like what he had encountered before, where at least his physical abilities were far superior to his opponent's. How was he supposed to fight this thing?

Move! Move! His mind screamed at his body.

He moaned and rolled off the car, trying to put something

between him and the monster. He need to buy some time, he needed to think. Unfortunately, the creature was not being cooperative. And then an idea came to him.

He felt the creature land on top of the car. It leaned over and looked down at him.

"You have lost your weapon, Hunter. Now I feed," it rumbled.

The creature grabbed him once again, and on instinct Christopher jumped. He reached into the seed of power inside of him and felt it rushing through his body. He sprang upwards as the creature grabbed empty air. He sped past the windows and cleared the top of the building, landing in a controlled crash on the roof. He quickly scrambled over to the edge and looked down.

The creature looked up at him in surprise, then it looked like its bestial muzzle was smiling. It jumped also, catching onto the side of the building with its huge claws and sending shards of brick and concrete to the ground below. It was running up the building like it was a vertical sidewalk.

So much for buying time.

He jumped to his feet and ran to the other side of the roof. He wondered if his predecessor, the Beast, had ever had to run from an enemy. Probably not, but that's what you get when you bestow the powers of Hell on a college kid who has no idea what he is doing.

He was halfway to the other side of the building when he heard the creature come over the roof's edge. Christopher didn't have to look back to know it was gaining on him. He jumped from the other edge and sailed over the street below to land on the other side. Moments after landing he heard the clawed feet of the creature land behind him.

He couldn't outrun it. He had lost the Weapon. This did not look good. He had to improvise.

A metal pipe came up from the roof below near a rooftop

access shed. He grabbed it and wrenched with both hands. It screeched in protest, but it was no match for his enhanced strength. The heavy metal bar came away in his hands. He turned to face the creature, holding the bar like a baseball bat.

The creature did not stop its charge, it came right at Christopher with claws extended. He swung at its head. The creature partially blocked the swing with its arm, the force of the blow bending the bar around the limb.

The creature let out a roar of pain and twisted its body, pulling the bar out of Christopher's hand and sending it off the edge of the roof.

So much for that weapon, thought Christopher. But he did notice that the creature's arm remained at its side. It might have been broken. *Take that mother fu...*

The creature's free hand shot out, grabbed Christopher by the shoulder and slammed him up against the wall of the shed.

Breathing hard and wounded, holding its massive broken arm close to its side and stomach, it was clearly weakened, but not enough to make much of a difference. It opened its drooling maw, dripping yellowish saliva and blood across Christopher's chest. Then its head shot forward.

Christopher was able to twist his body so that the monster missed his throat, but its teeth sank deep into his shoulder. Pain, far worse than he had experienced before, radiated from the wound. He cried out as the creature started twisting and tearing at the flesh, pulling it from his bones.

Then under the tearing of his flesh he felt something more, something far worse. Something deeper down than the simple severing of flesh and blood. A part of him that was more fundamental, more primal was being pulled out of him. It took him only a moment to realize it was his soul, the energy of his being.

As the creature tore at him, he felt his deepest thoughts and desires, his loves and hates were being taken from him. His darkest fears and greatest triumphs were laid bare. It was as though the core of his existence was being flailed. He began to scream and was not sure he would ever stop. All the energy and that was life to him was being taken, pillaged from him. It was a violation like no other.

The creature swallowed its bite and a part of Christopher was lost.

It opened its mouth wide to take another chomp, and all Christopher could do was watch in terror. The world was fading away from him, like he was tumbling down a black hole of nothing. His vision was failing him, for which he was glad. He hoped he would die before this thing was done eating his essence.

He felt rather than heard a fluttering like large wings above him. The creature paused and looked up, roaring in anger that its meal was being disturbed. Christopher followed its gaze, but all he saw was a large black blur with two fiery red dots come directly at him before he felt what could only be talons digging into his shoulders, both the good and injured one.

He screamed at the pain as he was lifted straight into the air and out of the surprised creature's grasp. The creature lunged at his feet, but whatever had him swooped away and its jaws missed.

Christopher looked down and saw his feet dangling over the building and streets as his carrier flew him back to where Hamlin and Eris were. That woke him from his world of pain.

He did not want to go back to where they were, that thing would just follow him and kill all of them. He looked up, trying to see what it was that carried him. But all he could see against the night sky were huge, bat-like wings and a mishmash of shadows. Then that too started to blur.

He was fading again, he could feel it. Something was wrong. He was weaker than he should be. The power inside was healing, he could feel it repairing his physical injuries. But there was something else damaged about him now, something that the power of Hell could not help him with.

As he felt his body come back in contact with the ground, he saw Hamlin rushing over, but the image was distant, like he was watching it happening to someone else. He lay on the ground trying to focus as darkness clouded his vision. Hamlin was talking to him, but he couldn't hear a thing.

The last thing he saw before fading into unconsciousness was the stuff of nightmares—a tall, skeletal being with huge-bat like wings sprouting from its back and leathery breast on its chest. Its obscenely long legs and arms were bone-like sticks ending at talons on both hands and feet. Its face was large and angular, smooth and almost feminine, but with a triangular mouth lined with needle sharp teeth. It must have been the thing that carried him.

His last thought as darkness consumed him was that it looked exactly what he imagined a demon would look like.

5

Anabelle looked down from the rooftop at the surprise below. Who would have thought he'd have a demon sidekick. *Maybe he was coming into his power faster than we expected*, she thought.

That small girl had transformed before her eyes into the winged monstrosity below. When she first appeared Anabelle had a moment of panic, as memory of her time below surfaced. Even now, gazing on the demon sent a shiver up her spine and awoke memories of pain and suffering. She would not go back.

The demon had just dropped the Hunter of Souls on the ground below. He looked unconscious. Her pet was only moments away, she could see him across the other rooftop. Now would be the moment to strike.

She staggered suddenly and caught herself on a nearby wall. She was weak. It was taking too much out of her to keep the mortals on this street from looking out of their windows. She had to constantly reinforce the suggestion that they stay in front of their TVs, or finish fixing their late night snacks, or start a heated argument with their significant other.

Maintaining the suggestion, even such a slight one, over such a large group of mortals was draining. And if the battle spilled over to another street again, there was no way she could keep up the illusion. She needed to end this, if the mortals saw what transpired it might upset certain members of her... family...and she did not want that at the moment. There was too much at stake.

Ammit landed in the street below her and started stalking towards the unconscious Hunter. The demon stood in his path. He could kill her, but not quickly enough. The mortal pulled out a gun and shot at him. He ignored it, bullets and the little pain they brought would mean nothing to him

She staggered again, suddenly very dizzy, and she could feel the power draining from her, her beauty was dimming. She needed to rest and recharge.

She reached out to Ammit.

Ammit, stop. Return to me.

Why my mistress? We have them. I want the rest of his soul.

Now is not the time. I cannot shield you from mortals any longer.

Then let them see, let them see what is coming for them. Ammit thought back at her and started walking once again toward the demon glaring at him.

No! The thought slammed into him almost physically. He stopped as though a leash had been pulled. You are ignorant and have no idea the consequences. We accomplished our goal to test them. Now, do as I say and return to me.

He turned and looked up at her. For a moment she could see the anger, the malice in his eyes. Then it was gone. He was no fool she thought, though he needs a shorter leash.

Then with a roar he sprang to the building she was on and

climbed up to join her on the roof. She released the hold she had on the mortals up and down the street. She collapsed, but Ammit was there to catch her. She hoped the demon would assume a mortal form quickly, but she was too weak to do anything about it. They were on their own for now. But next time she would kill the Hunter. And with that triumph she could usurp Golyat's position and assume control of the new Alliance.

6

Consciousness came to Christopher in a series of unconnected scenes. A flash of him being dragged and carried to a car and laid none too gently in the back. Then darkness until a vision of the ceiling of his home scrolling past. He was being carried, awkwardly, by two people. Hamlin's face swam into view above his. He thought Hamlin said something, but before Christopher could ask him what he had said everything went black again. He woke again, fading back to consciousness. The room where he lay—he thought it was his—was dark. A single lamp, set low, illuminated Eris' face. She was dozing in a chair next to him. And again he faded.

When he woke the next time, he was able to hold onto consciousness. He was in his room, he was sure now. Late afternoon sun filtered in through the window and sheer curtains. His whole body ached, but the healing had happened, his bones were whole once again and he didn't feel any cuts or major injuries. The power of Hell comes through again. But he still ached like his body was one giant bruise. Usually his supernatural healing left him feeling much better.

He realized he wasn't wearing his street clothes under his blankets. Somebody had undressed him and put him in his pajamas. And he was pretty sure that person wasn't Hamlin.

Eris sat by the side of the bed, looking at him anxiously. The skeletal creature flashed through his mind, and suddenly he remembered the battle and the creature that moved so fast, faster than him and had such strength. He remembered its bite, tearing more than just his flesh. He shuddered as he remembered how it had shrugged off his attacks. He had been no match for it, even with the Weapon and the Hell power inside of him. He also remembered the thing that had swooped down and plucked him out of the grasp of the creature, long talons cutting into his shoulders and carrying him to safety.

"It was you," Christopher said. "The thing that grabbed me and took me to safety."

She shook her head slightly. "It was her. The one inside me, Dark Eris. At least I assume."

"Assume?"

"I don't always remember when she takes control, and I think it's the same for her. Sometimes we are aware of what the other is doing. For me it's like memories, but sometimes they are too faded or obscure, so I can only make guesses as to what happened."

He tried to sit up. She moved forward to help him. He could see concern in her eyes and maybe a little fear. Perhaps she feared him after what she had seen.

"What do you remember then?" He asked gently.

She looked down as though unable to meet his eyes. "That creature had you, it... it was horrible. I could see it was hurting you. I felt like I needed to do something, but there was nothing I *could* do. When the thing chased you up the building, I realized that although there was nothing I could do maybe Dark Eris could. I grew angry. I was useless, and I needed Dark Eris to take over."

She sat back in a chair staring down at her hands with a frown on her face. She was clearly frustrated. Her voice shook slightly when she spoke again.

"I don't know what causes us to switch control most of the time, but that anger seemed to open a door somewhere inside me and let me summon her. No that's not quite right. I didn't summon her. It seems like we both are always waiting to take control of my body. Anger opened the door, and she came right in."

She looked at him again and grabbed his hand.

"But it was her that turned into... into, whatever it was. That was not me. I could feel my body change, twist and turn into the demon she became. I know she was doing it out of need, but it was not me, it was her."

That was when Christopher realized she was not afraid of him, she was worried he was afraid of her. He hurried to reassure her.

"I know it was her. It was obviously a demon, Dark Eris in the flesh," Christopher said trying to reassure her. It was hard for him to focus. Something was wrong, but he couldn't put a finger on it.

"How are you feeling?" she asked.

"I don't know," Christopher said and it was true. Something was missing. His body felt fine, but it was as though he was missing some vital organ. His body felt too hollow, that was the only way to describe it, although that was not quite right either. "How long have I been asleep?"

"Through the night and most of the day, it's about eight o'clock. You slept for almost twenty four hours."

"Jesus, I must have really been hurt. It never takes me that long to fully heal."

He was able to sit up, the ache was already starting to recede, but not the hollow feeling.

"What happened after I lost consciousness? Why didn't that thing finish me off? Was it because of Dark Eris?" Christopher asked, more to himself, but Eris answered.

"I don't think so. From what I can remember—and as I said I don't know how reliable that is—once you were safe on the ground the monster approached like it was going to attack again. But then it looked back, up at a building. It kept trying to come after you, and then hesitating. Like it was having an argument with itself."

"Or something up on that roof," Christopher said. "That would explain the scent I had of two dark souls. This thing and its master."

"I can't imagine that thing having a master. I don't think that thing Dark Eris turned into would have been able to fight it. And you, well you were no..." She let it trail off as she realized what she was saying.

"I was no match for it. All this power I'm supposed to have, and it overcame me like I was a child."

There was a knock at the door.

"Come in," Christopher called out, his voice sounding a little thin in his own ears.

It was Hamlin. He was still wearing the same rumpled suit as the night before and Christopher could see the dark circles under his eyes, he must have stayed the night here. For some reason that made Christopher feel a little better.

"Good to see you up kid. I was starting to get worried. I had no idea what we were going to tell the doctor if we had to take you to a hospital. Not sure they would go for you getting bitten by a monster while trying to whack it with your magic pocket knife."

"Doesn't sound nearly as impressive when you say it like that," Christopher said.

"That thing may have had your number, but you took a bad beating that no normal person could have survived. I'd call that pretty impressive." Hamlin sat down on a chair next to the bed on the opposite side from Eris, and he gave her an interesting look that Christopher would have described as suspicious. He couldn't fully blame Hamlin, he had seen more of that demonic creature she had become than Christopher had. "The question is what do we do now so that it doesn't happen again. Obviously it was a trap."

"You think? No wonder you were made detective, with a quick mind like that," Christopher said. He meant it as a joke, but it came off pretty harsh. He sighed. "I'm sorry, Hamlin. I know it sounds funny since I just inherited these powers a few weeks ago, but I'm not used to losing fights when in full Hellfire mode. It's making me a little frustrated."

Hamlin just nodded. "Yeah, an obvious trap and we can only assume it was set for you. The question is why? Not so much who. I guess we can assume it was one of those dark soul thingies you were supposed to be hunting down. But why would one of them set a trap?"

"Two of them. Remember when I said I could feel two dark souls?" Christopher asked. Hamlin nodded so Christopher filled him in on his and Eris' theory that there was something controlling the beast. "I don't see why they would either. My understanding is that in general they want to hide from the Hunter, I mean me, as long as possible because I am the only thing that can send them back to Hell."

"Well it looks like they're changing their M. O."

Christopher nodded. "I need to get to the Library and ask the

Librarian about this. He's our only source of information at the moment."

"Did it look like a werewolf to either of you guys?" Eris asked suddenly.

Christopher thought for a moment. "I suppose it was something like one from a movie. Large dog-like muzzle and claws, lots of hair, but it walked upright and had the musculature of a man, and a rather large one at that. But it looked too alien for a werewolf. I mean, its eyes were larger than any wolf I've seen and the teeth were much larger than any dog. And that leathery skin, not all fur. Almost like it was part lizard."

"Not to mention werewolves aren't real," Hamlin interjected.

"Like demons and Hell and magic people aren't real?" Eris asked.

"Well just because you and Christopher have some unusual um... abilities doesn't mean every little myth and story is real. I mean what's next, vampires?"

"If so, I hope they're the sparkly kind," Eris said. "But no, I was just thinking. Dark Eris mentioned something about a hellhound. Maybe that's what we're dealing with?"

Christopher sat back at that and stared at the ceiling. It made sense, as much as he didn't want to admit it. Eris' theory was just as good as any. Great, just great. More monsters, more mysteries, it was enough to give him a headache. A bigger one than he already had.

"Well, I think we're at a loss until we get more info," Christopher said. When no one spoke, he opened his eyes. They were staring at him, waiting.

"What?" he asked.

"We have no idea why they stopped attacking us...you, I mean. They, or it, or whatever could strike again at any moment. You need to go pay this library fellow a visit as soon as possible," Hamlin said.

"Yeah, yeah I know. I'll go there tonight." Christopher hoped they could not hear the reluctance in his voice. He was not comfortable with this power inside him, and this recent battle didn't inspire confidence.

"I was thinking more like now," Hamlin said, and when Christopher looked at him sharply he went on. "I know you're reluctant to use this power, and I think I can understand why. Hell, I've seen enough in the last few weeks to make most men shit their pants, I can only imagine what you're going through. But I don't think we have much time. I don't know why they tested you, but it was obvious they could have killed all of us. I don't think they'll wait long to strike again and when they do, I doubt they'll hold back."

Christopher looked long at Hamlin and then nodded. This was why he needed Hamlin, no matter what power he had, he needed a friend to be a rock and keep him centered.

"You're right, there's no time to waste. Where's the Book?" Christopher said. Suddenly, he had a moment of panic as he looked around for the Book and Weapon. He had been knocked unconscious. Had Eris or Hamlin picked them up?

He didn't need to worry. Eris opened the drawer on his night stand, both Book and Blade were there. He smiled his thanks to Eris and picked up the Book. He looked one last time at the others. Hamlin nodded encouragement at him.

Then Eris did a strange thing. She leaned in and kissed him on the cheek, near the corner of his mouth. "We'll be right here when you get back," she said, and for a moment, Christopher was sure she was blushing. Then her eyes turned dark.

"What are you waiting for, stud?" Dark Eris said with an all too toothy smile. "Don't worry, you have demon-girl here to watch over you."

Christopher swallowed hard and opened the book.

SURE TOOK YOU LONG ENOUGH, was written on the inside. Even as he read the words, they began to blur and everything faded to black.

7

Anabelle hated the basement. She didn't mind the dark, in fact, she preferred it. Night was the most sensual time of the day, and the darkness it brought created mysteries and hid that which you wanted hidden. Yes, the dark was for lovers and killers, and that is what made her love it so. The dark was a place for love and death, though she did not have much care for love. It was only the poor cousin to lust and obsession. And in those she was an expert.

It was the dirt, the musky scents of earth and concrete beneath her home that she disliked. The basement was large with a stone floor. The house above had been rebuilt and remodeled a number of times in the last two hundred years, but the basement had always remained, virtually untouched. The old stone walls held the smell of years mixed with the ancient odor of dirt long undisturbed.

The area of the basement near the stairs had been modernized to some extent. Modern water heater, electrical and plumbing, things of that nature. But just beyond the water heater and the old rusting coal storage bin was a nondescript door. It led to the true basement, in some ways the heart of the home.

Many had died there. Not even she knew all of them, since this home existed long before she had risen from Hell. When she opened the door to this area she could smell the old blood, the old terror. Dark stains still marked the stones on the ground where blood had been spilled and not fully cleaned. She could feel the remnants of those that had died here, hiding just beyond the corner of her vision. Trapped in this place. They had it easy she thought.

She had suffered a long torment in that place of desolation and depravity; but in her escape, she had acquired amazing gifts. She could control most men's hearts, give and take huge amounts of damage and pain and survive, perhaps forever. Yes, in Hell she had suffered, but here, with the gifts she had stolen from the infernal realm, she could rule. And of all those gifts, knowledge was fast becoming the most valuable.

For example, the young girl chained in the corner. Whimpering so sweetly. To most she was a runaway, a throwaway. She did not even know what she was. But Anabelle could see she was a witch, and a rare kind at that. She was a soul shaper. And she belonged to Anabelle.

Anabelle walked over to her now. She was dirty, her clothes filthy and stinking. Dirt and maybe a little blood smudged her skin. She had brown hair that hung in tangles down her face to about the middle of her chest. She had told Anabelle she was fifteen when they met, but her real age was probably closer to thirteen, or maybe fourteen. An iron collar was in place around her neck and from that a short chain extended to the wall. Overkill, of course, she was harmless, but it was all Anabelle had to restrain her.

She had said her name was Grace when Anabelle had found

her, back when she thought Anabelle wanted to help her get off the streets. Now she knew, however, Anabelle was not one to offer help. She took what she needed.

"Girl, I have a use for your talents," she said.

When the girl didn't look up, Anabelle grabbed her chin roughly and forced the girl to look her in the eyes. In the girl's eyes she saw only fear. Good.

"We have an unexpected gift that I need your help with," she said. Then to the darkness across the large cellar she said, "Come here, Ammit. You have something I need."

After a moment she could see the hulking figure of Ammit making his way out of the shadows. The girl screamed and tried to pull herself deeper into the wall. Anabelle chuckled and grasped the chain. She unlocked the end attached to the wall and pulled the girl towards the large wooden table in the center of the room.

"No! Please, no," the girl screamed. She pulled at the chain trying to break free, but Anabelle held it easily. Once she had determined that the girl's power was virtually dormant and the child had no idea of what she could accomplish with it, Anabelle knew she could control her, shape her just as the girl could shape souls, to do what she commanded.

"Hush! Quiet, girl," Anabelle said harshly and pulled on the chain, bringing the girl to heel as she would a mongrel. "You are perfectly safe. Ammit will not harm you as long as you serve me."

"Why have you brought me here mistress? Do you wish me to consume the girl?" asked Ammit. His growling like voice only made the girl struggle more.

"No. You have something for me, I believe?"

He tilted his head slightly as though confused in a very dog like gesture. Perhaps it would have been cute if it wasn't coming from a nine-foot tall, demonic wolf monster. "I have nothing," he said.

"Nonsense. I need the part of the Hunter's soul that you consumed," she said.

He looked surprised, or at least she thought he did, it was hard to tell on that grotesque face. "I do not understand?"

"You are part hellhound. Your job is to consume souls, it's what gives you strength, but you do not destroy what you consume. You simply store it. A soul cannot be destroyed so easily. On the plains of Hell, the hounds retrieved those that would seek escape. Your kind once roamed the mortal realm also as hounds for the Hunter, but that was forbidden long ago, I was told. You have the part of that boy's soul in you. And I, as the master of you, demand that you release it."

She said the last as a command. Ammit's eyes got wide and both of his massive clawed hands slammed down on the table, shaking it and making it creak. His stomach heaved and his mouth opened obscenely as though his jaw had become unhinged. Vomit spewed out onto the table, and the blood and flesh of his recent feasts fell in chunks out of his mouth.

The girl screamed again and danced back so that none of the reeking vomit would touch her. She pulled away but Anabelle just yanked her forward, while stepping back herself to avoid the fluids as they spilled on the ground. This was new to her also, and she hadn't quite known what to expect, but certainly not this mess.

Then, just as his heaving was about to be done, a ball of fleshy meat fell out. It was almost perfectly round and shimmered from the inside as though a strong candle burned on the inside.

"Quickly girl," Anabelle said and pulled a small crystal vial from her pocket. It was an old fashioned perfume vial. She hoped it would work. It was the only crystal she could find on such short notice. "Take the soul shard and get it into the vial."

The girl looked at her like she was crazy. Anabelle slapped her once across the face, hard enough to draw blood. The girl would have collapsed if the chain had not held her up.

"Listen bitch, dig into that ball of flesh. The soul will come to you, it is your gift. You will know how to shape it into the vial. It is in your blood."

The sobbing girl stared at the pulsating meat and looked as though she was going to throw up also. But she didn't move. Anabelle grabbed the back of her head and forced it towards the reeking tabletop.

The girl tentatively reached out with her fingers only to hesitate as they got close to it.

"Get on with it girl," Anabelle commanded.

The girl poked at it a couple of times until Anabelle hissed through her teeth. Then the girl took a deep breath and with bony hands started to peel it like some sort of flesh fruit.

Anabelle watched. She had heard of what a soul shaper could do, but she had never witnessed it. To anybody but a soul shaper, and a hellhound of course, the soul would be insubstantial and uncontrollable. To free it from the hound would send it slowly drifting back to its owner, or if the owner was dead it would simply fade and pass to the afterlife, either heaven or Hell. A soul shaper could control a soul, at least to some extent, and capture it in an appropriate container, hence the crystal vial.

Soul shapers can do more of course, much more. But this girl was just a beginner, it would take time for her to learn. For now, Anabelle could use the girl to get the soul shard into the container.

Ammit had slunk back to the shadows. The violence of his vomiting had obviously shaken him. This did not surprise Anabelle. He was, after all, only part-hellhound. The other part, the dark soul part, was still confused. And that was the way she liked it.

The girl dug into the flesh knot with both hands, pulling back the layers until the aura of the soul was visible. She let out a little gasp, and her eyes lit up for the first time.

"Quickly now, get it into the vial."

It was already starting to drift away from the table. The girl glanced at Anabelle and then gently reached out and cupped it in her hands. Then, intuitively, she rubbed her hands gently around it, as though making the world's most fragile snowball.

For five minutes Anabelle watched her, and the girl's eyes never left the soul. She worked on it like an artist lost in painting a masterpiece. Slowly, she reached out and picked up the vial with one hand while holding the soul shard in place with the other. Then, as though it was finding its way home, the shard of the Hunter's soul slid into the vial.

The girl held the vial as though it was the most fascinating thing in the world, her eyes wide with surprise or fear, perhaps a little of both. Anabelle knew this was a first for her, the girl had never known the talents she possessed. Anabelle would keep her, train her, and she would serve them well.

For now, she snatched the soul out of the girl's hand, surprising her. The girl let out a small yelp as though it hurt her to take it away. And perhaps it did. Anabelle did not know the details between a soul shaper and the soul it worked with. She just knew what they were capable of doing.

She held it up and examined it. There was not much to see, just a shimmer of light, like a candle flame flickering in a breeze. It wouldn't go out—souls are immortal—but it wouldn't get stronger or brighter until it could rejoin with the rest of itself.

And maybe it would. Maybe someday it would be complete again. Or maybe she would just keep it, use it somehow. Either way the Hunter would have to die.

8

Christopher had forgotten how hard and cold the stone floors of the Library were. He opened his eyes and tried to get them into focus as he slowly got to his feet. His arrivals here were nowhere near as bad as the first time, when his body had felt like it was being broken apart and put back together again with some sort of glue that had come directly from the fires of Hell. But he still felt he could work on an entrance that did not entail him waking up on the floor, feeling like he had one Hell of a hangover.

Around him the Library stretched off into the darkness. The walls were stone, castle like, and covered by wooden bookshelves, some reaching up into the shadows that obscured the ceiling. Other book shelves, more modest in height, but still much taller than Christopher, filled the large, empty room. He could not see them, but Christopher knew other doorways led to other rooms and hallways also filled with books and scrolls. The Library went on and on, presumably forever. In the limited amount of time he had spent here, Christopher had never seen every room. There was always another door or hallway.

Some of the books were modern-looking leather bounds or paperbacks, but further into the stacks could be found ancient scrolls and parchment paper written by hand. Once Christopher had found a wall that was covered in artwork and ancient carvings. The Librarian had told him that it may or may not have actually existed in the mortal realm, like everything here it was a metaphor for knowledge, both known and unknown. And the current representation was derived from Christopher's subconscious.

Which, based on the weird shit he found in here, made him think he was a deeply disturbed individual.

"Ah, the hero has returned," came a voice from behind him. He jumped and spun around, stumbling against the shelves. It was the Librarian.

The being that referred to itself as the Librarian towered over him, at least eight feet tall. He was cloaked head to toe in dark robes made of the same shadow essence that Christopher used to form his Hunter uniform. Christopher had never seen the Librarian's face or hands, not one piece of his actual body had ever appeared from underneath that robe.

"You need to stop sneaking up on me like that," Christopher said.

"I did not sneak up on you. You were facing the wrong way," the Librarian replied.

Christopher wished he could see the being's face. Sometimes he couldn't tell if the Librarian was being sincere or just messing with him.

"I also don't think belly flopping into the Library is a very dignified entrance for one of your stature," said the Librarian.

Now Christopher knew he was being messed with. "And what exactly is that stature?" Christopher asked.

"Keeper of the gates of Hell. Well, at least Keeper of the back door to Hell," said the Librarian.

Christopher sighed in disappointment. Usually the Librarian had cool, impressive sounding names for what he was. That one just sounded dirty.

"I was beginning to think you had forgotten about this place. I was getting so lonely, I was considering getting a cat."

"Look, I know it's been a while. It's a lot to take in. I can jump from rooftop to rooftop with almost no effort, I can move faster than humanly possible; and I'm stronger than any man, Hell any ten men. I heal so fast, I'm not sure I can even be killed. I can see and, unfortunately, smell the evil in all men's souls. I have even killed." Christopher looked down at that last one. A few weeks ago he would have laughed at the idea that he could hurt someone, let alone take a life. He knew that all those he had killed so far were evil and maybe even deserved it, but they were still men and women. Who was he to be the judge?

"You shouldn't think that way," the Librarian said softly, almost soothingly.

"I shouldn't?" Christopher said.

"Of course you can be killed. Come let's go to the assignment room," said the Librarian. Without waiting for an answer, he turned and headed towards a doorway that may not have been there moments before. Sometimes it seemed as though the structure of the Library would shift and change as needed.

"Wait. The last thing I need is a new assignment. They seem to be finding me at the moment."

That made the Librarian pause and turn slightly. "Interesting. All the more reason to visit the assignment room."

He kept walking and Christopher hurried to catch up. "I just wanted to see if you know anything about hellhounds, or maybe werewolf-hellhounds?"

The Librarian paused and turned around. "Werewolf-hellhounds?"

"Yes. We think we might be up against one. But we're not sure. What can you tell me about them?"

"You are in luck. I did my doctorate on Werewolf-hellhounds," the Librarian said. "I did my post graduate work studying alternate forms of lycanthropy at Harvard."

"Really?"

"No, not really. I am a construct of this library metaphor. Why are humans so gullible? We are here," the Librarian said.

Christopher was about to defend himself when he noticed the huge black door to the assignment room next to them. Like last time, it instantly made him uncomfortable. It was a deep black, like a starless night, almost sucking light into it. If you looked at it too long, it gave you the feeling that you were falling down a deep hole of nothingness. It was hypnotizing in its complete absence of, well, anything.

"Hunter? Are you well?" the Librarian asked.

Christopher shook himself, the Librarian's voice pulled him from the depths of the door. Hesitantly, like it was going to shock him, although he knew it wouldn't, he pushed on it. For anyone else, including the Librarian, the door would not open. But for him, it swung open almost effortlessly. Beyond was the assignment room.

It was a large room in the shape of a circle and against the walls giant, curved shelves held large, two-inch-thick books. In the center was a single stone pedestal upon which rested the current Hunter's journal. The books that surrounded them were past journals that noted all the dark souls that had escaped from Hell and how they were returned by the Beast, his predecessor. Although he now had one entry, his first prey, Rath. He had dispatched him to Hell a few weeks ago.

The journal was supposed to give him clues to help defeat these dark souls, some information about who they had been in life before descending to Hell. But for some reason, the book had never revealed his first target's past. He had been forced to wing-it with Rath, and he had almost died. The Librarian had assured him that was the first time he had ever seen the book fail the Hunter. The Beast had always had the information he needed. It appeared that for some reason, Christopher was not worthy.

Christopher approached the book with a sense of dread. He had no idea who wrote the entries into the book. Was it God? More likely the Devil, given his current occupation. Wasn't he supposed to be part of the Devil now? That's what he had been told, some sort of avatar. He didn't like that, it made him think that he was some sort of servant.

He had to look at the book though, there was really no choice. He had this whole Library of infinite knowledge, he supposed he should use as much of it as he was able. He reached the pedestal and looked down.

On the page the name *Ammit* was printed above a crude drawing. Rough though it was, it was obviously the creature that he had fought yesterday. Same large, hulking form covered in a mixture of hair and toughened skin, the outline of a muzzle with over-sized teeth, and wicked looking claws extending from its hands.

Once again there was no picture or information on what this thing was, or who it had been. He saw a detailed account of his ass-kicking by the thing of course, but no clues as to what or who it once was.

"I just fought this thing. It was why I was asking if you knew anything about hellhounds."

"If it is in there, then he is a dark soul. Hellhounds have no soul. It couldn't possibly be a hound. But may I ask why you thought it was?" The Librarian asked.

"The demon possessing the girl that lives with me said she recognized it."

"Demon girl... lives with you... I think you have some stuff to fill me in on," the Librarian said.

Christopher took a little joy in the fact that the Librarian seemed surprised and maybe a little flustered. The day was looking up. He went through the events of the last few days, getting the Librarian up to speed. At times it seemed like the Librarian was up to date on what was going on out in the real world, but at others he seemed to be completely ignorant. Holding this knowledge over the Librarian, who had access to such an immense source of knowledge and wisdom, made putting up with his incessant smugness and sarcasm worth it.

"Well, I can tell you if the name appears in this book, it is a dark soul, once human, that has escaped from Hell. It could not be a hellhound. At least not a true hellhound," the Librarian said.

"What do you mean by not a true hellhound?"

"To escape Hell is no easy thing. These books might make it seem like a lot have escaped, but when you realize they go back to the beginning of time, you can understand it is but a drop in the ocean of damned souls still in Hell. To get out of Hell, many of these dark souls will do anything to escape, sometimes they have to get creative. One might have found a way of combining itself with a hound."

"How would that help him escape?"

"It wouldn't, not directly. But the combination of a dark soul with hellhound would make a very powerful opponent. If a dark soul was to strike a bargain with a being either in Hell or in your mortal world—get some help as it were—the person who helped the dark soul would have a very powerful ally."

"So a dark soul merged with a hellhound? That might explain why it resembled a werewolf. Only I guess this would be called a werehound. You're saying he fused himself with a hellhound to make himself into a more valuable bargaining chip?" Christopher asked.

"Maybe. Or maybe something did it to the dark soul with or without its consent and then helped it escape."

Christopher looked back down at the book on the pedestal. He noticed that there was something around its neck. It looked like it could be a collar. As Christopher stared at it, he noticed there was a faint line coming from it. It was like it was just fading into existence, but it was still incredibly faint. It could simply have been a mistake of the artist, the pencil dragging across the pad. Except this artist didn't make mistakes.

The thin line went to the edge of the page. Christopher turned it. On the other side was a small drawing of a beautiful woman. Dark hair, striking eyes. It was just a drawing, but she seemed to reach out and grab him. In the flesh such a woman must be stunning.

It took him a good thirty seconds before he realized the line continued onto this page from the other. It ended at her hands. Above the drawing was the name Anabelle.

"I think I've found his friend. Someone named Anabelle holds his leash," Christopher said.

"This is not good."

The even more somber than usual tone of the Librarian made Christopher look up at him. But he could see nothing in the blackness of his hood.

"No shit. Now I'm dealing with two this time."

"No, Hunter. That is not what I mean. Never that I know of have dark souls worked together, at least not in so obvious a partnership. By their nature they are a selfish and suspicious group. They could never trust one another long enough to form any sort of bond. If they somehow start working together, well, not even the Beast had to contend with a threat that dire. If they unify, even a little bit, you are doomed."

"Wow, you are just awesome at those inspirational pep talks."

He looked down at the book again and flipped between the two pages. He had barely defeated his first dark soul a few weeks ago and had almost been killed by only the second one he had ever encountered. Now how was he supposed to defeat two at the same time?

"There is something however," The Librarian said, "but I am not exactly sure how we can use it to your advantage."

"At this point I can use any help I can get."

"Yes, well, hellhounds are under the dominion of the Beast, the Hunter of Lost Souls. They are the hunting dogs, so to speak, to complement the Hunter. Their original purpose was to assist the Beast in hunting down and dragging souls back to Hell. Their job was to consume the soul and bring it back to him."

"So these hounds are supposed to do as I say?"

"To some extent, but they have not roamed the mortal plane in a long time. And I don't know if a werehound falls under the dominion of the Hunter," the Librarian said.

"How did he control these things? Because the one I just fought didn't seem inclined to follow my direction. Unless it was to tear me apart."

"I do not know how he controlled them. Maybe it was some sort of innate gift. I don't know how to recreate it in you. Like I said before, no mortal has ever taken up the duties of the Beast."

"Yeah, yeah, I know. I'm the first of my kind and I have to learn as I go."

"Good thing it did not eat you though. It would have consumed your soul, and you might have been at the mercy of the dark soul that holds its leash."

"What if it just took a bite out of me?" Christopher asked.

The Librarian hesitated a moment. "Well, I don't know, but I would think that it would not be good. I suggest you avoid it."

"Too late," Christopher said and flexed his shoulder. It was still sore.

"Oh that's a pity. I suppose I will have to go through all this again with some other mortal after you die."

"I mean it. Inspirational speaker. You could make a lot of money," Christopher said.

"Your mortality is a problem, but there might be a more immediate concern," said the Librarian.

"Great, because I don't have enough to deal with at the moment," said Christopher.

"I don't know a lot about hellhounds, but I do know that similar to an earthly canine, if a hellhound were to get the scent or especially a taste of a soul, it would be able to track it just about anywhere."

"So you're saying that thing could track me down at any time?"

"I believe so, yes. One's soul leaves a sort of psychic residue, I think you used it to track Rath. The longer you stay somewhere the stronger the residue. And the easier you are to find."

"So you are saying that hiding out, say at my home, is not really a good idea?" Christopher did not like where this was going.

"Exactly. If you are at your home back in the mortal world, you would be easy for this creature to find any time it wishes. And that could be at any moment."

Christopher started towards the door. "That means both Hamlin and Eris are in danger too. I don't think that thing will ignore them."

"I agree you need to leave, but what of your dilemma? You have not learned how to stop this thing."

Christopher paused. "I can't take the time right now. I have to get back and warn them. We need to get out of that house. I'm a sitting duck, and my friends aren't much better off. Besides, you said yourself he didn't leave an instruction book lying around."

"No, he didn't. But we have the narrative of his life," the Librarian said, and with one robed arm, gestured to the walls of books filled with hunting journals, each one detailing the Beast's hunts from the beginning of time.

The Librarian was right. The answer might very well be in this encyclopedia of killing. He walked over to the wall, pulled down a journal, and flipped through it. There was a wealth of information in each of these books, not just for his immediate problem, but to learn the full extent of his power and maybe a way to control it so that he wouldn't lose his mind the next time he wielded the Weapon.

But not today. He put the journal back on the shelf. "It might all be here, but I don't have the time. I need to get back and get the Hell out of my house."

"Maybe I can help? If you allow me to stay for a little while, I can do some research. Perhaps I can uncover something about the hellhounds or the Beast's past that would help."

"I thought only I could enter this room," Christopher said.

"Yes, but we are already here. If you allow it, I could stay," the Librarian said. "At least I should be able to for a while. This is, after all, a construct of a library created by the power of the divine for your interpretation. You have some measure of control here. Maybe not for a long period, as we are both at the whim of your subconscious and how it interacts with the chaos of Hell, but perhaps long enough to find something."

Christopher nodded, it was worth a shot. He couldn't stay anyway. "I will return as soon as we are all somewhere safe."

He could read nothing on the Librarian, the hood too dark to read any facial expression, and he stood straight as ever, body language was out. There was a part of Christopher that worried giving this thing access to a forbidden room might be a mistake. This thing was a servant of Hell, after all. But he had no option. He needed to get back, but he needed answers just as much. He couldn't be two places at once.

He stepped out into the hall. In front of him was another door, not at all like the inky black one that led to the assignment room. Intuitively, he knew it was the door out. He looked back at the motionless Librarian one last time. Then he stepped through the door.

9

Anabelle was still admiring the soul shard trapped in the crystal vial when the intercom—her only other nod to the modern in the old basement—buzzed.

"Ma'am, there is a gentleman by the name of Golyat at the door asking for you. Actually, it appears he has just walked in. He does not seem happy, ma'am," Martin, her butler, said through the intercom. His voice was unsteady. Martin had seen many things in her service, things no mortal should see, still an angry Golyat would be intimidating.

"Damn, he must have heard something," she said to no one in particular. Into the intercom she said. "Thank you, tell him I will be there in a moment. Offer him a drink, but not the really good stuff. I'll see him in the dining room, that room should be large enough for him."

"Very well, ma'am," said the voice on the other end.

"Ammit," she said to the shadowed corner of the room. He stepped out into the light. "Golyat is sticking his nose in sooner than I thought. I'm not sure what he knows, but we are short on time. As much as I hate the risk, the time for subtlety is at an end. Track down the Hunter and bring me his soul. You may consume the souls of any of his friends."

What could only be described as a sickening grin spread across Ammit's muzzle, his teeth gleamed wetly in the small amount of light given off by the sole light bulb in the room. The girl shrank back from that toothy maw.

"But you must be careful to not be seen. Some witnesses we can contain, but don't attack where all the mortals can see. I have enough troubles with Golyat at the moment. The last thing we need is another reason for him to unite the Alliance against me."

Ammit nodded, his great clawed hand opening the door.

"And ware the demon bitch. I don't know what game she is playing, they can never be trusted, but for the moment she seems to be his ally. I don't think she is much of a threat to you one on one, but she is a puzzle piece to keep an eye on."

Ammit nodded his large bestial head and left the room quickly, darting into the shadow of the hallway. Anabelle looked down at the girl cowering by the wall.

"You did well today, and I am sure I will find uses for your talents in the future. I will send some food and water down shortly. Try to rest, you are still not used to flexing your power."

The girl said nothing. She stared at the floor as though the life had run out of her. *That would not do at all*, thought Anabelle. If she broke the girl too much, she would never embrace her full power. Anabelle would have to find some way to refresh the girl if she was to be of any use.

But that was a problem for later. For now, she had a much larger problem to deal with.

She made her way upstairs, stopping at the powder room to clean up a little after being in the dirty basement. She cleaned the cobwebs and dust out of her hair and then willed her aura to full force. It was one of her gifts, this aura of beauty, of desire. She had shaped it with her stolen Hell-power when she had fled that eternal prison.

No mortal could resist her when she chose, and only a few fellow former inmates had the will power to resist her seduction. Unfortunately, Golyat was one of them. But it did throw him off guard, make him a little easier for her suggestions. And she needed him as pliable as possible for the moment.

Upstairs the house held the traditional feel of its two-hundred-year life, but with modern and contemporary elements. It was, Anabelle liked to think, an accurate reflection of herself. If she wanted to rule in this modern world, she had to welcome the change, but her past was too important to her to forget. It was the life that had led her through Hell and back. Literally.

Rich hardwood floors, elegant finishes. And it was big, not as big as some of her other estates, but sizable, considering its proximity to the city. It had a large dining room with an oversized table that she hoped would put some space between the two of them now.

She opened the large double doors, expecting to see Golyat at the other end of the room by the door he would have come in. She did not expect him to be standing right before her, just inches from the doorway. She did not expect to be met with his huge, wall-like body and thick, clean shaven head, dead eyes staring at her with indifferent anger. Golyat was a giant, rotund was too simple of a word to describe his girth. He was as wide as several men and tall enough she thought he must bang his head on the top of doorways often. But he must have had a private tailor with a warehouse of fabric, because he was always dressed to perfection in suit and tie. He was the scariest, most well-dressed man she had ever met. Then again, he wasn't a man at all. He was one of Them, and the self-proclaimed leader at that.

"Well..." she barely got out before his hand shot out faster than a man that size should be able to move and caught hold of her throat. With effort similar to batting at a fly, he threw her across the room. She bounced once on the oversized table before sliding off and into the buffet against the far wall.

The hit stunned her. The buffet smashed as she went into it, and bits of serving ware and glass fell on her. Pain exploded through her back and ribs. He had moved so fast, she'd had no time to react. The pain and the surprise kept her from thinking straight. She slowly pulled herself out of the wreckage that had once been her furniture. Anger quickly replaced the pain. She could feel cuts on her arms and face, bruises were surely forming.

She touched her hand to her face gingerly. Her fingers came away red. Her lip was cut, as was one cheek. She could feel it already swelling. Her face! The bastard had damaged her face! It would heal of course, with her accelerated healing it would be as good as new by tomorrow, but that was not the point. He had destroyed her face.

She slowly got to her feet. A moan escaped her lips as she stood. It was a slow task with the pain biting at her the whole time.

"I believe it is an improvement. At least it will help keep you from being able to use your seduction on me while we have a chance to talk, you stupid bitch," Golyat growled.

His fist came down on the table. There was a low rumble, and then with a crack loud enough to shatter the large floor to ceiling windows, the large oak table that spanned the large hall split down the middle, its two halves collapsing over a jagged gash running up the middle of the three-inch-thick solid wood.

Anabelle used the wall to steady herself. He made no move to come around the now destroyed table. She concentrated on gathering herself together. She would never be able to defeat him one on one. She needed her wits about her.

"What have you done?" Golyat asked.

"Whatever do you mean, Golyat? You are the one who barged in here and struck me. You better know what I have done."

"I saw the reports. The creature that was seen by some, a hell-hound it has to be, somehow mutated by your magic," Golyat said.

She had never thought he'd have gotten wind of her machinations so fast. He must have eyes everywhere. Perhaps it was time to come clean. At least with part of her plan. He wouldn't kill her, he wouldn't dare. He could barely hold the Alliance together as it was.

"What have I done? I'll tell you what I have done. I haven't sat on my fat ass while a new Hunter is born. I haven't sat and waited while he grew into his power until he becomes a real force to fear," she said. She was letting her anger free and it felt good. She relished the anger and hatred as it flowed through her, tasting coppery on her tongue. "I acted. I am going to succeed where Rath failed and you are too afraid to even try."

She walked around the corner of the broken table, approaching him slowly, like a cat stalking prey. "I even used the power you experiment with, always testing, never willing to actually use. We could have an army of our kind marching over this world."

For the first time ever she saw surprise in Golyat's eyes. The pleasure it gave her was immense, better than sex. Maybe. "That's right Golyat. The Alliance might have found a way to pull our dark brethren from the depths of Hell, but I was the first one to put it to practical use."

"You actually opened the gate and retrieved a dark soul from Hell? And brought it to this world?" Golyat asked. "You are a fool."

This made her anger burn all the hotter.

"Fool? Me? Ever the General right, Golyat? Ever planning, never doing. Only I had the courage to do what had to be done. If we do not act now, this boy will only grow in power. And I was right, my creation easily defeated him."

"Really Anabelle? Then where is his head?"

That stopped her. She had expected him to fly into a rage. But this simple question threw her off, especially since she did not like the answer.

"I had only planned it as a test, just to see how much the Hunter had mastered his power. It turned out the Hunter was weaker than even I had expected. Ammit had him and would have finished him off, but I could not hold back the mortals around us. I distracted them as long as I could. Any longer and he would have been seen, and I did not think that prudent at this time."

"Perhaps the only smart move you made."

She ignored him. "Besides, the Hunter is a child. I now know we can defeat him anytime we wish. The plan served its purpose."

"So, let me get this straight. You wanted to observe and then wait and bide your time for the right moment? Is this not what you accuse me of? Laziness? How did you put it? I sat on my fat ass."

"I had no choice, the Alliance would have been after me if I had revealed so much to mortals. And the problem is solved now. Ammit is going after him as we speak. I expect his head within the hour."

"You are very confident, Anabelle. So was Rath. Obviously, you were able to use the gate that we have created. But hounds have no names, so did you free a hellhound or a dark soul?"

"I did both," Anabelle said and couldn't help raising her head a little in pride. "I was able to pluck an eternal sufferer from our former prison and fuse it with the essence of a hellhound."

"Well that is impressive, but how? The gate is incredibly unstable. How were you able to find a soul so quickly and force it into a hellhound? Where did you get that kind of power?"

She looked him in the eyes. "We all have our secrets we keep."

She wanted to keep her soul shaper pet a secret as long as possible.

Golyat picked up a chair and threw it through the window. He roared in rage. "You stupid bitch. You are forbidden to access the gate anymore. You have released another dark soul before we are ready."

"Calm down. I had to harvest a weak soul. I did not have time to choose. I grabbed the first one I found, and it jumped at the chance to escape, even giving up its essence of humanity. This soul was not like our kind, fighting to escape and earning their freedom. We, the Alliance of dark souls, are of a different breed. Ammit is nothing more than my puppy dog."

"And you would slay the Hunter of Lost Souls with a puppy," Golyat said. "He will fail. And then the Hunter will come after you," Golyat sighed. "I admit I might be moving slowly, but when a kid with no training dispatches one of our most powerful, like Rath, we have to proceed with caution, and you have shown very little. I will warn you. The gate must be kept secret, never before have we had the potential to retrieve dark souls from the bowels of Hell. It is the glue of this Alliance. Without it, we were few and easy prey for the Beast. With it, we are the beginning of an army and a new age for humanity."

He stepped forward, brushing the wrecked table aside as though it was made of paper. With that same impossible quickness, he was towering over her, his large hand catching her jaw and forcing her to look up at him, to meet his hate-filled eyes.

"If the Hunter finds out about the gate or anything happens to jeopardize its existence, I will personally split you in two. Hell will seem like paradise when I am through."

He turned and walked out of the room, ripping the heavy door off its hinges in his passing, as if it was made of cardboard. He had dismissed her as though she were nothing.

It was, all things considered, better than she had hoped for. She had cuts and bruises, her body ached, but it only gave her anger fuel. She would enjoy watching Golyat lose control of the Alliance when they heard how she had taken control and rid the world of their great Adversary. At the very least, she would gain enough support to make him think twice about coming into her own home and assaulting her.

She heard another crashing sound and knew she had to replace her front door as well. God how she hated him.

10

Christopher woke with a start. The book flew from his hands and he tried to sit up. Too quickly, pain from his recently healed wounds flared up. Dark Eris had been leaning over him, she sprang back from the bed and cried out in surprise, for a moment her face darkening and the shadow of the creature she had become yesterday passed over her. It was gone so quickly Christopher was not even sure he had seen it.

Hamlin had also jumped out of his chair, knocking it over.

"Holy shit, kid! Don't do that. I used to be a smoker. Almost gave me a heart attack," Hamlin said.

"I have to go. I have to get out of here," Christopher said and threw his legs over the side of the bed, winching as his stiff muscles reacted. It was just soreness, the essential healing was done.

"Now hold on kid, what did you find out?" Hamlin asked.

"That thing, that hellhound thing, it can track us, me that is, and the longer I stay in one place, the stronger the trail I leave for it. It could be here any moment. We have to move now!"

Christopher got to his feet a little gingerly, but the stiffness was working itself out. In a few moments he would be close to normal. Except he still felt hollow, as though missing an organ.

"Where are we supposed to go?"

"I don't know, a hotel or something. But we have to get out," realization suddenly hit Christopher. "I have to go. You two can't come with me."

"What the Hell are you talking about? Look, you're talking too fast. Take a moment to catch your breath..."

"It can track me Hamlin, not either of you. I'm what it wants, or what they want, and I am what it can track. Not you or Eris. If I head out, you guys can go on and be safe."

"Were would you go? Is any place safe place if this thing can track you?" Eris was back, the darkness completely gone.

"I don't know. The Librarian is trying to find answers, but all I know is that staying here puts us all in danger. I... I put us in danger. So I need to leave."

"Um, I hate to break it to you, but this is not the first time we have been in danger because of what you have become. And to think that now is any different makes no sense," Hamlin said.

"But it is different. Before we had no idea what we were up against, we didn't even know if we were up against anything when we went to the crime scene. But now we do. We know what that thing is capable of, and I might not be able to stop it," Christopher said and looked down, unable to meet Hamlin's eyes. "I might not be able to protect you."

"Hah, the day I need protection from a punk-ass college kid, even one with power from the Devil himself, is the day I quit the force and retire to Florida. And I hate humidity and Disney World. No dice kid, you're stuck with me," Hamlin said.

"And with me," Eris said.

"Well, there's no need for you to come along. I mean, I know you need my help but this isn't really your battle. You should just go somewhere and hide out for a while. I would come find you when this is over. I can even give you some money, you know, to cover expenses..." Christopher trailed off as the shadow once again overtook Eris' face. Dark Eris had returned and Christopher had the sudden suspicion that he had just fucked up.

"Go somewhere and hide out? Like a coward? Oh! And you want to give me some money? Well, we haven't even fucked and somehow you made me feel like your little whore," Dark Eris said, her facial features shifting as though the demonic visage was struggling to get through. But she held it back.

"What? No... I just didn't want you to have to get involved," Christopher said.

She stood up abruptly, and Christopher fell back onto the bed as she loomed over, her skin shifting and bulging as she strove to contain her demonic hatred.

"Involved? You mean like rescuing you from the monster? Helping you determine that it is some sort of hellhound? That kind of involved?"

"She has a point, kid. From what I've seen, she is able to take care of herself...and you...just fine," Hamlin said. But Christopher noticed that Hamlin had moved closer to him and had his hand on his gun. Christopher was not sure if it would even be effective against Dark Eris, but it was obvious that Hamlin didn't completely trust the demoness.

"I may have come to you for help, but where would you be without mine?" She asked.

Christopher nodded. "I know you can handle yourself, and you've more than helped me out. I just wanted to make it clear you don't owe me anything. I haven't solved your problem, and I don't even know if I'll be able to."

She seemed to soften, and her demonic nature stopped trying

to come out. "I know I need you to help me out, but that's not the only reason I want to help you."

"Why do you want to help?" Christopher asked suddenly curious. She showed up on his doorstep a couple weeks ago saying she needed his help. He was just a stranger to her, some guy that got stuck with a job he had no idea how to do. He had told her that from the first day, but she had stayed with him anyway. It didn't make a lot of sense.

Dark Eris stared at him as though surprised by the question. "I don't know... I." She stopped, unable to find the words. Dark Eris was never at a loss for words.

"Look, this is great and all, but I think we need to do as Christopher suggested and get the Hell out of Dodge. We can talk in more detail when we're someplace safe. I know of a couple police safe houses we might be able to borrow..."

A crash from the roof interrupted him. The crash was followed by the sound of heavy footfalls thumping across the ceiling.

"We're out of time," Christopher said and jumped up again from the bed. "Time to go." He grabbed the Weapon and Book from the bedside table.

Eris, Dark Eris had retreated, handed him his jeans with his wallet in it and a t shirt.

"Take the stairs at the back of the house. Go!" Christopher yelled.

Hamlin ran out into the hall, gun drawn, although they all knew the gun wouldn't hurt the werehound significantly. Eris was behind him and Christopher took up the rear. As they ran, he pulled the shadows towards him and formed his shadow jacket and clothes. It made him feel less naked to be in his "work" uniform.

They heard a crash from behind them, and Christopher knew

the creature had just come through his window. *Dammit, I just fixed it from last time*, he thought. They ran faster.

They made it to the top of the stairs before the door to his bedroom blew off its hinges and smashed into the wall on the opposite side of the hallway. Luckily, the top of the rear stairs, the servant stairs in days long gone, were around the corner from his room. The creature would pause for a second while it tried to determine which way they had gone. It was a large home with three different ways away from his room. But the hound could track him, they had only moments. They would never make it, not unless he bought them some time.

"Hamlin. Where is your car?" Christopher asked.

"Around the block, parking here sucks. Why?" Hamlin said.

Christopher tossed him his keys. "Mine's in the garage. I'll meet you in the alley." He handed his clothes to Eris.

"How?" she asked. "You couldn't stop it before?"

"Before I was trying to kill it, not slow it down. Now go."

Christopher gave her a shove and then turned back to the hallway.

"God dammit, kid," he heard Hamlin say, but they kept running down the stairs.

Christopher stepped into the hallway. The Hound saw him and made a deep, menacing sound. Christopher imagined it was the sound granite would make if it could howl. The Weapon exploded into a large sword in his hand. Power swirled along its blade and around his body. He could feel the Hellfire burning inside of him, purifying his hatred. It seemed like the Weapon's thirst for souls was ten times stronger than ever before. Christopher was overwhelmed. For a brief moment, he almost lost himself. It was like he was at a dark precipice, and at the bottom was all the anger and hatred he had ever felt. Falling in, giving in, would be the end of who he was. What scared him most was that part of him wanted to give up, and the power of the Weapon fed it. With a surge of will, he reasserted himself over the Weapon and held it in check.

But that hesitation was all the creature needed. It charged.

Christopher barely brought the weapon up in time. He didn't have time to strike. He lifted it, hoping to use it as a shield, and instantly the Weapon broadened into a large, wicked-looking axe. The creature's claws skittered against the axe head, sending up sparks of power. It stumbled to the side in surprise as power lashed out at it. It recovered with that same blinding speed that made even Christopher's enhanced reflexes seem sluggish. Before he could strike, the werehound jumped back, watching him wearily.

But they both knew it was just a matter of time. Christopher would not be able to defeat it one on one.

The creature moved in again, and Christopher swung the axe. It ducked under and struck Christopher with the back of its arm. Christopher flew through the hallway wall from the force of the blow, sending wood splinters and drywall dust everywhere. Pain shot up his back as he skidded across the floor of the guestroom and into an antique desk.

He rolled to his feet and brought the axe up moments before the werehound was on him. He swung as the creature charged, again it dodged out of the way of the massive blade. But this time Christopher reversed the strike faster and brought the blade back up as the creature struck. The edge of the Weapon cut into the creature's bicep, but the cut was shallow, and just as Christopher felt the Weapon latch onto its soul, the monster pulled away. The dark soul slipped away.

Christopher could almost hear the Weapon scream in frustration. The werehound jumped back across the room. The sting of Christopher's axe had shaken it up.

Christopher didn't wait for it to get its nerve back. He ran out of the room and down the hall towards the back stairwell. Before he could reach the stairs, the werehound exploded through the wall in from of him, blocking his path.

Knowing any hesitation would get him killed, Christopher immediately changed direction and charged through the door next to him into the bathroom. He would have to go through the window at the far side of the bathroom. He was three steps into the room when he heard the werehound come through the door behind him. It was big enough to take some of the doorway with it as it entered the bathroom.

Christopher was almost to the large window when he felt the claws sink into his back. The force of the blow spun him around. Without thinking, he gathered the power within him and leapt backwards. But the werehound was right on top of him and caught hold of Christopher with its massive claws. Together, they smashed through the window and out into the New York evening air, three stories above the ground.

The creature opened its jaws wide, obviously planning on taking a large chunk out of Christopher's neck, but Christopher knew it wasn't just his flesh he had to worry about. With a surge of desperate strength, he brought the axe up between them. The werehound's muzzle bounced off of it with a crackle of power and the monster was falling away from him.

He had no time to enjoy his relief. He slammed into the earth with a bone-jarring crash. If he had been strictly mortal, like he had been just a few weeks ago, his body would have been shattered, and he would be dead from such a fall. But with the power of Hell flowing through him, his body absorbed the damaged.

But it still hurt like a motherfucker. The air was kicked out of him, and for a brief moment the world spun.

Get the fuck up! A voice inside of him screamed. *It is going to be on you any second!*

He rolled to his feet with a moan only to see the werehound already on his own feet and slowly stalking forward. The Weapon in Christopher's hand flashed with power, and suddenly he was holding two slightly smaller axes, one in each hand. Apparently the Weapon felt quantity was what was needed here. They were still connected, Christopher could feel it, and both screamed at him with the hunger for more souls. Somehow he was again able to overcome their command and stay in control.

The werehound approached, and Christopher brought up both the blades. He had no idea how to fight with two axes, but then again he had no idea how to fight with one or the usual sword it became. He longed for the day when he might actually know what he was doing. But for right now he needed to focus on living to see that day.

The creature came in fast, claws out and jaw snapping. Christopher used the axes to block the blows, but that was all he could do. The creature was so fast, he could barely muster a defense, let alone any sort of attack. He focused on blocking the thing's muzzle, it could do the most damage. But the claws got through. He felt the claws slice through the skin on his right arm, causing him to lower the Weapon in that hand. The werehound tried to seize the advantage, but Christopher was able to bring the other blade up in time. The move, unfortunately, left his other side exposed, and the claws sunk into the skin across his ribs.

He sprang back out of the creature's reach, but he knew it was only a matter of time. He was bleeding from multiple cuts, and his healing did not seem to be keeping up with the rate at which the werehound was hurting him. He would not last much longer.

Then he heard the blaring of a horn behind the brick wall of his backyard. It was getting closer.

Gathering all his remaining energy, he swung the axes as quickly as he could at the monster. It avoided them easily, but was forced back. Hoping it was enough, Christopher turned and jumped over the wall behind him, expecting to feel the pain of claws digging into his back at any moment.

But he didn't.

He cleared the wall and landed on the ground just behind his car. It was slowing to a stop. That was no good.

"Don't stop!" Christopher said. "Keep going, dammit!"

"What?" Eris—or Dark Eris, Christopher couldn't tell—yelled out of the window.

"Keep moving! Go, go!"

Hamlin caught on. He hit the gas.

Christopher jumped towards the car just as the werehound cleared the wall and hit the ground less than twenty feet from where Christopher had landed. Axes in front of him, he smashed through the rear windshield of the car and fell into the back seat in a shower of broken glass. He immediately sat up and looked out the back window, just in time to see the werehound land on the trunk.

The Weapon shifted and was once again a short sword blade. The Weapon knew the large axe would be inefficient to wield in the backseat of a car.

Christopher swung at the werehound through the broken back window. He couldn't get much leverage because of the awkward angle, but the mere threat of the powerful blade caused the werehound to rear back. At that exact moment, Hamlin hit the gas and the car shot forward, sending the creature tumbling to the ground.

Christopher was glad he had convinced his dad to get the super charged version.

The were-hound rolled quickly to its feet and leapt again. Just as it was about to land, the car swerved and made a hard left out onto the main street. The werehound shot past the car and slammed into the side of a large truck, sending it skittering to the side.

Hamlin sped off down the street and made another sliding turn to the left. Fast as the car would let him, he turned down other streets in a slightly less aggressive manner, all the while putting more distance between them and the monster behind.

"Talk about defensive driving," Eris said. "Do you learn that stuff in cop school?"

"Some. The rest I picked up in my not so innocent youth," Hamlin said.

"We need to get off Manhattan as soon as possible, head towards the Lincoln tunnel," Christopher said.

"Are you crazy? This time in the evening? No, Holland tunnel is the best choice," Eris said.

"Neither," Hamlin said.

"I hear that Lincoln has gotten better..." Christopher started.

"Oh, I don't know," interrupted Hamlin, "do we listen to the rich kid who never had a job or the transient girl that doesn't own a car? I know, why don't we listen to the only guy in the car who has to commute every fucking day to work."

"Good point," Christopher acknowledged. Eris nodded her head.

"We are heading north. We need to put some distance between you and this thing so it can't hunt you down so quickly. We need some time to think," Hamlin said.

His words echoed Christopher's thoughts. Time to think, was that so much to ask?

11

"So, budget tight in the NYPD?" Eris asked.

Christopher had to admit she had a point. The apartment Hamlin had brought them to was a little on the rundown side. They had stopped at an apartment building just past the Bronx Zoo. It was small compared to some of the other buildings in the neighborhood and older as well. They were on the fourth floor with a great view of the other drab building across the street. A layer of dust covered the small dining table and most of the kitchen counters.

It was a one bedroom, with a kitchen, living area, and bathroom. At least it wasn't a studio, but if they were all going to sleep here, it would be tight.

It smelled of a mixture of disturbed dust and faint mildew. Christopher would have guessed it had been months since someone had been here to open the widows and let in some air. But it was safer than his house, at least for the moment.

"I picked one that wasn't in regular rotation, something off the NYPD grid or at least not at the top of the list," Hamlin said. "This one doesn't get much use. Kind of a reserve safe house. I think the only reason it’s still owned by the police is its virtually zero cost. I thought it our best chance to remain disturbed by my colleagues."

"It's not the police disturbing us I’m concerned about," Christopher mumbled.

"We'll be okay here, for a night anyway. It took that thing what? Twenty-four hours to find you at your house, and you said it would have an easier time finding you at a place you frequent. You've never been to this place,” Hamlin said. "In fact, have you ever even been to the Bronx?"

"Yeah, of course. But not very much."

"So we should be good here for at least a night. I got a few more places we could stay at over the next few nights. They're spread out around the city."

"Then what?" Christopher asked. "Head out of state? Run?"

Hamlin ignored him. "I'm gonna head out for some food. There's a grocery on the corner, I'll get us some snacks. Keep the door locked and keep quiet. The neighbors are going to be suspicious enough as it is that somebody is using this place again." He looked carefully up and down the hall before he left.

"You should go a little easy on him, it's not like it's his fault," Eris said as she sat in a chair by the window and gazed out.

Christopher sat carefully on the couch, his body sore. It seemed like just as his battle wounds were healing something happened to give him new ones.

"I know. I'm just tense. I hate this," Christopher said.

When she didn't say anything, he looked at her. She was quiet as she stared out the window. Then he noticed the tear running down her cheek.

"Hey, everything is going to be okay, you know," he said, although he was far from believing it. "We’ll figure this out."

"You're lying, but that's not why... not why."

Christopher stood up, ignoring the stabs of pain from his slowly healing wounds. He sat down again closer to her.

"What's wrong then?" asked Christopher.

"I... I tried, I really tried," she started.

"Tried what?" Christopher asked. He could see the aura of her soul, or rather the combination of two souls rippling around her, flowing against each other, but not mixing, like oil and water.

"When you were fighting the werehound, I tried to get Dark Eris to come... to take over I guess, but she wouldn't," she said. The tears were coming more freely.

"No, no don't be upset. This wasn't your battle, or Dark Eris' for that matter. This is my fight." Christopher was not sure if he should reach out for her. He wanted to, he wanted to comfort her, let her know everything would be alright. But she was right, it would be a lie. Still, he wanted to hold her, maybe even more for himself than for her. But he didn't, something stopped him. The image of Dark Eris in demonic form loomed in his mind.

"I really tried, I begged. At least I thought I did. It is so hard to describe how we... exist inside of my body together."

"It's okay," Christopher said.

"No, it's not. We should be helping," she said. "I don't think she knew what was going on. Sometimes, when you aren't the one in control, it's hard to understand what is happening. What I'm trying to say is, I don't think she abandoned us on purpose."

"No, of course not..."

"It was like she was hiding," Eris said and looked at Christopher suddenly. "But I don't understand what she would be hiding from. She is not the hiding type."

"True. She does seem to go at things head on. But I don't want you to beat yourself up like this. It isn't your fault this creature is after me, and it certainly isn't your fault that Dark Eris wouldn't listen to you."

It was then Christopher realized he had reached out and was holding her hand. But he did not pull it back. Somehow it felt right.

"I just feel so useless," Eris said suddenly seeming restless. She stood up and paced. "You have these powers and she has, well that demon thing, even Hamlin has his safe houses and cool logic. What can I do? Besides cry and be a burden."

"No, you're not a burden."

"I just wish I could do something, anything to help. You don't know how it feels to be so useless."

"But I do. Look at me, literally the Devil's bounty hunter, all this power and that thing swats me away like a fly. I mean it's destroyed my home, I'm on the run. Hell, I'm hiding out in a rundown apartment in the Bronx. Some emissary of the devil I turned out to be."

As he said it, his feelings of uselessness truly began to sink in. This had all been a mistake from the beginning. "I thought I could be this... this whatever it is that I am. I thought for a brief moment that it was important. But no, I was just a mistake. And now I have no clue what to do."

They both sat in silence until Hamlin returned from the store with food and supplies. They didn't speak, and they didn't let go of each other's hand.

12

Ammit slipped out of the shadows and into her bedroom silently. From the moment he entered the house, Anabelle knew he was there, of course, but it amazed her that something embodying such destructive power could be so quiet when it needed to be. Any mortal would have been surprised by the sudden arrival of the werehound.

He came up behind her and gently rested his massive claw on her shoulder. It should have been a heavy weight, but he held it there gently. She knew what it meant, what he wanted, but it was creepy. All males wanted her in some way, as well as many females for that matter, but at the same time it meant all males *wanted* her. It was her gift and curse rolled into one. She shuddered in disgust and shrugged off his claw.

"Do you have his head for me?" She asked, turning around. She let her dressing gown fall open, just enough to show off the inner swell of her breasts. She was disgusted, but control was more important at the moment. And she knew how to control men, human or otherwise.

"There was a problem," Ammit said.

With a grunt Anabelle pulled her robe closed, stood up and shoved him back. "A problem? You had a simple task, one you had almost accomplished before. What could have possibly gone wrong?"

He growled at her sudden change, but she was not worried. It was just typical male frustration. She used it like a weapon.

"He ran. I was expecting him to fight, but he ran like a coward."

"And why did you not catch him? You are faster, stronger," she said.

"I would have chased him down, but he had help."

"What? Those mortals that were there last time?"

Ammit looked down in shame, unable to meet his mistress' eyes.

"I thought him alone, but his friends showed up. They got away in a car," he said. The deep menacing rumble of his speech belied the slumped shame of his body.

Good. He should be ashamed.

"They got away in a car? You could not keep up with a car? Hell, in New York a cripple on crutches can catch up to a car in traffic," she said. This was not good, if she didn't get the hunter's head, and soon, Golyat would destroy her.

"I did catch up to the car, I almost had them," he growled. "But then I was thrown from the car and into another vehicle. By the time I was able to follow again, they had disappeared. Whoever was driving knows the streets well. I went from rooftop to rooftop, but I had lost them."

"How could you fail at this simple task? How can you lose them? Can't you track him now that you've tasted his soul?" she yelled. She knew she sounded out of control, but this was a disaster. She needed the boy dead as soon as possible.

"I can. Even as they disappeared, I could taste the meat of his soul on my tongue. But it will take time, and if he keeps moving, even longer. I thought it best to tell you what I know first. Besides, there were a lot of potential witnesses on the street. I had thought to kill him inside his home. I knew that you would not like such a disturbance, so I fled as soon as possible." he said.

She wanted to hit him, to beat and gouge at him. But that was not her way. Sometimes she hated her way. She reached out and gently touched his chest. Even hunched over in shame, his face was a little too far for her to reach comfortably. "You might have disappointed me in not killing him, but it was right for you to leave before the mortals understood what they were seeing."

He looked up at her touch, and she was certain that if he had a tail it would have wagged. "These friends of his, were they the same as the ones at your first encounter?"

"The demoness was there, I could see her. I did not see the driver. It could be the same man."

She nodded and then paced away in thought. She was quiet a long time as she thought through different scenarios. Tracking the hunter would take time, too much, she suspected. Golyat would be on her in seconds once he suspected she had not succeeded. For all she knew, he was on his way back to her home at this moment, although she doubted he had been able to place spies within her own household. They needed to draw him out, they needed bait. But the only bait she knew of was with him.

"Wait. The hunter is young," she said. She had the beginnings of an idea. Of all the escaped souls she had met since she had won her own freedom, only she had retained such an understanding of mortal emotions. She no longer suffered from them, but it was her gift to be able to manipulate them to her desire.

"Hardly more than a boy. I am disgusted I was unable to dispatch him easily," Ammit said.

"Mortals are weak and quite often stupid, especially the young.

This Hunter is something of an idealist, I believe. His father was a crusader. I wonder if he instilled any of his philosophies in his offspring."

"I see you have a plan. What is it you wish of me mistress?" Ammit asked.

"Begin hunting for him, but at the same time we can draw him out," she said.

"How?"

"Simple. Leave a pile of bodies up to his doorstep. Do what you are best at, kill and eat souls of the innocent. Not too many, maybe just one or two a night. Just enough let him know who it is that is doing it. If I understand our young man, he will come looking for you."

Ammit's muzzle-mouth spread into a toothy grin that would have caused any mortal to void their bowels on the spot. But Anabelle found it endearing. "With extreme pleasure mistress," Ammit said, drool already oozing from his mouth.

13

When Christopher arrived at the Library it was with his best landing yet. He only stumbled a few steps rather than falling face first into the stone. After catching himself on a stone bookcase, he waited a moment for the disorienting vertigo to fade before looking around.

The long hallway and tall stacks of books that made up this section of the Library seemed to be deserted. He could smell the surprisingly comforting fragrance of dusty stone mixed with the faint scent of ancient parchments. He thought he might have gotten the jump on the Librarian for once. The tall, shadowy figure was nowhere to be found. Perhaps Christopher could even sneak up on him for a change. His excitement at the prospect was short lived, however.

"Welcome, oh Great Condemner of the Sinful," the Librarian said from just behind him.

Christopher jumped forward and almost slammed into a large, solid looking shelf. It seemed to him that the Librarian had said that a little louder than necessary.

"Jesus Christ, you scared the shit out of me," Christopher said.

"I am not Jesus Christ, and I believe he would prefer to have nothing to do with our little operation. Conflict of interest," said the Librarian.

"Yeah, I bet. Have you found anything?"

The Librarian spun on his heels, if he had any—the dark robe hid his feet, and floated off down the hallway. "Come," he said as though Christopher was an afterthought.

After only a moment's hesitation Christopher followed after. He wasn't sure how this inter-dimensional library thing worked, but if he was somehow supposed to be the Librarian's boss, the guy sure as Hell didn't act like it.

"Did you find a way to defeat the werehound?" Christopher asked as they made their way deeper into the stacks. The Librarian seemed to be ignoring him.

Suddenly, the rows of shelves opened up to the familiar study area in the middle of the stacks. A long leather couch and several comfortable looking lounge chairs dominated the room, as well as a coffee table and a large desk covered with papers and old books. A fireplace with a large wooden mantle was set in one wall. While the study area looked the same as it had when he saw it before, the shelves that surrounded it looked older, it was obviously in a different section of the Library. Without the Librarian to lead he would never be able to find his way around in here.

"No," the Librarian said.

It had taken him so long to answer that Christopher had almost forgotten that he'd asked a question. His heart suddenly sank. He dropped into the most comfortable chair he could find with a defeated sigh.

"Great. I don't have much time before that thing comes after me again. You were right, it can hunt me down. We got away, but next time... well this might be the last time you see me."

"I said I did not find a way to defeat the werehound, but I did not say I found nothing of use."

Christopher looked up, pulling himself out of the pit of hopelessness he felt himself falling into.

"I may have found a lead. Tenuous at best, but something," the Librarian said and paused. The Librarian might be a metaphor or something, but Christopher had to admit he had a flare for the dramatic. "I had hoped to find more, but it appears my access to the assignment room is more limited than I expected. Soon after you left, I found it harder and harder to stay in that room. Eventually, I found myself outside the door."

"And that lead is?" Christopher asked.

"He had a house," the Librarian said.

"Who?" Christopher was confused even more than he usually was when talking to the Librarian.

"Who do you think? The Beast of course," the Librarian said with a sigh. "Try to keep up."

"He had a house?" This threw Christopher off. The thing he had met in the boiler room in the basement of his university did not seem like the type that needed a house, or sleep for that matter. But perhaps even the Devil incarnate needed some shut eye from time to time.

"Well, house might be too grand a term, more like a lair," the Librarian said. "In fact, I believe he had several, all over the world."

"Why? I mean did he even sleep?"

"I don't know about sleep, but as for the why, it appears even the Beast needed a home base, somewhere to heal wounds after a tough battle. Someplace to plan his next move."

"I wouldn't have thought any battle was tough for that dude. But I thought this library was a sort of home base?"

"The Library? As I have said before, this was not a Library for him. The way he accessed the information in the Book was completely different and much more efficient than any mortal mind," the Librarian said. "Also, as you are aware, you leave your body behind unprotected when you come here. Not a very intelligent tactic, I would think."

"But how is this a lead? What does this have to do with defeating a werehound?"

Christopher thought the Librarian shrugged, but it was hard to tell with the shadows draped about him.

"I don't know if it will help, but there may be something there that might help."

"Great. What? Do I go to his apartment and look through his fridge? Maybe he'll have a coffee table book on how to tame a hellhound?"

"Well, for starters it is not an average apartment, and there will most likely be more interesting stuff to look at than what he kept in the fridge. But if sarcasm is your best coping mechanism, please by all means, continue," the Librarian said.

Sarcasm was a coping mechanism for him? Christopher thought.

"The closest one," the Librarian continued, "is located under the Bronx zoo."

"Under the Bronx zoo?" That caught Christopher by surprise.

"Yes. I believe that is close to your current location?"

"But how can that be? I mean, wouldn't somebody have found it by now? Like workers at the zoo, or security, or someone?"

"Does it shock you that the lord of lies and obfuscation could hide something as radically complex as a door?"

"I guess not, just seems like there would be a lot of people around, and it's such a public place. Not my first choice for a lair for someone whose job it is to track down and kill escapees from Hell," Christopher said.

"Well, you are the Hunter now, you can put your lair anywhere you want. But this one was the abode of your predecessor and might have some clues that will help you fill his rather large shoes."

"I thought I was doing okay so far, at least until the werehound showed up," Christopher said. He knew it sounded defensive, but he was getting tired of being picked on. He had defeated a powerful dark soul and at least kept himself alive in the last two encounters with his latest adversary.

"Yes, you are doing well for a mortal child," the Librarian said as he stepped closer, looming over Christopher. "But the Beast would have brought the hellhound to heel the moment he saw it. It would be whimpering at his feet, not serving another dark soul. And the Beast would have banished the dark soul sharing its body back to Hell by now. You have much to learn before you are even a tenth of his power."

Christopher had sunk into the chair as much as he could as the Librarian had come closer. For a moment he thought the tall being was going to strike him. But the Librarian just stood there for a moment as though waiting for something. Then he sighed.

"But as I have said before, you are what we have to work with."

Christopher had the distinct feeling he was missing something.

"The entrance to the Beast's lair is in the Bronx River Park on the south side of the zoo, near Jungle World," the Librarian said. He stepped back from Christopher.

"What does it look like, the entrance, I mean?" Christopher asked.

"I don't know."

"You don't know? How am I supposed to find it? Is there a sign on it that says: Lair of Satan's Assistant?"

"I doubt it is even a door, at least not in the traditional sense," the Librarian said once again unfazed by Christopher's sarcasm. Sometimes he wondered why he even tried.

"So, I need to find a door that is not a door, hidden by what you basically said was the world's best deceiver, leading to an underground room under the zoo? Why does my life seem to get so much more complicated when I come to see you?"

"Oh, I suspect things will get even more complicated. Just think, you have only been the Devil's avatar for a few weeks, wait until you have centuries under your belt. Although, I'd say at the moment odds are, you won't have to worry about that," said the Librarian.

"Hey, I think..."

"I would imagine that the Beast must have used some sort of Hell power to help hide the door. I suspect you, as his successor, might be the one most able to find it."

14

Christopher woke with a start. It seemed even his returns from the Library to the real world were traumatic in some way. At least he was always sitting or lying down so falling on his face was not an issue. In this case he was lying down. He sat up slowly, letting the residual vertigo fade away.

Eris sat across from him, concern on her face.

"How'd it go?" She asked.

"Not much to go on, but something."

He heard a crash and then a string of curses from the other room.

Eris smiled. "Hamlin is trying to cook spaghetti. But I'm not sure he knows how to make anything that doesn't come frozen in a box."

Christopher returned her smile. It felt good, he hadn't stretched those muscles in a while. "Then we should go check on him before he burns the place down."

In the kitchen Hamlin was indeed making pasta. The smell filled the apartment and made Christopher's stomach grumble.

"Ah! Just in time," Hamlin said as they came out of the bedroom. "Dinner is served."

"Is he wearing an apron?" Christopher asked into Eris' ear. She nodded with a giggle.

"You know we could have just gotten take out," Christopher said, this time loud enough for Hamlin to hear.

"Nonsense, and miss out on my old family recipe?"

"But you're not Italian," Christopher said.

"Not to mention I saw the jars of sauce in the bag you brought home from the grocery," Eris said.

"Okay, you got me," Hamlin said and held up his hands. "It's just that we have been eating out a lot lately, and I thought a home cooked meal would, you know, boost morale."

"Kind of like a final meal?" Christopher asked and immediately regretted it.

Eris jabbed him in the gut. Hamlin looked down a little.

"I'm sorry, Hamlin," Christopher said. "Pasta sounds great and the smell is killing me."

Hamlin's faint smile returned, albeit a little more subdued. "You may call it pasta, but for me, it is good old spaghetti and meatballs."

As they dished up their plates and ate, they kept the conversation light as though they could all sense they needed a respite from the mounting tension. Eris was smiling more than she had in the past week. Even Hamlin seemed a little more relaxed, his constantly cynical edge dulled just a little bit. Hamlin didn't ask what he had found out at the Library, and Christopher didn't mention it. As dangerous as waiting was, they needed some time.

All too soon however, the tension broke back into their world. The light heartedness began to feel a little forced. Christopher could see Hamlin was straining not to ask questions about their next steps. It was time to talk about a plan.

"We need to finish up, I have a field trip planned for us," Christopher tried one last attempt to keep the feeling going. "We're heading to the zoo."

Hamlin choked a little on his pasta. "The zoo?"

Christopher quickly filled them in on what the Librarian told him. They seemed to be as concerned it was a wild goose chase as he was.

"At this point I don't see anything else to try," Christopher said.

"Why the zoo?" Eris asked.

Christopher shrugged.

"It makes some sense I guess. Empty at night, when he was probably most active. I doubt the animals would have bothered him. Probably lots of service tunnels and utility rooms underground," Hamlin said. "Besides, what better place for a Beast than under other beasts?"

Hamlin's phone rang. After a glance at it he said, "I have to take this. It's work." He stood up and walked a little way away.

Ten minutes later he came back into the room, and Christopher knew there was something wrong the moment he saw his face. Even his aura looked slightly weaker, almost defeated.

"They found two more bodies," he said. His former good cheer was gone. His tone was dry, Hamlin the jaded detective was back.

"You mean... from the werehound?" Eris asked.

But Christopher knew the answer. He got up from the table and looked out the window at the street below. Some kids were playing down there, riding their bikes. Others had chalk and were drawing pictures on the sidewalk. A few adults were out, sitting on their porch steps, watching the kids play. He saw nothing suspicious, no monster slinking through the afternoon shadows. The shifting colors of the kid's auras were not pure by any means, but they all still had a touch of innocence. Most of the darkness of their souls was imposed on them by their parents. It all seemed very normal. He dreamed of normal now-a-days.

"Yeah, same MO." Hamlin said. "Torn apart like fresh meat, very little actual flesh eaten."

"It is not meat he is looking for he finds his nourishment in deeper things," Christopher said quietly from near the window.

"Jesus," Eris said. "More homeless victims?"

"No," Hamlin said and almost fell into a chair. "One was a school teacher, the other a mechanic."

"Is that significant? Or are they just random victims?" Christopher asked.

"Well, regardless of the value you put on a human life, the first two victims were a homeless person and small time business owner with no family. The reality is that not many people will pay attention. You start having victims that have families and co-workers—people that will be missed—well, that ups the visibility. The press looks at it more closely, and people start to talk," Hamlin said. "What we don't know is if it was intentional or not. Maybe this thing just got too hungry to wait for you."

"No, I know why," Christopher said. "It's trying to draw me out."

"No. You don't know that," Eris said.

"Yes. Yes, I do. It can't hunt me fast enough, so it is doing what it thinks will draw me out. They are making sure I notice. Whoever is controlling it has sped up their timeline and doesn't want to wait for me."

"And we still have no idea what their end game is, or what the actual timeline is," Hamlin said.

"What we do know is that innocent people are dying because of me," Christopher said. He was still watching the children in the streets. They were already thinning out as each left for dinner, most likely.

"Bullshit, kid. Don't get all teary-eyed and melancholy. This ain't some movie, and you ain't up for an Oscar. They are dying because one of those dark souls released a monster on the city, pure and simple. You didn't ask for this."

"No, but I'm the one who's running away and hiding while that thing is out there. Yeah, yeah, I know even if I did confront it, I wouldn't last long. This was never meant for me. I should have never read the fucking Book."

"But you did, didn't you?" Dark Eris said. Christopher could see the darkness sweep over her eyes. "You opened it, and now you are what you are. You think this all a mistake, well maybe it is, you probably aren't cut out for this. Maybe you just got lucky on Rath, beginner's luck, and maybe now it's only a matter of time."

"Jesus, do you take career coaching lessons from a tall, dark librarian?" Christopher asked.

"Or maybe not," Dark Eris went on. "Maybe despite all evidence to the contrary, you are up for this. Maybe third time's a charm, and in your next battle with it you will send it scouring back to Hell. I would assume at this point it is suffering from over confidence anyway. The point is, you'll never know for sure until you try."

"I think what she's trying to say, to paraphrase a movie, is that you aren't the hero that the world deserves or even needs, you are the one it is stuck with," Hamlin said.

"I was never cut out to be a hero," Christopher whispered.

"Nobody is kid, not at first," Hamlin said. "Remember when this all started? You had your chance to run, but you didn't. Maybe it was the hunger for vengeance or some level of understanding of what this power means to you and everybody else. I don't know, but you didn't run then. And you aren't running now. We are just trying to figure all this shit out."

Christopher nodded. "Then let's go to the zoo and try to figure this shit out before it kills any more people."

15

"You're sure the door is in here?" Dark Eris said.

They were standing outside the park on the corner of 180th and Boston road. It was close to dusk and the sun stretched the shadows around them. Strangely peaceful considering what they were looking for. The smell of the river and fresh air was strong here, like an oasis in the middle of the densely packed city. The soft roar of the small waterfall just inside the park came through during lulls in traffic noise. Not so long ago, Christopher might have been spent a sunny afternoon like this one walking around the park looking for a nice place to sit by the water, not searching for the lair of the Beast of Hell.

The stink of sinful souls fouled up his sense of smell. It was as though even a place as nice as this had the stench of corruption about it. Of all his gifts, this was the one he hated the most. It took the hope of joy away from him. Everywhere he went, he was surrounded by the putrid smell of sin and evil.

"That's what the Librarian told me. Hidden somewhere in the park," Christopher said. Even as he said it, he gripped the small book in his pocket. It had taken the form of a small reference bible. It seemed the Book had a sense of irony.

"Well, they shut the gates around dusk, so we should get to work finding this thing," Hamlin said.

Christopher nodded and they went inside. Christopher caught Dark Eris' arm to get her attention and held her back briefly as Hamlin walked ahead.

"We don't have time right now, but don't do your disappearing act anytime soon. We need to talk."

She pulled her arm from his grip, but nodded. "Yeah, sure. Whatever."

The park was emptying, the last few stragglers wandering slowly out of the gates. He guessed they had thirty minutes or so before somebody would do a security sweep, and they would be asked to leave.

"Should we spread out or something?" asked Hamlin when they walked up next to him. "Although, I'm not sure what I should be looking for."

"Wouldn't do any good. It's hidden with some power that apparently only I can detect," Christopher said.

"What kind of power? I mean, is it invisible, or just disguised as something else?" Dark Eris asked.

"No idea. The Librarian seemed to think I could use my abilities to hunt it down."

"Then lead, on guy with the golden nose," she said with a flourish of her hand.

Christopher stepped forward, but he was not quite sure how to even begin. He started by testing the air with his nose. He blocked out the mundane scents and honed in on the supernatural ones. He could smell the taint of Dark Eris and the much fainter corruption on Hamlin's soul. He had expected that. What he had not expected, though, was the absence of the almost constant evil oppression he felt most places in the city.

Normally he felt it all around him, like a slimy film left over everything. The residue of the evil in all men's souls, thinned only by the goodness that could be found in most people. It was like being constantly around the smell of death, eventually you start to adapt, to ignore it. It takes a toll of course, adapting to something like that, turning it into the new normal, but it's what he had to do. There was no choice.

Here though...here things were a little different. Christopher reached out his hand and moved it through the air, trying to feel more, to sense more. He could feel that darkness of course, but it was less in here and was growing calmer as more people left the park. From the direction of the zoo he could sense the animals or rather, he could sense the absence of souls in the living creatures. They did not have souls, just pure animal instinct.

"I think I know why he made a home here, under the zoo," Christopher said. "The animals have no souls, they have no corruption inside of them, at least not naturally. Just instinct. Here he could breathe easier, literally, the stench of human evil is faint when the visitors are gone. It's an oasis for him."

"Great, but we need a door. Does this clarity give you some indication of where that might be?" Hamlin asked.

As they walked around the park, Christopher let his awareness spread outward. He had no idea what he was doing, but let instinct take over. The Hell-power inside of him flared up and then radiated outward. It was as though all his senses except sight spread over the ground around him. Touching, tasting, and smelling every surface. But it wasn't the mundane world he was sensing, it was the hidden. The realm of souls and the supernatural, the world of power and miracles.

Hamlin took a step back as though it suddenly made him

nervous to stand next to Christopher. Christopher didn't think Hamlin could see what he was doing. But he might be able to feel it or at lease sense a change in his demeanor. Dark Eris watched him intently, but she did not step back as he expanded his awareness. She seemed to be enjoying his display of power.

Once he felt confident, he pushed his awareness even further. He could taste Hamlin's soul. It contained that same taint of sin that he had tasted before. So far, Christopher's experience had shown him that all humans, even the kindest, have some level of darkness in them, it was the balance that made the difference.

Dark Eris was much more complex. He could see and smell the shifting shades of dark as they flowed through her aura, mixing with Eris' cleaner purity. For a moment, Christopher had thought the shades looked less distinct, the dark less black and the purity a little less clear. He wanted to touch that sin and see what secrets Dark Eris held, but he did not have time, and he knew that it would be a violation of her. He had read the secret sins of Hamlin's soul once before, out of necessity, but it was not a thing he wanted to repeat with those he considered friends. A demon friend though, that might warrant a deeper look when he could.

As his supernatural awareness washed over the park, he felt it weakening, like it was being spread thin. So there were limits to this sensing. He felt the souls of the last of the stragglers leaving the park and of the homeless looking for a place out of the way that they could hide and rest until the gates opened in the morning.

He touched upon the evil in their souls, but he did not investigate. Now was not the time to hunt mortals. He felt the weapon in his pocket cry out for souls as he tasted each one faintly. But he held it in check, even as he felt its fury grow with each taste.

Suddenly, the spread of his sense stopped as though they had hit a wall, and the Hell-power inside of him seemed to sputter.

The wound the werehound had given him flared with pain as though in mourning for a lost piece of himself. He fell to his knees and sucked air in through his teeth with a hiss.

Hamlin and Dark Eris rushed forward, catching him so that he did not fall forward. "Are you okay? What happened?"

"Something's wrong," Christopher said. "The bite, it hurts."

But that wasn't really it, Christopher knew. The pain of the bite wound was just a physical manifestation of the damage done inside. Something linked with the Hell-power inside him was damaged. Something was missing and it was weakening his power. But he wasn't sure how to articulate this to the others.

"It seems I may have found some limits to my power," Christopher said and pulled the awareness back in a little. Instantly it became more comfortable. "Help me up."

They hoisted him up and, after making sure he was steady on his feet, let him stand on his own.

"It doesn't seem like that bite has healed right. You sure you're up for this, kid?" Hamlin asked.

"Does it matter?" Christopher asked back, maybe a little harshly. "I don't have much choice. Eventually that thing will be after us."

Hamlin just nodded and stood back.

"We'll have to move around, apparently my range isn't what it used to be," Christopher said. He smiled when he said it, but no one returned it. For a brief moment he thought he saw concern on Dark Eris' face but then the familiar half-smirk returned. He thought he might have imagined it. Dark Eris wasn't one for showing concern.

Avoiding the few remaining people as best they could, they made their way around the park, Christopher gently searching as they did. Then, there was something.

Or rather it was nothing. Near the waterfall his awareness

suddenly slid over an area that wasn't there. That was the only way he could describe it. It was like a gap in the world, at least the supernatural one. One moment he was sensing both the good and bad around him and then, as his attention lingered near the stairs by the waterfall, he sensed an absence.

"I've found something over by the waterfall," Christopher said as he shifted focus back to the physical world. He was a little disoriented.

Hamlin grabbed his arm and steered him toward the river. "The stairs to the waterfall are just ahead."

The stairs started just above the water fall and went down along the shore a few feet. The waterfall itself was a small one, maybe ten or fifteen feet tall, but the roar was enough to drown out almost all other sounds. The short fence that separated the stairs from the short drop to the river shore had several signs warning against swimming and that the area beyond the small fence was off limits.

At the top of the stairs they stopped again and Christopher reached out with his power, looking for that same gap in the world. He felt it again, just below him. He looked over the edge. About fifteen feet below, the landing structure they were standing on met the rocky shore of the river. Whatever it was, it was down there.

Christopher looked around the park, it was deserted from what he could see and sense. Satisfied they were alone, he pulled the shadows to him, forming his hooded coat of shifting darkness.

"Trouble?" Hamlin asked, suddenly on guard.

"No. I thought it was best to be safe. The entrance is down there by the shore somewhere. I guess I could carry you down..." he said.

"Hell no. I can manage the climb and still maintain my dignity," Hamlin said.

"Suit yourself."

He turned to Dark Eris and held out his hand.

She smiled, and at first he thought he would get some scathing retort. But then she chuckled and jumped into his arms. He sprang over the edge and landed silently on the shore below. He set Dark Eris down on her feet and for a moment their faces were close, their bodies were close. The smile on Dark Eris' face dropped for just a moment and something like fear flickered to life. He was still in his heightened awareness, and he felt something reaching out between the two of them. It was a brief sensation of warmth that quickly turned into a scalding burn. She jerked away, scowling as though he had somehow insulted her.

He would never understand women, especially demonic ones. But he did not have time to ponder his ignorance regarding females, supernatural or otherwise.

He reached out with his power and instantly sensed the nothingness. It was a part of the natural rock wall that supported the stairs. He placed his hand against it, but felt only hard stone.

Hamlin landed next to him and dusted dirt off his hands and clothes from the climb. "Find anything?"

"Yeah, there's something odd with this wall," Christopher said.

Hamlin reached out and tapped the rock. "Seems pretty solid. Are we looking for a secret lever or something?"

"I don't know. I suppose we could look," Christopher said.

"Or maybe there's a key? Something only the Beast, or in this case you, might have in his possession?" Dark Eris asked.

Christopher looked at Hamlin who just shrugged his shoulders.

"He didn't give me key or anything like that...Oh wait, gotcha!"

Christopher pulled out the Book and Weapon.

"Not sure how you guys made it as far as you did without me. Not the brightest pair are you?"

Wisely, Christopher thought, they both ignored her. The Weapon remained a pocket knife. *Maybe it has a key that pops out like the saw or tiny scissors*? Just then the book twisted in his hand to become a metal plate covered with runes.

"Looks Aramaic," Dark Eris said from over his shoulder.

"You read Aramaic?" Christopher asked. Not that he even knew what that was, other than a really old language mentioned in *Monty Python and the Holy Grail.*

"No... I just... I don't know how I know. It just seemed to click," she said and stepped away from him towards the shore of the river. "Just open the door already."

Christopher held the plate out in front of him, looking for some sort of key hole that would fit the thing. Then there was a crack that they felt rather than heard over the roar of the falls. The stone face in front of him shimmered as though he was looking at it under water.

"Did you see that?" he asked.

"Felt something—like someone dropping a boulder on the ground, but didn't see anything," Hamlin said.

When Christopher looked at her, Dark Eris just nodded. "Yeah, same for me."

He reached his hand out to touch the now wavy surface of the stone. For a moment he felt a rush of power as he touched it, then he was sucked in.

16

He stumbled to the ground as though he had been yanked forward. He got to his feet quickly and spun around. He was in a tunnel lit by a string of faint light bulbs. It smelled of wet concrete and dirt. Behind him, the way he had come was a black wall swirling with shadows.

What was it with all the weird doorways with this guy? Christopher thought. Between this and the Library it would be nice to just find one that opens with a handle.

A moment later Hamlin came through. Christopher caught him before he could fall.

"Jesus Christ, kid. What the Hell was that?" Hamlin asked.

"I suspect that was moving through several feet of stone without actually passing through it," Christopher said.

"Well, I hope there's a normal door out of this place. I don't want to try that again."

Dark Eris came through next, stepping gracefully over the threshold.

"What?" She asked, noticing their looks.

They made their way down the hall. It looked like an old service tunnel. A couple of pipes carrying water or wires ran down the length. Weak, bare light bulbs were strung down its length.

"Question: who do you think changes these bulbs when they burn out?" Dark Eris asked.

There was only one turn before they found a door. A normal, steel door complete with handle.

"How far do you think we've come?" Christopher asked.

"Maybe four or five hundred feet. I'd imagine we're under the zoo proper at this point," Hamlin said.

Christopher opened the door and was immediately greeted by a musty scent. This door hadn't been open in a long time, and the air had gone stale. The room beyond was dark except for a faint glow from across the room, as well as a couple of blinking colored lights. He felt along the inside wall until he found a large switch that turned on the lights. The room was a large circle topped with a domed ceiling and walls made of concrete. There were no windows, so the only light came from the large light fixtures hanging from the high ceiling.

The room was large enough to house a family of elephants comfortably, but obviously it wasn't used for the animals. Against one wall was a bed and table. Nearby was a desk and a large safe. There was what looked like a kitchen area off to one side. Somebody had lived here, obviously it had been his predecessor.

The faint light he had seen earlier was coming from a wall of monitors on stands near the middle of the rooms. The blinking colored lights had come from the server rack that stood nearby. Below the monitor wall was a large desk. It looked like an IT guy's dream setup.

"Congratulations," Hamlin said. "You have your own bat cave."

Christopher walked over to the computer rack.

"Why do you think he had all this?" Hamlin mused aloud.

"Well if I had to guess, I would say he was taking advantage of modern conveniences to help hunt down his prey," Christopher said. "I've been starting to worry that we've been thinking too small. So far everything we've had to deal with is in New York. But as much as I love the city, I don't think that every escaped soul from Hell ends up in just this place. It's got to be a worldwide thing. If we go on the assumption that he was the only Hunter on duty, he would need a way to monitor the whole world. The internet would be a useful tool."

"Okay sure, he sets up a Facebook page and sends friend requests to all his Hell-spawn pals. Gives a whole new meaning to catfishing, but whatever. He would've had to have some way to travel quickly around the world, and if your abilities are any indication he couldn't fly. That's a lot of air miles to rack up."

"The other question is, how did he set this all up?" Christopher said and sat down the in the chair. He started flipping on the machines. "I mean, this isn't the movies. I could be wrong, but he didn't seem like the type to have a lot of assistants, and he didn't seem like the tech-savvy type when I met him. More of the kill-them-all-and-let-Hell-sort-it-out type. So how did he build such a high tech lair?"

"This might help explain it," Dark Eris said and held up a piece of paper from the desk. "He owns the zoo."

"That can't be right," Hamlin said. "The zoo is a nonprofit. Nobody owns it."

"Well then, maybe he is a big donor. These papers mention huge amounts of money that went into the construction and remodeling of parts of the zoo," she said. "And from the looks of it, he had a lot of say in the design. A lot of these papers are requests for approval."

"Well, that might explain it. Between his money and power, he could probably have manipulated the powers that be for this place," Christopher said. "Actually, makes me feel a little better, seeing that he had to use mundane means. It's not all magic and killing people."

"Now I'm really curious about what's in that safe," Hamlin said.

He went over to investigate it while Christopher continued to boot up the system. Only one screen lit up, and it was asking for the password.

Well so much for this being easy.

He had no idea what the password was, so he went over to the desk and safe with the others.

"It weird," Hamlin said as Christopher came up behind him. "There is no actual way to input a combination of any sort. No dial, no digital reader. No wires running to it, so I don't think there's a remote interface."

"It has a handle," Christopher said and tried it. It didn't budge. "Rock solid."

"Almost as if it was a onetime deal," Dark Eris said.

"What do you mean?" Hamlin asked.

"Well, like you seal something up and never open it again. A permanent solution."

"But why put something in a safe that you never intend to get to again? Why not just throw it away? Shred it, or whatever," Christopher said.

Hamlin knocked on the side, it made a dull thump. "Well, it's got to be a custom safe. I wouldn't think they would sell safes you can only get into with brute force. This safe looks solid as Hell. I can't imagine what kind of strength or power you would need. Not something you could bring down here easily..." Hamlin trailed off as he looked at Christopher, realization dawning. "You're right, girl. It was a onetime use."

Christopher caught on too. "Stand back."

He pulled the Weapon from his pocket. It screamed to life and shifted into a large axe. It was similar to the one he had fought the werehound with, but less battle-ready looking. It was thicker, more like a tool than a fighting weapon. Power crackled up and down its length.

Christopher stoked the Hell power inside of him, shrugging off the nagging suspicion that despite the huge amount of energy that flowed through his body, he was weaker than normal. Power radiated around him, jumping from the Weapon to his body, coursing through his shadow clothes.

But the desire, the hunger, was stoked as well. The need for the Weapon to consume souls washed over him. He had starved it for a while now, and the hunger was nauseatingly powerful. He tried to rein the power in, but it was as though he was numb. The need to kill was rising up in him from the Hell power, the Weapon was calling out to it and it was answering.

Trying to control it was like pulling at the reins of a horse, only to have them slip through your fingers. He tried to warn the others that they were in danger, but the power distorted his senses. Through a haze he saw himself raising the axe high above Hamlin as he crouched against the wall. He was yelling something but Christopher could not hear. The only sound he heard was the pounding of blood through his ears.

Hamlin had his gun out, but that only stoked Christopher's rage more. It was like he was suddenly two people, one the bystander unable to intervene, the other an axe wielding maniac. There was no sound, Hamlin was still yelling, his gun aimed at Christopher's chest. The roar of his Hell power crackled around him. The will of the Weapon had taken control of his body. He was a marionette and the power of Hell and hatred was pulling the strings.

Somehow he was weaker, he had always been able to control

the Book and Weapon before. But the power was starved for a soul, and it would take the closest one.

Suddenly Eris was in front of him screaming. She stood between him and Hamlin, tears streaming down her face, arms raised up as though defending him from Christopher's blow. The sight of her, the sight of them in fear, and the thought that he was the cause of that fear caused him to pause. The uncontrollable power inside of him was about to take the lives of the only other people that knew what he was. The only others who could be there for him.

And he was about to kill them both and condemn them to Hell forever.

His will surged anew. With new strength he seized back control of his body and muscles. But the axe was already falling, the power screaming for flesh and soul. With a wrenching motion that was deeper in the soul than the strength of mere muscle, he changed the angle of descent and it came down on the edge of the safe.

With a sound that was a blend of metal twisting against metal, and shrieks of anger, the axe bit deep into the safe. The door burst open as the axe cut through, sending large chunks of reinforced steel flying.

As soon as the axe had completed its arc, Christopher sent it flying off across the room before collapsing in exhaustion. He felt like he had just fought the hardest battle of his life. Harder than the fight with the werehound. The darkness was coming for him, the haze of unconsciousness was on him. It was going to take him, he had no fight left. He glanced over at Hamlin and Eris huddled against the wall, looking at him as though he was a madman. The last thing he saw before passing out was the fear in their eyes, and he was suddenly scared too. He needed them. Maybe now more than ever.

17

Ammit lifted its head from the bloody remains of what had once been a cab driver. The cab was on its side next to the train yard where he had dragged the body. Claw marks ran down one side, and the driver's door was torn off. His prey had tried to drive away when he attacked. He liked it when they fought back or tried to escape, it gave him a chance to play with his food.

He supposed someone might have seen him, tearing apart the cab as it barreled down the road, although the area was not very populated and those that were nearby had learned to keep their drapes closed when they heard noises outside. Nobody wanted to be a witness to a drug deal gone bad, or worse.

He supposed there might be cameras in this train yard. Maybe even security guards heading his way at this very moment.

Good. More food.

He released the soul he had just consumed. He felt its warmth spreading through him. Each one he ate made him feel stronger and more powerful. It was the soul he was after, but he even enjoyed the simple things, like the coppery taste of human blood or the way the soft bones crunched in his jaws. If he could, he would gorge himself on this delicacy.

And why couldn't he? Why did his mistress put restrictions on his feast? Who cares if the mortals saw him? What could they possible do to him?

He loved his mistress, but she was a coward. She was too careful. He could have killed this great Hunter that first night if she didn't have this fear of mortals finding out, or her fear of the thing she called the Alliance. He would not defy his mistress, he loved her, but he could take liberties with how he interpreted her orders. He would not let his chance to kill the Hunter slip away again.

He sniffed at the air. He was close to the zoo, he could smell the animals with his mundane senses, but he was also close to his true prey. Ammit could smell the Hunter with his other senses. He was nearby. Somewhere in the area and close, very close. So close it was frustrating.

With a roar he slammed his shoulder into a nearby train car. It lifted off the tracks and tumbled over, pulling the next car attached to it off the tracks also. That car leaned also, but stayed upright.

Power. Yes, he was getting stronger with each mouthful. He needed more souls. His mistress' limit was only two per night, but that was just an approximation. Surely one or two more wouldn't hurt? It would just make him stronger as her champion.

Then he smelled it again, or rather felt it. A sudden tug on the power inside him. Ammit licked at the air, his large tongue sending slimy tendrils of drool flying through the air. It had the same taste as that small chunk of soul he had torn off the boy. It drifted over him like a cloud of power. It was the Hunter, Ammit had caught his scent again.

Something had happened. The Hunter had used power and it amplified his footprint to Ammit. The air was alive with the stink of it.

Interesting, thought Ammit, tilting his head in a very dog-like gesture, *it came from the direction of the zoo*. Had the Hunter thought to hide himself with the animals in the zoo? Did he somehow think that would throw Ammit off? Then he was a fool. He would tear the zoo apart looking for the boy.

Or, he thought and paused. He looked down at the human blood all over his hands and dripping from his muzzle to the ground. Or, Ammit could feed tonight and then tomorrow draw him out. His mistress had thought the Hunter cares for these soft, fleshy mortals. Instead of killing unsatisfying animals while he searched, tomorrow he could simply gorge on the humans visiting the zoo. If he truly cares about these mortals, the Hunter will come and try to stop him. He would be the dessert to Ammit's feast of souls.

His mistress would never agree to this. But after the Hunter was dead, what need would there be for their kind to hide? This would be a magnificent way to announce themselves to the world. Yes, once she understood, once she saw, his mistress would be pleased with him. He would be the courage she needed. It was all so simple.

He heard a noise over by the train car. Ammit's head swiveled as he tried to focus in on the sound. He smelled meat.

"Help!" cried a weak voice from the car that hadn't tipped over completely.

Ammit saw a hand appear outside the door as whoever was inside tried to climb out. Probably some hobo spending the night in the car.

"Help!" the man cried again. "Is somebody out there? I need help!"

Ammit's muzzle lips tried to come up in a smile, but he just bared his teeth like a rabid animal.

Oh, he would help him.

18

"I seem to be making a habit of this," Christopher said in little more than a croak when he woke up on the bed in the corner of the lair.

Eris handed him a cup of tea. "I found some supplies in a storage area. Only a little food, but there was some tea. Seems our Beast had a little refinement in him. Habit of what?"

"Waking up with you taking care of me," Christopher said and sipped the tea. She smiled at him. It seemed to warm him more than the tea.

Hamlin walked out from one of the adjacent rooms. He stopped when he saw Christopher was awake. For a brief moment Christopher could see a flash of fear, then it was gone. But it wasn't just fear. Christopher could see the emotions playing out through his aura. It was something more like worry. Hamlin tried to hide it with a smile. Christopher couldn't decide which was worse, the fear or Hamlin smiling.

"I'm sorry... I lost it... I," Christopher stammered.

"Look kid," Hamlin said and came closer to the bed. "I can't even imagine the burden you have. That power fighting with you all the time, it must be unbearable."

"But I almost killed you. No, I almost sent you straight to Hell."

"Well, I'm pretty sure I'm on my way there with or without your help. The important thing is you didn't strike me."

"Only because Eris was there. I was out of control," Christopher said.

"It was because you still had enough control that when Eris stood in the way you could stop, force yourself unconscious rather than strike. I could see it, the battle you were waging was taking a terrible toll," Hamlin said.

"It's getting stronger, the power in the Weapon and the power inside me. The more I starve it for souls, the more it tries to take over when it has the chance."

"Then we don't use it unless you have dark souls to give it. When you have a bunch of baddies or one in particular baddie you whip it out," Hamlin said, as though that solved all their problems. "It's either that, or you feed it regularly."

"It's more though. Something's different. Ever since that thing took a chunk out of me, I feel like I'm not all here. Like I'm less of what I was. My control over the power is weakened. I think that thing took a piece of me, of my soul, and I don't think that kind of shit heals."

"Maybe when you stop it, you can get back whatever it took from you," Eris said.

"Maybe," Christopher said, but he wasn't sure he believed it. He looked up at Hamlin. "Hamlin, I'm sorry."

Hamlin gave his more normal half smile. "I know, kid. We'll figure this shit out, but let's keep your sword in your pocket until either the bad guys are knocking down the door, or you're confident you can control it."

Christopher nodded, but he couldn't help but notice the detective kept some distance between him and the bed.

"But enough of this. While you were pulling a Rip Van Winkle on the bed, Eris and I did some poking around. There was a lot of stuff in the safe. Including the password to the computer," Hamlin said. Behind him, Christopher could see the wall of computer monitors had sprung to life. Images played across the screens. Most were too dark to distinguish, and many had the green tint of night vision. It took him only a moment to realize he was looking at the zoo at night.

"He tapped into the security system?" Christopher asked.

"Yeah, and that's just the tip of the iceberg, but I know jack shit about computer stuff."

"There's more," Eris said and then nodded for Hamlin to go on.

"Well, I'm glad you're sitting down. Kid, you're rich," Hamlin said.

"I guess, but I don't like to think of it in that way." Christopher said.

"No, I mean like rich-rich. There are all sorts of financial documents, everything from charitable organizations to real estate to Swiss bank accounts. All of it, somehow in your dad's name."

"Holy shit! How much, and how is it in my Dad's name?" Christopher asked. He was stunned and he was exhausted. This was just one more shock to the system.

"Not sure exactly, I'm no accountant, but it's a shit-ton. Much of it in real estate. Since it's in your dad's name and you're his sole heir, it all belongs to you. I mean, once we have the lawyers go over it and taxes are taken out. "

Eris grabbed a rolled up piece of paper off a huge stack on the floor in front of the safe. Next to the safe was a blackened and twisted piece of metal he hadn't seen when they first arrived. It took him a moment to realize it was the four-inch steel door of the safe. He shuddered again. He had been moments away from unleashing that power on Hamlin.

Eris unrolled the large piece of paper on his bed. "I found this map, and it looks like you own property all over the world," she said.

Christopher looked at the map. It looked like a satellite blow up of the whole planet. Red dots were spread everywhere. Most major cities had at least one, sometimes more, as did every country.

"Lairs," Christopher said. He knew he was adopting the term they had used for this one. Somehow, it just seemed appropriate.

"There's one in Vegas. I've never been. I say we book plane tickets now," Christopher said. He felt he had never needed a vacation more than he did at the very moment. He wondered how long they would have until the werehound caught up to him. He figured at least enough time for him to catch a show.

"It's overrated, besides, there's more. You up for moving about?" Hamlin asked.

"Sure," Christopher climbed to his feet. Eris helped him up, but he didn't really need it. He felt emotionally exhausted, but physically he was way better than he had been the last time he woke up from unconsciousness. "But for the record, I don't believe you about Vegas."

They walked over to a large door on the other side of the room. It was also steel and looked almost as heavy as the vault door. Christopher was instantly on guard, he didn't trust doors when they involved his predecessor. They had a way of not behaving correctly.

Hamlin opened it and gestured for Christopher to enter. "Don't worry. I've already been inside. It's weird, but it didn't kill me."

The other room was large and square. There was no furniture. The walls were different than the other room, they were made of roughhewn stone with symbols carved into them. The carvings gave off a faint glow.

As Christopher stepped in, they flared to life. The room was still gloomy, but it had brightened noticeably.

"Well, that didn't happen when I came in here before," Hamlin said from behind him.

That was when Christopher noticed he had walked all the way into the room. The room was, in a word, awesome. Light still from an unknown source played along the carvings like they were alive. There were only two other things in the room besides the intricately carved walls: a frame, like something that would have held a full length mirror, only it was empty as though the mirror had been removed or broken, and a small pedestal with a cube about the size of a Rubik's Cube on it.

"What is this stuff?" Christopher asked, not really expecting an answer.

"Not sure, but I've seen *Hellraiser*, so I ain't going anywhere near that cube," Hamlin said.

"What's a Hellraiser?" Christopher asked.

Hamlin just shook his head. "Kids today, what the Hell is the world coming to when kids don't know the classics. Never mind, but as an emissary from Hell, the movie should be right up your alley."

"I think it's also a map," Eris said. She had come in behind Hamlin.

She walked over to the wall and traced a carving, and Christopher noticed that some of the carvings were not glowing with the mysterious light. Now that she mentioned it, it did seem like the non-glowing carvings outlined countries. Dots were spread around the countries with incandescent lines connecting them to each other. He had a feeling he knew what the dots represented.

"The lairs," he said to no one in particular.

It made sense. The lairs in the bigger cities had more lines stretching out from them to connect to other dots around the world. Once he started looking at the whole picture, it began to look a lot like the maps in the back of airline magazines where the airline showed all their routes. He thought he might have a guess as to what the purpose of this room was, but he had no idea how to operate it.

"That's interesting," Hamlin said, He was staring above the door. "I didn't notice that before."

Christopher followed his gaze. There was a small stone above the door. The name 'Bronx" was carved into it. "It's so he could confirm where he was."

"Come again?" Hamlin asked.

Eris smiled. "Ah yes, it makes sense now. But how does it work?"

Christopher examined the cube on the pedestal. It looked as though it was made of one single piece of glass-polished metal. There were no breaks or seams.

"Somebody want to let me in on the secret?" Hamlin asked.

Christopher touched the cube gingerly. It was warm, as though heated by an internal power. The Hellpower inside of him surged forward, but not in the uncontrolled, wild way that almost caused him to kill Hamlin. It was as though it was reaching out to a kindred spirit. And when the two powers met, the room started vibrating gently, not like an earthquake, but like a large power waking up.

The cube moved and Christopher jerked his hand back. It moved first one way, then the next in a seemingly random pattern on the stone platform upon which it rested. Then, as the rumbling got louder, it stopped its random jerking movements and lifted into the air. From within the hovering cube, a light emerged as though the cube was really a crystalline structure with a bright light in the center.

The center of the stone frame, just a few feet from the cube, darkened. In moments it was too opaque to see through, and the area inside was filled by swirling shadows, similar to the door they had come through when they entered the lair.

"I think it's a way to travel, but I am not sure how to operate it," Christopher said. Strangely, this display of power didn't make him nervous. Everything else he had experienced in the last few weeks had shaken him up—the power of the Book, the seed of Hell power inside of him, and of course the soul thirsty single mindedness of the Weapon. This was different, he had no doubt it was created with the power of Hell, just like everything else he had seen since opening the Book, but rather than fear, he felt fascination.

"What? You mean you step through that inky stuff and you end up somewhere else?" Hamlin asked.

"Yeah, maybe," Christopher said.

"It would make sense," Eris said. "As much as it might seem so at times, I doubt all escaped souls from Hell would take up New York as their residence. They must be all over the world, and I don't see him booking airline flights everywhere. That would take too much time."

"Besides, nowadays they wouldn't let him take the Weapon on board, even in its pocket knife form," Christopher said. He suddenly felt a huge weight on his shoulders. It was enough for him to moan and lean against the wall with sudden weakness.

"What's wrong?" Hamlin asked.

"Nothing...I mean, everything. It just suddenly became clear to me. Like I said before, up to this point we have been thinking locally about this job. Now this...this thing just drove home how this is a global thing. I will have to hunt over the entire world. How can one guy do that? Especially a mistake like me?"

"Now hold on, kid. We don't even know if this really is a device to travel. And even if it is, we just have to hold it together and take it one step at a time."

"You're right. We don't know for sure what this thing is," Christopher said. "Time to find out."

He approached the cube and carefully touched it again with his hand. Again, it felt as though the power inside of him reached out to touch whatever power resided in the stone. Once the two powers met, the wall map flared to life. Or one area of it did, anyway. He felt no pain or danger, just the flow of power between himself and the cube. With building confidence, he placed his whole hand on top of it, as though holding it from the top.

The area on the map grew even brighter and tendrils of power drifted from the wall to the cube. Eris, who was closest to that area of the wall, examined it. She chuckled. "Makes sense. I think it's Vegas. The last place you were thinking about."

"Well, I guess there's only one way to find out. Although this wasn't exactly the way I thought my first trip would go," Christopher said.

"We can get you strippers and shots next time," Hamlin said. "Are you sure about this?"

"That's why we came, right? I mean, I don't know if this device will help me fight the werehound, but we did come to learn as much as we could about what I'm supposed to be doing. This seems like an important tool."

"I suppose," Hamlin said a little reluctantly.

Christopher let go of the cube. The faint flow of power lines continued to move from the wall to the cube. He walked towards the black doorway. With one quick look back at Hamlin, whose face was covered with a concerned scowl, and Eris, whose smile seemed a little more in awe than afraid, he stepped through the doorway.

As he entered the blackness, there was a great rushing sound like the roar of a river, but it wasn't through his ears that he heard it. It was as though the rumbling noise he had heard in the room was all around him, vibrating though his whole body. There was nothing around him, just darkness, and utterly complete blackness, not of night, but of emptiness. He also had a sense that the blackness stretched on forever, infinite darkness. For that brief second of nothingness, he was suddenly afraid. Afraid it would never end.

Then he was standing in a room similar to the one he had just left. The same carved walls, but the stone was slightly different. A similar cube floated above the pedestal in the center of the room. There were some differences besides the color of the stone. The pedestal, for example, was a little taller and narrower that the one in the Bronx. Speaking of which. He looked above the door.

"Well I'll be damned," Christopher said.

Above the exit door was a carved stone with the name Las Vegas on it. He was tempted to leave the room, have a look around at this lair and maybe of the city outside. But he had to get back quickly, they would be worried. Before returning he had one last test.

He grabbed hold of the floating cube. The tendrils of power that had been snaking towards what looked like New York on the map drifted quickly to a new location. For this test he had thought he should try something further away, out of the country. He decided on Paris.

He was not sure exactly what he should do, so he tried to picture things that made him think of Paris. He envisioned the Eiffel Tower and the glass pyramid outside the Louvre. The power lines connecting the cube to the wall slid quickly across the map. From where he stood, it looked like a carving of France.

He stepped through the black door once again. He had that same sensation of infinity and that roaring through his body and then he was standing in another cube room. This one was much older. The stone walls were more worn and cracked, but still functional as the tendrils of power reaching from the wall to the floating cube proved. A thick layer of dust covered the ground around the pedestal. It seems the Beast had not been here in a while to clean.

Above the door leading out was another carved stone, but this time it was in a script Christopher did not recognize. He thought it might be Latin. It might be Paris, but since he didn't read Latin it was impossible to tell. The only solution was to peek outside.

The door from this room was also different from the one in New York. For one thing, the whole room appeared older, including the door. This made sense, the city was much older. The door was also made from stone. There was no handle, just an old partially rusted metal lever in the wall next to it. It looked like it might still work, so it must have been a fairly modern replacement.

Only one way to find out.

He pulled the lever, and the door swung outward with a great grinding sound. It moved slowly, but surely. Whatever mechanism controlled it seemed to have survived the ages. He looked through the door and realized a flaw in his plan.

It was pitch black, and he had no light. The room he was in was lit faintly by the power in the walls and cube. Enough to see his way about the room, but not strong enough to penetrate the darkness beyond the door.

Hoping to find a light switch, he stepped cautiously into the darkness. It smelled dusty and faintly of incense. He reached along the wall, blindly looking for a light switch and discovered the wall was covered with protrusions, like random rocks jutting out from the wall, some with smooth round surfaces. But no light switch.

Gradually, his eyesight adjusted, and the light from the cube room was enough for him to see faint shapes on the wall of the room. Then he had an idea.

Without touching the Weapon in his pocket, he drew on the power inside of him. He wrapped himself in the Hell power. In the past it had given him enhanced physical abilities, and this time was no different. Apparently, one of his gifts was the ability to see better in the dark. Suddenly, the room beyond became clear.

The walls were made of bones, human bones. From floor to ceiling skulls, femurs, humerus, and other indistinct anatomy parts covered the walls. The wall he had touched looking for a switch was covered with skulls as well. With a startled cry, he jumped back into the cube room and pulled the lever.

"What the fuck was that?" Christopher said out loud over the sound of the door closing. The Beast dude was way more fucked up than he had thought. Who keeps all those bones in their home or lair?

A creature born of Hell I guess, thought Christopher. Were those all dead Dark Souls? Or were they mortals? What was he doing with all those bodies? Why would he keep bodies like a mausoleum?

It slowly dawned on him. Not a mausoleum, catacombs. This lair *was* in Paris, specifically in the famous catacombs under the city.

He leaned against the wall in relief and was thankful nobody was there to see the Hunter of Lost Souls, Lord of Damnation, Bringer of Hell on Earth scream like a little girl when he saw a bunch of old bodies.

It was time to get back.

He placed his palm on the cube and opened a door back to New York.

They ran at him when he got back. Hamlin slapped him on the back, relief relaxing his face. "Jesus kid, we thought we'd lost you."

Eris had tears running down her cheeks. She held onto him for a noticeably long time.

"What's going on? I was only gone a few minutes." Christopher asked.

"A few moments after you went through, the room just suddenly went dead," Hamlin said. "The light, the sounds, everything. The cube fell back to the pedestal."

"We were worried you had died," Eris said.

"No, I was fine. But I did get to Vegas and then took a side trip to Paris," Christopher said.

"Paris?" Hamlin asked.

"Yeah, as a test."

"I've always wanted to go to Paris," Eris said. "How was it?"

"Dead. Literally. The Lair is in the catacombs under the city. I didn't really get a chance to look around."

"Ew," Eris said.

"I think it's safe to assume that all the locations on the map are connected by this... whatever it is. And we can travel to all the points. But not all the points are as large as this. The one in the catacombs was just a cube room from what I could tell."

Hamlin nodded, but something about his posture was different, something was off. Then he realized Hamlin was exhausted. He looked over at Eris and could tell she was running on fumes herself.

"We need to figure out next steps," Hamlin started.

"Next step is for you guys to get some rest. I've had a couple of unfortunate naps, but you guys have been pushing it. You two need some sleep, and then we plan next steps. I think we learned a lot about my predecessor here and found a cool toy, but I'm not sure it helps us defeat the monster chasing me."

"Hell, with that thing you could run forever and he would never catch up to you," Hamlin said.

"No I can't. I really can't. It doesn't matter what I think anymore, I have no choice. Whether I am ready or not, it doesn't matter. The stakes are raised, my eyes are opened, and my world just got a whole lot bigger. I need to find a way to stop this thing. I need to master this power. From Hell or not, this power is all that is standing between humanity and Hell on earth."

19

Anabelle was pacing back and forth in her living room. She ignored the luxurious carpet gently cradling her delicate toes, any other day that would have been her favorite part of being in this room. The afternoon sun blazed into the room through the large floor-to-ceiling windows. On any other day she would have loved the sunlight warming her body. But today it just hurt her eyes.

Her normally perfect hair was escaping in loose strands from her ponytail. Her flawless skin shifted from smooth porcelain to cracked and bleeding cadaver gray, the occasional puss-leaking sore sprouting on her face. She let her glamour flicker on and off as she walked and thought, or tried to think. One moment she was the beautiful, powerful woman all men loved and desired, the next she was the twisted and deformed crone of her true self. If she hadn't been alone, she would have held her glamour in place with an iron hand. She would never allow another to see her true figure. But not today, not right now. Right now she was worried. No, that was too weak. She was terrified.

This was taking too long and becoming too messy.

Ammit was becoming too careless, too confident. It was spiraling out of her control. Ammit was killing, the bodies were piling up and it had only been two days. Already the media was all over it, local and national news reporting the mangled bodies mauled by a horrible, vicious animal that no expert could identify. Bear was loose! Tigers in New York! The news ran with anything they could find on it.

Golyat would have seen it by now. He would be calling. No, he would be *coming* for her any moment. She had broken the laws, she and her creation had exposed them. Part of her tried to dwell on what went wrong. Where had she lost control of the beast? She could almost hear Golyat telling her it was because she dabbled in things she did not understand.

That made her laugh, although it came out more like a hysterical giggle.

They all dabbled in things they did not understand.

She had to run. This was stupid. She had waited, hoping the Ammit would come back before doing more damage. She had thought he would come back for guidance. She needed to gain control again, she could make this right. She could rule the council. If all she did was hold it together.

But there was another reason she waited. She waited for him. The only man she had ever truly loved, truly desired. And it had taken her to Hell and back to know what real desire was. She knew it deep down, that was why she waited. She needed him right now. And like in all great fairy tales it happened.

"Why do you fret, love?" came a voice from the shadows. Shadows that should not exist in the middle of the afternoon, shadows that shouldn't exist in the bright open room in which she stood. Shadows that existed nonetheless.

She knew the voice, like honey over the top and the hottest of spice underneath. The owner of that voice was tall, powerful and more handsome than any man, mortal or otherwise, she had ever met. Simple words from him, just the tone was enough to make her fall apart. She pulled her glamour tight about her but also fell to the ground simply from relief. He had come to her. He would take her up in those strong arms, effortlessly holding her against his chest. It was there that she found her greatest happiness. She would gladly claw her way out of Hell a hundred times just to be held in this man's arms.

And he was there, lifting her and then crushing her against his chest in that good way that only a lover would understand.

"There, there love. What is the matter? Why do you shake so?" the man asked.

"Oh Jax, it's all a mess. Our plan, it's so messy," she said. A part of her hated how weak she was around this man. But mostly she didn't care, he loved her and would protect her. If she couldn't trust him, then it was all over.

"Shhhh love, it will all be over soon," Jax said.

"No, no you don't understand," she pulled back and looked up at him. God he was handsome. Dark hair, darker than the shadows around him. Eyes so blue that they had to be carved out of sapphire. Strong jaw and chiseled face. He was perfect and she knew, from her own experience, that it was not glamour, this was his true face. "Ammit, the one you instructed me to create, has become a liability. He is running amok in the city, killing indiscriminately."

"Love, you must calm yourself," Jax crooned, and she did start to feel calmer. Jax was here now, he would tell her what to do.

"I... I was worried you wouldn't come back. That you had helped me start my plan in motion and... and deserted me."

"No, no love. Never. I would never leave you for long. That is why I returned, I had hoped to rejoin you at your moment of triumph. But I find you like this. How it pains me to see my love this way."

"I know. I know, but that beast you taught me how to make with the soul shaper. I thought I could control it, like I do every other man. But it is taking too long to find the Hunter."

"Is the Hunter this powerful then? I had thought to return and see you leading the Alliance. Has the boy grown with such strength?"

She laughed, again with more than a little hysteria, and wiped away tears. "No, that's just it. He is weak, like a baby. We almost had him once, but we let him get away. After that he has evaded us with a combination of dumb luck and help from his mortal friends."

Jax stroked her head and instantly she was soothed. He kissed her on the head with lips both gentle and cold. That was him, warmth in his voice, but his body was always cold like stone. He even smelled like stone mingled with herbs. Most of their kind knew only ugliness and stink, their time in Hell either corrupting or purifying them, depending on whom you asked, beyond their mortal transgressions. With Jax, though, it was different. He knew beauty and he had shown it to her whenever possible. He was one of the ancients, she did not know when he had escaped Hell, but it was long before she had, long before any in the current Alliance had. Somehow he had evaded the Beast. He had more knowledge than all of them combined she thought.

"We have to go. You have to take me away from here. Golyat will be here soon. He will destroy me for exposing us like this. Without the head of the Hunter I will have nothing to prove myself with. He will send me back to Hell!" Her voice had been growing steadily louder as she spoke until the last came out as a scream. She was losing control again.

"Shh love, I know. I know, but you must calm yourself. Yes, Golyat is coming."

He held her close again, gently stroking her hair.

"So you will take me with you," she said, relief flooding through her. "We can leave the country, he will never find us if we stay hidden. We could find a small home in Europe, or maybe something on the beach."

"No, love. You misunderstand. Golyat is coming, I have seen this. He will hurt you. I don't know if he will send you to Hell, but there will be so much pain you might wish he did send you back."

It took her a second to realize what he was saying. The warmth she usually found in his words was gone, all that remained was cold. In shock she tried to push him away, but his arms seemed to become stone, like the coldness of his body. She struggled and pushed, but he only held her closer.

"What do you mean? I don't understand. Jax? Jax? Let me go," she cried.

"It didn't go exactly according to my plan, but these things seldom do, right love? I can see you don't understand and I'm disappointed in your surprise, especially from someone with your talents of deceit. Did you not think it could be used against you?" He chuckled, even less like honey and more like cold stone on stone. "Ah, the arrogance! No wonder I fell in love with you."

"But...but if you love me then why do you do this?" She was still trying to understand. She was confused, where had this all gone wrong?

"Oh I do, love. I love you truly, you can't walk this earth as long as I have and not understand love. It's just that love and hate are not opposites and as much as I love, I really, deep-down hate. And... well... I love to hate," he said.

"You're mad! That doesn't make any sense," She said.

"Of course you would say that. You don't understand. Let me keep it simple. I love you, and I love that you served my purpose in moving my plan along, and now I love that that purpose is at an end. There is only one problem."

Jax pulled her up against his chest, lifting her closer to his face. He put his mouth against her ear and whispered.

"You see love, when Golyat gets here he will punish you, he will torture you. He will want you to talk about everything you know. And you know what? You'll tell him everything. I know this because I have seen it. But I am not ready for Goylat to know about me."

She pushed at his chest, but even her enhanced strength was no match for him. She screamed. She called up her glamour, but it was as though he was ready for everything she did. He knew what move she would make before she made it. He held her easily, he dismissed her power almost as easily.

"But there is an easy fix that won't spoil the fun for any of us. Give us a kiss, love," Jax whispered.

Suddenly she felt his tongue in her ear, an impossibly long tongue. It slithered and crawled up her ear canal, piercing her eardrum and wriggling into her head. It was a sensation like he was licking her mind, pulling off bits and memories, tearing through any mental barriers she might have had. She was fully exposed, and he took what he wanted. He slurped her memories from her mind. He seemed to savor some, but she could not remember what they were. Soon it was too hard to hold on to consciousness. Her body and soul were going into a kind of shock, shutting down on her while he scooped away parts of her. Eventually, the darkness consumed her. Her last thought was of confusion—What was going on? What was happening?

When he was done, Jax dropped her motionless body to the ground. Her chest moved slightly, she was still alive.

"Sorry about that love, nasty bit of business, but necessary. I can't have the Alliance poking its nose in where it doesn't belong at the moment. But don't worry. You see, in the end, I win. Not the silly Alliance of dark souls, not the boy Hunter they are so afraid off. Me, I win. I know, I've seen it."

20

Christopher was the only one awake, which was fine by him. Those two had watched over him many times when he was exhausted and recovering. It was the least he could do. Granted, most of his sleep recently had been the result of getting his ass kicked by either a monster or his own sword, but at least he had gotten a little shut eye along the way.

After a quick trip in the cube room to the Vegas lair—which was rather large and would need some time to fully explore—to grab some extra mattresses, they had fallen asleep instantly, despite the protest of the detective.

Christopher had only convinced him to sleep by telling him they could figure out the next move as soon as they got some rest. Hamlin had called into work, assured them he was still alive and working on a case, and then promptly fell asleep. Eris had been seconds behind him.

Now Christopher sat in a chair, bathed by the glow of the monitors. He had spent some time on the computer, hoping for at least a video game. Nothing. Although it didn't surprise him, the Beast had been all business. He didn't know what half the software did. He could only guess most of it was illegal, maybe for hacking into systems? He was as tech savvy as any twenty-one-year-old, but he had gotten a C in the only real computer class he had taken. So after spending a little time on Facebook, he sat back and watched the security cameras.

He glanced at the two of them from time to time, their peaceful faces also illuminated faintly by the monitors. It wasn't really the both of them, though, he could admit he spent more time looking at Eris. It was hard to believe that a demon and an innocent girl both shared that body. She looked so calm in her sleep, relaxed as though there was no homicidal monster chasing them.

He was at once thankful she was with him and angry she was here. If he was supposed to be protecting humans, albeit in a roundabout way, shouldn't he start with his friends? The demoness he could understand. This was a part of her world. She understood what she was getting into, at least to some extent, but not Eris. She was not built for this kind of stuff.

He had made a decision. Once they woke he would send them away, at least until he had stopped the werehound. They would try the same arguments they had used when running from the thing, but this time it didn't matter. They had tried to find a way to stop the creature and they had failed. He would keep looking, but eventually he was going to have to go toe to toe with the creature. Especially now.

He had seen the news on his computer screens. It was killing more indiscriminately. The media had picked it up. It seemed the current theory was that a pack of wild dogs was terrorizing New York. It was hard to watch the newscasters' faces when they were reading that off the teleprompter. They didn't believe it, but there was no other possible explanation, so they said it with a straight face.

No officials had suggested staying inside, but the newscasters had no problem suggesting people stay off the streets until these rabid hounds were found. But nobody was listening. The security cameras at the zoo told him that much. It was late afternoon on a Saturday, and the place was packed. Kids and their parents everywhere. Running, screaming. Really screaming.

What the fuck?

Christopher leaned in closer to one of the monitors. This one showed the exit from one of the animal theaters. People were running out, adults dragging their kids or just picking them up and running. Mouths wide open in silent screams on his screen. He had no audio, but Christopher didn't need it to know they were screaming in panic.

Quickly as he was able for one who had just started using the system, he tried to switch to a camera that was in the theater. After clicking through several other cameras, where people walked, oblivious to the panic in the center of the zoo, he landed on the right camera angle.

"Holy shit, get up!" Christopher said loudly.

There on the screen he could see the werehound. Not hiding in the shadows, not peering through the foliage. No. He was standing in the center of the stage, holding the lifeless body of an animal trainer in one hand and the trainer's decapitated head in the other. Blood had splattered most of the stage. The birds in the cages behind the monster were going crazy, smashing against their cages and screeching their silent cries of fear.

"What? What is going on?" Hamlin rolled up from the mattress, staggering a little with sleep. Eris stretched and yawned. The panic in Christopher's voice had not sunk in yet.

"It's here," Christopher said and pointed at the monitor.

"Jesus," Hamlin said. "What the Hell is he doing?"

"Killing. Just what he was meant to do."

"But in the open like that? I mean he's on a fucking stage."

"I guess they've decided they waited long enough."

"Oh my god," Eris exclaimed from behind them. She had finally woken up and her face was a mask of terror. "Did it track us here already?"

"I think it must have tracked me at least to the zoo. I'm guessing it or its master decided that killing innocents would draw me out faster than trying to find my exact location. And they are correct. I have to go."

"But we don't have an answer on how to stop it. What are you going to do?" Eris asked.

Even as they watched the thing jumped from the stage onto the last of the people trying to run from the amphitheater. He grabbed hold of another man, his claws impaled through the man's back as the monster pulled him close to take a bite out of the screaming man's side.

"I don't know, but I can't just watch and do nothing," Christopher said.

"Kid, if that thing kills you, it's all over. We know there is more going on than just some monster roaming the streets. If you die, there is nothing to stop the real threat, the masters that stand behind this thing," Hamlin said.

"Chris..." Eris started.

"No, I'm done talking," Christopher said suddenly. He was sick from what he was watching. It was all because of him. People were dying simply for bait. "Time to fight."

He grabbed Eris by the arms. "Dark Eris? Are you in there?" He said and shook her.

"What are you doing?" Eris cried out. She tried to pull away from him, but he held her fast.

"You just come and go as you please don't you," Christopher said. The anger in his voice was intended for Dark Eris, but it was only Eris that gazed back at him with tears in her eyes. "Dammit, come out! We fucking need you. I need you."

For a moment Eris gazed at him, then the tears spilled over and she slumped in his arms. He pushed her away. He knew it wasn't Eris' fault, but it didn't matter, at this very moment, she and Dark Eris were one and the same. He didn't have time to comfort her. He had to stop this thing, and it looked like Dark Eris would be of no help.

Hamlin looked at him coldly for a moment then nodded. "Kind of harsh kid, but go."

Christopher ran through the door that led to the access tunnel for the zoo. They had scouted it earlier. It would put him out just inside the zoo, next to Jungle World. As he ran, he pulled the shadows close about him, forming his hooded coat. He hoped the shadow garment completely obscured his face. He had no choice but to confront this thing in the middle of a crowded zoo. So much for the secret Hunter routine.

21

Ammit decided he liked the pure terror. The screams were a beautiful sound, they inspired a kind of lust in him. Feasting on souls was what drove him, but feasting on the souls of the terrified just added something to it. A special sauce for his meal.

He had stalked through the bushes and forest, the animals of the exhibits running from him, until he had found just the right place. An outdoor theater. Humans filled the place, watching animals perform for their amusement.

They were of all ages, but many of them were children, the sweetest of meat. He would save those as a dessert. A trainer stood on stage with a bird on its hand. Without warning, the bird took flight and started squawking hysterically before diving into its own cage. It must have caught Ammit's scent and was going to the only safe place it knew. The other birds also began screeching and squawking, creating a cacophony of bird noises. Cages rattled as they fought to escape or bounced around in pure panic. They knew what stalked from the trees. But Ammit had no desire for them, it was the sweet meat of human souls he craved.

The trainer stared at the panicked birds in stunned silence before speaking to no one in particular.

"What's got them all riled up so..." The trainer started but never finished.

With a roar Ammit had jumped from the trees, shredding through the light netting that surrounded the stage. The birds in cages cringed back, the ones on open perches broke from their training and flew away, batting against the netting in a desperate attempt to get away.

The human trainer had been stunned, but the look of surprise quickly turned to sheer terror as she was confronted with the full eight feet of bestial rage that was Ammit.

The trainer was quickly ripped in two, and Ammit relished the screams of the humans in the stands as he tore into his meal. He went straight for the soul this time. He didn't linger on the flesh as he might usually do, enjoying the whole meal. He had too many souls to capture and eat this day. He consumed the trainer's soul and let it infuse him. He could feel the extra nourishment increase his power. Then he turned to the other humans streaming out of the amphitheater.

He roared at their retreating backs and held the head of the trainer in one hand, the body in the other. Pleasure washed over him. He wanted to kill the boy Hunter, but Ammit wouldn't mind if he took his time getting here. He was enjoying the hors d'oeuvres before the main course.

22

After running through two access tunnels, both with secret doors cleverly hidden and locked from the inside, Christopher made it to the employee access tunnel that ran only a short distance before opening to the outside. The door he came through was hidden by a fake landscape and a wall with an "Employees Only" sign on it.

He jumped over the wall and landed in the middle of a walking path. He knew there would be people around, but he had no choice. Hopefully they did not see where he had come from. As he landed, the shadows intensified around him despite the fact it was still daylight. Tendrils of power and darkness flowed around him. The people that had been calmly strolling the path scattered with startled screams.

He ignored them, he did not have time to worry about the show he was making. After a moment to get his bearings, he leapt into the air in the direction of the World of Birds attraction. He hoped the monster was still there.

He soared through the air and for a brief moment thought he

might actually be flying, but then gravity took over and he headed down. That's when he realized his error. He had not picked a landing spot. In the city, jumping from building to building, it was easy to see where his power would take him. Here, in his hurry to stop the werehound, he had leapt before he looked and now as he hurtled down toward the trees, he had no idea what was down there.

Acting on something similar to instinct, the power that wrapped around him reached out through the trees just ahead of him. He felt something and again trusting in the power, he pulled himself towards it. Instantly, his angle of descent changed, and he plunged through the edge of the trees only to crash onto the only structure in the area. The top of the zoo monorail.

His bands of shadowy power pulled him towards it, and he landed in a heap on the top of the monorail car, shaking it. The people on board who had seen his decent screamed, others who had just felt the shaking cried out. The more enterprising of them in the cars ahead had their phones out and were taking pictures of him. No time to waste.

He got to his feet as fast as he could, gathered his power about him again and jumped. This time, although he couldn't see where he was going, he let his Hell power unfold before him. The tendrils of power found solid places to latch onto, pulling and shoving him, allowing him to stay in the air longer.

He was stunned by this new power. It was as though he could feel the ground. Not the details, but the basic shape of the world around him. He pushed off the ground in one direction or pulled in another. It allowed him to change paths in midair. He almost laughed out loud. He would have, but he could not forget his destination and what waited for him there. His joy at this new found power sobered up quickly.

Below him he could see the people on the walking paths

looking up at him. Most stood in shock, some also had their phones out and took pictures. Animals in their pens took cover as he passed over.

It was not flying, however, and he had to come down at some point. He directed his descent to a walking path and landed. Power emanated from him as he came down with a deep boom, like a small shock wave, it knocked some of the people around him back.

The people near him cried out in surprise, but it took him only a moment to realize it wasn't just him. Zoo visitors were running past him in panic, screams filling the air. Some people just stared in shock between Christopher and the flow of people running from further up the path.

He must be close.

Christopher heard a roar from up ahead.

Very close.

With another leap he sailed over the World of Birds building in front of him. He stretched his power out again, still trying to understand this new ability and what he could do. Then he felt it. He felt the huge spot of dark power on the ground. That had to be it.

He landed on the roof of a building. From the sounds of frantic squawking beneath him, he knew it must be the birds. From the top he could see the pavement below. And the creature was looking right at him. Of course, it could feel him, track him. It knew he was coming. There would be no element of surprise for Christopher.

The thing was covered in blood, and bits of flesh still clung to its claws. It looked up at Christopher, and its lips pulled back in the horrible parody of a grin, crimson teeth glistening wetly with blood. Through its eyes and the shifting motley darkness of its soul, Christopher could see it. What had been bestial before was now madness. The fusion of hellhound and human soul was driving it crazy. Then with a roar, which sounded suspiciously like a laugh, it turned and leaped into the air. Christopher knew where it was going and he was filled with dread.

It was heading to the center of the zoo, the area with the highest concentration of visitors. He had hoped to fight it here, where most of the visitors had been scared off, but that was not the creature's plan. It was mad with blood lust. Apparently Christopher was no longer enough for it, it was greedy.

Christopher jumped after it, using his new ability to control his power to guide himself on a steadier course, but the creature was faster and made it to the park area in the center of the zoo before him.

Zoo visitors scattered from the beast that had just landed, their late afternoon picnics and snack breaks disrupted by the eight-foot-tall monster in their midst, but apparently the monsters snack break had just begun. It grabbed hold of the nearest human it could find, a man who had just pushed his wife away as the creature's claw struck.

Christopher saw it lift the screaming man towards its gaping maw. He pushed off with his power and slammed into the ground just behind the werehound. He stayed on his feet this time and let his rage flow from him. The shock wave of his landing was enhanced as his Hell power rolled away from him in a great wave. The ground heaved, and the very fabric of reality seemed to ripple with his power. It threw the civilians back, knocking them over and pushing them away from the center of the park.

The creature was also knocked off balance and dropped the man in surprise. The power wave sent the man sprawling a few feet away, out of the creature's reach. But the werehound didn't seem to care. It turned to face Christopher, still wearing that same manic wolf-grin on its face.

"Ah, the main course," it said with a voice so powerful and deep it almost shook the ground.

Something was different Christopher realized. The monster seemed bigger, although it was the same size. And then Christopher understood, it was the creature's aura. Its aura, though thick with the stench of evil and corruption, was pulsing with vitality. While Christopher had been running and barely recovering from his wounds, this thing had been growing in power, consuming souls and becoming stronger.

That's just great, thought Christopher, like I wasn't at a serious disadvantage already.

"I almost ate you late time Hunter. I would have, but they wouldn't let me," the creature said.

"Who wouldn't let you? Who are you?"

"I am Ammit, the Eater of Souls," Ammit said. "And *they* are the ones who created me. Or one of them did, anyway."

"Why? Just to destroy me?" Christopher asked.

"It does not matter. I have already tasted you, and now I will consume you, I will make you forever a part of me." Ammit looked around at the last of the humans running out of the zoo. "It was so easy. She knew you would care for this... this... food. I was hoping you would be harder to hunt and kill than this."

Christopher could feel the Weapon screaming at him, it burned in his pocket. It wanted blood and souls to take to Hell. Christopher was afraid of it, afraid of it taking control again like it had in the lair. But he had no choice. He could not defeat this Ammit without it.

He freed the Weapon from his pocket, and it instantly transformed into a sword. Power shot along its blade and mixed with the streams of Hell power cloaking Christopher. He could feel the will of the sword coming over him like a wave. He fought against it, forcing it under his control. He was able to master it this time, maybe only because he was ready for it, but he could still feel something was wrong, some piece of weakness inside of him.

Ammit snarled and launched himself at Christopher. The Hell power surged inside of him, and with blinding speed Christopher jumped to the side and struck out with the Weapon.

But even with Christopher's enhanced speed, Ammit's hand struck out, the claws hit the blade and deflected it. The force of Ammit's blow almost knocked the Weapon from Christopher's hand, but he was able to hold on.

Christopher tried to recover quickly, but the monster was faster. His claws came back around and struck Christopher. Luckily it was the back of the creature's hand, otherwise the claws would have ripped him to shreds. Instead, pain slammed into his chest, and he was knocked back about twenty feet, where he landed on his ass.

He sat there stunned for a moment before scrambling to his feet expecting a second, final blow from Ammit. But none came.

When he had regained his feet, he spun to face the monster with his sword up. But Ammit was just standing there. He was still smiling that vicious grin.

"I don't normally play with my food, but I think this time I will make an exception," Ammit said. "And when I am done, I will look for the young ones to have for dessert. The pure souls are the juiciest."

Fueled by a burst of anger, the Hell power flowed through Christopher. He leapt at Ammit, the Weapon coming down in blows as fast as he could. Ammit fell back under the onslaught, and Christopher was rewarded by roar of surprise coming from the monster.

But it was a short lived triumph. Ammit recovered quickly. Claws, like short steel blades, moved in a blur even at Christopher's enhanced speed. Soon Christopher realized he was being played with again.

This thing had such power. He would never defeat it toe to toe. He jumped back to buy some time and reached out with his shadows. Tendrils of power snaked from his body, and he jumped into the air using the power in this new found way to guide himself higher.

Ammit launched himself into the air, howling as he hurtled straight at Christopher. Christopher pushed off with his power and shifted out of the way at the last moment. Ammit sailed past him with a surprised yelp and slammed into the side of a large stone building. Parts of the stone facade shattered around Ammit, and he plummeted to the ground.

Christopher used the power again to pull himself in the direction of Ammit's landing spot at the base of the building. He landed at the same time Ammit crashed into the ground. Christopher struck with the Weapon. But Ammit was quicker, he was rolling as soon as he hit. Christopher's blade missed its head, but sliced into its shoulder. It was not a deep wound, but Christopher could feel the tug of the dark soul inside as the Weapon snagged its prize.

For one brief moment Christopher saw it. The two beings inhabiting a single body, a body made of pure power. The dark creature, the true hellhound, subservient to the twisted dark soul inside. The entities blended, but it was the corrupt desire of the dark soul that drove its blood lust.

Then it was gone. The cut was too shallow, and the blade lost its hold on the dark soul. It snapped back, and Ammit howled with pain. Its arm flew out as it jumped to its feet and caught Christopher in the chest before he could bring the sword around again.

Christopher sailed through the air, landing on concrete and

skidding across the paved walking area. His Hellpower whipped about him, stopping him. He got to his feet quickly, he was beginning to learn to use the shadow aura of power around him as an extension of his body. He was like a gangly teenager experiencing a growth spurt with it. It didn't always move as he had planned. And he didn't have time to practice with it now.

He spun towards Ammit, just as the creature slammed into him with its shoulder, like a linebacker making a tackle. The air rushed from Christopher's lungs, and the Weapon flew from his hands. Instantly, he was unarmed.

Gasping for breath, he gripped his fist in his hand and slammed it down on what he hoped was Ammit's neck. The monster was so large it was hard to tell. Ammit grunted but didn't let go or alter his trajectory. Christopher slammed his fist against him over and over. Hellpower infused his blows, and he knew it was doing some sort of damage, but the monster held him. Then Christopher slammed into a wall. His head snapped back and smacked the stone with a crack. Everything went fuzzy for a moment.

The power flowed through him, healing his wounds quickly, but he was still dazed. The world was spinning, and after a moment, he realized he was looking at the darkening sky. It moved across his vision. He was being dragged across the park. He shook his head, trying to regain his senses. Where was Ammit taking him?

The claws tightened around his leg, and he was spun around and then thrown into the air. Christopher didn't know exactly where he was, but he reached out with his power, searching the ground. Now was his chance to get away. But Ammit was on him again, claws tearing into the flesh of his side and he was being dragged down. He tried one last grasp with a tendril of power to push off of something, but then he was slammed into stone ground with the combined force of Ammit and gravity.

Close by he heard the barking of a sea lion. He had been bashed against the stone island in the middle of the sea lion enclosure. Stone shattered beneath him even as his own bones cracked, and then he was underwater. Drowning.

The landing had dazed him some more, he was not even sure exactly which way was up. He struggled weakly in what he thought was the direction of air, but claws like iron weights held him down. Then he was lifted up, and Ammit's face filled his vision. He sputtered and coughed, trying to catch some air into his lungs.

"Little boy Hunter," Ammit roared. "You are nothing. You are not worthy to lick my mistress's boots."

He was underwater again, caught off guard and water filling his mouth. Then he was lifted out.

"Was it worth protecting the humans? You could have hidden, maybe that would have been some more sport. It might have even taken me a while to find you if you had kept moving. But you are weak. Just like all the other mortals. You don't deserve the Eden. I will fill my stomach with your kind."

Christopher was under again. He couldn't focus his thoughts, blood from his head-wound filled the water around him. He was weakening quickly. The power, slowed by the missing part of him, struggled to heal him fast enough, but the damage was too great. It was a losing battle.

He was no match for this thing, he never had been. He was foolish to think he could ever be this, this Hunter of Dark Souls. This was a job meant for a supernatural being, something with real power. He was playing at something that beings thousands of years old had mastered before him. It was silly. The real Beast, the real Hunter could have brought this thing to heel instantly.

He was lifted out again.

"And now I will know your soul, it will reside forever in my gut. Maybe someday I will shit you out," the creature said and opened a maw dripping with viscous saliva for one massive bite. But it didn't bite.

It looked up in shock and a moment later talons dug into Ammit's shoulders, and he was ripped away from Christopher. And Christopher was once again plunged into the water.

Released from the werehound's grasp, he searched around him wildly for the ground or surface so he could orient himself. His lungs felt like they were half full of water.

Why do I end up almost drowning whenever I am fighting these fuckers? He thought.

His hand brushed up against the stone of the sea lion island, and he pulled himself out of the water. He lay there gasping for a moment until the sounds of a struggle close by reached him through his coughing. He rolled over on his back.

On the main sea lion island, Dark Eris in her demonic form fought with Ammit. She hovered above him, diving in and scraping him with her talons periodically. He knew he needed to help her, but he was unsure of how. Neither one of them was a match for this soul-infused monster. But he would do what he could, it was Dark Eris for fuck sake.

He moved and the world spun, he steadied himself against the stone. He was far worse than he had ever been, he could feel the blood pouring from multiple wounds. Shattered bones were mending slowly, the pain intense.

He was a broken man. What could he possibly do against this thing? The Beast, his predecessor, had been fearsome. Christopher remembered the power he felt in its presence. He had been scared and confused when the Beast had summoned him to an audience that day in the boiler room. Christopher understood that had been what it was. And when the Beast had given him the task to deliver the Book and Weapon to his father, he had still been confused and terrified, but there was no denying a command from a being like that...

Something clicked inside Christopher's head. Almost, there was still something he was missing. The Hellfire inside of him leapt up so strongly that it felt like he burned on the inside.

On the other island he could see that Ammit had caught hold of Dark Eris by the leg and was pulling her down.

"I will tear you apart you harpy," Ammit roared. He slammed her down against the concrete island.

The power loomed up inside of Christopher and opened before him like a chasm. He had always controlled it, forced it as best he could with his will. It had always been a wrestling match, but each day it grew stronger. With Hamlin it had almost completely overtaken him. Christopher had thought that was the answer, this terrible power had to be controlled, to be channeled. But maybe he had been wrong, maybe all along he had been failing to see the solution.

Dark Eris was almost dead, he would be next. There was only one option. He had to stop fighting this power. In his own mind, in his own soul, he let himself fall into the chasm. And the power of Hell washed over him.

23

He didn't try to control the power, he didn't try to hold it in check. He let it run its course. He let it cut its burning path through him. He could feel it awakening things inside, things dormant, things primal. He could feel its hatred, its anger, but beyond that he could feel something like justice or maybe the idea of just punishment. That was the basis of Hell, was it not? It wasn't mindless evil, that was for the dark souls. Hell had purpose, and that purpose now flooded Christopher's being.

He felt his muscles contracting, his bones seemed to heal and harden. He cried out in anger. He was no slaughterer, he was not the cruel hunter. He was the condemner of the deserving.

He could feel his heart beating so hard in his chest he thought it would explode. He cried out again, but this time in relief. It was as though his burden was lifted. When he stopped denying the power, it was as though a thousand pounds were lifted off of him. This was what he was, what he was meant to be. The power was the answer. To punish the evil and to kill in righteous anger.

The power of Hell, now free to flow, lifted him off the ground with tendrils of force until he stood on that lone island in the sea lion habitat. Lightening and bands of energy curled about him.

Across from him Ammit stood over Dark Eris, one claw extended, prepared for a final strike. Ammit did not see him, his single-minded madness shut everything out around him. The claw started to descend.

"No," Christopher spoke the command.

It boomed out from him, causing the souls of anyone in earshot to cower. He heard screams from some humans still trapped nearby. But he ignored them. He had spoken a command, and he expected to be obeyed.

The werehound's hand stopped in mid-blow as though frozen. It looked at Christopher and snarled.

He understood now. The secret he had been looking for, the mystery of how the Beast would have stopped this thing. The way to command hellhounds had always been there. There was no trick, it simply was.

He was the Lord of Damnation.

All Christopher had to do was believe it and embrace his power. The hellhound part of that monster would obey him as its master.

With another snarl the werehound pulled its arm back to its side and stood upright. Then it let lose a blood-curdling howl before turning to face Christopher.

Now the dark soul part was another matter. Christopher doubted it wanted to go back to Hell. He leapt into the air, letting his power flow around to propel him quickly toward where the Weapon rested on the ground. The monster was almost as quick, but Christopher reached the Weapon first. He picked it up, and it immediately flared to new life. Christopher let its power run its course, no controlling this time. He could feel its unholy desire boil over into his body. They understood each other now, and with that understanding came a level of control he had never had. The Weapon and he were one. He was the Weapon, the embodiment of Hell. The Book and he were one. His mistake had always been to see the separation. But no more.

Ammit lunged at him. Christopher put his hand in the air palm out. A simple gesture, but it was all it took.

The hellhound inside of Ammit obeyed and halted. Ammit's body contorted and rippled as he struggled for control. Given enough time Ammit would have control again, never to the same level—the hound would always seek to do Christopher's bidding —but eventually he could be a threat. Except Christopher would not let that happen.

The sword flashed. Ammit raised his arms to ward off the blow, but the Weapon cut cleanly through, severing his arms. Christopher reversed his cut, slicing upwards through the creature's torso. The Weapon hooked onto the dark soul cleanly this time and with a great, flesh-tearing sound the soul snapped free of the body and was sucked into the Weapon with a flare of power.

The body fell, but even before it hit the ground it had burst into a combination of bright lights and dark shadows. The shadow pieces dissolved slowly as though reluctant. Christopher didn't blame them, they were souls the werehound had consumed that were destined for Hell. The bright lights flew to all corners of the park like some great fireworks display before exploding into joyous burst of color. They were the souls destined for heaven.

Dark Eris!

Christopher turned and raced back to the island in the sea lion habitat. She was gone. No, she had changed back to her human form and fallen behind one of the stones. He found her leaning against the rock, bruised and injured, but still alive. Her eyes opened at his approach. It was Eris.

"Thank you," Christopher said and gently touched her cheek. "Are you okay?"

"That is one of your stupider questions, luckily I have come to expect them. You look different, by the way."

"Can you walk?"

"I'd rather not," Eris said.

Christopher lifted her gently off the ground. He drew shadows around her, in case anyone was looking. He was standing on top of the stone island. Night had fallen. Sirens in the distance told him it was time to go.

It was over. All the soul lights were out and all the shadows dissolved. All, save one—the largest of the shadows.

It was the hellhound.

"Come," Christopher commanded.

The hound drifted forward as though unsure, but unable to disobey. It was without form. It had no eyes, but he knew it looked at him expectantly.

"They are without form on this plane, until granted by their master," Eris said or maybe it had been Dark Eris, she had closed her eyes and drifted to sleep so he could not tell.

He had to give it a form? He saw a sign a few feet away. It had a giraffe on it. No, that would not do, next to it was picture of a monkey. No, that seemed like more trouble. Then he saw another animal and knew it was the right call.

The shadow lengthened and thickened. Four black legs sprouted from the blob and a long, inky tail drifted out of it. In moments a large black panther stood just on the other side of the sea lion fence. Its eyes blazed with Hellfire and it let out a roar that Christopher could have sworn was pure joy.

Yes. That form will do nicely.

Flashes of light from behind him drew his attention. A group of zoo visitors stood against the building, all of them with their phones out. Another group, zoo employees he suspected, watched from the window of the administration building, phones in hand.

"Damn," he said. "Shit just got real."

He pulled Eris close and summoned the hellhound—or rather, Hellcat—to his side. The Hellcat dissolved into shadow again and joined the power swirling about him. He could feel it close by him, and for second he thought it might be purring. Nah, had to be his imagination.

He leapt into the air and disappeared into the night. At least, he hoped he did. The civilians had gotten enough video footage of him already.

24

The large double door to the Dark Soul's house was already off its hinges and on the marble floor of the entryway when they arrived. Christopher walked in, draped in shadow and Weapon held high. At his side was Ammit, Christopher had looked up the name and thought it appropriate, so he had kept it for the Hellcat. Besides, it was a girl's name, and he had a feeling that the cat was a girl.

Behind them stood Hamlin and Eris. Hamlin had his gun out, ready, for what they were not sure. Ammit had led them here when Christopher had told her to find the master of the dark soul with whom she had shared a body. He had expected maybe a battle, or at least a trap. But not this.

The door was crushed inward as though by a great force, leaves and dirt blown in by the wind told them that this had been done at least a day or two ago. Blood splattered the walls, and more doors leading off the entry were damaged or completely ripped out. Claw marks gouged the walls.

"Looks like there's been a big scuffle," Hamlin said.

"Captain Understatement speaks again," Eris said.

"Well, we've got to search the place," Hamlin said. "Any ideas on what this thing might look like?"

"I have no idea. All I know is they have a piece of my soul," Christopher said. "It could look like anything. I just hope I know it when I see it."

They searched through the deserted house. Ammit padded ahead of them at times, searching quicker. The place was huge. They found a few bodies—servants Christopher guessed— but no piece of his soul. They decided to split up, still, an hour later they had nothing.

Christopher found Hamlin in the living room. He had long since sheathed the Weapon. There was no danger here, not anymore.

"It's not here, they would not leave something like that behind," Christopher said. "How are we supposed to find it?"

Ammit came into the room, and an idea came to him. Hellhounds can track down a lost soul when they have taken a bite. Could they do it in reverse? Track back to the piece of soul? Seemed like it should work.

"Hey guys, I found something," Eris called from the other room.

He and Hamlin entered the study to find her standing at a desk. The study looked like it had been torn apart. Paper was scattered everywhere, some of the charred remnants in the fireplace. Books that had once lined the custom bookshelves lay in piles on the floor. A wall safe was open, the door torn off the hinges, the contents, or what was left of them spilled out on the floor. Eris held up a manila folder with a few sheets of paper in it.

"I found this tucked under the desk. I think it fell there, and whoever ransacked this place missed it," she glanced down at the page. "Do either of you know what the Alliance is?" She said, looking up at them.

25

"We are so fucked," Christopher said.

He was drunk and he didn't care. They had come back to his home and covered what holes they could with tarp and boards. Then they sat in front of the TV watching the craziness unfold. Ammit curled up in the corner near where Christopher sat and faded in and out of shadows.

Some said it was two large animals fighting at the zoo, but they could not answer what animals. Others thought it was a gang firefight that had broken out. There were a multitude of theories spreading. But they all stopped once the footage was shown.

That's when the religious fanatics chimed in. It was the end of times. Two demons duking it out. It was the beginning of the rapture. To others it was two monsters from another universe, but they were out-cried by those that knew for sure it was aliens.

But to Christopher's horror the one idea that seemed to strike the biggest nerve, that seemed to stick with everybody was a statement a ten-year-old boy who had been in that group of tourists near the sea lion enclosure. When he had been interviewed afterward, they had asked this boy what he thought had happen.

He had simply said. "A bad guy was there, a monster, and he was trying to kill everyone, and then this other guy came and saved us. You know like a superhero."

Christopher groaned every time he heard that clip and took another belt of whiskey.

"Facebook is blowing up. All my newsfeed shows is video of our fight. Some really good photos too," Eris said.

"You have a Facebook account? I don't even have one," Hamlin said.

"Of course I have one. Even a possessed demon girl needs a social life," she said and rolled her eyes. "And I'm not surprised you don't have a Facebook account. I bet you'd still have a flip phone if it hadn't finally died on you." She looked at Christopher. "Old people, right?"

Christopher gave her a weak smile.

"Well, I can't say I know what this means," Hamlin said nodding towards the TV. "But I think you might have just been introduced to the world."

"Shit. That is the last thing I need. I've grown in power, I feel it. The battle with the werehound, and ultimately with myself, taught me a lot. But I'm still just starting out. I'm gonna make a lot of mistakes, and the last thing I need is a world stage. I don't know, maybe they'll just forget, you know, over time?"

"Sorry kid, I don't know much, but I think people have a hard time forgetting about things like this. That boy said it best, some people are going to see you as some sort of superhero. Others may see you as a monster or demon—no offense, Dark Eris—but they won't forget. They'll just misunderstand. It's the nature of humanity," Hamlin said.

"Don't worry detective, Dark Eris isn't here right now," Eris said.

"The question now kid is, what's our next step?" Hamlin asked.

"I've been thinking about that," Christopher said. He put down his drink and picked up the Book. "This last fight made me realize that I've been getting lucky. I had thought the power was enough and had gotten a little cocky with it. But when that monster came along, I was way out of my league. I think my next step is some sort of training."

"Training? You mean like join some sort of martial arts club?"

Christopher smiled. "No. I was hoping for something a little more ambitious."

"Then what? Where are you going to find training for the right hand of the Devil?" Eris asked.

"I don't know, but I think I know who to ask," Christopher said and looked down at the Book.

26

Anabelle was in a dark place. Beneath her aching body the ground was hard and cold, leeching the heat out of her flesh. Her once flawless flesh was now covered in sores and cracked skin. Her glamour was gone. If the light had been on and someone was nearby, she would have looked like a hag to them. But she was weak and broken, she could not wake her power. It was over, she had lost. Ammit had gone mad and ruined everything. But what scared her the most is that she could not quite remember what exactly he had ruined. Her memories were gone, just like her power. But unlike her power, she did not think they would ever be back.

A door opened and light poured in, piercing the darkness. She squinted at the sudden brightness, then a large form blocked out the light, like the moon eclipsing the sun.

Golyat.

He had done this too her. Locked her down here, hurt and tortured her. Asking his questions over and over again, punishing her, he said. She hated him. But most of all she hated that she wished she could tell him everything. She wished she could tell him all about what she had been up to these past few weeks. But she couldn't, it was all gone. She even tried to make things up to stop the pain. But no. He was relentless.

And now Golyat was back. To begin again.

He reached down and pulled her to her feet. Even on her feet, Golyat towered over her. He was a large man, it made sense that he had been known as a giant.

She felt a click on her neck, and she understood that he had just connected a chain to her collar. He wanted her to be sure of her new position.

She could see around the room now in light from the doorway. A steel table with straps, she could remember that. She had been tied down. Next to it was a rolling table with wicked instruments of torture. Not the normal kind you see in the movies. These were snatched straight from Hell. The tools were more organic than steel and writhed in little pools of putrid liquid. They had been used on her, she could remember that now. She screamed as the memories came flooding back. Of being strapped down, of the cuts and incisions those living tools of pain had caused. They had been in her, and she screamed again as she remembered them moving through her cutting, rending, tearing.

Golyat slapped her hard, though at a mere fraction of his strength. The blow stunned her, and she quieted immediately. With a satisfied grunt he turned and walked out the room, yanking on her chain. She staggered forward and coughed as the collar wrenched at her throat. The hallway outside was brightly lit, and she had to shield her eyes at the glare.

He dragged her down the hallway behind him like a reluctant puppy. She grasped at the wall to hold herself upright. She could barely walk, her body was so weak. This was also the moment she realized she was nude. The shame did not bother her, she was no prude, but the feeling of exposure did.

When her eyes became adjusted to the light, she could tell they were in a service tunnel underground. After a few turns and another locked door they arrived at a loading elevator. It looked familiar and a new kind of fear started sneaking up on her.

The elevator opened and they got in. Inside one side of the door was lit up like a Christmas tree with all the floor buttons. That was when she realized where they were and what was about to happen. He pushed the button for the top floor.

She began to sob. Of course he would do this, this final humiliation. She slid down the corner to sit on the floor. She sobbed, and he ignored her.

The door opened and Golyat yanked her to her feet. He had not talked to her once since he had questioned her. She knew it was his way of telling her how much she was beneath him. But he didn't have to speak, she knew what came next.

They stepped out into the penthouse suite, it was more of a corporate penthouse. It was one of the meeting places of the Alliance. She was sure there was a meeting called tonight. And she would be his trophy. The memories of details were gone, but she did remember that she had acted to gain the upper hand with the Alliance. Although, how she could have was a mystery to her. For some reason, she thought she could steal the leadership away from him. That had been foolish, as she could now attest. If anything, she had given him a boost of prestige. She was his slave.

He opened the door to the conference room and pushed her through the doorway. As she went through, he casually yanked on the chain, and she fell to the ground kneeling at the feet of the five other dark souls that sat around a table. She heard a couple chuckles and at least one tsk tsk. She knew them all but she could not look them in the eyes. She was exposed, she didn't even have her glamour to hide behind.

Five members of the Alliance of dark souls sat around the large conference table. The smell of sweat and blood was stronger than usual in the room. The room was also darker than usual, only a few faint lights in the ceiling illuminated the great table. They all sat as far from each other as they could. Arguments and rage were the norm in this place, and the distance itself a form of protection.

Never had so many of them gathered in one place. Several must have traveled from out of the country.

"Let this be a lesson to you all," Golyat said as he took his place at the head of the table. "You may not recognize her, but this is our beautiful Anabelle."

There were more gasps at this, several had not recognized her. Her shame only grew.

"Yes, the most beautiful of us has been reduced to this," Golyat said.

"What happened to her?" One of them asked. Annabelle did not raise her eyes, so she could not be sure, but she thought it might have been Andre Lavolier, the Alligator King. She was glad she did not have to gaze into his reptilian eyes. They had always unnerved her.

"Therein lies the warning," Golyat said. "She thought she would act on her own, gain power here in this room by preempting our move against the boy Hunter. She disobeyed the Alliance, and this is what happens."

"The boy did this to her?" Another dark soul asked.

"I like to think that she did this to herself, but yes, her plans were defeated by the Hunter."

"She is the one that created this hellhound? She is the one that exposed us to the world? It is all over the news," a dark souls said.

"Scientists try to explain it. To the average person it is a glimpse into the supernatural. It will be hard to go back to the shadows after this."

From his accent she thought he might have been Draug. He was a long way from Eastern Europe.

"Then he grows strong fast. This is the second of us he has defeated," one of the dark souls said.

"You said he was just scratching the surface, Golyat? How then was he able to do this?" Another asked

"I will admit he has grown stronger much faster than I had anticipated. As I said, this is the first time we have had a mortal Adversary. Nobody knows the rules here. But we are still in the much stronger position," he said and laid his hands on the table. "For one thing, no matter how quickly he is learning, he is still a babe to the power. There is no way he understands the full extent of it yet. For another, we have a gift from our Anabelle here."

He nodded to another door and as though on cue, it opened and a pretty young lady stepped out. It took Anabelle a moment to realize who it was. Her soul shaper wore a gray and black dress, she was clean and had obviously had her makeup and hair done. It looked like she had even been fed recently.

The soul shaper looked around the room nervously at the dark powers who sat there. She almost turned and ran back into the room behind her. But then Golyat caught her eye, and his silent command made her stay and fearfully make her way to his side until she stood above Anabelle.

There was more than a little satisfaction in those eyes as they gazed down at her.

"Well, I can see she is a witch, but how exactly does that help us?" Draug asked in a rumble.

"She is not just a witch, but a soul shaper. Untrained, but

potent," Golyat said and there was a short murmur of approval. But Draug was not impressed.

"But again, how does that help us now?"

"Because we also have this."

Golyat reached into his coat pocket and pulled out a small crystal vial. It glowed with an inner light.

"Is that..."

"Yes," Golyat said. "It is a shard of the Hunter's soul."

He put the vial down on the table for all to see, but it was not far from his reach. There was no trust in this room.

"You see, brothers, we have the advantage here. Between this and the Relic, he will not be able to stop us," Golyat said and turned to the huddled woman on the floor. "And yes, Anabelle did expose us. But I wonder if it is now time to show the world what evil really is, maybe it's time to give it a face. Our face."

THE DEMON COLLECTOR

BOOK THREE OF THE HAND OF PERDITION

1

The coffee shop was warm and inviting. Christmas music played quietly over the speakers, the rich, earthy smells of coffee and pumpkin spice hung strong in the air. The store was crowded with shoppers taking a break from hectic malls and shopping centers. They talked loudly, as though they were at a bar, not a small coffee shop catering to the wealthier clientele of this area. For Christopher, however, the cozy scene could not cover the rotten stench of his prey.

Christopher might have looked a little out of place. He wore a simple outfit: jeans, t-shirt and a hoodie, his brown hair, a little too long, sticking out from under that hood. His college kid home for Christmas break look contrasted starkly with the hip well-dressed young men who sat around him. And maybe he looked a little too serious, maybe people would think he was having trouble with his classes or a break up with a girlfriend. He was certainly too young to have serious problems, problems that most people only found in nightmares.

The thing most people would have noticed, if any of them even bothered to look at him, was that on such a cold winter night he did not appear to have a coat. Nothing hung from the coat hook just above his head, nor from the back of his chair. It was too cold to not have a jacket; the weather was verging on a blizzard.

It was not that Christopher had no coat; he simply had no choice but to leave it outside—it *was* the outside. It was the shadows that kept him warm at night. It was the dark that had become his new home.

It had been his new home ever since he had opened the Book, ever since he had accepted the Weapon. It had become his home the moment he had become the Hunter of Lost Souls, the Lord of Damnation, and a hundred other titles his predecessor had been called. Now he hunted souls escaped from Hell. A bounty hunter so to speak, only he wasn't paid, not with money; his only reward was knowing if he did nothing, the world as he knew it would be destroyed as evil seeped back into the world a thousand times stronger than when it left.

That and vengeance. He had been paid in blood when his new gifts had allowed him to take vengeance on those who had killed his family. If he had to admit it, that was the coin that had sealed the deal. Revenge. But now he knew, as much as he loved his family, it was a steep price to pay. An eternity of hatred and anger.

He held the coffee close to his face, breathing in the scent the way a detective might have smeared Vicks under his nose at a particularly grisly crime scene. Unfortunately, the coffee had little effect. This wasn't a physical smell, this was a rot of the soul.

His eyes swept over the crowd, his vision awash in the color of auras. He had gotten better at it, learning to read the souls of others. This woman was happy, her kids were coming soon, home for the holidays, it would be the highlight of her year. Her husband, sitting next to her and grinning like a madman, was happy, but not because of the kids; he was anticipating the next encounter with his side chick, his mind full of sexual delights.

Another woman smiled and laughed with her friends, a pile of packages next to her. All the while lines of stress permeated her aura as, in the back of her mind, she tried to figure out how she would pay for all this.

An older, well-dressed man sat by himself slowly sipping a coffee, trying to decide if this would finally be the year he killed himself. He couldn't decide if anybody would care.

It was draining sometimes. Christopher could see the happiness in them vaguely, sadness he could see with great detail, but the evil, the evil he could *feel*. Evil was his stock and trade—understanding it, knowing where it led, what it did. These were the tools that let him do his job.

It wasn't just sight; in fact, that was the least reliable of his senses. He could *smell* evil. Not the little wrongs—petty thefts, little lies and abuses—at least not enough to matter. Death, murder, hatred, torture—these were the things he could smell, and they stank.

The worst was the scent of a dark soul. These were the most malevolent of human souls, condemned to Hell on their death. The strongest of them sometimes found a way out, escapees from the eternal prison, but only the strongest could claw their way back to earth. They came changed, twisted even worse than before, bringing with them dark powers and mysteries. These were his prey.

And he had the scent.

His prey stood up from his table, where he had been reading the newspaper. Calmly sipping his coffee. He too was a little different from the crowd. He wore a puffy jacket and filled it out with his large and roly-poly shape. His hair was inky black and sat on his head like a helmet. His eyebrows were thin, his nose pointed, his mouth small as though his overall face was too small for his head. He wore round wire rim glasses. His skin—what little was exposed, he wore gloves, so that left just his neck and head—glistened in the low light as though he was sweating. All in all, he looked disgusting. But that was nothing compared to how he smelled.

His soul was rotting inside him like a maggot devouring an apple core. Christopher could see that the black smear of his soul lacked any humanity. This was his prey, his bounty.

He should have known what the mortal had done to be condemned to Hell, but for some reason, that piece was still locked away from him. The journal that gave him his targets had left that page blank. But there was no doubt this thing, returned from Hell, would kill, torture, and spread his suffering to any who crossed his path.

After the man passed his table, Christopher rose to follow his prey. Once outside the coffee shop the man, despite his large size, strode quickly off down the street. Christopher followed, but he didn't have to stay too close, he had the scent and could have followed the man from a mile away.

At a moment when no one was watching Christopher reached out for the shadows and pulled them around him into the long, hooded coat that had become his uniform. He hated that the shadow coat was so warm and comforting to him.

He also reached out through the shadow looking, feeling. Then the hellcat was there, also strangely comforting. She hid in the shadows, not taking form yet. He commanded her to hide when they were out in the city. It was hard to remain discrete with a huge black panther walking at your side.

Christopher followed him for a few blocks. It was bitter cold and the snow was coming down hard, but it was no blizzard as the weatherman had suggested. Otherwise that coffee shop would never have been so full. He was moving away from the hustle of the shopping area, which was good; fewer people meant less chance of innocents being hurt. And less chance of him being recognized. Not that he worried about revealing his true identity; his uniform and the depth of shadow inside his hood hid his face. No, the last thing he wanted was to be recognized again as the hero of the Brooklyn Zoo. The YouTube video of him defeating the werehellhound was still one of the highest viewed and had the most likes, despite critics complaining that it was all fake.

He wished it had all been fake. Now everybody was waiting for the next appearance of this hero. He was no hero, just a man that had taken vengeance too far and now paid the price every day.

Christopher didn't know where the dark soul was headed, but it didn't matter; he would never make it. The man made an abrupt turn down a little used alley. This was unexpected and Christopher wondered if he had been noticed. This also didn't matter; he had to strike now anyway, it was the right moment. It would be nice, to be prepared for an ambush.

Christopher entered the alley ready for anything. The man had stopped mid-way along the narrow street. It was a true alley, there were a few windows in the walls, a couple of little used fire escapes and a handful of dumpsters near loading doors. It was deserted. Perfect. But his prey had paused, obviously waiting for him. Not perfect.

The large man turned slowly to face Christopher.

"So, you are the one they warned me about," the man said. His hissed his S's and Christopher thought it was the way a snake would sound if it could speak.

"They?" Christopher asked. "Who are they?"

The man just smiled and slowly removed his coat. Underneath his coat four other appendages curled up against his torso. As the coat was removed they stretched out, elongated and thin like the legs of an insect, and had an extra joint not shared by anything human. His arms, which had been covered by the puffy coat looked the same, now that they were uncovered. At the end of each glistened a long knife.

He was not fat; the coat had just concealed his folded arms. In fact, he was quite slim. His shoulders had been slumped forward, but now he stood up straight, his torso fully stretched. His legs kinked backward under his pants, like his knees just decided to fold the other way. He looked like the result of a spider mating with a human. The freakishly long appendages stretched out until they filled the alley. Each arm moved independently, snaking a blade back and forth.

This was new, sort of. Christopher had only starting hunting, but usually his targets were humanoids. Creepy as shit, but human shaped. Only the werehellhound he had fought had been a monster, and that was because it was dark soul fused with a Hellhound.

Christopher pulled out the Weapon. In his pocket and when not needed, it assumed a non-threatening form. Usually a Swiss Army knife. As soon as he pulled it out, as soon as it sensed a soul to consume, it transformed into the most effective weapon Christopher could use at the moment. The only problem was that Christopher didn't have direct control over it; it made the decision to become whatever it thought it needed to be. But since it had been doing this a lot longer than Christopher, he was okay letting it call the shots.

This time it became the sword he was becoming used to. The pocket knife twisted in his hand, but never enough to cause him to drop it, and exploded into a large blade. Bands of power, like bolts of lightning, traveled up and down the blade. Energy poured off of it in waves. Despite the bright illumination coming off the weapon, the shadows of the alley deepened as the Lord of Damnation unleashed his weapon.

Even the spider creature took a step back when confronted with such raw power. The hatred in the Weapon rose up and threatened to consume Christopher, but he was ready for it. This was not his first rodeo. He had learned how to ride it, though not to control it. The fury of Hell could not be fully controlled; there was no spigot he could turn off and on when needed. But he had learned to direct its flow through him and put it to use, rather than simply killing anything with a soul in a five-mile radius. Still, it was a constant battle inside him, and several times he had almost lost it. He had learned since his initiation, but he was no master like his predecessor.

"That is a pretty thing you have there. But do you know how to use it?" The monster asked rhetorically. He didn't wait for an answer before charging at Christopher like a Ginsu-wielding Cuisinart.

Christopher brought his blade up just in time. He felt a quick tinge of pain from his shoulder, the one the Hellhound had taken a bite out of weeks ago. Unlike all his other wounds, it had never completely healed. Despite the old pain he was able to block two of the knives, but it was impossible to stop all six arms. He felt a slice across his abdomen, another across his non-sword arm. They weren't deep, but they weren't just flesh wounds either. The weapon itself was of no use, preferring to only be on the offense, despite the danger to the wielder.

Christopher jumped back, the hell power inside of him carrying him more than twenty feet. Far enough to disengage. He could feel his body quickly trying to heal the lacerations. But the creature was already on him, blades flashing. Christopher's blade wanted souls and darted forward, but there were too many knives. For each cut he blocked, two got through, slicing away at him. In moments he had slices along his arm, gut, and legs. It occurred to him that the dark soul was just playing with him. Any of these cuts could have been deeper. He was holding back.

Christopher had underestimated this prey and was now paying the price. It had him up against the wall, knives flashing, and despite the power of his weapon, he was always a step behind. The raw brute power of his weapon was no match for the skill of this multi-blade wielding monster. Fortunately, the Weapon wasn't his only option.

Though weakened by the myriad of cuts, Christopher leaped into the air and, propelled by his hell power, he soared upward fifty feet. He reached through the shadow and sent out tendrils of power; they caught hold of the walls and pulled him along the alley. Shadows and waves of power surrounded him like a dark fog, and then he was on the ground at other end of the alley.

The dark soul was right behind him. Its appendages stretched out to hook into both sides of the alley, and it scurried forward like a freakishly large spider walking upright. Honestly, Christopher had no idea how he slept at night, given the nightmarish things he had seen. Perhaps it was because his waking hours were so full of them.

The Weapon shifted again in his hands. It became longer and round, still aglow with barely contained power; it had become a javelin. Christopher, wasting no time, threw it. It was a clumsy throw, an attempt at mimicking what he had seen on TV. He had never had any training with the weapon, but improvisation had worked before. Only that time he had been fighting mortal gang members, not an escapee from Hell. Still, the power was there, and the javelin left his hand, streaking toward the many-armed creature.

And missed.

His opponent ducked, and the javelin bounced harmlessly off the wall behind it and clattered to the ground.

"Shit," said Christopher.

It came at him, blades whipping through the air. He was about jump towards the top of the building in a last-ditch effort to get away when he heard a growl. His adversary must have heard it also because he paused. Briefly, but long enough.

Hellcat pounced. The sleek black blur detached from the shadow and transformed into a huge black panther in the air. It landed on the dark soul's back, its claws digging into the monster's flesh. Its powerful jaws clamped onto a shoulder, and Christopher could hear the spider thing's collar bone snap.

The creature cried out and fell to its knees from the unexpected blow from behind. All of its knife-wielding hands scrabbled for the giant panther now feasting on its flesh. And more than simple flesh, Hellcat was tearing into its tainted soul. The man bellowed again in pain.

Despite all the cuts and blood loss, Christopher raced around the screaming creature, trying to get to the Weapon. Already the knives were finding Hellcat's flesh and doing damage. Hellcat was tougher than the animal it took its form from, but Christopher couldn't take the chance that it would outlast this thing. He needed to take advantage of the distraction.

He reached the Weapon just as the man-spider slammed its back against the brick wall, knocking the giant cat off. But eight-legs was too late, Christopher was there.

The Weapon had shifted once more into a sword and sliced through the air, leaving a trail bright with crackling energy. It sunk into the creature's flesh like butter, and Christopher could feel the pleasure emanating off the weapon as it gorged on the soul. The being screamed a high-pitched shriek of horror and pain. As the blade left the creature's body, it pulled with it the twisted soul that lived inside. It emerged from the body reluctantly in gooey strings, like rotten taffy. Finally, it snapped free and the Weapon sucked it up like a sponge.

The body that the dark soul once inhabited turned black and rotten, instantly dissolving into a pile of slimy parts that was rapidly turning from a pile to a puddle. The sword thrummed with energy; it wanted more. It always wanted more. Christopher allowed its desire to become his. He felt it rush through him, and subconsciously he raised the sword as lines of power radiated off of it and lit up the alley. Then he calmed himself, and because they were one, the Weapon calmed too.

He used to fight it, wrestle with it and the power and need it drove through him. But Christopher had learned he and it were joined, and it was best to embrace its power and its need. This allowed him to control himself and focus the power in the Weapon. Still, although he was learning how to control this massive power, he had a long way to go and it wouldn't take much for him to lose control again.

As he breathed in and out slowly, the rage inside himself and the Weapon leaked away to a more manageable level. The desire to take souls was not as strong.

Then Hellcat growled a warning and Christopher spun around, the Weapon raised and power surging, but not the mindless soul hunger from before. A boy—really, a young man about Christopher's age—stood out on a fire escape. He wore flannel pajama bottoms and a t-shirt. The window next to him was open, despite the freezing temperature. Christopher guessed that he lived in the building. He had his phone up, taking a video.

"Shit," Christopher muttered.

Once he saw he had been spotted, he immediately lowered the phone.

"You're him, aren't you? The hero from the Bronx?" The young man asked.

Hellcat growled louder and the young man took a step back. "I didn't...I mean I thought... I'm sorry I didn't mean to bother you."

"I'm no hero," Christopher said, letting the full might of his power shine through. "I am the Hunter of Lost Souls. I condemn dark ones back to Hell. I am no hero." He pulled the shadows closer about him letting his power radiate from him. Hellcat padded to his side. The blade flared with a last surge of power and then transformed back into a Swiss army knife.

The young man turned pale. "Please don't kill me. I'm so sorry."

Christopher could see and smell the young man's soul. It was the dirty gray of your average mortal. He hid no great evil. The young man was actually a breath of fresh air after dealing with the dark soul, the stench of which still burned in his nostrils.

"I only take the deserving. You are not corrupt enough. For now." Christopher added that last part because it wasn't a long journey from dirty gray to black spots.

"Come," said Christopher to Hellcat. The large black panther growled one last time at the man on the fire escape before leaping into the shadows surrounding Christopher and dissolving into their depths. Christopher leapt straight into the air at least fifty feet up to the roof. Once there, he leapt off the edge of the building to the next roof.

From rooftop to rooftop he traveled, his shadows reaching out to propel him along whenever needed. This was his preferred way of traveling. And tonight, it took him home quickly.

2

"Oh, look at that, another YouTube video," Dark Eris said as Christopher came through the office window. He banished his shadow uniform as soon as he was safely inside. The home office used to be his dad's and was traditional looking: masculine dark wood, leather couches and chairs, and floor to ceiling bookcases that held old leather books. Christopher had always like the smell of the place, leather and old books with just a hint of burned wood from the large fireplace. Hellcat curled up by the fireplace. There wasn't even a fire. A large flat screen had been installed over it, used mostly for video games.

A large desk dominated the room, also dark wood, with a decidedly untraditional computer monitor sitting on top of it. Eris sat at the computer now. She was small and looked almost fragile, but Christopher knew she was anything but. Her jet-black hair fell about her shoulders, partially obscuring the tattoos that covered her neck and, Christopher presumed, more of her body. She had tattoo sleeves as well, but he hadn't seen much beyond that, unfortunately. Christopher had to admit she was hot despite the whole split personality thing.

Christopher decided the cat had the right idea and fell into the soft chair next to her. With his shadow coat gone he could see the damage to his clothes. His jeans and hoodie were almost in shreds and covered in dark stains of blood. Through the multitude of holes pink, freshly healed skin covered in rust red blood could be seen. The bleeding had stopped, but he looked like he had been in a slaughterhouse explosion.

"It happened what, ten minutes ago, and it's already posted with thousands of views," Dark Eris said. "You really need to check your surroundings before going into hero mode. Or at the very least take the goddamn phone away..." she finally looked at him and abruptly stopped. He saw the subtle shift in her that meant Dark Eris had faded and now Eris was in control. He had learned to tell who she was from her body language. And then there were her eyes. They darkened to almost black when Dark Eris was piloting. It could be tricky being friends with a demon and a girl sharing a single body. "Holy shit! Are you okay?"

"I'm no hero," Christopher said.

She got up from the desk and came over to the chair. She started poking at the almost healed wounds. There wasn't really anything she could do, but he didn't mind her concern. "Did it do this to you?" she asked.

"Yeah. It's nothing really, just a lot of shallow cuts. Painful, but no real damage."

"This is only the second one since you fought the werehell-hound. The last one was much easier," Eris said.

"The last one had assumed the shape of a child. Thank god nobody recorded that. The whole world would hate me."

"My point is, you need some sort of training. I mean, what if these things get harder to kill? You're fast and powerful, but if you don't know how to use your weapon, what happens when you run into somebody that does and is also fast and powerful?"

"I've got Hellcat to save me. Don't I, girl?" Christopher reached down and stroked the cat's massive head. She stretched out her neck and raised her head to give him better access. She made a sound that sounded suspiciously like a purr. He thought he had read somewhere that big cats like panthers can't purr. Ironically, it seemed the ones from Hell didn't know that.

"You know what I mean. She got you out of this one, but what if she hadn't been there or was hurt herself? You didn't stand a chance against this guy's knives. I saw the video, remember, so you can't talk your way out of this one. You need someone to teach you how to use that thing."

"I could join a local kendo class, but I don't think anyone is gonna want to spar with a sword that will rip your soul out and send it directly to hell. Besides, what do I do when it decides to be an ax or a spear or any of a hundred other weapons? That would be an awful lot of martial arts classes."

"Don't be an asshole. You know I wasn't suggesting going to a strip mall and joining the local martial arts club."

"Sorry, rough day," Christopher said and picked at his shredded clothes.

"Well don't take it out on me. What about your Library friend? Didn't you say you were going to ask if he had a solution? I mean for a guy with access to all the knowledge in the world, you seem very reluctant to use it," Eris said.

"Fine, I'll ask the Librarian. But I bet he's just going to give me some annoying sarcastic remark. That's what he does."

"Didn't you tell us that he was created from your subconscious or something? Something about how he was created out of part of you?" At some point during the conversation she had switched from Eris to Dark Eris again.

"Something like that, I guess." Christopher said.

"Then I guess you have only one person to blame."

"Alright I get it; I'll ask him the next time I'm in the Library." Christopher said.

The Library was a sort of extra-dimensional space Christopher found himself transported to whenever he opened the Book, which was a portal to the repository of all the knowledge that exists in the world. The problem is it is so vast and complex it makes it next to impossible for Christopher to utilize it properly. The Librarian had told him it takes on a different metaphor depending on who possesses the Book. There had been only one other owner, his predecessor—the Beast, as he was called—a being that had existed from the beginning of time. The Library, he was told, was never made for a mortal mind, and that was why it had such an inefficient design for him. Christopher found it hard not to take that as an insult.

"You look like shit, and I suspect you're getting dried blood all over the chair. You need a shower," Dark Eris said.

Their switching had become more common place it seemed, changing control positions more often. But he was too tired to think of what that might mean right now. A shower sounded perfect and... "A drink. A shower and a drink. That's what I need."

"That does sound good," Eris said. "Make me one too. After your shower." She wrinkled her nose a little as though he smelled bad and then turned back to the computer.

Realizing there was no sympathy to be had here, Christopher left for the shower. Forty-five minutes later he was back in the chair freshly washed—the blood had been a pain to scrape off—and not nearly as sore as when he had come through the window.

His ability to heal was incredibly useful, but it still felt different. Weaker in some way that was hard to describe. It seemed that every time he hunted he found new strengths and abilities with his power, but through it all he felt something was missing. It was hard to describe or even point to where exactly it was affecting him, and that is why it was hard to talk to Hamlin, Eris, or Dark Eris about it. It had started when he fought the werehellhound. The only way to describe it was that something was missing, and it seemed like something important.

3

The air inside the old church was hot, thick and filled with moans and wailing. Like some kind of sauna for the damned. Late evening sunlight trickled in through the spaces between the boards covering the windows. It had been hastily done, the boarding of the windows, using all the spare wood they could find, even breaking apart one of the pews. Still, there was no glass so the screams got out; the children of the village could hear.

Antonio knew that some of the children, the braver ones, would climb on top of each other to try and get a peek inside. It had become a game to some of them, daring each other to peek in the demon house, as they called it. It had once been a church, the center of the community, a place of worship and peace. A place of comfort. Now Antonio thought it would be forever known as the demon house, earth's own little corner of hell. A place of death and rot.

And it did stink. Death, decay, the smell of sick and sweat. Incense burned, but there was not enough to cover the disturbing smells. Antonio didn't think there was enough incense in the world for that.

Candles burned throughout the church, struggling to illuminate the dark corners left behind by the thin beams of light. Dust motes, like swarms of insects, danced through the weak beams of light. This place, once cleaned so regularly, had never been so dirty. Pews had been moved back from the front of the church haphazardly as though they had been pushed back by some wild force. Despite that, several of the pews had people in them.

Antonio's mother was there, the tears on her face streaming past her wailing mouth. His father was dead, which was a mercy. His father would not have to see this, not have to be disgusted. His sister was there, her arms around their mother, holding her as though at any moment she would spring forward toward the front of the church. His sister was beautiful; the man that marries her will be lucky, he thought, because she is the beauty that is hidden. She looked at him now with hatred in her eyes. That hurt, but he understood it.

Other people, many family, and of course it was all family in a town this small, sat at other pews. They all looked to varying degrees tired, stressed, weak. But it had been a long battle. Hopefully soon to be over.

There was a lot of blood here, splattered throughout the church. Most of it human, although at least one chicken had been slaughtered. They were getting desperate and turning toward the old ways. Most of the blood surrounded the bed at the front of the church. The bodies of the priest and his assistant had been removed by Antonio's uncles and a cousin.

Antonio wanted to tell them all to forget it, it was over; he was no more. They should leave, abandon the village and let him rot here in his own little hell. But they never would. This wasn't just about him; this was a battle testing their faith and they would not give up. Besides, he couldn't speak, the demon had taken over. Antonio was now simply a passenger in his own body.

He could feel though; he could feel his pain-soaked body. It felt as though it was giving out, but he knew that was just him losing control to the demon inside. He hoped he would not remain conscious for much longer, he hoped it was death that awaited him as the demon took more and more of him. Hoped is the word, it was all he had left.

He was chained to an iron-framed bed, which was in turn chained to the floor. He had only been brought here in the last few days. He didn't know exactly how long it had been. Time flows differently when you are not who you should be, when wickedness hijacks your body. It was a last-ditch effort, as was the priest who had flown in all the way from the Vatican. They had been here as a formality it seems, to investigate the need for an official exorcism. The priest had not believed, not until the demon in Antonio had torn the good father apart with Antonio's bare hands when he had leaned just a little too close.

He was thirsty, so thirsty, but none would approach him with water. Again, he didn't blame them. They would pray, but they would not touch. It was death to touch him.

Alicia was there. That was probably the worst part. She was there watching as the thing took over his body. A body that he had been planning to commit to her just next year. He was eighteen and they would have been married. They were so young and it would have been so grand. He was healthy and would be off to the university next year, and she would have been by his side.

Then he had caught this sickness of the soul. Dreams ended, nightmares began.

Why did she have to watch? He wanted to scream at her to leave, tell her that he was ashamed and that if she had ever loved him she would run away now and forget he ever existed. He had loved her innocence, but now she had been exposed to such evil, such twisted things the demon had done through his voice and his body. He screamed silently inside.

And the demon just laughed.

The wailing, the crying, the praying had reached another peak. It went in cycles as the friends and family ran out of energy and had to rest or try to eat outside the building; the stench in the desecrated church held too much death to eat inside.

The screaming, the praying at full volume, the futile cries for the demon to get out filled the room with frustrated energy. Now Antonio wanted it to stop; all of it was too much, just too much. He wanted them all to leave, leave him to his slow death. And Antonio knew the demon could feel his suffering, and that's why it did nothing to stop his family's display of desperate frustration. He could feel the tears running down his cheek, but it was all the demon would allow him. It had placed the crazed Cheshire grin on his face. So now he had a mad, grinning, crying face to display to his family.

Just as he felt his ears would start to bleed from the constant praying and wailing of his family, the door to the little shack of a church flew open with a crack and a bang. It was as though a gun had gone off. There was sudden silence as everybody took a startled look back at the door. Antonio even felt surprise coming from the demon inside, and then a sort of amused curiosity.

A man stepped in from the startlingly bright outside. The dull interior of the church had made his eyes sensitive to the light, although Antonio thought dimness might just come from the demon. On TV monsters always hated the light. The transition from bright to murky made it hard to see the man at first. He was not a tall man, short in fact. Slightly pudgy, maybe a bit of a gut, but not fat.

"Oh, pardon me," he said and turned to close the door. Much gentler than he had opened it.

Antonio's eyes adjusted back to the dark interior illumination almost instantly. The man's face was pale, to the point that Antonio thought he was albino. He thought the man was not old, maybe in his forties, but the pale skin, dark rings around the eyes, making them deep-set like a skull, made him look ancient. Antonio had the impression that the man was bald although he wore a wide-brimmed black hat on his head. It looked like a flat cowboy hat.

Perfectly round wire frame glasses sat on the edge of those sunken eye sockets, making his eyes appear much larger than they were. This was all the more disconcerting because of the depth of his eyes. But what jumped out most to Antonio, and probably everyone else in the room, was that he was wearing the black clothes and white collar of a priest. He carried a bag, similar to an old doctor's bag, the kind used to make house calls.

Despite what happened to the last priest, hope once again rose in Antonio. Was this a backup? The actual exorcist? Would this new priest be able to rid him of the demon?

The demon snorted in derision through Antonio's nose as though he had been listening to his thoughts. Which it probably was.

"No hope, just another toy," spoke the demon through Antonio. It was a quiet rasping sound, not Antonio's voice at all.

The priest gazed around the room. "Well, this is a turn out," he said. "I suppose there is little else to entertain in this god-forsaken village."

The villagers bristled at that, but Antonio knew the priest was right. It was a god-forsaken type of place. He would have laughed ironically if he could.

"Father, we are a god-fearing people, please do not speak so,"

Antonio's grandmother spoke. "Have you come to help our poor boy, Antonio?"

Saying his name released a new torrent of sobs and wailing from her and then the rest of his family. The man raised an eyebrow and pursed his lips as though considering the request. And that is when Antonio knew this was no priest. Hope sunk out of him.

"Yes," the man said. "Yes, I have come to help you, so to speak." As he spoke he seemed to grow in confidence as though he was deciding it was a good idea on the spot.

"You will drive the demon from my baby?" Antonio's mother asked. "Please, we are lost. We need to see the way out."

"I promise, I will remove the demon from this body," the priest said.

"Come here priest, I am hungry," the demon said. "I have tasted the blood of a thousand priests, I have ruled nations, I have..."

"Nope, 'fraid not" said the priest as he came toward the bed. "You have done none of those things. You are nothing more than a jumped-up imp."

Antonio could feel the demon's surprise. The amusement was gone. "How dare you, weak human, mortal slave."

"You see the problem with you low level annoyances is that you give all demons a bad name. I mean look at this shit. Looks like a scene right out of The Exorcist. Do they use it as some sort of training video in Hell for you bottom dwellers?"

The priest had stopped just out of the reach, as though he knew exactly how far the demon in Antonio could move. He set his bag on a small table nearby.

The demon sat up and strained against the chain around its neck. "You forget your place, mortal."

"I forget nothing. You are nothing. I have dealt with a thousand of your kind, and none have ever gotten the best of me. Normally I wouldn't even bother with something as pitiful as you. I came to this village expecting a greater prize for my collection. I'm doing this because I simply have nothing else to do and I am bored. You are hardly more than a snack."

Antonio felt the shock of the demon. Shock that was slowly turning to something resembling fear. Antonio had no clue what was going on, but he took a simple joy in the demon's fear.

"You are the one? The one they call The Collector?" the demon asked through Antonio's lips.

"I am," the man said and stepped into the circle of death around the bed. The demon growled and leapt at the priest. The priest didn't try to defend himself, he didn't even flinch; he simply closed his eyes and opened his hands, palms up. The demon's hands had just touched the priest's throat when they stopped. Power surged from the priest's hand, and the demon was stopped.

Powerful hands of light and smoke wrapped around Antonio's arms. The amorphous clouds attached to those smoky hands coalesced instantly into two hideously demonic shapes on either side of Antonio. They were the incarnation of the demon Antonio sensed inside his body.

They were two huge creatures of twisted sinew and flesh as though parts of their vaguely humanoid shape had been turned inside out and made into skin. Exoskeleton parts of the outside punctured their skin, seamlessly melding with the bone inside. Their skulls were elongated, and horns like twisted dreadlocks sprouted from their heads, twining together and coming to an uneven point at the back. Their jaws were large and distended as though they regularly took large bites from their prey. Wicked, sharp looking teeth, curved backwards like a shark, lined their mouths.

This was a visual of the demon within him, Antonio knew.

One of these things was what had taken him, dominated him completely.

They dragged Antonio's body back onto the bed. The demon within screamed and kicked, but it couldn't overcome two of its own kind. The room had erupted into chaos as soon as the other monsters had appeared. A few caught on that the priest was no priest. They came forward, perhaps thinking they could take him down and avoid the devil's pets in the process. They were wrong.

The man faced Antonio's family and friends and once more closed his eyes and turned his palms upward. Two more demons, smaller than the others, leapt from his hands and into the crowd. These were different, all teeth and claws. They cut into the villagers like a scythe through grass.

Blood flew and bones snapped. The screams of his family and friends ripped through what was left of Antonio. He tried to hide, to pull himself back from the scene, but the demon within kept his eyes open and Antonio couldn't look away.

Some of them tried to escape, but the pews, which had been moved to make room for the bed, were now pressed so closely together they were practically a jumble. Only a small aisle down the center was open; most tried to make it out that way, but there were too many bodies jammed together. The demon fell into them. Others tried to climb over the pews, but most of them tripped or fell and were easily victims of the other demon.

While his pet demons slaughtered the villagers, the priest that was not a priest pulled off his jacket, calmly folded it, and placed it on a chair near the bed. Then he rolled up his sleeves as though he was about to engage in messy work.

The demon inside Antonio tried to escape. It was trying to leave his body and return to hell. Antonio could feel it. But it couldn't run, apparently un-possessing a person is not a spur of the moment thing. The demons holding Antonio's body must have felt it too. They tensed and bore down on his arms, snapping the bone. Antonio felt the pain and would have screamed if he could have.

"You are his slaves, his little pets," the demon inside Antonio said. "You are pathetic and weak."

One of the demons responded in a language that should have been meaningless to Antonio, but with the demon inside him he could understand the words, "As you will be. We have no choice and neither do you. So swallow that pride, it has no place here."

"No, I will not be his," the Antonio demon said.

"Yes, yes you will, you will all be mine eventually," the no-priest said. He had moved the small table close to the bed and opened his bag. He pulled out several quasi-surgical instruments and lined them up neatly. "Shall we begin?"

He held up a knife with a wicked looking blade that turned inward like a butcher's hook and let some of the faint light glint off it. He examined it as though he could measure the blade's sharpness simply by looking at it.

The Antonio demon twisted and turned violently despite the broken bones, but The Collector's assistant demons held on. The man with the sunken eyes leaned over the writhing body and looked directly at Antonio. "Whoever is inside there. This will be painful. I'm sorry about this, but not too sorry. To be honest, I kind of like this part. On the bright side, it will all be over soon."

The man with the sunken eyes held the knife aloft, facing downward in his palm. Then he plunged it into Antonio's chest, just below his heart. The demon inside let out a scream and struggled even harder, the last throes of a doomed creature. Antonio also cried out, albeit silently. He cried because of the pain, but mostly because the blade missed his heart. On purpose, the man was keeping him alive. The man sliced downward on Antonio's torso, splitting him open in a clumsy evisceration.

Once the blade reached Antonio's groin, the man, although Antonio no longer thought he was truly a man, went to work more carefully on his chest, cutting through the rib cage, but not damaging his heart.

The Antonio demon spit blood at The Collector. It splattered against his face, but he didn't seem to mind or even notice. Pain, beyond what even the last few days had brought, washed over Antonio.

He just wanted it to be over.

Once the rib cage was cut through, the man put the knife down and picked up an object that look like a vice. He placed the device between the cracked ribs and started cranking, pulling Antonio's ribs apart.

Any normal man in this situation would have been dead, but the demon inside kept Antonio's body alive. With a crack, his chest popped open and the back of the rib cage cracked near the spine.

"There we go," said The Collector.

Antonio could not pass out to escape the pain, so his mind did the next best thing. He went insane. The strain of the last few days, the conscious defilement of his body, it was all too much. Reality slipped from him.

Once the ribs snapped the man removed the vice from the chest cavity. Then after a quick survey of the open body, and an assurance that the heart was still beating, he plunged his hands into the organs. Using just his fingers at first, he sifted through the large and small intestine, searching and feeling his way through. He pulled chunks out once he had searched through it, tossing the still warm tubing over the side of the chest, where it fell to the floor, still attached. The man began chanting. It was a deep, droning sound, so different than his speaking voice. It rumbled and growled and bit. He chanted ancient words of power in a language long forgotten. This Antonio knew through the demon inside.

Not finding what he was looking for, he moved his way up, ripping up kidneys, the liver, and any other organ that did not have whatever treasure he was looking for. It was just after he reached the diaphragm that he seemed to find it. All the while he chanted.

Through crazed eyes, his and the demon's, Antonio could see some sort of glowing object reflected in the glasses framing those sunken eyes. Antonio thought the lights were pretty, the way they danced and swirled in that reflection. He knew intuitively that was the demon inside him. It was so beautiful. Then it winked out.

"Oh no you don't, you little bastard," the man said, breaking his chant briefly before resuming.

He dug into Antonio's body with a passion. Ripping though his innards, chasing after that little bit of glowing. Flesh and organs flews as the man ripped through his body. Blood from the man's frantic digging covered the walls and dripped down the large crucifix above the bed.

"Gotcha," said the man, once more breaking his rhythmic chant.

With a final yank the man pulled free the glowing form. The Collector cupped it in his hand. Wispy mist and cloud-like energy swirled around a glowing center. The clouds of power wrapped around the Collector's hand.

Antonio saw this in his last moment through dying eyes. There was a certain mercy in this. Despite what the man had done, he had granted Antonio the one thing his family never would have. His broken mind couldn't handle the details of what had just happened or what they meant, and he no longer cared what or who this man was. He had been granted release and he took it. In the end he was once again only Antonio. That was his last thought as the light left his eyes.

The man known as the Collector slurped up the demon's essence like it was an oyster. It tried to pull away, to fight him, but the man had control. The essence was formless, stolen from its vessel. There was nothing it could do.

A slurp and then it was gone.

The man turned his head up and basked as the demon was absorbed into his collection. He felt power and vitality flow through his body. It was nice, this treat, but it was no meal. He would need to collect another one soon; he was never truly satiated.

He looked at his hands dripping with blood. His shirt and pants were also splattered with the stuff. He could feel it drying in his hair and on his face. He supposed there wasn't an acceptable restroom around here to clean up in. He shook his arms a couple of times to get off the worst of it and then picked up his tools and put them in his bag. He could clean them later.

When he was done he turned to the two demons standing in the middle of the room. He knew they hated him, and he didn't care. They were his. He walked over to them, carefully stepping over the bodies and trying not to slip in the wet blood pooling on the floor. When he reached them, he thrust his hand into one chest. Its form sunk in as though the demon was a hologram. The man clutched at the throbbing ball of source inside and squeezed. The demon looked up and bellowed, then dissolved into the same wispy, smoky shape he had pulled out of the boy. He slurped it up.

He repeated the same process with the other demon; this one uttered a high screech of pain as it collapsed in on itself. That taken care of he made his way to the door, once again doing his best not to step in pools of blood or trip on a severed arm.

At the door he noticed one of the congregation was still alive. It was a woman; she was covered in blood, but alive. For the moment. Then he noticed it was the boy's mother. Her eyes were wide and her lips opened and closed soundlessly as though she was talking on mute.

"You see? I did remove the demon from his body. He is free now, I have brought him peace," The Collector said. He patted her cheek softly, leaving a smear of her son's blood across her face. Her lips just kept moving. "What's that? I can't hear you. I believe I deserve a thank you? What? None? You are a rude people."

He turned and stepped out of the front door. The sun was down, which was for the best; he wasn't really a fan. With the sun down the air had grown cooler, definitely better than the sauna like heat that had been inside the church.

He was about to step off the raised porch of the church when he saw the man. Although mountain might be a better name for the huge thing that stood quietly across the rocky church yard. He was a giant in height and was even more massive in breadth, the size of two large basketball players standing sided by side. He wore a pale suit, an expensive one that fit him perfectly, but just barely. The Collector could tell most of that mass was muscle, not fat.

And the big man was like him. The Collector could tell. They had both escaped the same eternal prison. They were brothers in a way. The Collector wondered briefly if he should kill him.

"Are you the one they call the Collector?" The big man asked.

"Yes. What are you doing here?"

"My name is Golyat and I am recruiting."

4

Christopher stumbled as he entered the Library. The transition from the real world to this extra dimensional pocket was never a smooth one. In fact, it usually felt violent, as though he was being ripped out of one world and shoved into another. It was disorienting and slightly nauseating and despite the improvement in his landings, it was still a pain in the ass. Although it was never as life changing as that first trip.

This time, as the Library took form around him he stumbled forward, searching for support with his hands out. They found cloth and he clutched at it even before the shelves and books around him came into focus. He thought the cloth was draped over some sort of pillar or a curtain perhaps, and he was certain he would have fallen to his knees, perhaps even his face, if not for the thick material.

The Library solidified and Christopher looked up. They weren't curtains at all; he was clutching the robes of the very tall Librarian. Christopher couldn't tell if the Librarian was looking down at him—his cowl hid his face in deep shadow—but he was pretty sure there was a glare in there somewhere.

"Oh great, a hugger," The Librarian said.

Christopher pulled away as though the Librarian was on fire. "To what do I owe this touchy feely visit?" asked the Librarian.

"I fell," Christopher said.

"Ah, a clumsy hugger, the girls must love you."

Christopher held his tongue, knowing that whatever he said would only dig the sarcasm hole deeper. Besides, if he was stuck all alone in a never-ending library, Christopher suspected he'd be an asshole too.

And the Library was vast, infinite from what Christopher could tell. Huge stone rooms and passageways lined with shelves, each loaded with books, scrolls, and in some cases, stone tablets. Row upon row the book shelves stretched to a ceiling so high it was often obscured in darkness. He had walked the halls several times, examining the odds and ends. It wasn't just books there were objects as well, objects that must have imparted some sort of information. Some had engravings and were obvious, but once he had found a skull, only vaguely human shaped.

It also had a comfortable study area with desks and soft reading chairs. Perhaps it was more than one, Christopher wasn't sure, but the study always seemed to be close by when he needed it, no matter which room he was in at the time.

It was frustrating, having all this information around him, but only being able to access a small part of it, one drip at a time, usually filtered through the Librarian's research. But with a non-existent—or at least one he was not aware of—indexing system, and books written in multiple ancient, dead languages, it was impossible for Christopher to use it effectively. The Librarian said it was because of his limited human mind and that his successor had much more efficient access.

But he suspected that was just the Librarian being an asshole again.

The Librarian himself—at least Christopher was working under the assumption that it was a he—was even more of an enigma. Merely an extension of the Library and shaped to some extent by Christopher's subconscious, the Librarian technically didn't even exist.

And perhaps he really didn't.

Christopher had never seen his skin or any clothes beneath those long robes. Where his face should be there was nothing but shadow. The same with the ends of his sleeves; where his hand should be just dark holes.

"You look...off," said the Librarian.

"Why thank you. That might have been the nicest thing you have ever said to me."

"You seem weaker, thinner than last time," the Librarian said.

"Yeah, I've been off lately. Maybe it's just a flu bug or something."

But they both knew it wasn't a bug. It had something to do with his fight with the werehellhound a few months ago. Specifically, its bite and what it had taken from him.

"Come," the Librarian said and turned abruptly before gliding down the aisle. He didn't really walk as far as Christopher could tell; he floated on whatever legs he had beneath the thick robes. Christopher followed after, still a little dizzy from the trip.

They turned at the end of the aisle, and there was the comfortable sitting area: a desk, a couple of chairs and a coffee table. Christopher collapsed into one of the chairs. He always felt slightly drained when he came to the Library, as though the journey took something out of him, but this time it felt stronger, as if it was getting harder to make the transition. Or perhaps he was catching something. Or perhaps it was all in his head. It was all still so new he didn't know what he was supposed to feel.

"Again I ask, to what do I owe the pleasure?"

"Something we talked about before. I need some help," Christopher began. And then winced and waited for the stinging insult.

"Don't worry, that one was too easy. I'll let it go," the Librarian said.

"I mean with training."

"Ah, did you encounter some baddie that you couldn't just beat into submission with your sword? Need something more in your repertoire than a wood cutting ax-chop? You must have pulled it off somehow being that you are here and not lying shredded to pieces in the gutter."

"Hey, I'm not that useless. I have hunted down several dark souls and returned them to Hell. And don't forget I dammed Rath. And he was able to kill my predecessor, so I can't be all that bad," Christopher said. And it was true, he had a lot to learn, but he had overcome a lot too. He was doing a job never intended for a mortal. He deserved some kind of acknowledgment.

The Librarian was quiet for a moment, his expression invisible, then he said, "Perhaps."

"Perhaps? Perhaps what?"

"Perhaps Rath killed the Beast and perhaps not," the Librarian said.

"What are you talking about? Of course he died. That's why I'm here, isn't it?" Christopher said.

"Yes, well, of course he died and you mistakenly inherited his power, but what proof do you have that Rath was the one that killed him?"

Christopher opened his mouth to respond then paused and closed it. Rath had been his first real test when he took the job of the Hunter. But his only proof was that Rath had told him he had killed the beast. He had just believed him.

"Rath told me," Christopher said, but it sounded hollow in his own ears.

"Ah yes, and he is the trustworthy type? Recent escapee from Hell trying to kill you? Seems legit," the Librarian said.

"So, he didn't kill the Beast?"

"I don't know. I am just pointing out the unreliability of your source. It does seem to me that a creature able to kill a being with experience stretching back to the beginning of time, a being with thousands of years practice, fully in control of an immense power you are just starting to understand, would not be so easily dispatched by a kid swinging a sword like a baseball bat."

"So, what you're saying is that either Rath did kill him and I just got lucky, or Rath lied and the thing that did kill my predecessor is still out there?"

"Yes," said the Librarian, "and I wouldn't count on the idea that Rath did it. It seems the less likely of the two."

Christopher leaned back into the soft chair and rubbed his eyes. He suddenly felt very tired. He needed a moment to assimilate this new threat. Up until now he only had to worry about his prey and some mysterious group of dark souls that called themselves the Alliance. He still had very little information on them besides their name. Now he had to start looking over his shoulder for a powerful, rogue dark soul that might come after him?

Not for the first time, and definitely not the last, he wished he could just get rid of the Book and Weapon and go back to school where he had been safe. Where his biggest problem was getting a paper done on time or passing a test, not "which horrible monster was he going to fight to the death today?" But he had been down this road before; he knew he couldn't quit, so that left only one option.

"All the more reason I need help. I can't just rely on getting lucky with my ax-chop technique, as you put it."

"Hmm. Well, you took that realization fairly well. It's not every day you are told you might be hunted by a being that killed the world's greatest killer. There may be hope for you yet."

Christopher gave him a wane smile. "Now *that* might be the nicest thing you have ever said to me."

"Well since we've established you will probably be killed at any moment, I do take pity on you. I am not completely heartless."

Christopher's smile dropped.

"Now let's see what we can do about getting you some training."

The Librarian spun on his heels and glided off down an aisle. Christopher jumped up to follow. The Librarian turned right and then left down other rows. They wound their way deeper and deeper into the labyrinthine aisles of books and tables. The air smelled of dust and age. This place had come into existence the moment he had opened the Book, but it felt as old as a medieval castle. Christopher quickly became lost and disoriented in the maze and dark. Occasional lamps, torches or even candles stuck in a shelf or on top of a bookcase lit the way, and made the shadows around the stacks dance. Christopher made sure to keep up with the Librarian; if he lost sight of him, Christopher would never find his way back.

"The problem is your mind is too feeble," the Librarian said.

Christopher just rolled his eyes.

"It was never designed to interpret what was stored here. It is too much for it to take. It would drive you mad, but we can give it a try."

"Drive me mad? I don't know about this..."

"We will start small, that way if there is any damage it will be minor," the Librarian went on.

"Look, maybe I can just hire someone..."

"Here we are." The Librarian had stopped at a shelf and pulled a book off. Even as he grabbed the book Christopher still couldn't see his hand; the long sleeve of his robe draped over it covering his fingers. The book itself was a plain, standard leather-bound tome with no title or any markings on the outside. “This is the knowledge of Miyamoto Musashi."

"Wasn't he Japan's most famous samurai or something like that? I think I read the book he wrote. I don't remember it being quite so thick. Besides, reading books does not seem to be an efficient way of training."

"You misunderstand, this is not a copy of his book, this is a representation of his knowledge. In contains everything about him, everything he did or thought, or anything anybody thought about him. None of these books are really books in the traditional sense."

Christopher must have looked puzzled because the Librarian sighed and tried again.

"Have you seen the Matrix?"

"The movie? Yeah. I loved it," Christopher said. "The sequels sucked."

"And you remember when they plugged him into the computer and downloaded all those martial arts directly into his brain?"

"Yes. Are we going to do something like that? Because that would be awesome. I wouldn't have to spend time learning it."

"No. We can't do that because your brain isn't wired to understand this place at that level. It would blow your mind, in the bad way. That is, however, the closest way I can describe how it is supposed to happen. Your predecessor could pull what he needed when he needed it. It wasn't exactly like in that movie, but close."

Christopher was disappointed; for a moment he thought this

would be easy. He should know better by now. "So, what do we do? How do I get this knowledge?"

"A compromise, I think. Partially the old fashioned way, partially using the power of the Library. It is probably better if I just showed you."

He handed Christopher the book.

"Open it," the Librarian said.

Christopher stared at the book in his hand. It seemed normal, like some sort of fancy edition of an old classic novel. He moved it around nervously from hand to hand, feeling the cover and spine as if touching it would give him some clue as to what would happen. He didn't think it would be as simple as written words. The last mysterious book he opened turned him into damnation incarnate.

"Okay, here goes," Christopher said with one last look at the Librarian. The look was returned with cavernous darkness from under the hood. *Fucking ultimate poker player*. He opened the book.

5

Then he was standing in a field surrounded by trees. A faint breeze washed over him, carrying the scent of flowers and a hint of wood smoke. He could hear birds and other animals scurrying about in the nearby trees and brush. There must have been a stream or small river not too far away; he heard the gurgling of water washing over stone.

It was definitely not Central Park. In fact, the landscape looked different from any he had ever seen. And the air, despite the smell of burning wood, was fresher than he had ever experienced. Crisp and clean. The land around him was so full of life, he could feel it. He wanted to lie down and stretch out in the sun. That was the other thing. It was summer here, but back in New York it was the dead of winter. This couldn't be real.

He was dressed in the same t-shirt, hoodie and jeans he had been wearing in the Library and in turn in his bed back home, where he had entered the Library. Which made him wonder, was he in yet another pocket universe like the Library, or was this the same universe as the Library? It was starting to make his head hurt.

As a test he reached out with his power and tried to pull the shadows to him, trying to clothe himself in his uniform. Nothing came; he could feel the power in him, waiting, writhing, but it was as though it was not allowed to come out.

He turned slowly in a circle, trying to get some sense of where he was. His foot caught on something and when he looked down, he saw the open book at his feet. Despite the breeze its pages didn't move, nor did they seem to have any writing on them. He turned completely around and looked up.

There, almost close enough to touch, was a mountain, the air so clear it appeared massive and towered over him. It took him a moment to realize he recognized it. Mount Fuji. He had seen it in pictures.

"This is my favorite place," said a voice from behind him.

Christopher spun to see a short man in baggy black pants and what looked like a kimono with a print of trees and Mount Fuji on it. Christopher had no experience in Japanese clothes, but the clothes looked old, as though the man had stepped from some ancient painting. He was a small man, perhaps in his fifties, but he had an ageless face, he could have been seventy. He also had a white cloth over his head like a bandanna, although Christopher was sure there was a proper name for it.

The man held two large wooden sticks, one in each hand. They were long and carved into a vague katana shape; Christopher suspected they were some sort of practice sword. He tossed one at Christopher's feet.

"You are Miyamoto Musashi?" Christopher asked. He made no move to pick up the practice sword.

"In a way. I am all that he ever was, I am all his knowledge. As I understand it, I exist to teach you. This is somehow a way for you to understand, to experience."

"So you are going to train me? Show me how to fight with my Weapon?" Christopher asked.

"I am going to show you how to master yourself and to win in all battles. Now pick up your bokken," Musashi said and pointed to the wooden sword at Christopher's feet.

"Wait. Right here? Now? And how are you able to speak English?"

"Yes. Right here, right now and there are no languages here."

Musashi sprang forward, his sword whipping through the air, and struck Christopher's arm. Christopher yelped and staggered to the side, clutching his arm. The area where the sword had hit him stung and felt deeply bruise, but not broken.

"What the fuck? I'm not ready. I still have some questions. Jesus Christ that hurt."

"No time for questions. We only have a few hours today," Musashi said circling around him.

"A few hours? I can't—."

WHACK!

The bokken came down on his right thigh. Harder this time, the pain excruciating. Christopher fell down as his leg gave out. His bokken was near and he scooped it up, using it as a cane to get back to his feet.

Musashi's bokken sliced through the air and knocked Christopher's bokken out from underneath him. His leverage gone Christopher once again stumble to the ground. Despite the pain, his leg wasn't broken, and Christopher climbed once again to his feet, this time keeping the wooden sword between him and Musashi.

Musashi straightened up, coming out of his fighting stance. "That is much better. We will talk, we will wander this forest, and we shall fight. In time you will learn all I have to teach. When we are done for the day, all you need to do is close the book."

Musashi nodded to the open book lying in the field.

"Shall we start at the beginning?"

Hours later Christopher was not sure he had the energy to crawl to the book, let alone close it. He lay on the grass. He didn't have to look to know his body was covered with bruises and welts. He didn't think anything was broken, but you couldn't tell that from the pain.

He had spent the afternoon 'training' but he was pretty sure the only thing he got better at was turning black and blue. At one point they had paused in his relentless beating to eat. They walked over to a small cook fire surrounded by a camp site just inside the trees.

There were two mats by the fire to sit on while Musashi dished up rice and some sort of fish. The rice was rougher that Christopher was used to, but with more flavor. It was not processed like the grains he was accustom to eating. The fish, too, had more flavor than he expected.

"Did you catch this yourself?" Christopher asked. He had been trying to make conversation all day, but Musashi had limited himself to terse words about his stance, or how he was moving, or how he held his stick—bokken—too low or too high or too centered.

Musashi said nothing. It seemed that even on lunch break it was to be the silent treatment.

"Is the weather always like this?" Christopher tried again, half-heartedly. Then to his surprise Musashi spoke.

"You are not ready to speak," he said. "You do not have skill."

"Skill? What about questions? Shouldn't I be able to ask questions?"

Musashi made a barking sound. It took Christopher a moment to realize he was laughing.

"You don't even know what questions to ask; therefore, it is useless. Do no useless action," Musashi said, and he spoke no more during lunch.

And now Christopher lay staring at the beautiful sky, and he thought the greatest thing in the world was the breeze that drifted over him.

"You did not do very well," Musashi said.

No shit.

"But I see a way forward in you," Musashi said. "Next time you will do better."

"Next time? Next time? Fuck that. We are done. I'd rather take my chances going against a dark soul with my hands tied behind my back."

Musashi turned and walked towards the trees. "Next time try not to fall so much."

Motherfucker.

Christopher rolled over to say something to him, but he had already disappeared. Christopher spied the book about ten feet away and crawled to it. He took one last deep breath of the clean, pure air and then winced as his ribs tightened in pain around his chest. He closed the book.

And he was once again lying on the carpet in the Library. The robes of the Librarian were inches from his face. He moaned. The pain was less here, but it wasn't gone. It was as though the transition from ancient Japan back to the Library fast forwarded his healing a few days.

"Was it fun?" the Librarian asked.

"Not exactly the word I would have used for it."

"Well, maybe next time."

"Next time? He said the same thing. You don't mean, like, tomorrow?" Christopher asked.

"No, no. I was thinking there is this one Cossack from the fifteenth-century, greatest warrior of his generation, for tomorrow."

"Wait a different guy? I get a different teacher each day?" Christopher asked.

"Yes, my idea was to use the knowledge of the Library to have you trained by the greatest warriors that have ever lived. But not a different one each day, at least not after the first few days. I wanted you to sample several different styles before you commit to a plan to work with them. One teacher would never be enough. Your weapons and powers are diverse; no one mortal can show you your potential," said the Librarian.

"You sound like a personal trainer trying to sell me a training package," Christopher said. "Besides there's no way I can spend what? Five hours a day here? I don't have that kind of time, we need something faster."

"You didn't spend five hours there, at least not of real time. As I said, the Library is conforming to your mortal mind. With your predecessor, accessing the information was almost instantaneous. For you, when you experience the knowledge here, it is also instantaneous, but you have to process it at a normal rate."

"Process it? So, no time passed from when I opened the book to when I came back?"

"On my end it just looked like you opened the book a moment ago and then fell. But you do that a lot, so I wasn't concerned. I would think that if you came here once a day you could get four to six hours of training in before your body collapses."

Christopher had thought that Eris might be worried about him—he had never stayed in the library for this long—but according to the Librarian he had been here only a few minutes.

This was all very, very weird. He needed to learn, but every day with an unlimited number of teachers. Would this actually work?

"Will this even work?" Christopher asked. "I mean this is just my spirit thing, not my body. If this is all in my head, how will my body get in sync?"

"Good question, I suppose that would be more of an on-the-job part of the training. Putting into use what you learn here. Nobody ever said hunting down escaped souls from Hell would be easy."

"I'll have to think about this. It's a lot to take in," Christopher said.

"I understand. This all must be a shock to you; you've had such a simple mundane life up until this point," the Librarian said.

"Whatever," Christopher said and walked to the exit door; it had appeared at some point after he had returned from ancient Japan.

"You don't want to go to the journal room and pick up a new hunt?" the Librarian asked.

“Not tonight, I just finished one and need a night off. I'm gonna be here tomorrow anyway, right? Besides lately they have a way of finding me."

He opened the door and stepped back into the normal world.

6

Christopher returned from the Library to the lair. His little home away from home deep beneath the Bronx zoo. They had redecorated and repurposed some rooms, but it still looked like a large bomb shelter.

The bed he was in was shoved into a corner. It was in the main room so the others, either Eris/Dark Eris or Hamlin, could watch him. He was his most vulnerable when he was visiting the Library. His spirit went to that other realm, but his body stayed and was at the mercy of anybody around him.

That is why he used the lair when traveling to the Library: it was his most secure location. At least in New York. His successor had built lairs throughout the world, all of them now his, accessible by the cube room, as they called it. In that room he was able to transport, teleport really, to any of the others. He had journeyed to many other countries over the last few weeks, although he didn't leave the lairs for the most part. It was an impressive set up, but then again, his predecessor had been Satan's emissary on earth, so he had access to a lot of resources.

The lair itself, at least the New York one, was a fairly large underground complex, well hidden behind both technology and supernatural security. The direct way to access it was through a mystic door near the river that only opened for him or rather, the one bearing the Book. The main chamber was dominated by a mass of computers and wires at the center, like something out of a hacker movie. They were learning to use it, but slowly. At this point, its primary use was for video games.

It had a kitchen, guest rooms, storage and a bathroom. It was comfortable, albeit spartan. He had bought some rugs off Amazon, but it didn't compare to his home in the city. He thought of this place as his office.

Hamlin, the NYPD detective who had become, for lack of a better word, his partner in...well, whatever it is his life had become, was sitting at the computer stack now working at something. He wore the same rumpled brown suit he always wore, tie pulled loose and collar unbuttoned. He had the perpetual look of a man who had just smelled something and didn't like it at all. He was a walking cliché.

Eris sat at the desk near his bed, feet up, phone in hand, earbuds in. Probably watching a video. Despite the fact they were in a concrete lined lair, under the zoo, watching over him while he traveled to another world, it all seemed rather normal.

Hellcat was curled up on the bed. In fact, she took up most of the bed and covered his feet. She was so dark, she looked like a shadow covering the lower half of the bed. He reached down to scratch her behind the ear. She stretched her head out in appreciation, and made the quiet rumbling noise he had come to think of as purring.

Eris was the first to notice he had returned. She smiled at him and pulled out her earbuds. "Welcome back," she said. "That was quick. Did you get any advice on how to find someone to teach you?"

He could tell by her body language that it was Eris he was speaking with, not Dark Eris. For some reason her smile almost took his mind away from the remaining aches and pains he carried over from his first training session. He was still sore, but it was residual and he could already feel his body soothing the rest of it away. He was not sure what the implications were that his body could feel the pain that only his spirit had experienced.

"You could say that," Christopher said and sat on the edge of the bed. "The Librarian's idea is to have me learn from the greatest warriors that have ever lived."

"Sounds impressive," she said and by her shifting tone he thought she had switched to Dark Eris. "How's he going to pull that off?"

"He already did," Christopher said and then proceeded to tell her about the few hours he had training with Musashi or the ghost of Musashi, or whatever it was exactly. Of course, he left out the part about how badly he did and how badly he was beaten.

"So, hours passed for you while you were training, but only thirty or so minutes passed by here while we waited? How'd he pull-off that little trick?" Dark Eris asked. Christopher noticed Hamlin had turned away from the computers and was listening in.

"I don't think the Librarian *did* anything. It has to do with how I access the information in the Book. Being human, apparently, I can't take the direct route; I have to learn it the old fashioned way. Somehow it slows down my perception so I have the time to absorb it."

"Well did you learn anything?" Hamlin asked.

"Yes, well no, I mean probably not. It was only my first day."

"So, you plan on doing this again? How often?"

"I guess I'll try to go every day," Christopher said and then shuddered when he thought of the pain he was in for. "But it won't be easy."

"It never is, it's a good idea though. You need all the help you can get," Hamlin said.

"Yeah, if the help doesn't kill me," Christopher said.

Christopher stood up and stretched, the pain had faded at this point but the stretching still felt good. Hamlin had turned back to the computer and was scrolling through news articles. Hamlin wasn't much of a computer guy, so Christopher was surprised to see him pecking at the keyboard and looking intently at the screen. Christopher glanced at Dark Eris while nodding toward Hamlin. She just shrugged and pulled a beer out of the fridge.

Christopher was suddenly aware of how thirsty he was and went to join her.

"What are you up to?" Christopher asked Hamlin as he popped open the bottle.

"Hmm?" Hamlin said distractedly, and then he pulled himself away from the screen. "Have you ever heard of the Days of Chaos?"

"Yeah, I think I heard something about that. Something about some hackers or anarchists or something. Some big event they have planned?"

"Sort of. NYPD got a threat assessment alert about it. It was fairly vague. They think it's mostly a hoax, some internet urban legend, but it's widespread enough that some small fringe group might get wound up. No real terrorist threat or anything like that. Just small time," Hamlin said.

"But you're not convinced?" Christopher asked.

"I just don't know. That's why I'm here, this rig is a better set up than my work laptop. And the programs your predecessor created are so useful. It makes searching the web much easier; it can almost anticipate what I need to know.

"But yeah, I'm not completely convinced. Seems too well organized. It's not just one day, it's a series of days of worldwide chaos, whatever that means. Only the first day is posted. No cities are really named except this first one, Mexico City. Just vague threats of violence and mayhem."

"Days of Chaos seems more of an anarchist theme than a terrorist one. Maybe a major hack?"

"Well according to the internet, it won't be computer systems or at least not just computers. There is a lot of talk about bloodshed and killing the 'jail keepers of society'. The people behind it have a manifesto, it's online too. Seems to be the usual stuff about the government conspiracies— they're tracking everything, the government is behind everything bad that has ever happened."

"That does sound like anarchist or terrorist shit. We hate the American government and all that stuff," Dark Eris said.

"That's just it. It isn't just the U.S. This movement is against all government, any sort of control," Hamlin said. "But it's really just a website and a lot of posts on forums, no real evidence that they are actually going to do anything."

Christopher had finished his beer, grabbed another, and sat down in the other chair at the computer station. "Are you thinking there's any connection with, you know, my job? Or this Alliance thing? Is that why you're here talking about it?"

Weeks ago, they had found a few documents at a dark soul's house referring to some sort of group that calls itself The Alliance. Christopher was afraid some dark souls had banded together. It was hard enough to hunt them down and face them one-on-one. If they were working together, they would become an even bigger threat.

"No, nothing about this Alliance thing. I checked all the databases I could get access too, nothing. Whoever or whatever they are, they're invisible. And no, I don't have proof of any connection between the Days of Chaos and your... hunting activities, but..."

"But?" Christopher asked.

"But I just have this feeling in my gut that it's something bigger than just a handful of crazies talking big on the internet."

"And you trust your gut?"

Hamlin turned from the screen and looked Christopher in the eyes. "I always trust my gut. But it's more than that. Here, look at one of the websites."

Hamlin clicked on a link and a page appeared. It was a fairly simple page. The standard stylized picture of Guy Fawkes at the top and a long-winded post below. But at the top, above the picture was a line of symbols. They had a vaguely occult look to them, no pentagrams or other stereotypical symbols, but definitely archaic looking.

"The language of the Angels," Eris said from behind them. As Christopher looked at her she shifted to Dark Eris, "Or demons, depending on how you look at it."

"What? That's real? They have a language?" Christopher asked.

"Well, it's the original language; I don't know if it was actually created by angels or demons. Despite being a demon, I'm not that old. It is from before my time. From the time before mortals. Call it whatever you want, but the point is it was the first language."

"Is it common? I've heard of all the new-agey stuff with it, but I don't think that is authentic," said Hamlin.

Dark Eris frowned. Christopher knew she did not like talking about her past and her time in Hell in particular. "Like I said, things are cloudy about my past, especially what Hell was like. But from what I can remember you can barely even find it in Hell, not that writing is all that common there anyway. I can't even remember it, just enough to recognize the symbols."

"Can you translate this page maybe?" Hamlin asked.

Now her face screwed up in anger. "I don't know, not off the top of my head. All I can tell you is it isn't good. Something big, bad, and ancient. I'm getting a headache."

And with that she was gone. Her eyes changed and Eris was once again staring at them. "What?" she asked, a confused smile on her face. "You're looking at me like I just told you the end of the world is approaching. Oh, did *she* say something bad?"

Once again Christopher wondered how a demon and a human could live together in one mind. Sometimes they seemed to know what happened when the other was in control, other times they seem completely clueless.

"Not exactly the end of the world. At least, hopefully not." Christopher got her up to speed quickly on the ancient writing.

"Well then I'm trusting my gut more and more. If this is some ancient, mystical writing then there is a good chance it does have something to do with you and your work. I mean you working for Hell and all," said Hamlin.

"I don't work for Hell, at least not directly."

"Well you sure as hell don't work for the other guy," Hamlin said.

"So, what if this *is* somehow connected to me? What should I do?" Christopher asked.

"Still working on that part," Hamlin said.

"Where and when is the first Day of Chaos supposed to happen?" Eris asked.

"It all starts in Mexico in three days."

"Mexico? Perfect. We need a vacation."

"So, you're suggesting we go to Mexico and just hang out to see what happens?" Christopher asked.

"Yeah. Why not? I mean if something happens and a dark soul

is involved you will be there; if not, then worst case is we spend a few days relaxing in the sun, drinking margaritas. I really don't see a downside. I don't know if you guys noticed, but it's freezing out there. A few days in the sun would be good for us. Especially you, Mr. Pasty-face detective."

"Everybody is pale in New York in the winter," Hamlin said.

"Exactly. All the more reason to go."

"Fuck it, I'm in," Christopher said. "If this is nothing, like most people think, then worst-case we have some sun and fun. If this is somehow related to my new job, then I need to be there anyways. I might as well have a little fun and relax. It's not like I have anything else to do."

"That's right, you can bring the Book with you and train every day," Hamlin said.

Christopher groaned. "Thanks for reminding me. So much for a relaxing couple of days."

"So, we're really going to Mexico? Awesome! When?" Eris asked.

Christopher shrugged. "I suppose anytime we want. I'm pretty sure there's a lair in Mexico City, so the cube room can take us there."

Now it was Hamlin's turn to groan. "Why can't we just take a plane? Also, I'm not even sure I can get the time off."

"You have to get over your fear of traveling through the cube room. I've tried it over a dozen times now with no problems. And don't you have so much time off saved up they're threatening to take away your vacation if you don't actually start using it?"

"Maybe, but there's a lot of work to do. We're still guessing about these Days of Chaos. I need to be here where I can keep an eye on things."

"The action starts in Mexico, that's where shit is going down.

It's the best place to 'keep an eye on things'. No matter what happens down there we can make it back to New York instantly."

"I just don't think it's a good idea to approach this as a vacation," Hamlin said.

"So, it's settled. We go, pack, and meet back here in a couple of hours so we can head out on our," Christopher paused and nodded to Hamlin, "working vacation."

7

Juan looked up and rubbed his eyes. Despite the two large screens, the lines of code were small and starting to blur together. But he couldn't stop, no that would be no good—though he couldn't remember why—and then he was thinking about the code again, that wandering train of thought cut off. His hands flew over the keyboard, bending the systems, the networks to his will. The will of an eighteen-year-old kid. He wanted to laugh; how silly they would look when he and his team brought it all down.

Ten minutes later he was once again distracted. Sweat dripped past his glasses and down his nose. The drop ran across his lip and his focus was interrupted. He was hungry. This time he didn't just look up, he stood up and stepped away from the computer. It was hard pulling away from the PC: like a heroin addict stepping away from his stash. He must be doing so something right. He had never felt this pull before. He loved the hack, but it was never quite this compelling.

He looked around the room, trying to shake off this feeling.

The room had two other hackers, set up like he was with a PC—top of the line for all of them apparently—a desk, and a comfy chair. He hadn't been aware they were in the room. He was so into the hack that he never even registered them. Christ, he had been focused. It seemed unnatural, that kind of focus.

The room had no windows, just cold cinder block walls. And despite the AC vents in the ceiling circulating air, the room stank. It smelled like old sweat and Funyuns. He looked at the others sitting in their chairs, staring intently at their own screens. They had not stirred when he moved; they didn't talk, at least not verbally. They were in constant contact via messaging at their PCs, but they never said an actual word to each other.

Their clothes were dirty, hair greasy and uncombed. They must have been in this little room for a long time. He couldn't remember how long. He looked down at himself. He was wearing jeans and a T shirt and he could smell that they hadn't been washed in a while. How long had they been down here?

The other end of the room was a glass wall with a door and beyond that an even larger room full of servers, blinking various colored lights and humming along. He knew that these systems were the most powerful in the world. In that, the man had not lied.

He remembered the man. The man with the pitch-black glasses that looked as though they would suck up all the light when he entered a room. His slicked-back hair and expensive suit. And he remembered the words the man had told him. At least he thought he did.

They were one and the same, the man had said. They loved his fight against the injustice that declared itself justice, against all the corrupt governments and corporations that destroyed the world and the humans that populated it.

He could hack, they had said. He would have access to unlimited resources, the best equipment. He would be given the opportunity to do that which he craved the most.

Tear it down. Tear it all down.

Destroy the world of the overlord politicians. Take everything away and remake it all in their image. They loved him, they wanted him on their side in the coming battle.

He popped his neck and stretched. Everything after that was hazy. They had come here he thought—though he didn't remember it—to this safe place. He didn't remember where here was, still in Mexico? Or was it South America?

Something was not right. He needed to pee or gets some air or something. His mind was fuzzy; all he could clearly feel was that he needed a break.

There was a door at the rear of the room, opposite the glass wall. He cautiously opened it and peered out. Behind him, the others didn't look up from their screens. The room beyond the door was a small combination living room and kitchen.

The living room part had a couch, some chairs, and a stack of dusty looking magazines on the coffee table. A couple of reading lamps. The kitchen portion had all the basics including a fridge and stove top. The furniture, the cupboards, the linoleum all looked old and dirty.

He remembered it vaguely, this is where they prepared their simple meals. The table in the kitchen was also unused. Usually they just grabbed their food and went back to their computers. But he didn't remember it being this drab. There were two doors against one wall. He knew that one led to his room, really a bunkhouse he shared with the others he now recalled. The other door was to a bathroom they also shared.

There were no windows, just cold concrete walls and one final door. No, not a door, an elevator. This was where they lived for... he was not sure, but he thought it had been a long time.

There was a man in the room and Juan was slightly startled that it had taken him this long to notice. He wore khaki clothes with a black bulletproof vest. A ball cap on his head said 'Security' across the front. A patch on his shoulder said the same thing. A belt containing the usual assortment of security tools, including a holstered pistol was at his waist. Next to him an assault rifle lay against the wall.

He had been playing with his phone, but lowered it when Juan entered. The security guard nodded slowly, watching him.

Was the guard always in the room? He couldn't remember.

He nodded back and then went to use the bathroom. When he returned to the room the guard's eyes followed him intently. He was suddenly thirsty. There was bottled water in the fridge, he grabbed one and took a long drink, then glanced at the elevator.

"I," Juan started and then paused to clear his throat. His voice was raw and rough, unused. Again, he thought to himself, how long had he been here? "I need some air."

The security guard glanced at the elevator and then back at his phone. He typed briefly and then looked back at Juan. They stared at each other for almost a minute. Juan was trying to think of what else to say, but words were hard, they slid off his tongue before having a chance to form.

The guard's phone beeped. He looked down briefly and then nodded at him.

Juan pressed the elevator call button and waited. It moaned and creaked to life with a metallic screech like he had woken a giant bird. Then it was gone and the elevator ground to a halt. When the doors opened Juan expected to see a rusted-out cage, but it wasn't that bad, just a dingy metal box. He didn't remember it being so bad when he came down. Those memories were a blur. He felt it was a good sign that he remembered anything at all.

There were only two floor buttons in the elevator, the floor he was on and up. He pressed the button, the doors shut and the elevator ground its way up towards the surface. At least he thought it was the surface, that seemed right.

The doors opened to reveal a wooden structure—rickety at best, a wooden shack. The elevator itself was a metal box inside this wooden one. Light pierced through the gaps between the boards that made up the doorway and walls. It hurt his eyes and it was hot, sauna hot, like this wasn't even a shack, but an oven to cook hackers who stood there too long.

There was nothing inside the shack except for the elevator. Part of him knew the shack was just cover for the elevator. It wasn't supposed to be here and was hidden. He didn't know how he knew this, and he was beginning to suspect he wasn't supposed to.

He stepped through the doorway and into a narrow hall, also striped with streaks of sunlight through gaping slats. He tripped as he went through as though stumbling on a stone or concrete riser, but when he looked down he saw nothing, just dirt. Down the hallway was a door hanging from bent hinges.

He pushed opened the door, squinting at the intense light. It felt like the sun was resting on the earth itself, it was so bright. He wanted to let his eyes adjust, but the heat inside was too intense. He needed to get out. He stumbled out with his eyes scrunched shut.

He felt gravel and dirt grind under his feet, and as his eyes adjusted to the light he understood why. He was in the middle of nowhere. Scrub brush, rock, and dirt stretched off into the distance in all directions. The only manmade object in sight was the shack. Nothing else but desert.

He spun in a circle several times. Nothing.

Not even a dirt road. How had he gotten here? Did they fly him in? He couldn't remember.

And it was flat, no hills or mountains in the distance, just unending flat desert.

He tasted salt and while he was sweating profusely, it was tears he was tasting. He was crying. He didn't know why exactly. He was confused, scared maybe? But not sad. It was something deeper inside of him he thought, something that somehow understood a little of what was happening, and it was sad. This scared him even more.

Through shimmering heat waves and tears he saw something moving. A man, from nowhere, coming out of the distance. He hadn't been there a moment ago, and Juan had no idea where he could have possibly come from. The world tilted, and for a brief moment he was surrounded by buildings: small, squat things that looked abandoned. He thought he recognized it briefly, graffiti, corrugated metal, chipped plaster and brick. It was some sort of slum. He knew this place he thought. And he knew at some level this was the truth.

Then it was gone. Then the sun and desert were back and the buildings were gone. Even the memory of what he had seen was slowly fading. It was all sun and heat and dust. This was the new truth.

As the man drew closer Juan could see it was the same short, slim man with deep black sunglasses and slicked back hair who had recruited him.

"Juan," he said, "How goes it in the trenches? How goes the good fight?"

He had a grin from ear to ear, as though his face was splitting apart, that showed a lot of teeth.

"Um," tried Juan. His thoughts were growing murky again. Any clarity he was experiencing was slowly draining away.

"You guys getting everything you need?" The man asked as he put his arm around Juan; he had to stretch his arm out to reach his shoulder. He turned Juan back towards the shack. They slowly started walking back.

"I don't... I'm not sure why I'm here," Juan said.

"What? Why, the same reason we're all here. We want to change the world, cleanse it by fire, purify it."

"But I'm not sure I want to be here..."

"Of course you do, Juan," the man said; his words seemed to take on a serpentine quality. They snaked their way into his head, twisting and turning through his thoughts. Jumbling them up in their wake.

"We will bring down the oppressor, those who think they are better than the rest of us. Those that rule for the sake of lining their own pockets. Those that stand on the broken backs of the workers. You are here my boy, because you are a hero."

The man was right of course, part of him wanted to think it wasn't that simple, but the thought-snakes quickly jumbled that up. They were on the forefront of the revolution. His kind were leading the way into the new world. Already his mind was working on how they could leverage the systems he and his brothers had infiltrated. How they could usher in the downfall of the corrupt world government.

As they stepped into the building with its gleaming metal and glass walls, its coffee shop with the fresh baked pastries, its beautiful paintings and sculptures in the lobby and most importantly the welcoming air conditioning—Juan had no idea why he had been so hot—he grew excited to get back to his beautiful office and his PC.

The lobby was full of people and alive with hustle and bustle. They were all on the same team working together to bring down the... the...

"Corruption that is destroying the humanity in us," the man said as the elevator arrived. Juan stepped on, but the slim man held back. "We are so close Juan, the work you have done and will do is a tribute to your love of our cause. You must now go back to your desk and help lead us to victory."

"What about you? Are you not coming?"

"Alas, I don't get to do the fun, exciting stuff you guys get to. I just don't have your talents. My task is the boring one, somewhat bureaucratic it seems. I go to meet one of our benefactors. The fight costs money, at least until we throw off the yoke of capitalism, and my job is to keep it flowing."

Juan nodded vaguely, that made sense. The doors started to close and the man's hand shot out, catching one side. The door slid back open and a small piece of paper appeared in the man's hand.

"One small task for you Juan. Please send this message to the email address also on the note."

"What is it?" He took the small slip of paper. It contained a series of numbers and letters. Coordinates it looked like.

"Just a little something to add some excitement, up the stakes a little. Don't worry, it is all for the cause."

The doors closed on that grinning, toothy smile. Juan pressed the button. There was only one, which was odd, but not really important. He had to get back to his desk. There was work to do, important work and everybody in this building—no, the entire world—was counting on him to do it.

He looked down at the simple message. It seemed important, something about it, the odd request. Then he slipped it into his pocket. Important work, very important work.

8

The man smiled until the elevator door closed. Then the smile dropped, replaced by a scowl. The glamour had weakened on this one, he would have to watch that. None of the others had come out of it, this boy was special. He would have to watch him. He would have killed him outright, but he was their most talented and the man needed him. Sort of.

The man left the abandon house. He wasn't worried he'd be seen; the area around the black house was deserted. The slums were full of vermin, but not this area. The buildings here were owned by Golyat and his kind. The boy had seen a desert landscape, an extra layer of glamour wrapped around him as a safety precaution, and the man had briefly entered the glamour. Now he used a handkerchief to dab at the sweat forming on his brow as though it had been real.

It was time that was a nuisance, time lost dealing with the pawns. Then he smiled, he had a meeting to attend. It would be a fun one; he liked playing pretend.

The man opened a hole in space there in the street and

stepped into the Currents. With one step he disappeared from the world and passed through the wall that separates everything from nothing. He was surrounded by the ebb and flow of energy. He could see nothing in this place, he could feel everything. Energy and power swirled by, sending him spinning off. He was nothing at the moment, at least nothing physical, just one of many flows of energy.

He flowed into a current of energy and within seconds—although there was no such thing as time here—he was where he needed to be. He opened another door in the wall between the nothing and the something and stepped out.

He was in a room—an office bathroom to be exact—and he was alone, although he glanced under the stalls to be sure. All the better, he didn't have to explain his sudden arrival. He glanced in the mirror and took a moment to straighten his suit. His skin rippled slightly as he made some adjustments. He was not fond of this body, but it would do for now.

Outside of the bathroom was a small lobby, ornate but not ostentatious. Very neat and clean, just how the man liked it. It was not his building, of course; he was the visitor here. And that was also just how the man liked it.

The lobby was like the building: new, modern. Lots of metals with a tasteful splash of wood here and there. And it smelled new. New and fresh. The man knew it was mostly just chemicals, but he loved that smell. Too bad it would all be gone soon. A pile of rubble to be gazed upon. That thought soured him; now all he saw was what was to be, the destruction. It wouldn't be as new then.

It was also empty, the receptionist gone for the evening and all the employees for the cover business also gone, at least on this floor. The janitors would not be here for at least another couple of hours. This was as planned; it would not do for prying eyes to see who was meeting here.

The man pushed open both double doors—he liked to make an entrance—to the conference room across the lobby and strode inside. Golyat, his enormous human form taking up much of the window, turned from the view outside.

The man glanced out the window behind Golyat, but all he saw in his mind was the destruction of this city. The buildings beyond razed, bodies everywhere bloated with rot, the survivors fighting each other, the small petty wars as mankind chose to either fade away or rebuild itself, starting from the ground up.

This is what the man saw when he looked at the world.

"That was an awfully long time to take a piss," Golyat said.

"Sorry, lots of coffee. The fuel of the productive," the man said.

Golyat grunted and then turned back to the window. "Are your teams ready? Have they infiltrated all the systems?"

"Almost. And we will be all set in time for day one as planned."

"You'll forgive me Mr... Stone. While I can appreciate your confidence, too much is riding on this for me to blindly take your word. I will need details."

"But you hired me to handle the details, Mr. Smith. Building up multiple hacker groups distributed globally takes time. We are on track. The teams in Europe, Asia, the US and Africa are set up and almost in control of the necessary infrastructure. I just got back from the Mexico City installation a couple of days ago and they will be ready in two days when we start."

"And the ground teams?"

"That was much easier. Set up websites in the deep web so they think they're on to something, some real conspiracy. Spread some fake news. Rile up the bleeding snowflakes with talk of injustice and taking back the establishment. On the other side: groom the racism, feed the fear of immigrants, threaten to take their guns away. Mix in a little drugs and anti-racism and you have yourself a riot waiting to happen. Just point it at something and down it goes."

"The key is that the two groups are in sync. The protesters by themselves are a bonfire if directed correctly; coordinate that with the failure of vital infrastructure and my own... special forces...and the whole world burns."

"Our goals are the same, Mr. Smith," the man said.

Golyat grunted again. "I doubt that, Mr. Stone. You want money and material power built from the wreckage of the world. I have other goals. Goals you would never understand."

The man kept his face still, but inside he smiled. He understood Golyat. He understood him very well.

"Speaking of money," The man said. He didn't really care about the money, but he had to keep up appearances. "We will need more. Just another five million."

Golyat laughed. "Is that all? Done. I do find it odd though, that you are so concerned with money when you know it will be useless as the Days progress. We aren't talking total destruction of civilization, but extreme economic disruption is unavoidable. It will take a long time to stabilize again. Do you have your doubts? Something I should be worried about?"

But 'Mr. Stone' was thinking of total destruction.

"Not at all Mr. Smith. I have my uses for the funds, as long as they are timely. In the future to come, trade goods will be just as valuable as cash. My people and I still have a few days left to stock our warehouse. Besides, I bought some servers on credit. Dell and HP don't know the world is going to end soon.

"My only concern, and I don't even know if it is founded, is regarding this hero of the Bronx Zoo everybody is buzzing about. You had mentioned him before, but I dismissed it as urban myth until I saw the other videos. I don't know what he is, but will he be a problem?"

"No, he is nothing more than a boy with a few talents and some gimmicky special effects. I am in the process of dealing with him as we speak. Besides, he has no reason to believe that the Days of Chaos isn't just some ordinary protest. He is fed through the news like the rest of the world. And now we control the news."

The man nodded dutifully again. All the while knowing Golyat was wrong. In fact, he was counting on it. Christopher was a threat to Golyat, fortunately he could be manipulated just as easily as the big man. That's what made this game so fun.

"The end of the world," Golyat mused. "Rebirth, really. I hope for your sake your teams are ready, that the unrest is sown and will reach fever pitch at the right time. Because my people are ready, and if you fail they will just as easily deal with you."

The man tried to look properly scared, but he was thankful for the sunglasses. It was hard to fake something you have never felt. Golyat had no understanding of who he was talking to. To him, the man was just another mortal looking to make a buck and maybe end up in a position of power in Golyat's new world. And Golyat's people did not worry him at all. They weren't a threat worth acknowledging.

In the end it did not matter whether the world burned or not. All that mattered to the man was that he won. And he would win, of that he was sure. He had seen it.

9

Hamlin, Eris, and Christopher stood in the cube room in the lair. Hellcat trotted by Christopher's side. The soft blue light radiating from the carved lines on the wall gave some illumination, but it was still murky and the strange lighting made everything seem slightly off.

It was a large room; a pedestal with a cube on it and a stone frame, similar to what might be used to hold a mirror, were the only objects in it. The walls were covered with an intricate carving of a map of the world, which was in turn covered by lines connecting cities, seemingly random areas of the world. Christopher still thought it looked like a stone version of the airline map you find in the back of airline magazines.

The pedestal holding the cube was a plain narrow platform. As far as they could tell, the cube was the main catalyst to activate the door to other places. For all Christopher knew it could be the only thing needed and the room and frame were just for convenience. It the end Christopher had no idea how it worked at all.

The plan was to only be in Mexico City for a few days then

after confirming there was nothing mysterious about these Days of Chaos, enjoy the beach for the long weekend before heading back. It was December and even the resort areas would be a little bit chillier than normal, but anything would beat New York in winter.

They had all brought bags, one each, except for Eris. She was carrying two, but Christopher wasn't sure if she needed extra stuff or if it counted as one for each Eris. All he knew was that he wasn't going to say anything. Hamlin had also brought a bird.

"Really? Were you a miner in a previous life?" Eris asked.

Hamlin held up the small cage. "I'm not about to step through any magic door without checking it first. I'm the only, you know, normal human in this group. Taking risks like this might be cool for you supernatural folks, but I ain't taking any chances."

"What are you gonna do with the bird after?" Christopher asked.

"I'm gonna let it go. I made sure at the pet store that it was a species native to Mexico. I may be an asshole sometimes, but I ain't that cruel."

Christopher shrugged. "Let's get started."

He grabbed the smooth cube by the top and felt the Hellpower inside of him reach out to it. Instantly the room darkened and seem to come alive with the hum of power. On the wall, the path from New York to Mexico City started to glow brighter. Christopher released the cube and it began to spin, floating into the air and jerking in random directions before pausing in the middle. The floating crystal began to glow with an internal light. The darkness within the stone picture frame started to move as though black liquid was rippling across the surface of a mirror.

"We'll do the bird thing. You guys will have to go first. It closes right after me," Christopher said.

Hamlin held the bird cage out on the end of a mop handle he had borrowed from a zoo janitor's closet. Carefully, he let it pass through the shimmering surface. With a squawk the bird went through. Hamlin held it there for moment and then pulled it back.

The bird was unharmed, although it did flutter about in irritation. It squawked a few more times to make sure they knew how pissed it was before finally calming down.

"Well, that's that. Seems like it's okay for non-employees of hell to travel by cube," Christopher said. "Who goes first?"

Brushing up against him with a smile that let him know who was in charge, Dark Eris grabbed her bags and stepped through the portal as though she had done it a thousand times.

"Well, I can't let the girl show me up. There better be one hell of a strong margarita waiting for me on the other side," Hamlin said then picked up his bag and stepped through, not quite as confidently as Dark Eris.

The others safely through, Christopher picked up his bag and nodded to Hellcat. She padded up to his side. He scratched her head and together they stepped through.

The room on the other side looked the same. Carved in the cement above the door was the word Mexico.

"Anybody dead?" asked Christopher.

"Yeah, yeah. I got it. It worked," said Hamlin.

"Well let's see where we are exactly," Christopher opened the door. The room beyond was similar to the one they had just left, but about half the size. There was a small computer station, a kitchen, and a few other doors that probably led to bedrooms and a bathroom. The air was stale and old-smelling, but not as bad as it would be if it had been closed up for a few years. There must have been some sort of ventilation. The appliances and PC were only a few years old.

"He must have maintained this one," Hamlin said. He blew the dust off the monitor. "Somewhat."

"We can boot up the PC and see if he has the same security set up. Might give us an idea where we are when we climb out of the lair," Christopher suggested.

"Come on. Let's just get out of here. I need a drink even if we're not on the beach," Dark Eris said. "You can handle whatever is out there."

She said the last with a wink. He didn't like when she acted this way. It seemed fake, teasing for the sake of teasing. Or like an act she could fall back on when she was nervous, although it was hard to think of Dark Eris as the nervous type. All the same, a part of Christopher didn't want to disappoint her. Maybe they should just head out.

"Let's take this one step at a time," Hamlin said, rescuing Christopher. Christopher shook it off, it was disconcerting that he was so different when he was around her.

It turned out they were below the airport. The security cameras, accessible via the computer station, showed people moving up and down terminals to gate after gate. The Mexican version of the TSA were stationed throughout.

"Well, it's impressive that the Beast could maintain this lair right under the nose of airport security," Hamlin said.

"Honestly, I'm impressed that he could maintain this at all. I mean if any more of the lairs are like this, with this kind of tech set up, it would be like maintaining a corporate IT department. I've never run one, but it is obvious he had to have help of some sort," Christopher said.

"Maybe it's in that stack of paperwork back at the Bronx lair you never go through," Eris said. "Just like the accountant you never visit, or the lawyers, or any of the other professionals set up to manage your vast inheritance."

"Yeah, but it's so boring."

"Children, children," Hamlin interrupted. "Let's at least wait until we are out in the fresh air before the fighting begins. It looks like the coast is clear, or at least we know what we are walking into. We should probably get to the surface."

It turns out that was quicker than they had thought. The main door out was not really a door, more of a doorway that looked like it had been bricked up with cinder blocks. Like the door in the other lair, when they touched it, one by one, they found themselves in a service tunnel. On this side there was no door, just the cinder block wall.

Christopher reached out with his power sniffing at the air. Again, like the hidden entrance to the Bronx zoo lair, he could feel the presence of the doorway. He would always be able to find it. He was certain that if he were to hold the Book close to the door, it would turn into a similar key and allow them access.

"Fade," he commanded Hellcat. With a low rumbling noise in her throat she dissolved into the shadows. He knew she would be near when he called, but it wouldn't do to walk through the airport with a huge black panther by his side.

The service tunnel went on in a straight line for a few hundred feet, and he suspected the lair itself was somewhere under the tarmac. The tunnel sloped up slightly, and eventually they could hear the noise of planes moving past overhead. After a few twists and turns they found themselves at an exit from the tunnel system near a public restroom. They were in the terminal just beyond security and customs.

"Well, that makes things much easier. No awkward questions," Hamlin said.

They had brought their passports of course. Eris didn't have a real one, but between Hamlin's street connections and Christopher's money, they had gotten her the best forgery money could buy.

They made their way out of the airport as quickly as they could. It was the one place they would be stopped and questioned.

But they played the part of tourists as best they could. Once outside they found a taxi.

"Where to sir?" the driver asked as they got in the back seat. Hamlin took the front.

"The Four Seasons Hotel," Christopher responded when Hamlin didn't. He had booked them the nicest place he could think of; it was supposed to be a vacation after all. He noticed Hamlin looking back at him with raised eyebrow. Dark Eris was looking at him with a smirk on her face. "What? I told you they would probably speak English. They get a lot of tourists."

"What was that sir?" the driver asked.

"My friends here were surprised that you speak English so well, no accent that I can tell."

Now it was the drivers turn to look at him oddly.

"Kid, you weren't speaking English when you talked to our driver. It sounded like fluent Spanish to me. But what do I know, I'm just a stupid gringo."

"Ah yes, gringo. Now that I understand," said the driver with a laugh.

It was true. It felt so natural that he didn't even know he was doing it. Now that he realized what was going on, it was obvious; he had been speaking Spanish. He switched to it now.

"You can understand me? I'm, ah, testing my Spanish."

"Yes sir, not even an accent. Sounds like you were born here."

"Now that is a nice gift, maybe your most practical one," Hamlin said.

Dark Eris' hand found his thigh. "I think the Latin languages are sexy."

Any other time Christopher would have responded to that hand, but he was engrossed in his new ability. "I can speak Russian," he said in Russian. "And apparently, I speak Japanese well, and I can speak Korean without much trouble." He said in their respective languages.

Language after language came out of his mouth. Every one he could think of he realized he could speak and understand. The driver was giving him an increasingly more worried look.

"Quick call out some languages," Christopher said.

"Swahili," Hamlin said.

"Bostonian," Dark Eris said, and was rewarded with a chuckle from Hamlin.

Christopher looked out the window and described things speaking in every language imaginable. He was pretty sure it annoyed the hell out of everyone else in the car.

"This wasn't exactly what I had in mind when I imagined a work vacation," Eris said as the cab left the airport, and Christopher had to agree with her. It was the middle of winter, but he hoped the coastal area would be a little warmer. It was cooler here in the city.

This area of Mexico's capital was dirty and run down, the slums butting up against the airport. He knew from the little reading he had done that the true slums were on the other side and were considered one of the world's biggest.

The conditions got better as they drove into the city. Soon he had to admit it looked like any other big city. He was not sure what he expected to see. He knew there wouldn't be taco stands on every corner—he wasn't that sheltered—but he supposed he expected more of an old world feel. Mexico City was a modern city. But not entirely. The deeper he looked the more was revealed. There was plenty of old world blended with modern skyscrapers. Towering glass and steel architecture blended in with old traditions. There were more colors too, it made the place seem alive. He wouldn't say it was better than his own New York, but he thought he could learn to like it here.

But then there were the crowds, seemingly out of place. This impression was confirmed by the swearing of the driver; as they drove through the city center it became clear why there were so many people. Protests. A mass of people blocked streets and slowed traffic to a crawl. It did not appear to be an out of hand riot, but it was a large group.

"These damn protests, always fucking up the traffic," the driver said.

"Does this happen a lot?" Hamlin asked.

"This, no not a lot. But I think some people are all fired up about the government in general. Everybody has a different complaint, and it appears that all this anger is bubbling up around the same time. An unpleasant coincidence. Sure makes my life hard."

While the driver spoke a combination of broken English—apparently he spoke it well enough to communicate with tourists—and Spanish. Christopher translated when necessary.

"Coincidence or organized?" Hamlin asked. "I have seen protests and riots up close. As a beat cop I had to be right in the thick of things a few times. This doesn't look right to me."

He was looking out of the window and pointed to a group. "See that group there?" Many people were standing around as though not sure they should be there, while a handful of people dressed in dark clothes and hooded sweatshirts, some wearing bandanas to cover their faces, walked amongst them yelling out slogans and swinging signs. "It looks like some confused individuals wandering about with a handful of fanatics trying to get them all riled up."

"So, you think this whole thing, all these people are fake?" Christopher asked.

"No, I'm not saying these protesters don't have a gripe against the government. I'm just saying that this gathering seems to be...

facilitated. And my guess is the group facilitating it wouldn't care if it turned into a full-scale riot."

"You think there's a connection with this Days of Chaos thing? Maybe they *are* trying to create riots around the world?"

"It would kind of fit with the MO of an online activist presence. The question is how good are they at creating riots? Could be mostly talk. I mean, I'm not saying the riots can't turn bloody, but seems pretty tame in the grand scheme of things. It's not like the world hasn't seen its fair share of riots."

"Thank fucking god," Christopher said and sank back into his seat.

"Well, riots are no laughing matter; I mean, there is often violence and tons of damage..." Hamlin started.

"No, No. I know what can happen, and I'm not happy about it or the violence that might come. But it is sounding more and more like this is a civil, mundane matter. No need for a sword wielding, soul-damning guy with barely a clue about what's going on. Maybe this can turn into a real vacation."

"Maybe," Hamlin said, but didn't sound convinced. "Let's keep our eyes open just in case."

10

The Collector stood in the shadows of the cell block common room. It was night in the prison and the lights were low, not off—it was a prison—but low, leaving plenty of dark places for him to do his work. It smelled in this place. Dank and musky like mold gone unchecked. Harsh unpleasant scents of old sweat mingled with the smell of unflushed toilets. He could smell fear beneath the unwashed bodies as well as anger...no, hatred. That was good, it made him smile.

But most of all he could smell the madness driving that hate. It was no normal prison the Collector had chosen. It was a prison for the insane, the criminals so twisted the deepest, darkest Mexican prison was not right for them. You had to be a special type of mad to make it here, a madness he could cultivate.

Insanity, anger, hatred, suffering. It was the perfect breeding ground for evil. Fertile ground and he had the seeds. They were inside of him, his collection of seeds. He loved the way they felt, he loved the power and strength they gave him. Golyat had wanted him to give his collection away, his beautiful demon seeds. He would never do that, they were a part of him now.

But he would plant them. Temporarily. Here he could plant them and they would flourish. They would serve his and Golyat's bidding that way. They would be his army; every revolution needs an army after all. Then, when they were done, he would discard the shells they had grown into and bring them once again inside him, where they belonged.

It was hot in here, as though the concrete building absorbed all the heat during the day so there was no respite in cool night air. Outside might be perfect right now, but inside it still felt like a sauna. He did not want to be here during the day. Luckily, he wouldn't have to be. His task was short. He could be long gone before morning.

There were cameras, but one of his collection had taken care of that for him. It had a gift with electronics, a knack for making them do what it wanted, and it wanted whatever he wanted. There were guards, of course, across the expanse of the common room in their own little room with large glass windows. They would need to be dispatched.

The Collector raised his hand, palm up, and a glowing point of energy appeared on it. He tossed it like a ball a few feet in front of him, toward the guard.

As it sailed through the air it changed. The small dot of light expanded, becoming a large ball of power. Then it shifted, elongated, growing easily to the size of a large man. The mass changed again, becoming recognizable as some sort of man-shaped beast. It was well over six feet tall, but hunched over as though the weight of its heavily muscled shoulders and back overpowered its spine. It was hairless, its skin rough like it had been grown from trees and stone.

Powerful legs formed, coalescing as it ran. In less than a

second it was at the guard booth. There was a moment when the guards looked up and saw the thing, fist pulled back to punch through the glass. But there was no time to react, no time to process what they were seeing before it roared and smashed its fist through the heavily reinforced window.

The glass exploded inward, and the guards raised their hands to protect themselves from the flying shards; they didn't see the demon in those final moments. They didn't see its slobbering mouth full of razor teeth. They didn't see the deep hatred and anger radiating from its searing eyes. They did hear the bone-chilling roar just before its clawed hands grabbed them and pulled them toward its massive mouth.

The Collector liked to think that, although it was fast, they had time to feel the pain before the demon ripped them apart. This thought made him smile.

The inmates were up and at the doors. The noise of the crashing glass and destruction had awakened them. Those that were sane enough to show interest stood at their doors, some wearing pajamas, some underwear, some even nude. Still half asleep, some stared in shock, others cheered, and others screamed words at nobody. Some grabbed the bars and rattled them. One man started to take wild runs at his cell door, slamming his face into the bars each time; soon blood dripped from his nose

The one closest to The Collector pointed and giggled. "I told you so," said the insane man. "I told you they existed."

He was a little man with a short beard and longish wild hair. He wore some sort of pajamas, dingy with grime and sweat stains. His eyes darted about as though he was having trouble focusing on any one thing.

"This one seems like a good place to start," The Collector mumbled. He raised his hand again and another glowing ball appeared in his palm. This one he blew on gently. It drifted lightly through the air, like a bubble, as the screams of the dying guards faded away and cacophony of sounds from the mad humans around him grew.

The giggling mad man noticed the bubble of power and smiled. He turned from the spraying blood of the guards being torn apart to watch it approach. He smiled at its beauty. The ball floated at him and he stepped back letting it into his cell.

Once past the bars, however, it kept moving toward him. The smile slowly left the little man's face. The ball moved a little faster, and the little man backed away until he was up against his bunk.

"No, no, not me! There are others, go after them," he said nodding to the other inmates who were still hooting and hollering at the show of death and bloodshed they had just witnessed. But the bubble drifted closer. The man's eyes widened in fear, the whites of his eyes big and shiny with tears.

"No, no! NO!" he repeated, each word getting louder, more hysterical. Then the bubble floated into his chest. He let out one long, final scream and the bubble slowly sank into him. The scream was like no other, the scream of an ending.

Even the other inmates, across the spectrum of sanity, paused in their bloody cheers. The demons finished their grim task and then paused, awaiting instruction. Slowly, as though just discovering the sound came from one of their own, the prisoners turned toward that final screech.

As the bubble disappeared into his chest, the scream stopped. His eyes rolled back into his head and blood drained from his face. He staggered, his body tried to keep him upright, but only for a moment. He fell to the ground, his vibrating as though in a seizure, but impossibly fast. He became a blur as his body heaved up and down, as though something inside was trying to get out. Then it all stopped and he lay there on the ground.

His skin was pale, almost translucent, with black veins

threaded through his skin. His eyes were sunken as though he had not slept in a year. His chest moved up and down slowly, and a rattling sound came from deep within his chest.

The ward had become quiet. Those that could see inside the cell watched the transformation; others, who couldn't see in, watched the man with the bubbles as he looked on, a grin on his face.

With a snarl, the possessed man was off the floor, slamming into the bars of his cell. He grabbed hold of the bars with fingers, longer than before, elongated and thin. He rattled the metal bars, shaking them back and forth, pulling and pounding into them. His face, though still recognizably human, had become bestial. His mouth wider, more wolfen, and lined with sharp teeth. A large red tongue glistening with a yellow puss-like saliva lolled out of its mouth, drool dripping to the floor.

It still held madness in its eyes, but there was something more: something dark, angry, and ready to destroy. It was the demon inside. The seed had taken hold. Demons could exist in the mortal world without a host of course—the guards on this ward had experienced that—but not indefinitely and not without expending extra energy to hold their essence together. To create an army, you needed fleshy hosts—raw meat and fuel.

The creature howled and pulled at the bars. They bent and twisted under its hands.

"Shhh," said the Collector. "You will be out soon enough. You will all be out soon enough."

The creature stopped howling immediately and hung onto the twisted bars, panting heavily. It waited for instructions from the Collector.

The Collector raised his hands palms up. Bubbles of power formed on his hands and floated away as though on a gentle breeze. They poured from his palms like a bubble machine, bright beautiful colors, floating throughout the ward.

Some of the inmates, those least in control of their faculties, giggled at the colorful show. But even they stopped as bubbles drifted closer. The floating globes of power slowly spread out, each one narrowing in on a target. Soon, the bubbles entered cells.

Then the screams began.

At first just screams and yell of panic, then of terror, then they turned to cries of pain. One by one what had happened to the first prisoner was repeated.

The Collector walked the ward smiling, laughing at the antics of his little seeds. They clawed at the bars that held them in, or shredded their mattresses. Each was transformed, but each was different, beautiful in its own way.

When all the bubbles had found their hosts, when all the howls and yelling had reached their peak, the Collector looked to the demon in the walls. The gremlins that did the tech work. "Open it all up," he said.

In moments all the doors slid open with a rattle and a bang. The horde piled out; a wave of half-human, half-beast creatures flowed from the cells, swirling about the Collector. He spread his arms, laughing loudly. They swarmed about him in a frenzy, but did not harm him. They never would. They were part of his collection after all.

The doors to the ward slid open and the Collector pointed towards them. "Time to go children, time to remake the world. And don't worry. There are plenty of other prisoners to play with along the way."

The Collector smiled as they almost danced their way out of the ward.

11

"He's here," said the soul shaper as she burst into the dining room.

Golyat looked up from the paper he was reading. The New York Times, not one of these Mexican rags. He had it brought to him from the local market. The latest news was important now, to gauge the unrest, the fire they were stoking. Yes, he did get most of his news from online, but there was something satisfying about holding real paper. Or maybe he was just old-fashioned. He could remember a time when paper was as valuable as gold.

She stared at him across the large dining table. Everything was large in this house, this hacienda. Golyat hated small places. He tolerated cars, but only for short periods. He only flew in private jets so he would have room, space around him.

That is why he had purchased this hacienda in the Polanco district of Mexico City. It was one of the largest single homes in the city, filling the entire city block. Soaring ceilings, large double doors throughout, classic regional architecture. Beautiful and opulent, just the way Golyat liked it.

The table stretched out before him could easily seat twenty. The chandelier above, the furniture along the side of the room were all ornate enough to boarder on ostentatious. Three plates, empty except for the scraps of his breakfast, sat on the table in front of him. Moments before they had been filled with eggs, bacon, and all manner of other breakfast food. He was a large man with a large appetite, he ate about five times the average human. The chair he sat it was also large, custom-made and big enough to fit two normal men.

Although it was early, he was already wearing a suit, dressed for the day. His suits were his pride and joy, custom tailored for him by the world's best tailors. He had stashed a large cache of them underground for his use after the end of the world. He will be the best-dressed person during the apocalypse.

"Grace, my girl, how many times must I tell you to knock before bursting in like that?"

Grace was the witch and soul shaper he had claimed from Anabelle after she failed to dispatch the new Hunter of Lost Souls. Besides that failure, she had violated the trust and rules of the Alliance by using their resources without permission. Although even Golyat would admit 'trust and rules' were a stretch.

Grace was a young girl with talent well beyond her age. She was fourteen, and when he had inherited her she had been mostly dirt and bruises: a weak and mousy child, afraid of everything. She had suffered for a long time with Annabelle; the woman had viewed her like a garden tool: use it as much as possible and when it breaks, throw it away and get a new one. In truth, she was a tool to Golyat as well, but like any tool, if you take care of it—clean it up, keep it well maintained—it can last a long time. Only when you are done with your project do you throw it away.

He had cleaned her up, given her clothes—she wore jeans and a t-shirt for the moment, but she had a whole wardrobe of beautiful things—fed her well, and she blossomed. Both in beauty and in power. She had blond hair, no longer brown from caked-in dirt as it was when he had first rescued her. Her pale skin held just a hint of color, not the pasty dullness of malnutrition and having been kept in a dark basement. Her eyes were still meek and fearful, he had seen to that, but they also now held an edge to them as though she was starting to see a glimmer of her power and what she could do with it.

Her control was becoming better; soon she would be able to manipulate the shard of the Hunter's soul they had taken from him. Then the Hunter himself would be Golyat's tool. One he could be less gentle with and still last a million lifetimes.

"I'm sorry sir...I didn't mean to... I'm..." Grace stammered, suddenly that fearful girl she had been.

"Steady girl. I will not beat you this time, but you must remember these things."

She nodded her head, visibly relieved. He did not beat her as much as Anabelle and he didn't usually treat her as dirt, but when he did beat her, she never forgot the lesson.

"I'm sorry, I just thought you should know. He's here."

"Who, my girl?" Although as he asked, Golyat already thought he knew the answer.

"The Hunter sir," she said quietly. Grace was across the room from him, but she winced as she said it, ready for him to strike out of anger. He held back when he did hit her—he would kill her with one strike otherwise—but the blows were devastating nonetheless, leaving her broken for days at a time.

"Here? In Mexico?" He asked.

She nodded. "Here in Mexico City."

"You have felt this?"

Again, she nodded, eyes downcast. "Yes. I had been feeling

something odd all night. This morning I touched the shard of his soul as I practiced. That's when I knew he was nearby."

Golyat stood, the chair creaked in relief as his massive bulk lifted off of it. "How could that be? There's no way he could know."

He stood up and walked to the window overlooking part of the city. He stared intently as though he might be able to spot the boy. "How did this happen?" It was possible that the new Hunter had resources he was unaware of, but unlikely. More likely the boy picked up a clue or was directly told by a traitor in the Alliance. That last thought disturbed him the most.

"I don't know how he found out, Mr. Golyat, but he's here now. I can feel it when I touch the shard of his soul. It calls to him although he might not know it. He might even be drawn to it."

"It can't be coincidence, girl. Nobody comes to Mexico City in winter for a vacation. Most likely we are betrayed. I will have my people look for him. In the morning we leave for the ruins, the work there is almost done." He looked at Grace, as though he would smile, but he didn't. He never smiled. "You have done well, girl. Now go and practice more with the shard. It doesn't matter that he is here, he is still a boy. He would have tried to fight us at some point anyway. And now we have a secret weapon."

"What is that, Mr. Golyat?"

He approached her slowly until he towered over her by several feet. He could see the fear in her eyes. "Why you, my dear, of course. If he somehow manages to defeat all that we have for him, then you will be the final act. You will make him ours. But first let's take the opportunity to send him an appetizer. I'll have my people start at the nicer hotels; he has money now and like any kid, I bet he's itching to use it."

12

Christopher was on his third margarita, top shelf tequila. Why not, he reasoned; he was loaded. Maybe it was his fourth, he had lost count. But he deserved it. Only a few hours ago he had gone through his second training session at the Library.

This time the session had been with a charming Cossack who didn't try to hide his joy in beating Christopher. Musashi had at least tried to keep from laughing at him.

This time there was no forest. Christopher had found himself in the steppes—eastern Russia, probably. The cold air, once again more vibrant than reality, cut into his skin like daggers of ice.

A man, wearing red baggy trousers, a heavy brown shirt, and thick vest, stepped from nowhere it seemed. He had a thick mustache and several days' growth of beard on his cheeks and chin. He carried two curved swords. He looked pissed.

"You know what this is, what we do?" the man asked.

"Yes. I mean, I've done this once before."

"Good, then we begin."

He tossed one of the sheathed swords to Christopher. Caught

by surprise, he wasn't fast enough and fumbled the catch, dropping it in the most spectacular way possible.

"This will be a long day," the man said. "Now pick it up."

He lifted his blade as though to strike. Christopher snatched the blade off the ground and clumsily pulled it from its sheath. "Wait! We are using real swords? Shouldn't we use practice ones?"

The man hesitated as though confused. "Why? You cannot die here."

"Yes, but I'll still feel it if you cut my arm off."

"But pain is good; it is the best teacher. You are lucky to learn in such a way." The man raised his sword again to strike.

"Wait!" Christopher frantically thought of something to stall him. He wasn't ready for live blade practice. "I don't even know your name?"

"True. I am Ivan Platov, and I will cut you a lot today, but you will be stronger for it."

Now, sitting in the hotel bar, still feeling all the cuts and bruises slowly fade away, he wasn't sure he was any stronger.

"Might want to go easy on those margaritas; technically the vacation part of this trip hasn't even started yet," Eris said. She was nursing her own margarita, and appeared to be better restrained, it was only her second.

They sat in the hotel restaurant on the top floor of the building. Large windows gave amazing views of the city below. It had recently been remodeled and had a modern, straight-line feel too it. Spanish music quietly played in the background. The low murmuring of the other patrons and the occasional clink of plates from the kitchen added to the atmosphere.

The food, too, smelled amazing when Christopher forced himself to focus on it. Though, when he didn't focus, he could smell more than the food in the kitchen; he opened himself up to smelling the corruption of the souls around him. And that scent was not pleasant. He had gotten better at switching that skill off when he didn't need it. But still, all it took was a stray thought about the people around him or a good sniff and then it was there. He could smell the slick oily scent of the man next to him who had stolen millions from his clients to fund his sex tourism to countries where his unique desires were catered to. Christopher didn't want to dive too deeply into that. Or the odor coming off the soul of a woman who killed her first child out of frustration and framed her first husband for the crime. He shut these things out as much as possible; to not do so would drive him mad.

Of course, not all of the patrons had such a stench around them. Most were just average, a blend of good and bad, good choices and wrong ones. For the average person Christopher would have to look deep into the shifting pattern of their soul to read anything about their sins.

Then there were the good. The innocent child sitting with her parents was fresh and pure, with only the hint of a stain on her soul. Probably some minor transgression, not yet strong enough to corrupt her scent.

He had once told Hamlin that this ability he had to see and smell the weight of a person's soul was like spending life walking through a beautiful flower garden fertilized with shit.

Christopher looked at his cell phone for the time. "Where's Hamlin? I thought he would be joining us."

He had gotten them each their own suite on the same floor as his, best they had available. When they had come down, Hamlin had said he would be right behind them.

Eris shrugged, "I don't know, but I think we're doing great by ourselves," she said with a faint smile on her lips. "Where's Hellcat?"

"Upstairs sleeping on the bed. I told her to fade if housekeeping came."

Eris laughed, "That would be awesome. Can you imagine the maid walking in and seeing a giant panther on the bed?"

"Yeah, it would be horrible. They'd probably make me pay a pet deposit or something."

This got another laugh out of Eris and he joined in, finally starting to feel the stress of the day slip away. It had been nice, just talking as though they were normal people. They talked about the simple stuff: how cool the hotel was, what they thought about the city. That slid into discussion of the future, hopes and dreams. The normal stuff you talk about with friends. It was hard though, Eris' lack of memory made every subject somewhat tricky for her; with no history to fall back on, she could only give her thoughts in the moment. Sometimes she struggled visibly and Christopher's heart went out to her. They couldn't avoid the dark cloud over them. He had to say something.

"Look, I know that I haven't been really attentive to your... problem. I mean I know I'm supposed to be helping you and Dark Eris separate, or de-possess, whatever you want to call it," Christopher started.

"It's okay Chris, we've been really busy, with, you know, hunting down bad guys and saving people and all that."

"Yeah but it must be hard, two people trapped in the same body."

"It is," she said looking down at her hands, "but it's hard to describe. I don't want to say we're getting used to it, but it is getting easier I guess. I don't know, I told you I don't understand it exactly. Sometimes..."

Despite the dimly lit restaurant, Christopher could see the transformation as Eris was replaced by Dark Eris. The only physical changed was the darkening of her eyes, but it was the shift in body language that really gave it away.

"...It's like we're sisters," Dark Eris finished. She tossed back the margarita, risky considering the potential brain freeze. "Enough of this sweet stuff, I need something harder." She winked at him.

"Sisters?" That took Christopher by surprise. "I thought you couldn't wait to be rid of each other?"

"Oh, I still think she wants to be separated; me too, although I am a little less enthusiastic since I would just end up back in Hell. But I think it's safe to say we are getting somewhat used to each other. Not perfectly, but then again sisters fight. We're beginning to understand each other a little more."

"You would have to return to Hell?" He wasn't sure how he felt about that. It might be her rightful place and they had only been together a short time, but he thought he would miss her if she wasn't part of the team.

"Yes, I'd have no choice. Demons don't exist long in the mortal world without possessing a body. We eventually lose our hold on the world and sink into Hell."

"Is that the only reason you want to stay?"

She raised an amused eyebrow at him and seemed like she was about to say something sarcastic when she paused. Her smile dropped and suddenly she looked serious or maybe concerned.

"No, there is something more. At first, we thought this was some sort of dumb luck, some mystic occurrence that just decided to fuck with us. I mean, we had no idea how it happened, no one to ask, no help except I remembered you, or the existence of your office at least. I could remember that, I had no idea it was you, of course; I was expecting the Beast, but there you were."

"And I'm no help."

"So far," Eris said, she had switched back and a smile had returned to her face, "But I have faith in you."

"She was telling me that something had changed in your um... condition. She said at first you thought this was just dumb luck?"

"Maybe. Yes, there's something different. We don't think it's dumb luck anymore. It is so hard to talk about. We are starting to feel like we have a purpose."

"A purpose? Like what?"

"I don't know. I told, you it's so hard to describe and so confusing."

She suddenly looked so sad he wanted to reach out to her. He settled for placing his hand on top of hers. As soon as they touched she looked at him and the sadness seemed to disappear.

"The only thing I do know is that I...we...like being with you. Just like this, here and now, just talking."

Christopher was stunned by the admission. He stuttered, not sure what to say, but before he had a chance to get something out it was too late.

"Am I interrupting anything?" Hamlin asked with a glance at their touching hands.

For some reason this made them both yank their hands back as if burned. "No, no, we were just waiting for you."

"Good because I'm starving. Sitting around all day staring at a laptop is exhausting."

"Did you figure anything out? Any ideas about what's going to happen?"

"No, but various protesting has picked up all around the world. The internet, social networking thingies and all that are all going crazy. The more I read it the more I think it's somehow artificial. I mean some of it just seems so contrived, so fake."

"You don't spend much time online, do you?" Christopher asked. "What you just said is the definition of the internet."

"Yeah, yeah. I know, but I just got this gut feeling. I mean it's like every activist group for every cause decided to protest at the same time. I read a couple of articles that the groups themselves don't really understand what exactly they are protesting."

"Well I guess we'll be here if something does happen, but I

really think it will just be some malware and the typical protest we've been seeing."

"And the cryptic ancient writing on the website?" Eris asked.

"Now that does seem strange, but maybe they just found the writing somewhere and thought it would be cool. Make it look more ominous or something. Either way I need to use the bathroom." Christopher pushed back his chair and stood. The room wavered a little, the alcohol was catching up to him.

"You okay kid?" Hamlin asked.

"Yeah, just feel'n it a little, but hey, it's a vacation."

"Not yet it ain't. Take it easy on the liquor."

"Okay dad," Christopher said and instantly wished he hadn't.

"Listen Chris..." Hamlin started.

"I got to piss," Christopher said and stepped away from the table. He was a little unsteady as he made his way through the tables to the side of the restaurant where the bathroom hallway was. Next to him large floor to ceiling windows displayed the city lit up at night. It was a beautiful view.

Christopher turned away from the window and was about to enter the hallway leading to the bathroom when he saw a man staring at him from near the kitchen door. It was the maître d'. He held a cell phone to his ear and his eyes did not leave Christopher. He couldn't make out what the maître d' was saying, but from the look on his face it couldn't be good. Did he miss a dress code? He knew he should have brought a jacket.

Then he smelled it, the stench of evil rolled over him and he could see the man's soul. There was a gray cloud around him, like the average person. But this one had a black core that shot tendrils of darkness throughout the cloud like a spider web. It reminded him a little of what he saw when he had looked at Eris' aura, but this was different. Whatever darkness was inside of this man had complete control over him. He was possessed, and Christopher could see the possessor only cared about one thing. Killing.

The maître d', still staring at him, put his phone in his pocket and started running straight at him. Not like a casual jogger: no, this was more like sprinter. He was instantly running at full speed. Whether it was the alcohol or just the sight of a waiter suddenly running at him, he was caught off guard and his reaction was slow. Like a linebacker with a clear shot at the quarterback, the man charged at him. Before Christopher's brain could figure out a response, the man was on him.

He slammed into Christopher. The impact was powerful and he staggered back. Even in his slightly inebriated state, no mortal man would have been able to send him flying back so easily. Christopher needed no other confirmation that this was no mortal man.

Up close it was obvious. His human features were twisting, shaping themselves into some hideous parody of a human face. The man's eyes were bloodshot and laced with black lines, his jaw was a great square thing, lined with also square, but no doubt sharp, teeth. Drool, yellow like milky puss, dribbled up through his bared teeth. But most of this was lost on Christopher as the glass exploded outward behind him and he sailed out into the night air with the maître d' attached.

He acted on his new instincts, reaching out to the shadows nearby. He pulled the darkness close as he fell, forming his hooded jacket in shifting shades of gray and black.

The demon clawed at him, nails digging gashes into his chest as it tried to hold on to his shadow clothes and the natural shirt underneath it. Its oversized square jaw opened to bite his face off. Christopher brought up his hands in time, grasping the thing's throat and pushing back its snapping jaw. Its teeth came together with a loud crack, like the world's largest bear trap just closed an inch from his nose.

The building was tall, but they were falling fast. He couldn't take his eyes off the demon to see how close they were to the street below. Blindly he stretched his power out. Shadow billowed around him and power crackled through it. Dark tendrils shot out from the shadow, trying to find a building edge to hold on to. He had been practicing with this recently discovered ability and was able to move quickly through cities using the power of Hell inside him to almost fly between buildings.

But he was not actually able to fly, the ground was only a small miscalculation away, and he had never used the power when drunk. The shadow tendrils grasped at the building, but his inebriated state seemed to reflect in his control of this power. At last it grasped briefly and their fall was slowed. Another tendril of shadow billowed out and tried to find purchase on the building. They were jerked to the side as it attached to a building. He was off from the alcohol and his attention was focused on keeping those large teeth from biting off his face, but for a moment he thought it had worked, their fall would be stopped.

Then he slammed into metal and glass as he collapsed into the roof of a car. It felt as if his back was breaking. His head bounced off the crushed roof, sending the world spinning. For a moment he thought he had shattered every bone in his body. All he could pay attention to was the pain and the lack of air in his lungs. He had lost contact with the demon, but luckily it seemed it had also been thrown clear.

It could be on him any second. That thought helped him focus. He tried to sit up, but couldn't, and for one horrible moment he was worried he *had* broken his back and he was now paralyzed. Then he moved and gasped. Air flooded back into his chest, causing a whole new burst of pain. Movement was coming back slowly, too slowly. Every moment he couldn't move left him defenseless against that thing. After a few more seconds he tried to sit up again.

There were gasps around him. He was surrounded by onlookers, cell phones out, staring at him with various looks of shock, terror, and excitement on their faces.

"Are you him?" cried a small voice close enough to Christopher to hear over the chaotic noise of the crowd. "The one that saved New York from the monster? I've seen you on YouTube. You are him, aren't you?"

It was a kid, maybe twelve years old. He was a brave one. The adults stood away from him, close enough for cameras, but far enough to run if they needed. He breathed a sigh of relief that his shadow uniform still covered him in coat and hood. His identity was still safe.

"Are you going to kill him?" the boy asked and looked at the ground behind Christopher. The demon-possessed body of the matre d' was slowly getting to his feet.

"Yes," he said. Then turned back to the kid. "Run boy. Run as fast as you can."

The kid must have heard something in his voice, because his face turned a pale white as it drained of blood. Then he ran, faster than Christopher had ever seen a kid run. The boy disappeared into the crowd.

He crawled off the car; he hoped it was a dignified crawl. The demon was on his feet and growing steadier by the second. Christopher stood, for a moment using the car as a brace. But already the pain was fading. It wasn't his fast healing, although that had kicked in. No, it was the seed of Hell flaring up inside, burning out every thought but violence. What little inebriation left in him was burned away too.

And with the seed of hate came the dreaded desire to take

souls, to feed on them. He could smell the corruption around him intermingling with the more balanced souls. His hand subconsciously grasped the Weapon disguised as a Swiss Army knife in his pocket. It practically jumped into his hand, and the pang of soul hunger that stirred inside of him reminded him how long it had been since he had harvested.

The Weapon transformed as he pulled it out, morphing in his hands to become a sword. Power radiated from him and his weapon, sending pulses of vibrations through the street. Bands of power arched from him, and scarred the ground where they hit.

The Weapon ached to dig into the crowd, anything with a taint on its soul would do. The Weapon only saw darkness or purity, not shades of gray. The power had him in its grip and he knew not to try and fight it, instead he let it flow through him. He did not try to suppress it as he had in the past, he channeled it.

The strongest smell of corruption came from the man the demon had possessed. He looked at the man's aura and took a strong whiff even as the demon smiled at him, preparing to strike. He could see the sins of the mortal whose shell the demon inhabited. He could see and smell the theft and petty crime, but more importantly he could taste the murder, the lack of remorse. And this is what damned him.

The demon hesitated as though assessing his own health. Despite the energy and power radiating off of him, Christopher held himself up with the broken car, he was still so weak. He sunk down a little as though the simple act of holding the blade was dragging him down. That was all the sign the demon needed. It took the bait. It charged at him: its fingers lengthened into claws, its large jaw distended and glistening with drool.

Just as he was within arm's reach of those claws, Christopher swept the Weapon up, cleaving though the human shell that housed the demon. The blade cut cleanly, leaving two halves neatly separated. The human soul clung to the sword as it was ripped from the quickly dying body. It pulled away like stringy goo, clinging futilely to the skin husk, then snapped away as the last glimmer left the man's eyes.

The Weapon slurped it up like a favorite meal, but it had been a while since the Weapon and the Hell power inside of him had been fed, so it did little but whet the appetite.

There was some hesitant clapping from the crowd, but also some retching. Most stood in silence, their looks telling him they weren't sure if he was the hero or villain. The authorities would be here soon. Probably not good to stand around. He was about to look for a quick exit that didn't involve him running through the crowd—he was afraid in his weakened state he might not be able to control his unnatural hunger—when he noticed something interesting about the body.

He bent down and, using the edge of the sword, he sliced through the maître d' uniform and exposing the body's neck and torso. The man was covered with tattoos. They looked gang related, though he was no expert.

"Prison tattoos," someone said from the crowd. When Christopher stood and looked at the man who spoke, the man took a step back.

"How do you know?" Christopher asked. He was speaking in Spanish again, but also subconsciously altering his voice, filling it with power and darkness.

The man lifted his shirt. Across his chest were similar markings, but not nearly so many. The dead man was covered almost completely with them. Except for his head and hands.

"And from the looks of them he was one bad motherfucker, or a sick one anyway. You don't earn some of those for little stuff. I know; I regret mine."

Christopher looked at his soul and sniffed the air. The man's aura had its fair share of dark blemishes, some not just little things. The hunger rose up in him so suddenly it took him by surprise, and he found himself striding toward the man, Weapon flaring to life, power billowing around him.

The man gasped at the look in Christopher's face. He stepped back, grabbing a young boy whom Christopher hadn't seen, and shoved the kid behind him, pushing him away.

"Run Miguel, run quick and tell your momma I love you both. Now run."

The simple act of redemption, small in the grand scheme of things, was all it took to make Christopher hesitate. And that bought him the time he needed to refocus the need, the blood lust that overwhelmed him.

Then he saw the brightly glowing bubble.

It slipped out of the exposed chest of the dead man; it floated aimlessly at first as though caught on a gentle breeze. Then, discovering its target, it drifted quickly toward the opposite side of the crowd. A man waited there, hand outstretched, a smile on his face. He wore the clothes of a priest and a wide brimmed hat, glasses perched on his nose. Deep-set eyes gave his face a skull like appearance.

The glowing bubble landed on the man's palm, sunk quickly into his skin, and the man sighed. The power flared and Christopher looked at the man's aura. It was pitch black and instantly he could smell the horrible scent of corruption. This man was a dark soul.

Hunger washed over Christopher. The Weapon surged with power, and a fresh burst of energy ran through it. It needed to feed. Knowing he could not stop it, Christopher focused his hunger and rage. He would harvest this man’s soul.

The smiling man stepped back into the crowd. He was short, and as the crowd closed around him, he disappeared. But Christopher could still smell the taint of his soul. With a roar he raised the Weapon, preparing to spring into the crowd after him. Behind him there were gasps and screams. Christopher ignored them; the mortals were not his concern. But the crowd did not part in front of him. Power raged around him; they should have been running in fear.

And they would have, if they had been mortal. The people that had surrounded the retreating man started to shift and change. Claws replaced fingers; large, grinning jaws lined with sharp teeth replaced mouths. Their bodies shifted and twisted in ways no human could; they grew more vile and disgusting every moment. The dark soul had brought an army of demons with him.

"Well fuck me," Christopher said.

13

With a collection of snarls, roars, screeches and high-pitched squeals, the horde of demons surged toward him. And here stood Christopher, Lord of Damnation, with two whole days of official training. There was no way he could take them all on. Besides, he didn't know if all the human souls trapped in those bodies deserved to spend eternity in Hell. They may not all be murderers like the first one.

The Weapon shifted in his hand and then he was carrying a huge scythe. Once again, the Weapon had no compunction against killing, guilty or innocent.

Behind him bystanders were scattering. Screams of fear and confusion were almost as loud as the bellowing horde. It was chaos all around him. He had no choice. He let the hatred and violence roll over him from the seed of Hell inside.

He swung the scythe as the first row of demon soldiers reached him. It sliced into the group, cutting through muscle and bone. Each time it cut, it snagged a soul and slurped it up like an oyster.

Bodies, sliced in half, or spilling out their intestines from huge gashes across their torso, fell to the ground as the blade of the Weapon cut through, ripping out the mortal soul and sending it to Hell.

The first two rows of demons fell to the scythe before the rest paused. They were vicious, but not stupid creatures. They spread out, trying to surround him. There was more room now that the humans had fled, but he was sure there were plenty of people in the buildings around him with their phones, recording everything.

As soon as he was surrounded they charged in. He spun in a circle, the scythe gleefully tearing souls from the bodies. They pulled back, but they had the numbers. They would coordinate eventually, and he would be overwhelmed.

He saw the glowing balls floating up from the fallen demons, all drifting quickly on the breeze in one direction. Christopher was sure it was back to the skull-faced man. He was their master.

They came again and this time they were fast. He managed to kill many with the scythe, but then they were inside the radius of the blade. The Weapon shifted again, back into a long sword.

He brought it up, plunging it into a demon, then ripped it out only to swing at another. A claw clamped down on his shoulder. Something heavy landed on his back. He threw his shoulders back, tossing the piggy-backing demon from him, but it was just replaced with another.

A demon latched onto his arm. He yelled in pain and surprise, then pulled it close and struck with the Weapon, severing its head from its body. The pommel of the blade had become a small spike, Christopher used it to drive into a demon skull. There were so many, each time he struck one or two more took its place.

Teeth sank into his shoulder almost causing him to drop the Weapon. He thought maybe he could jump, spring away and regroup. But there were so many massed around him, holding him, weighing him down. He had little choice. Soon they would pull him down to his knees and he would bleed to death. He gathered his power for one big push.

Then he heard a screech that cut through the noise of the demons around him. Even the demons paused, startled. From above, a great winged beast was swooping toward them.

Despite the pain Christopher smiled. Long, emaciated skeleton body, oversized head with bony skin pulled too tight across it, black leathery wings. It was his girl, Dark Eris, in her demonic form. Much more bad ass than these minor demons, he thought.

She landed with a thud, her talons clicking on the asphalt. She was tall in her demon avatar, ten feet at least, her torso thick and bony, like her skin had become her exoskeleton. Her arms and legs were thin things, compared to the rest of her body, but he knew from experience they were powerful despite not seeming to have any muscle. Her sunken eyes glowed with a deep fire, and a long slimy tongue dangled from her gaping mouth.

The demons watched her warily for a moment, as if unsure what to do. Christopher had the feeling that she somehow outranked them in the hierarchy of Hell. He was being swarmed by low-level demons and she was a boss demon.

A group broke away from the pack attacking him and charged at Dark Eris, although they seemed a little unsure of themselves. But Christopher had little time to watch, the remaining demons swarmed over him again.

He swung the Weapon; it would alternated between a longer blade when he was making sweeping cuts and a short blade for stabbing. He caught one by the neck and tossed it to the back of the pack. He would have sliced it, but his blade was already hilt-deep in another. He constantly spun, relying on his Hell-fueled speed and power rather than any real skill, striking and dodging, waving the blade in an attempt to keep them from completely burying him.

He couldn't see how Dark Eris was faring, though he could hear the screams of pain and a large number of glowing balls of power were drifting up from her kill zone. The occasional demon was tossed way up in the air only to come crashing down on its brethren.

Although there were two of them now, it was not great odds against this many opponents. Despite his lack of training, he could have taken on any one of these demons mono y mono, but the sheer number was too much. Already he was slowing, the pain from a hundred different bites and claw wounds draining his energy. His healing couldn't keep up.

He was thinking that maybe he could work his way over to Dark Eris so they could make a last stand together, when darkness shot out of the shadows at the base of the hotel.

The large bolt of blackness plunged directly into the group of demons surrounding him. With a roar that shattered windows, Hellcat ripped through the demons like they were cat treats. Biting and throwing back the horde, she made her way to Christopher. If he hadn't been desperately trying to stay alive under the mass of demons, he would have cheered. He still didn't know if they would survive, but their odds just got better.

Hellcat jumped from demon to demon like they were stepping stones, taking out a large piece of a shoulder here, half a scalp there. Her claws shredded demon skin and dark, almost black, blood dripped from her jaw.

The demons fell back; the onslaught of the Hellcat made them pause. Warily they backed away from the large panther that had just destroyed a half-dozen of them.

Then, just as they seemed to be regaining their courage, they suddenly froze as though listening to some far away voice. As one they turned and ran in all different directions, scattering into what was left of the crowd, which now stood much further away, cellphones still out.

Christopher fell to one knee in exhaustion. He couldn't chase after them, although he knew where they were headed or rather, to whom. Hellcat gave chase until he called her back. Dark Eris also looked pretty beat up. It was hard to tell on such a gruesome visage, but she seemed to have her fair share of gashes and bite marks. With a nod at him and an ear-piercing shriek, she launched herself into the air and soared up to the night sky.

Christopher got slowly to his feet. The ever-present Hell power still flowed through him, causing black, swelling clouds to billow around him. The Weapon burned with energy. It had gorged itself on souls. It wanted more, but it was sated enough for Christopher to will it back into its pocket knife shape. He slipped it into his pocket.

He was the center of attention. The crowd, larger than before, was slowly coming back now that the immediate danger was gone. Christopher looked around and saw cars abandoned in the road. Some were just left in place, others sat at odd angles as if the owners had tried to turn around and then, when the real fight began, just ran. He saw a few heads pop up from the back seats, some had taken cover it seems.

Then he heard a clap, then another. He turned to look at the crowd as more clapping started. Not a lot, most of the crowd just looked confused. He knew what they were thinking. Was he a good guy? Had he brought the monsters? Was he a bad guy?

Not even Christopher was sure of the answer to that.

In the distance he could hear sirens. That was his cue. The battle had seemed to last forever, but only a few minutes had elapsed since he fell from the building.

"Fade," he commanded Hellcat after giving her a scratch behind the ear; she deserved that at least for saving his life. She dissolved into the shadows around him. Then he jumped. Tendrils of power stretched out around him giving him a boost, propelling him up into the night sky.

14

"Well, I guess we established that whatever is going on is in my jurisdiction. The normal police won't be able to handle this. Hell, I'm not sure I can," Christopher said. "So much for the vacation half of this working vacation."

He was lying on the couch in his suite. A room service tray was on the coffee table next to him, his food barely touched. He knew he should eat, but he had no appetite. Not after almost dying. Eris had done the most damage to the tray, devouring the food like she hadn't eaten in days. She was weak, paler than usual, and weary, but obviously still had an appetite.

He knew how she felt, he still hurt from the battle. The wounds were mostly healed; no scars were left to show the fight even happened, but his body still ached: muscles, tendons, and also something more. He had that sense of missing something, a sense of emptiness in part of him. The feeling came and went over the last few months, but lately he was feeling it more and more, usually after a fight or anything that made him tired or wounded.

"Yeah, I was really hoping this was just your run-of-the-mill, mundane political chaos and terrorism," Hamlin said. He was pouring a whiskey for Christopher—his third since the fight—and one for himself. "I was looking forward to the vacation too." He handed the drink to Christopher. "I needed some sleep."

"Who are you kidding? You just wanted to show off your new Speedo on the beaches. Get those ladies all fired up." They both chuckled.

"You might want to go easy on that Chris, you don't want to be caught off guard again. Remember, somehow they know you're here; they could be back at any minute," Eris said quietly and somewhat ominously.

Hamlin sighed and after a long forlorn look at the glass, put it down. "She's right," he said.

"I know," Christopher said and then downed the drink in one gulp. "All the more reason."

"Sometimes you can be a real asshole," Eris said.

"Thanks, Dark Eris, I'll take that under advisement."

"I'm not her, I'm me," Eris said.

That startled Christopher. Eris was usually less confrontational. He turned to look at her.

"So you are." Then he returned to gazing at the ceiling. He felt emptier.

"What exactly did you guys fight back there? I mean are we sure they were demons?" Hamlin asked.

"Yes, it was definitely demons," Dark Eris said; she had switched again. To Christopher she said, "Yes, it's Dark Eris this time, you ass." She stood and walked over to the bed.

"Although things are...fuzzy from my past, I know a possessed human when I see it. The glowing bubbles of energy leaving the bodies after you killed them was their demonic essence."

"Hey, I wasn't the only one killing people out there. I seem to remember some big ugly, bastard fighting alongside me."

"Whoa kid, watch it," even stoic Hamlin seemed taken back.

Dark Eris paused and looked down at Christopher. Dark Eris could be cold, mean, full of hate—she was a demon after all—but there was something different in her eyes when she looked at Christopher; something he had never seen before in her. It took him a moment to realize it was hurt. But before he could say anything, or even apologize she went on.

"But they didn't just dissipate and pass back to Hell. They stuck around. That's not normal; something is able to keep them here on earth. Not only keep them here, but force them to work together."

"Force them? Is it possible they're just ganging up? Maybe they're part of this Alliance we heard of, you know...working together?" Hamlin asked.

"No, demons don't work that way. We're loaners. Honestly most of us can't stand our own kind. Sometimes a few of us more powerful ones will work together on some project, but that's only as a necessity. To have so many low-level demons fighting together is almost unheard of. No, this army was not their idea; something is forcing them."

"I think I know what, or I guess, who was controlling them," Christopher said. "I saw a man just before the battle started, right after I killed the one that pushed me out of the window. He was dressed in priest's clothes and the demon sphere went right to him as if called. He was a dark soul."

"Jesus. One of these things has the ability to control an army of demons?" Hamlin said. Now he did pick up his glass and take a long drink.

"Those were fairly weak demons," Dark Eris said, "and you saw what they were capable of. If he found a way to control the more powerful ones," She paused and looked at Christopher. "More ugly bastards like me, then he would be even more of a threat."

Christopher looked away; he couldn't look her in the eye. He wanted to apologize, but couldn't. "Why are they possessing humans? Why not just show up and start killing, or whatever it is they are trying to accomplish?"

"Demons are children of Hell. They don't really belong here, as much as they wish they did. We can manifest for short times, but eventually this world will reject us, the fabric of this reality thins, and we are forced back to Hell. By possessing a human, we can extend the time here almost indefinitely depending on how we use the mortal shell. If we abuse it or alter it too much, it too will start to reject us. Usually we destroy it before it gets to that point."

"As much as we need to talk this out," Hamlin said. He was looking down at the new smart phone that Eris had made him buy, tapping at the screen like it had buttons three inches thick. "Eris is right, those things could be back at any moment. We need to get out of here."

"I suppose I could get us another hotel room," Christopher offered.

"We don't even know how they found you. They might be able to hack hotel reservation systems. I think we need to hole up in the lair. Or maybe I could pull some strings with a contact I have in Interpol and get us a safe house."

"This is like the Bronx all over again. You cops and your safe houses. What's wrong with just using the lair?"

"Nothing. The only downside I see is that while it's great for hiding, going in and out of the airport all day might be suspicious. But I was thinking, we didn't look around the whole place; I wouldn't be surprised if we found a back door. Just like the one in the Bronx. It would make sense that your predecessor liked to hedge his bets with escapes routes. In fact, I wouldn't be surprised if the one we took through the airport wasn't even the front door."

"A back door? If not in the airport then where?" Christopher asked.

"I'm not sure," Hamlin said a little sheepishly. "But if I were to guess, I would say a slightly less regulated part of town."

"Shit," Dark Eris said. She was looking at her phone. "Near the airport? Unregulated? I hope you don't mean what I think you mean."

"It won't be that bad," said Hamlin.

"What am I missing?" Christopher asked, eyes darting between the two of them.

"He's talking about Neza-Chalco-Itza, the world's largest slum."

"This is all just guess work," Hamlin said. "I'm just going on gut and what we know about this Beast's lairs, which ain't a whole hell of a lot."

Christopher looked around at the room forlornly. Five-star hotel to slum, he was going to miss this. "Well let's get going. Eris is right, they could be back any minute."

15

The Collector stepped from the shadows as though he had just appeared, but Golyat had known he was there despite his use of shadow travel. One of his pets must have taught him that secret trick. Still, he arrived quietly with none of the sickness that path can leave with a traveler. He had some skill.

Golyat waited for the Collector to reveal himself. He sat patiently on the couch—though for someone of his girth, it was more like a chair—near the fire that warded off the chill in the night air. This was his favorite room in the house; he would sip his drink and stare into the fire, sometimes for hours, as though he could read his fortune in its flickering light. It was dark, always dark in this room. The only light came from the fire.

He didn't know why the Collector remained silent for so long, perhaps to size him up? The Alliance was fragile and maybe he was trying to gage Golyat, maybe already planning how he would strike, planning what would be required. Too much, Golyat would say; too much is required to defeat me.

"I know what happened. I watched the news," Golyat said and took a long sip of his drink.

"Yes Golyat. He had companions with him, companions I was not aware of," The Collector replied.

There was something in his voice that made Golyat turn his massive head and neck and look at him.

"There was a demon with him. A thing of beauty, she fought against her own kind. I like that fierce independence."

"Ha," Golyat laughed. "Are you in love? Do you desire this demon?"

The Collector seemed to be ignoring him. "I must add her to my collection, I must make her mine. What power she would give me..."

Golyat hid his disgust. This one creeped him out. "Eye on the ball, eye on the ball. You can have her once we have taken care of the young hunter. Tell me what happened tonight, the news was not as detailed as I would have liked."

The Collector nodded, reluctantly it seemed to Golyat, then he recounted what had happened.

"It seems the boy hunter is more accomplished than we thought. His power is growing. And that Hellhound; it wouldn't even be a factor if not for Anabelle's stupidity." Golyat said. "It is best he involved himself in our plans, it will force our hand. We will make him ours or kill him."

"So, you have a plan then?"

"Yes, and a secret weapon or two."

"And what of me? What is my part?"

"Same as it always has been, go and build your army. The Days are almost upon us."

The Collector stepped back into the shadows.

"One other thing," Golyat said. "You might want to watch your back. He has your scent now. It might take the boy a little bit to understand that, but eventually he will come for you."

The Collector grinned as the shadows closed around him.

"I know."

16

Getting back into the lair was as easy as getting out. They simply had to wait until no one was looking before ducking into the service tunnel. The entrance was strategically located to avoid security cameras, it might have been the only blind spot in the entire airport. His predecessor had planned it well.

They slipped through the little-used tunnels to the lair entrance; despite its invisibility Christopher knew exactly where it was, it called to him. He fished the Book out of his pocket, and it shifted in his hands to become a key: not a modern cut key, but a large, archaic hunk of iron. It took only a moment for Christopher to find the keyhole that had appeared in the wall. With a quick turn, the door opened and they were in.

Once inside the main room Hamlin said, "Kid you look for the back door. Frankly, I'm kicking myself that we didn't check this place out more thoroughly when we arrived. I guess I wanted the vacation to start as much as you guys did. Getting soft in my old age."

"Got it," Christopher said. He put his bag down on the couch. "What are you going to do?"

"I'm gonna play with the computer and see what I can see. Check the news, that sort of thing."

Hellcat slipped from the shadows now that they were away from any prying eyes. She rubbed up against Eris, demanding some attention. No house cat, Hellcat was taller than Eris' waist and almost knocked her over, but Eris just smiled and gave her a vigorous scratching around the ears.

"Want to join me in poking around the place?" Christopher asked Eris.

She hesitated for only a moment before nodding wordlessly, but it was enough to let Christopher know she was still pissed about what he had said at the hotel.

They walked off down a corridor they knew led to the bathrooms, but had other doors they hadn't opened. It turned out one did, indeed, open onto a long hallway. Hellcat padded quietly behind them.

"This looks promising," Christopher said with a smile. Eris didn't return it.

"Eris," Christopher started, "I'm sorry I said what I said back there. I'm just not myself lately, I mean, I guess... fuck, I have no idea what I'm trying to say. I'm... I'm..."

"Lost?" Eris asked quietly.

That caused him to pause. He stopped and froze in place. That was it, that word described everything he was feeling. "Yeah, that's it. That's the word for it. Only it's not all at once. It's like I'm slowly getting more and more lost. Some feelings are becoming blurry. I don't know, maybe the power is changing me or something."

"Maybe the nature of who you are changed. In some ways you're not really human anymore."

That was another blow. She thought he was losing his humanity. And she was probably right, how could he not, when his main job was to kill, destroy, and damn.

"But I don't think that's it," she said. She must have seen the confusion on his face, because she tried to clarify. "You are a good person Chris, that's why I agreed with Dark Eris to reach out to you for help. We watched you and I just knew you were a good person, a good person in an impossible situation. No, I think this is more to do with the chunk of your soul that the were-hellhound took out of you and what the Librarian said about it."

"Yeah, since that happened, things have been different. The power inside me has felt different. Not that I knew what the hell I was doing before, but after that fight... it has been harder to control and everything just seems more and more distant. It's changing me, slowly. I can feel it."

"It's as though you were wounded and it isn't healing. It's festering," she said.

"Like I'm rotting from the inside," he said. "In the spirit sense."

He stopped and leaned against the wall, suddenly feeling tired and sick.

She reached out and touched his face gently. "I want to help you so badly, but I can't. I just don't know what I can do. I wish there was something I could kill to take away this pain."

Christopher looked up sharply at that. That's when he saw the hardened lines, the firmness and confidence, but most of all the dark eyes. At some point Eris had changed to Dark Eris in their conversation. Now it was Dark Eris who held the concern and sadness in her eyes. It was the demon inside that was touching his face, it was the demon with the tear sliding down her cheek.

Taking notice of her hand on his cheek, she pulled it away slowly, staring at it like it had betrayed her. Then she brought it quickly down to her side, gave Christopher one of her disdainful smiles, and quickly brushed away the tears.

"More tears...I swear Eris cries over everything. Why did I get stuck with such a weak human? This hallway seems to go some distance, I think we might be on to something," she said and walked briskly down the hallway, leaving a stunned Christopher to wonder what exactly he had just seen. "Move your ass."

Christopher shook it off and caught up with her. She was right. The hallway was long it had to lead somewhere. After a few hundred feet it ended at a brick wall. She looked at him expectantly.

"I think we found our back door," Dark Eris said.

Again, he simply touched the wall and, with a rush of unsteadying power, found himself on the other side. Dark Eris was moments behind him. They were in another tunnel. Old, worn brick covered the walls that stretched off into the dark. Despite his heightened ability to see through darkness—a useful side-effect of his powers—Christopher couldn't see to the end.

"Looks like it might be an abandoned sewer, or perhaps an old access tunnel. Either way it's heading south, into the slum area. It's hard to judge, but we might be at the edge of the airport."

Dark Eris nodded and they moved on. It was a long walk before they found a set of stairs leading up. The stairs were as old as the tunnel, the brick and concrete crumbling away, but they were still intact enough to use. The tunnel continued on, and the scent of sewage grew stronger.

"I think the stink is coming from whatever is down that tunnel. I suggest we take the stairs, before we end up in sewer sludge. These are new shoes," Dark Eris said.

At the top of the stairs was a rusted metal door. It creaked loudly as Christopher pushed against it. It wasn't locked, but it felt almost rusted in place. It eventually popped and swung free with a grating sound.

"Not used very often," Christopher mumbled.

"Could be some of the Beast's old magic keeping people away. Like a subtle deterrent," Dark Eris said.

Beyond lay a semi-collapsed hallway. One side was mostly caved in with just enough room for a single person to squeeze past the rubble.

"And no one is stupid enough to try and take shelter in a tunnel that is about to collapse."

Christopher reached out, touched the debris, and gave it a shove.

"Watch it!" Dark Eris said and backed toward the door, eying the ceiling nervously. "What the fuck are you doing?"

Christopher shoved again, nothing moved. "Just as I thought, cosmetic. The tunnel is stable, but made to look like it could collapse at any moment. My predecessor was pretty clever."

He squeezed past the rubble, Dark Eris following. The hallway beyond was short and he could see light from ahead. "I think this is the exit."

It was a doorway that opened onto a street. A street like none Christopher had ever seen. The first thing—like a slap in the face—was the overpowering smell of rotting trash. It littered the streets, piles of garbage lumped up against a wall. He saw a handful of people sleeping against another wall, the homeless in the slums. The buildings themselves were little more than large sheds stacked atop each other. There were larger structures: long-abandoned mansions, now overrun by tenants filling each room.

Noise and lights moved in the structures. Apparently, the slums were awake through the night. Christopher could hear laughter, yelling, and sobs in the distance. The sounds of mothers yelling at their children and men laughing echoed through the streets. In some ways it felt more alive than New York. But all it took was one whiff, and Christopher realized it wasn't home.

There was death in the air, a constant cloud of it hung over this town.

He could smell the spiritual corruption too. Evil hung over this place, but it mixed with a strange kindness and happiness. There was a strong sense of wrongness here, but it was simpler and distinct from the good. It was different from New York, or even Mexico City proper. Christopher could only guess it was evil born out of survival.

But the darkness was there, and suddenly Christopher felt the hunger to hunt. Almost subconsciously he started to reach out to the shadows, began pulling them toward him. Shaping them into his jacket and hood. A hand reached out and clutched his arm.

"What are you doing? This was just reconnaissance," Dark Eris said. "You can't go off hunting and killing right now."

She was right, Christopher realized. He started to nod when he caught a new scent. It was a putrid soul stink that he recognized. It wafted faintly down the street. It was the soul stench of the Demon Collector. Instantly, the Weapon was in his hand. But before it could change and flare to life Dark Eris grabbed his arm again. This time wrenching it and spinning him around. Then she slapped him, not a human get-your-attention slap; this was a full-on demon bitch slap. Christopher reeled back.

"Don't go rogue on me now Chris. Get your shit together," she said.

Rage surged through him, but the pain cut through it, and he was able to push it back down. He let go of the shadows and put away the Weapon, and then leaned against the wall.

"Thanks. I don't know what happened. I caught the scent of the dark soul, and the next thing I knew the power jumped at me, almost like it was excited."

"You mean the dark soul controlling the demons? You were able to get his scent?

"Yeah, he's here, somewhere in these slums. I need to go after him, get to him before he strikes at us again, or is able to pull off whatever this Day of Chaos is."

"What you need to do is get to the Library and see if you can get any information. The last time you saw him, you were almost overrun by an army of demons. Unless you know something we don't, there's no reason to suspect it would turn out any different this time. Hell, it could be a trap."

"I hadn't thought of that," Christopher said quietly. "Thanks for stopping me."

"No problem. Usually when you go off like that, you cause us a lot of trouble. I'm just glad I was able to stop you."

It was true, Christopher realized. She had slapped him and he had calmed instantly. In the past when the hatred and anger overtook him, he was either overcome or he was able to push it back with great effort and a much longer struggle. He had thought it was just the pain of her slap that had brought him back, but now he was thinking it was something more...or rather less,—her touch. The pain of the slap just completed the job.

"Let's get back to the lair so you can go off and visit your Library and maybe get some answers," Dark Eris said.

And before he could say anything, she had disappeared back through the rusted door.

17

This was not her room. The one she liked was back at the hacienda, but Golyat had told her this one would do for now. And she should not question Golyat, he made her hurt when she did that. Still, he was better than the horrid woman who had kept her locked up in that basement. At least he gave her things, clothes and food, let her sleep in a bed. He was good to her when he wasn't being bad to her.

She wasn't sure why they were here. Something about finding ancient artifacts. Something in these ruins was important for the Alliance. Some sort of power. Golyat had said they'd found it, and even now it was being shipped out of here to some place far away. He said they would have to stay much longer.

She didn't like it here; this room was not a good place. Its ancient stone walls seemed to press in on her. It gave Grace a slight panic like she would turn to find the doorway gone and she would be trapped forever. She had screamed the first time he had left her alone in here...until he had hurt her. It was her fault, with all the screaming. She deserved it.

The room was small, but big enough, she supposed. The bedding was very simple—a mattress with a sleeping bag on it—but it was clean. A table stood against one wall, her work station Golyat had called it. Various metal tools were spread across it: vials of obscure, and in some cases mythological, substances sat in a rack. Stacks of books, almost all of which she could not read, were on the desk and stacked against one wall.

All of this Golyat had obtained for her, telling her it was the tools of her trade. But she had no idea what her trade was. They told her she was a witch, a soul shaper, but they never told her what exactly that meant. She knew she was very important, but not as important as the glowing vile resting gently in her palms—the vial that contained the soul shard of the one they called The Hunter.

And her task was to master it. She didn't know exactly what that meant, but she was learning. She sat in a chair and stared at the shard cradled it in her hands. She reached out with... something. Her mind, her soul, she didn't know; she just did what felt right. Some part of her reached out and wrapped itself around the essence inside. She caressed it.

Like she had done so many nights before she gently probed it, poking at it and watching it react. She could sense that it was protecting itself. The soul was no easy thing to understand, its complexities far beyond anything she was ready for. But Golyat had made it clear she must understand it as soon as possible.

She continued her examination, working instinctively. Her own special magic, backed by emotion, seemed to have the biggest effect on it. So she had started feeding her power—her probing tool as it were—anger, hatred, and fear: big emotions she could easily access. They came to her naturally. They were a part of who she was, and she understood these primal emotions better than anything else.

And so it was these feelings she injected into the shard of the Hunter's soul. Most of the time it didn't work, finding a chink in the armor he had built around himself was difficult; but every once in a while, she succeeded and a little part of her power seeped in before the shard could block her once again.

It had gone on like this for days. She searched and searched, poking the soul. It would defend itself, ever shifting. But each time she was able to insert a dark thought or hateful emotion, it weakened just a little bit. It became just a little bit easier to find that next chink in its armor.

Though she did not understand how, she knew that when she weakened the shard, the corruption reflected back on the rest of the soul. The part still in the Hunter. When she damaged this shard, she struck out at the Hunter. And that pleased Golyat, so that pleased her.

She was winning. She just needed time. Unfortunately, that was not how Golyat saw it. He needed her to master her soul-shaping as soon as possible. He was afraid. She could feel it in his black and blighted soul.

He wouldn't say it and she never would mention it, she had felt his anger and his beatings too many times, but he was afraid of this Hunter.

And that made her curious. What could cause such fear in one as powerful as Golyat? She did not know exactly what he was, but Golyat had a dark power at such depths she couldn't even fathom.

She poked again at the soul shard, hoping to make another hit. Though Golyat had been patient so far, Grace knew that he would soon want her to demonstrate progress.

She thought she might have some glimmer of control now. She gazed deep into the soul shard trying to see into it with something more than her eyes. Then she felt it.

"He's close," she whispered. Perhaps Golyat would have his

demonstration sooner than she had thought. And she would finally see the Hunter in person. She would see how he matched up against the little piece of him she had now. "Come Hunter, let me see the full you."

18

Christopher arrived standing at the Library. This was a first. Usually he was so disoriented when he crossed over, he ended up flat on his face. It was also getting less painful, both physically and spiritually, when he traveled to the Library. He wasn't sure that was a good thing: did it mean he was becoming used to the power, or was he becoming more jaded? In the past it had felt like a cleansing of the soul; now, it was just another piece of his new life.

Whatever the reason, he had arrived standing, not on the ground looking up at a smug Librarian. Speaking of which, Christopher thought, where was he? If he isn't here to see this for once...

Christopher turned and immediately ran into tall, dark, and shadowy. Apparently, the Librarian had been standing right behind him. Christopher cried out in surprise and tripped over the edge of rug and went down, landing on his back.

"Don't do that! You scared the shit out of me," the Librarian said.

"Scared the shit out of you? God dammit," Christopher said getting to his feet.

"God doesn't damn, you do," the Librarian said. "Or they do it to themselves? There are all sorts of ethical theories on the subject we could discuss. So, did you come here to discuss philosophy? I assume it isn't for another round of training so soon. You were badly beaten up the last time."

"Thanks, but really if you're not planning to take a career as a motivational speaker, you should at least write a book."

Christopher rubbed his tail bone. "I wanted to look at the Hunter's Journal. I need some information on a new dark soul that I just encountered."

"Certainly," The Librarian turned and floated away. Christopher trailed after. He might have been able to find the journal room by himself, but he'd rather not take the chance of losing himself in such a vast space. They passed through several large rooms the size of cavernous stone warehouses, and walked down a long hall finally ending up in front of the door only he could open.

The door was large as though made for giants, and black: not a painted black, but a darkness so deep no light could reflect off of it. He was used to the sense of vertigo it gave him every time he approached it, but that didn't make the entrance any easier. When he walked toward it he felt like he was falling into something. Something not right. It opened instantly at his touch.

Inside was the room that held the journal of his predecessor, the Beast. The walls were lined with past volumes of hunts, thousands of them. He had read through some, discovering his predecessor was truly ruthless, but also smart and well versed in his job and it just confirmed what a noob Christopher really was.

In the center of the room was a pedestal, and on it lay the current Hunter's Journal. It was open and Christopher suspected he would find it turned to the page he needed, the page of his latest dark soul. It was always disconcerting to look in that book. It was like a history of evil laid out in one place. While not all of humanity's woes were chronicled here, the vast majority of significant horrific events had a dark soul as its source, either before the soul had descended to Hell or after it had escaped.

Christopher approached the journal. He expected to see what he always did: merely faint outlines and little or no text describing the prey. The Librarian had told him the journal was supposed to be a sort of background on who, or what, he was hunting. It was a way for the Hunter to learn about his prey, what made them tick. The idea being he might find some insight into killing the dark soul, some weakness.

The only problem was that it didn't seem to work for him. Whether it was because Christopher was mortal, new to his role, or just plain didn't know how to turn the damn thing on, the journal gave him no background. It only captured notes on what he had done in his hunting, no history of the dark soul.

So, he was stunned when he looked down at the book and saw staring back at him a fully detailed drawing of the dark soul he had encountered in the streets of Mexico City.

"Well, fuck me," Christopher said quietly.

It was all there: the priest clothes, the wide brimmed hat, his short, slightly paunchy body topped by his round face, and the sunken, black rimmed eyes. He could see details he hadn't seen before; the priest raiment looked old, anachronistic. Wire glasses and an old bag that seemed out of place in modern time.

There was only one picture. It seemed he looked the same before and after escaping Hell. Only his inside had changed for the worse. Above the picture was a name: Fredrick Bailey, aka The Demon Collector. There was more text also; it appeared to be a snippet of his life story.

"Well that's more like it," the Librarian said from over his shoulder. "I knew you could do it."

Patronizing tone aside, the Librarian was right. It did seem like the journal was finally giving up its secrets. Despite all of his screw ups Christopher was progressing. At least, whatever powered the books thought so anyway.

"It even lists his alias," Christopher said to himself.

"Yes, what part of "all the information in the universe" did you not get?" the Librarian said. "If it is knowledge, it is somewhere in this Library."

"Really? Can you direct me to the knowledge on how to make a metaphorical Librarian shut the fuck up?"

The Librarian said, "I'll be outside in the hallway if you need me."

Then he turned abruptly and floated out of the room. Christopher almost said something. Almost. Then he let it go. He needed to read through these notes on the Collector, he didn't have time to coddle the Librarian. The book in his hands was calling out to him. He quickly read through the short passage. It read like a cross between encyclopedia entry and horror novel. It even had a title: The Damnation of Fredrick Bailey.

Fredrick Bailey was born 1831 and raised in the Old Brewery in the Five Points area of New York. From the moment he was born his life was a constant fight for survival, a fight that he was in no condition to win. He was a pale, sickly child who should never have made it out of infancy. At the time, the New York slum rivaled London's own decaying urban sprawl. Overcrowding and incredibly unsanitary conditions led to rampant disease and suffering. Death was everywhere.

Into this the Collector was born. Smaller than average and weaker than the others around him, no one expected him to survive. But he did, day by day. Early on he did this by staying away from the worst elements of the neighborhood.

But it was not always enough. Even he could not keep away from the hell that was Five Points. He was regularly beaten and raped. The slum, the bottom of the vast pond of humanity, was where the worst of the scum eventually settled. Everyone started out as a victim in Five Points, and everyone had a choice: remain a victim forever or evolve into something more.

The Collector chose the latter.

Eventually he was pulled into the gangs; service to them was the only way to survive. He never rose high in the ranks, staying a low-level errand runner. He didn't have the strength to become any sort of leader. However, despite being weak and small, he never got sick and he never turned down a job. He earned a reputation as being smart, efficient, loyal, and best of all, submissive.

"No wonder he's such a freak," Christopher said out loud. His early life read like he was the poster boy of serial killers.

The first major turning point happened when he was eleven years old. A priest had come to the Old Brewery. He came to save he said, he came to teach, but he also came to satiate his unholy lust. This priest had a taste for the exotic: pain and suffering as well as the occasional sexual dalliance. By day he lectured and taught the children who ran on the street, giving them something to hope for. He destroyed those hopes at night.

The Collector was drawn to him, listened to his words, and tried to understand what kind of god would create this world. The priest took him under his wing, gave him food and knowledge with one hand, and took his pleasure with the other. It was the story of the Last Supper that caught The Collector's young mind. It was the idea of eating the body of a god to gain some insight into the world, to be saved, and for The Collector that meant power.

As this corrupt and false priest pulled the boy further and

further into his disturbed nighttime world, the Collector twisted the stories of the bible with the realities of his life. Soon the priest invited his protégé to join him in the delights of torturing the flesh in service to the soul. His own soul. Pain and suffering became confused with consumption and personal power. He began to think that, if he only knew where to look, he could find the seat of power in every living thing.

In his warped mind he developed a fantastical theory: if he could find and consume the part of an animal that held its power, say, the stealth of a cat or the flight of a bird, he could take on that power, just as the disciples had taken the god-child's.

The second turning point came when fantasy became his reality: he began capturing animals and dissecting them in search of what it was that gave them their power. When he thought he had found it, he would eat it, hoping—no, knowing—he would get a piece of that power.

When his theory didn't work, he assumed it was because he hadn't found the right part. He just needed to keep looking.

His priestly mentor knew the boy was insane, but kept him close because he was a good, pliable partner. His young partner was taking more and more interest in their nocturnal activities, delighting in the torture, though not in the pain, that the priest enjoyed inflicting on their victims. The boy wanted to cut to the chase, tear into the body, and look past the pain etched on their faces.

The next turning point came when the Collector realized that the reason he couldn't find what he was looking for—he was not an animal. He needed to look inside a human: there he would find the power he sought.

One night as the priest lay sweating and breathing heavily on the thin sheets of the tenement bed, the beaten body of a young woman moaning in pain next to him, the Collector made his move. He crept to the side of the barely conscious woman and, with the precision of a doctor, he sliced into her.

The priest thought to stop him; they had killed many people of course, but that had always been in the throes of passion. It was the cold calculation that startled him. But it also excited him. He watched as the boy cut into the girl and sifted through her entrails as though looking for a treasure. Watching the Collector work, he thought, was almost a thing of beauty.

"Aha," the boy cried out and ripped a piece of something, some slick organ, out of the woman's torso and slurped it into his mouth, the woman's dead eyes staring at the ceiling.

The boy Collector looked at the priest, trying to wipe the blood off his face with the back of his hand, but instead left a wet smear across his lips and chin. "Am I prettier?"

"Yes, my boy, yes you are beautiful," the priest said, lust shining in his eyes. He didn't know what the boy was talking about, but he knew what he wanted. He reached out and pulled the boy to him.

.

The boy, emboldened, set about on his new task. Together they found their victims: the priest to enjoy the sport of their dying, the boy to collect their power when they were finished.

By the time the boy was in his teens they had amassed quite a pile of bodies without anybody noticing. Why not? It was just Five Points, nobody there was worth paying attention to. Death had taken up permanent residence in the neighborhood and nobody outside cared.

The Collector had found his place in the world, his task and mission. He still ran errands for the gangs for money and took on the occasional higher profile jobs, like killing for money. But his real love was his nights with the priest, working in partnership.

All that came crashing down the night the priest died. Fredrick Bailey was fifteen the night it happened. It started like any other of weekly diversions. But tonight, it was one victim too many for the priest. They had found their target, pulled her into an alley and began their fun.

But they had gotten over confident, cocky even, and neither of them saw the strength in their victim's eyes. They wounded and they tortured, but they did not break this one. The Collector left his knife next to her as he turned to his hands for more of a tactile delight of her skin. Through the haze of pain, she saw her chance. She grasped the knife and before either could react, the blade came down in the priest's eye. He screeched in horror as the tip punctured the orb.

Then she pulled the knife back and struck again, then again, and again, each time finding a new soft spot on the priest. The Collector watched in horror as the priest's screams grew weaker and weaker. Then they stopped, and he could do nothing. It was as though the concept of the priest, his mentor, his only family, dying could not register. It was an impossible thing and he had no answer for it.

The woman turned to him, eyes wild with madness and vengeance. He knew her then. She was Mad Molly, one of Jake Callum's women. Jake was a ranking member of a heavy hitting Five Points gang.

She lunged at him, but she was weak from the fun they had been having with her and the Collector, roused from his frozen state, was able to dodge away and make a run for the door. He was quick and nimble, it was his trademark after all. He was able to get away from her.

But there was no getting away from what he had done. He had left her alive and she would tell, she would tell everyone. Five Points was always dangerous, but when Jake heard what he had done, *saw* what he had done to his woman, it would become fatal.

Reeling from the loss of the only other person he had ever

cared about, the Collector had an idea. He cleaned himself up the best he could while keeping his head down. Word came to him that people were looking for him. He had little time.

Cleaned up, he took what money he had—crime does pay when done right—and went to the seminary. With luck, some quick thinking, the mention of his priest mentor, and most of his money, he was allowed in. He was to be a priest.

And it suited him. He relished his studies, but seen through the filter of his own damaged life, they had very little to do with heavenly salvation. In fact, it was at the seminary he discovered demonology. This, he believed, was where the real power lay. A good god in the sky was nice for the weak, but he had seen evil up close every day. He had embraced it and found strength in it. Demons, the Devil—this is where the real power was. This was what he had to tap.

He played the part of the good priest, stuck to his studies and soaked up all the knowledge he could. Not just theology, but a wide range of subjects. He became a scholar. Soon he came to the attention of those who ran the school and he was looked upon as a prodigy, someone who could go far in the priesthood. He did not care for the politics of it all, but he did enjoy the indulgence they allowed him to pursue his other areas of interest. Soon he became the seminary's resident expert on demons and the realm of Hell.

And through it all he continued his other, nocturnal games, searching for some glimmer of power. He stalked the other slums, keeping away from the Old Brewery and his old neighborhood as much as possible. He killed a large man, thinking he would gain the man's strength. He killed a keen business man slumming for the evening, thinking he might gain his business sense.

He gained none of these things of course, but in his mind, it was because he was just missing some key process or step. Once he completed his work he would find this power.

In his studies it occurred to him that the power he sought lay in the soul. He believed it was tied to the evil in all men. So, he changed his process to try and draw the evil out of his victims before eviscerating them. He turned to the tools of his mentor, torturing them as the priest had done.

It was not enough. He collected scores of victims, but never found the power inside. His failure and frustration was taking a toll. He delved deeper into occult mysteries and became careless, failing to hide the intensity of his research.

When his superiors noticed, they grew concerned that his studies were consuming him and may not be entirely godly. They told him it was time to take a break, to move on into other areas of theological study. He was forbidden to study the nature of demonic corruption so closely.

By now Fredrick Bailey knew that the priests had no clue about the nature of true evil, its real beauty, it's real power. He ignored their warning, hiding his true calling from them. His killing became more frantic as he adopted occult rituals into his torture and murdering. He got sloppy covering his research, and after repeatedly ignoring warnings from the church, he was defrocked and released from the priesthood.

Angry at the priests' ignorance and the lack of progress in his collection, the Collector left New York. He traveled the country visiting the smaller rural settlements mostly in the Midwest territories. Here he was safe playing the part of the traveling priest, creating one lie or another as to why he was traveling. These small towns were so far removed, by the time someone had thought to check his priestly credentials, he was already gone, having accepted what charity the community could give him. He always had food available to him, and enough money tithed to him to buy what he needed.

And of course, he never stopped collecting. This is how he

thought of it now: finding what he needed, what he wanted, in others and then adding them to his collection. He could remember most of the victims...how they looked, how the smelled. But now he had a bigger purpose. Rather than taking their power, he wanted to sacrifice what they were for what he could be. He tracked down ritual after ritual, and when he couldn't find any more he made up new ones. However, he was unable to summon a demon, to get that taste of real power, until the day he died.

Why this day was different he would never know. He had just left a community the day before, eating dinner at a farm house on the outskirts of the town, a place far enough away that no one heard the screams of the husband and children that lived there as the collector killed them, weakening them with poison then bashing in their heads with an ax handle. Far enough that the nearest neighbors would not see or smell the smoke until morning when he set their house ablaze.

He took with him the wife and mother, barely conscious from the poison, but alive. He was not ready for her to be dead yet. In the night, he rode deep into the forest of the Kansas territory, far enough from the road to not be discovered, but close enough to find his way back when he was done.

He found a suitably flat clearing and set about his work. He knew rituals that embraced the world below needed to be precise and specific. But by now his need to collect power overwhelmed any sense of caution. He had become ruthless and brutal, all subtlety gone. He worked frantically, as though he was racing against time to finish his collection.

Perhaps it was this angry frustration, or maybe it was the new twist to the ritual he had worked out, whatever the reason, when his blade opened her up in sacrifice surrounded by the archaic symbols he had learned over the years, something heard his call.

A wind picked up slowly, growing to a long howl. It shook the trees as it passed through, leaves in the tall branches rustled loudly at the power of the wind. There was no reason for it, this wind, and he knew something, finally, was happening.

He smelled the rot and fester that could only mean something dark was coming, something powerful. He heard a moan, a low-pitched sound of menace.

This was it, this was what he had started. He smiled, and as the wind grew and the stench of death filled the air, he began to giggle. A part of him had given up hope, told him to forget this silly pursuit. But now it was all coming true. His giggle turned into a laugh, uncontrolled and maniacal.

A dark mass formed above the woman's body. Inky black smoke drifted up from her pooling blood as though it burned. It pulled together drifting higher and higher. Whatever it was becoming it was tall, gigantic. He sobered for a moment. A part of Fredrick Bailey knew this was dangerous, this was something from the other side of Hell, but he didn't care. He was finally coming face to face with his life's work. Everything he had done had led to this moment.

Then he laughed again, a deep belly-laugh of pure joy even as the thing took solid shape. Its skull-like visage and long, spindly appendages looked like they had been stretched out on some sort of torture rack; the demon appeared exactly as he had pictured it. It would be a great start to his collection.

He was still laughing hysterically when the demon noticed him. Then, ignoring the protective binding circles the Collector had painstakingly created around it, it reached out one thin but powerful arm, grabbed Fredrick and lifted him off the ground by the neck.

Putrid breath washed over him as it brought him to its mouth. Thin leathery skin pulled tight against its skull and outlined each bone that made up its oversized head. It looked at him with eyes no human could read, but Fredrick the Demon Collector thought it wanted an explanation. The claw around his throat was tight, but he could squeak out sounds.

"I'm going to collect you," the Collector said.

The demon bit his head off.

This was the life and damnation of Fredrick Bailey.

Christopher leaned back, suddenly realizing a chair had materialized and he was sitting in it. Engrossed in the text he hadn't even noticed.

At some point while escaping from hell Bailey had learned how to actually collect the demons and use their power. It took going to hell and back to achieve his dream. Christopher flipped the page. At the top of the next page was a time.

AT LARGE: 5 Years, 26 Days, 5 Hours, 34 Minutes, 10 Seconds.

As Christopher watched, the ink of the seconds shifted and flowed, incrementing second by second.

So, The Collector has been loose from hell for over five years. Had he really collected an army that big in five years? That seemed like a lot of demons to find here on earth.

He set the book down on the pedestal and found the Librarian out in the hall.

"Do you know how many demons roam earth at any given time?" Christopher asked him.

"I would not know the exact count, but it would be no more than a handful. Too many would have caused... concern in the mortal world."

"That's not enough," Christopher said to himself.

"Interesting, most people would agree that one is more than enough."

"No. I just meant that this Fredrick Bailey already has an army under his control, but he has only been out for five years. He couldn't have collected that many."

"An army?"

"Well, I encountered dozens trying to fight me, it could have been as much as a hundred. And that's just what attacked me. Who knows how many he has in reserve?"

"Having a hundred demons, or even just a dozen, obeying your command would easily make him the most dangerous dark soul on earth, or at least the one capable of the most blatant destruction."

"But how could he have that many? You just said there are only a handful active at any... shit," Christopher said. There was one way he could have so many. "He must have brought them with him."

"Interesting, but human souls are at a distinct... disadvantage in Hell. I don't know how he would be able to gather so many. It would be quite a feat."

"It does seem like there is something odd going on. There seem to be more fugitives from Hell than ever before..."

"Well to be fair, the human population is growing," the Librarian interjected.

"...at least some are banding together. You also said they had never done that before. Even going so far as to attack me, the office of the Hunter to be exact, directly. I assume that has never happened before either."

"Yes, most of the dark souls strove to hide and avoid the Beast. He was greatly feared. I just assumed it was because they saw you as a weak, pitiful little human not up to the task..."

"Hey..."

"But it does seem like there is something more going on."

"Yeah," Christopher said, ignoring the Librarian's *pitiful little human* comment. "Like some sort of mismanagement down below."

"You might be right, it does seem like something is going on," the Librarian said. "But you do realized Hell is not physically 'down below'."

"Yes, I'm not an idiot."

The librarian said nothing.

"So, what do you suggest?" Christopher asked.

"I think it is in everyone's best interest if you stop this Demon Collector before he destroys the world."

"Have I ever told you how insightful you are?"

"You want insightful?" the Librarian asked. "How about this. You have had what? A couple of days of training? An army of demons will kick your ass."

"But they didn't. I had help from Hellcat and Dark Eris, but I survived," Christopher said.

"Exactly."

It took a moment for what the Librarian was saying to sink in, but when it did he suddenly felt sick to his stomach. "He let me win."

"Yes. Even your predecessor, one of the greatest warriors of all time, would have been hard pressed to survive such an attack. I mean I admire your confidence but really, an army of demons?"

"Okay, Okay, I get it. I was being a sucker. How the hell am I supposed to stop him? Up until now it has been one on one, or at least one at a time. How does one man fight an army?"

"Well for starters, you are not a man. Not only a man anyway. You have all the power of hell behind you."

"What does that even mean? What good does it all do if I don't know how to use it? No matter how powerful I am, or think I am, I will get overrun by a demon army."

The Librarian remained quiet. Perhaps there was nothing more to say.

"Perhaps you should consider a less direct assault? Subtlety can be its own type of power. Surprise its own weapon," said the Librarian.

"He's gonna know I'm coming. Like you said, he set this up by letting me get away. It's got to be a trap."

"Of course it is, and you will probably end up dead and the world will end, but that's a poor excuse for not trying. If you try, at least you go down swinging."

"I'm leaving before you completely destroy any confidence I might be able to muster," said Christopher. He turned for the exit door that had appeared near him. It was always there when he needed it, but he never saw it until he looked.

"Remember, direct approach, you die. Try to sneak up behind him."

"Right, thanks again for your pearls of wisdom," Christopher said and stepped through the door.

19

"Well, the Demon Collector fellow seems like a high-class guy, epitome of human evolution," Hamlin said.

"Yeah, and that was just the stuff he did before dying and going to Hell. I'm sure since his escape he's done even worse. I mean, that perverted need mixed with whatever powers he could have dragged back from Hell..." Christopher said.

He was sprawled on the couch in the lair. He stared blankly at the stone-gray walls trying to clear his mind. He had a whiskey near him, it was his second since returning from the Library. It hadn't escape him that he was drinking a lot more now, but he thought it was to be expected. Being the embodiment of Damnation caused a lot of stress.

He had to hunt, he knew that, but he needed a moment to think and to speak with the others, although he wasn't sure why; it's not like they had any idea what he was going through. They didn't understand his stress. He felt Eris' eyes on him from across the sitting area. She watched him with a frown on her face. What the hell was that all about?

"So, what are we going to do?" Hamlin asked.

"We? Since when did you get the Hell power?"

Hamlin frowned. "Okay kid, what are *you* going to do?"

"I don't have much of a choice. I need to hunt the Demon Collector down and stop him."

"No," Eris said suddenly. "You can't, not in your... condition."

"My condition?" asked Christopher.

Eris had stood up and shifted from foot to foot. "Yes, your condition. I have been trying to tell you. You're not you. You are becoming something else, something not...good. We... you need to fix that first. I think hunting isn't a good idea until we fix what's wrong with you."

"'What is wrong with me?' What is wrong with me? I'll admit there is something...off...since the bite from the werehellhound," said Christopher. There was a short whining sound from Hell Cat. "No, I don't blame you, girl. The dark soul was controlling you until my command," Christopher continued, then turned back to Eris. "But I don't have time to go 'fix me'. Today is this first day of chaos. I have to stop the Collector before his army destroys everything."

Eris folded her arms and looked down at him, somehow fiercer than Dark Eris had ever looked. "You need your soul back or you won't be able to stop what is coming. You're too weak and vulnerable in this condition..."

"ENOUGH," Christopher commanded. He rose from his seat, and darkness gathered around him; clouds of dark mist filled the room. He felt the power flowing though him, arcing out and painting the room in flashes of blue and white. The shadows had pulled to him and he was once more wrapped in his hooded coat. He towered over Eris.

But it was not Eris that stared back at him. Dark Eris didn't blink, her face a stoic mask as she faced him. She wasn't moving. She just stood there daring him to do something.

"Christopher!" Hamlin shouted.

"I'm going to hunt. I will harvest his soul."

He turned and gathered the shadows close about him so that they couldn't see his face, but he could see the hurt and anger on their faces.

He had no time for that. The rage had him now, its power coursing through him. Better to forget them, better to forget her. He summoned Hellcat to his side and she flowed into the shadows around him, somewhat reluctantly he felt. Great. Was she was against him now too? But at least she was backing him up. Not calling him weak and vulnerable.

He left the lair heading down the tunnel to the slum. He would stalk the streets, try to catch the scent of the dark soul. He flowed through the sewer tunnel, letting the shadows carry him along, pulling and pushing so that he almost floated. He leapt up the stairs and slammed open the metal door; it screamed in protest with rusted hinges and twisting metal.

On the other side of the door he paused. If he appeared on the streets like this, he would be recognized, at least as the character from the YouTube videos. Word would spread, and no doubt the Collector would hear. The Librarian was right; the Collector might be waiting for him, but he didn't need to announce his presence. He still might have the advantage of surprise.

Christopher released the shadows and they fell back into place. He kept the coat however, shaping it into a black hoodie. He still couldn't afford to show his face, not to mention that a white man walking the streets of a Mexican slum might seem a little out of place. His control of shadow was still fairly rudimentary, but it was enough to keep his face in the dark.

"Fade," he commanded Hellcat. She obediently disappeared into the shadows.

Looking less like hell on earth, he exited the building and stepped onto the streets of Neza-Chalco-Izta. The streets of the slum were not loud like the streets of New York, but the noise was constant. It was still early in the evening, just after seven. The sun had set, but people still roamed the street.

Christopher thought of it as a street, but it was more of a concrete slab. Several inhabitants looked at him, startled by his sudden and out of place appearance. But for the most part he was ignored. The buildings were old, decrepit. Where they were falling down, cinder blocks and corrugated metal sheets filled the holes. Tarps stretched across exposed roofs and open second-floor doorways. Sheets, not curtains, filled most windows. But in contrast, even in the dark, he could see that some of the cinder blocks were painted bright colors. He could see art: street graffiti mostly, but a lot of it was artistic, not destructive. Despite the impoverished conditions, some took pride in what they had.

Music played in the distance, traditional perhaps, but it was hard to tell. Another radio playing more modern pop songs was closer. TVs, audible through open windows, also jumbled into the mix. He could hear arguments and laughter.

And the smells. There was the expected odor of trash, his heightened senses could detect it clearly, but there were also the smells of dinners cooking: fragrant foods filled with spices filled the air—along with the more unpleasant smells.

As Christopher passed he shifted his vision, scanning the pedestrians about him. Weighing their souls almost automatically. He could see their sins, and there were many and they were horrible for some, but he could also the goodness, the love of life. He saw the ones dragged down by drugs or crime, he saw the ones that had given up and embraced the corruption, but he had also seen the ones that fought on, that nurtured that spark of life to lead them out of whatever darkness they had been surrounded by. Yes, there was extreme poverty here, but there was also community. Death held a place here, but that seemed to make life all the more important.

Still, poverty bred evil and he found it here more than anywhere else he had been. Whether it was the families that had sold children into sex trafficking, the murderers that walked the streets, the drug gangs that poisoned and killed, there were plenty here who deserved the judgment of damnation. He sorted through it all, looking past the mortal sins to the darkness behind. He searched for the dark soul.

Christopher walked the streets trying to catch the scent of the Collector. It didn't take him long. Instinctively he ran through what he knew of him, this Fredrick Bailey. As he mentally thumbed through the life told in the journal, it hit him. The stench of the dark soul cut through the smells that permeated the slums. The scent was stronger than before, not because he thought his prey was closer; it was more like the scent was clearer. It was as if knowing something about Fredrick Bailey's life and damnation somehow attuned him to the dark soul.

He could taste the soul-stench on his tongue. It was disgusting, but also distinctive. He could almost taste what his prey was thinking. It was unending thirst for collecting his objects of power.

"Jesus, he's worse than a Pokémon player," Christopher mumbled to himself. He almost giggled, but then caught himself. It would not do for the Lord of Damnation to be seen giggling.

He sped up after he caught the scent. The hunger to take a soul was growing stronger and pushing him faster and faster. He looked inside the people he encountered, searching their souls for the telltale sign of demonic taint.

He found murder and death, he found abuse and hate. He

found injustice and self-loathing. He found the sadistic and the just plain angry. But no demonic blemish on a soul, just normal mortal malevolence. It wasn't until he was deep in the slums, still following the scent of the Collector—the spore of the dark soul getting stronger with each step—that he spotted his first demon.

It stood in a window gazing down at the street. Christopher saw it before it saw him, and he ducked back into an alley. All the streets were alleys, but at least he had the cover of a wall. He peeked around the corner to confirm he had not been seen. He hoped that out of full costume he might not be recognizable, just another dude in a hoodie. The last thing he wanted to do was get himself noticed.

"And what the fuck do we have here," came a voice from behind him.

Christopher spun, but was able to resist releasing the Weapon or pulling the shadows to him. Behind him stood two men—large and made mostly of muscle, heads shaved, skin covered with tattoos. In the dark Christopher could see the tattoos clearly; he couldn't understand them, but he knew what it meant. These men were part of a gang.

"Oh great," he said.

"Was that English, motherfucker?" The leader glanced at Christopher's hands. Christopher had ensured that his face was not visible, but his hands were another matter. "What the fuck is an American white boy doing in our little community?"

At first Christopher tried to think up a good lie. Something about being with a charity group, trying to do research for a documentary. But he didn't really have time for all that, and they would probably just want to kill him anyway. He settled for the direct approach.

He looked into their auras, sifting through their souls, and what he found made his stomach turn. He moved quickly, before they could react. He caught the younger of the two men, not much more than a boy, by the neck and threw him against the wall of the alley. The man smacked against it and slid down, stunned.

The shadows came instantly by his command and draped him in his long coat and hood. The Hunter of Lost Souls, Lord of Damnation stood before the gang members in his full glory.

The thug had not moved; it had happened too fast. His mouth hung open in shock and terror. Christopher switched to Spanish.

A growl let him know Hellcat was with him, by his side. The gang member's eyes shifted briefly to the giant panther as she coalesced from the shadows. Panic and terror played across his face. He must have realized who Christopher was.

"You are Carlos Garcia. You murdered at least ten men and raped countless women. You think power over people through terror is true power. You are wrong,"

Christopher stepped closer to the thug, who backed away, pressing himself against the wall as though trying to bury himself in the brick.

"You are him, aren't you? You aren't going to do anything, right? I mean you're the good guy, man," the man pleaded.

"But the worst?" Christopher continued. "The worst is what you did to your mother, to your sister. You killed your own mother while she slept and then you quietly went into your little sister's room and raped her."

"How? There's no way you could have known about that shit. No way!"

"But I do, just as I know when you were tired of her, you sold her. First to your friends and then to anybody with enough pesos."

The man had slid to the ground, still trying to sink away. He had his hands up as though that could stop Christopher.

"No, I can explain. I mean that's not what happened. You can't do this! You're the good guy," the man pleaded again.

"You don't need to explain Carlos. I know you, the real you."

Christopher had pulled the Weapon out. It transformed into a large, wicked-looking knife crackling with power and hunger.

"And for the record, I am far from a good guy."

Christopher caught him by the neck and lifted. He brought the knife down, slicing through muscle, bone, and soul. He felt the blade snag the man's soul, and the gang member's eyes widened with fear and the sudden realization that there are fates worse than dying. In the next instance, his soul was sucked into the blade and the life went out of his eyes.

Christopher dropped the lifeless body and turned to the stunned young man lying on the ground. His soul was different. Christopher looked through it, tasting his life. It was a bad one, filled with abuse: horrible torture first from his father, then from the gang that forced him to join. He was not innocent, but he was not in the league of the hard-core thug whose soul Christopher had just eviscerated.

And Christopher didn't care.

The hunger was on him stronger than before and his will to fight it was weaker, so much weaker. This was a gang member. If he wasn't truly corrupt, he someday would be. He had done his fair share of crimes. He deserved damnation. It was Christopher's job to judge him, to condemn him to eternal Hell.

There was something wrong here: he knew it, could sense it. But he was beyond that. He alone had the right to pass judgment, he could not be wrong. The lust was on him and the part of him that had kept this...need...in check was weak.

"Please," the man pleaded. Just as the other had. "I don't want to die. This is all wrong."

"No," Christopher spoke calmly. "It is so right. I condemn you to eternal damnation."

The blade flashed and took the young man's soul. Blood from

the vicious cut splattered along the wall of the alley. The lifeless body sank to the ground as the Hunter of Lost Souls reveled in the taking.

The hunger was still on Christopher, but there were no immediate souls around to take. The Weapon wanted him to run into the streets taking souls. This was the slums; there were no innocents in the slums.

But even as he thought that, he heard the music again. He heard laughter, he smelled the dinners cooking. He forced the logic, the realization that this place was not inherently evil. Not everyone deserves damnation, no matter how much it might seem like it.

He put the Weapon away; without victims nearby the lust was manageable. Hellcat, sensing she was to hide again, faded into the shadows. He looked down at his latest victim. The need to harvest had receded, leaving in its place nausea. There was something wrong here. He had done something wrong.

No, he told himself. *You did your job.*

Yes, the man deserved his judgment; Christopher had made the right decision. Besides, he didn't have time for this. He glanced back at the alley entrance. What were the chances the demon in the window hadn't notice this display of power?

Christopher looked around the corner. The window was empty. He had his answer. The demon had seen something and was off to report to its master.

"Shit," he said.

He once more dismissed the shadows of his coat until he was again dressed only in a hoodie. He had to assume the Collector knew he was coming, but he didn't need to stand out like a sore thumb.

He picked up the scent again and walked deeper into the slum. The streets became narrower, darker as though the smaller they got the less light they drew in. There were few streetlights in general around here, but as he followed the scent there was less light, fewer people: as though they subconsciously knew to avoid this area.

The buildings were more run down here. Cracked and crumbling, they looked like they could fall in at any moment. Dirt and trash lay thicker here on the streets, and where there wasn't trash there was brick rubble where the walls had partially come down. No music played, no laughter. The bright colors and decorations were gone now. Just gray and dingy buildings.

It wasn't completely quiet. He could hear the occasional cough or incoherent grunt. Just moments before, the noises he heard had been the sounds of life; here, it was the sound of the dying.

He knew he was getting close, the stench of wrongness was incredibly strong here. He kept to the shadows, stretching them to provide him some cover. They would be watching for him, he knew, but he had to get as close as he could. He just hoped he wouldn't be fighting through a horde of demons for that last ten feet.

Then he turned a corner and realized he had found it. He quickly ducked back behind the house he had just passed.

It was a building, five stories high, the tallest building around. It wasn't a free-standing home, like some of the decaying structures in this area, but a building very much like a townhouse. The structures on either side had been reduced to rubble, making this one appear stark and alone.

The walls were dark gray—darker than everything around it, giving the impression it was almost black. It had two upper windows and one wide front door. It had the appearance of a face with black, rotting teeth. Nothing moved around it, almost as if this area was a ghost town. Not two streets over there had been people: worn out, destitute people seemingly drained of life, but still they were there. Here was emptiness.

There had to be guards, somebody keeping watch, but Christopher saw no one in the windows or on the roof, demon or otherwise. This was the house, it had to be; the trail of the Collector led right to it. Christopher could taste the evil essence on his tongue. It was thick around this building, but it looked deserted.

He skirted around the outside, hidden in the shadows and shelter of the deserted homes that surrounded the black house. Originally, the black house had shared walls with the homes on either side, so there were no windows or doors on those walls, just the dark gray stone. There were more windows in the back and a door: all heavily boarded up. No entry there.

Throughout his reconnaissance Christopher felt eyes on him, watching his every move, but he saw no one. If there were demons outside of that home, he would have been able to feel it, smell them if they were close enough. If the Collector truly had an army there would be some sign; they wouldn't all fit inside that black house.

He wasn't an idiot. He knew it was probably a trap, but he had no choice, he would have to spring it.

20

"My God," Hamlin whispered.

He stared dumbfounded at the screens. He had several news channels open. Facebook was also open, several accounts streaming at once. Twitter was spewing short messages across another screen. Hamlin was no tech whiz, but he could get the sites up and running with all the applications on the system. Eris had helped him with social media sites.

"What? Anything happening?" Eris asked.

She stood behind him at the kitchen counter, fixing them sandwiches. She wasn't really hungry after the fight with Chris, but she had to do something to keep herself busy. She put down the mayo after hearing the tone in Hamlin's voice.

"Yes. Dear God, yes."

"Well what? What the hell is going on?" She had come around the counter to look over his shoulder. She could see the video feeds filled with people running and screaming.

"Chaos, pure chaos," Hamlin said.

The scary thing was Hamlin didn't know the true extent of

what had happened. A few minutes ago, it had been a quiet peaceful evening. He had started to entertain the thought that this Day of Chaos was just an internet hoax, maybe a gimmick to get them down here. He could focus on Christopher and his hunt. Not that the boy seemed to want them involved. Then it all started, and he watch with growing horror as is unfolded in real time across the internet.

First the power went down; not everywhere, but in a few select infrastructure points. Prisons lost their alarms, hospitals lost primary, and in some cases, secondary power. The airport above lost power throughout the building and the runways. According to the news feeds, the air traffic controller computers were operational, but that was followed quickly by a tweet from the airport saying midair collisions had occurred and it appeared the software had been hacked; it could not be trusted.

Police and fire stations went dark. He saw footage of an officer, his computer system in the car blank. He was yelling something into the mic on his portable radio.

Buses were down. Some routes were operational, but according to Twitter, they had lost contact with dispatch. Cell service had also gone down, but not data service. And that was odd. The internet, cell data service, these things were still up. Social media was the only form of reliable communication. That meant something. This was intentional.

"This is it, the big hack from the group. This is Days of Chaos," Hamlin said. "The extent of this hacking is unprecedented. I mean, it looks like it's targeting every vital infrastructure component: transportation, emergency services, everything."

They heard a distant boom and the lair shook slightly.

"Jesus Christ! I think that was a plane crashing."

"Is it everywhere, or just Mexico City?"

"Just here, I think. I'm not seeing anything from any other

country other than reaction to what is happening here. Just like they said, today was the first Day of Chaos and the target was Mexico City. I never thought they meant all of Mexico City."

Eris pointed and Hamlin turned back the screen. The image of Guy Fawkes was popping up on social media feeds. Below the images were more symbols taken from the first language. And below, that more words in English. And they chilled Hamlin to the bone.

NOW THE REAL HACKING BEGINS

"That doesn't sound good," Eris said.

Hamlin was frantically clicking with the mouse. More windows would open, capturing live video streams from people on the ground.

"Dammit! I wish I knew how to work this thing. We need a computer guy!"

"A computer guy?" Eris asked.

"Yeah, you know. Some tech guy to run all this shit. Like in the movies."

"No problem. I'll run a Craig's list ad. Wanted: computer guy like in the movies. Use the latest hacking and illegal tools in service to the gatekeeper of Hell. Team player needed. Must be okay working with demons and panthers made of shadows."

Hamlin could tell he was now talking to Dark Eris. He ignored her.

On the screen something changed. When the power went out as the chaos started, large groups of protesters out on the streets cheered—believing, Hamlin suspected, that this was all part of the protest. And it was. Just not in the way they thought. When the lights went out and the security systems failed, the crowd, already amped up, turned ugly.

On the screen Hamlin watched as a window was smashed by a trash can. Then a car was smashed and stripped. The protests were turning into a riot. Most of this was captured on phone cameras. Some was captured by news cameras that were streaming directly to their websites.

All around the city videos popped up with the same signs of destruction. The entire city was turning into a riot. But it was no natural riot.

"They're doing this," Hamlin said.

"How?" Dark Eris asked. "I understand the hacking, but how are they escalating the riots?"

"Riots, by their nature, are a gas-fire just waiting for a spark. You seed the protests with enough of your people—or real extremists—and that's your match. Right now, it's just a few sparks. My biggest concern is what they are going to use to stoke the flames. Riots will calm down as authorities start taking control."

"But the authorities are crippled by the cyber-attack," Dark Eris said.

"Exactly, but I have a horrible feeling there is something more about to happen, something to take all of this to another level."

"The demon army," Dark Eris said.

"I think we are going to see a sudden escalation in bloodshed."

As if taking a cue from Hamlin on the screen, a phone camera caught a protester leaping onto a police officer in riot gear, driving him to the ground. Before the other officers could react and come to the assistance of their colleague, the protester screamed like a wild animal and bashed the officer's head against the ground. The riot helmet split open from the impact, and the officer's body went limp.

"There," Dark Eris said and pointed at the screen. "That is no mortal. There's a demon inside there, controlling him."

As several officers swooped in to assist, the protester struck out, knocking the officer back into his colleagues. For a moment it was as though everyone was shocked by this sudden display of violence, everybody held their breath for a split second. Then it was all fear and anger.

More protesters broke through and attacked the police. Police batons whipped through the air and more than a few pulled out guns. As more demon-possessed protesters charged the police, gunfire rang out into the crowd.

"Jesus," Hamlin whispered. Similar scenes played out on other video feeds. Some news crews had set up and found a way to stream directly to the internet on battery power. Everywhere, police and protesters—instigated by demonic forces and, Hamlin suspected, paid mercenaries in disguise—clashed and violence erupted.

The governor had brought in military troops to back up the limited police force, but standard riot procedure was soon abandoned and deadly weapons came out.

"Whoever is responsible for this has a lot of money. Enough to hire an army of mercenaries or fund an extreme activist group, or both," he said.

"And is well connected with the supernatural. Obviously, the Collector is a part of all this," Dark Eris said.

"The Alliance, whatever that is exactly, they have to be behind this. And they went to extremes to make sure the world sees it."

"By the way," Dark Eris said. "You have mail."

"What?" Hamlin looked at the email program. It did indeed indicate he had one unopened email. The message was cryptic. A string of numbers and a note:

Careful... this is obviously a trap.

It was followed by a smiley face and a poop emoji.

"What the fuck is that?" Hamlin asked.

"That's called an emoji..."

"I know what the fuck that is! I meant what are the numbers?"

Hamlin thought for a moment and then it clicked. "They're coordinates."

Quickly he copy-pasted the string of numbers and letters into Google Maps. A pin popped up in the middle of the slums.

Dark Eris stood back. "It's got to be where Chris is going, right? It can't be a coincidence. He's walking into a trap. I knew it. We tried to tell him."

"We don't even know who sent the email. It could have been anybody."

"Not anybody. Somebody who knows who Christopher is and his fucking email, they obviously know more about what is going on than we do. Send the coordinates to my cell."

Dark Eris turned to leave at a run.

"What the hell are you doing?" Hamlin asked.

"Going to save the asshole. Again."

"And what the hell am I supposed to do?"

"I don't know. Try to figure out who sent the email."

Then she was gone. Hamlin just stared at the keyboard. He had never felt so helpless.

21

Christopher shaped the shadows once again into coat and hood. No point in hiding; they knew he was coming and there were no mortals around to shock. Then he leapt to the top of the home, shadows and dark energy billowing out from him, covering the roof as he landed.

Still nothing. He was beginning to hope something would attack him. He was getting creeped out. When this sort of thing happened in the movies, it was a bad sign.

There was a hatch, like a trapdoor, on the roof. He opened it up and gazed into the darkness below. There was nothing really to see, it was a simple empty room.

He dropped down, Weapon out. It flared to life as a longsword, bright with power. The room he had dropped down into was dark, as though there were no windows. The light from the trap door in the ceiling cast a brick of light onto the ground where he stood. But just beyond his arm's reach, the light died as though sucked up by the shadows.

There was something wrong. It wasn't natural darkness, and

his eyesight struggled to penetrate the shadows around him. Normally Christopher was at home in the dark, at least since he had taken up the Book and Weapon. But this was just wrong. The power arcing from his blade gave him some light. The walls seemed to be covered with some sort of lumpy substance, much thicker than mold.

And the smell. The scent of rot filled the room. The place smelled more like a rendering factory than an old abandoned home. The scent of the slums outside were a rose garden compared to this place. The air was so heavy he could taste the decay on his tongue. He wanted to vomit. Not really the image he wanted to portray as the Lord of Damnation.

He slowly became aware of a sound. Or perhaps many sounds. Rhythmic, but out of sync with each other. It was the sound of a breath. No, it was the sound of a hundred people breathing. Even as he realized what it was, it grew louder. Then there were other sounds. Moans and grunts from his right, whispered talking to his left.

He spun, blade up, but nothing was there—just the horrid smell and lumpy walls. Then a scream, a wail, pierced through the breathing sound. The moans grew louder.

And Christopher realized he was in the scariest haunted house of all time—which was saying a lot considering his job was dealing with what were technically ghosts.

He heard a sickening wet, organic sound, like flesh tearing. He spun towards the disturbing noise, blade held high. A figure, vaguely humanoid, peeled itself away from the wall as though it had been attached. It was a pale, white thing with black veins, as though oil pumped through its body. As Christopher watched it jerked, its leg—the foot still attached to the wall—pulled free, leaving behind a moist, skin covered wallpaper. Then its eyes opened.

Baleful red eyes glared at him. Suddenly there were eyes all around him, covering the walls. He could hear the same squishing sound as the room came alive with writhing bodies, pulling themselves from the walls. The first stood before Christopher and grinned, its large mouth stretched to fit dozens of sharp, glistening teeth.

It had once been human, but now only shared a vague resemblance. Its face was split, its massive mouth covering the bottom half, while above, small, but brightly glowing red dots served as eyes. Its arms were long gangly things that ended in finger-like claws. It was nude; originally a woman, its breasts lay shriveled against its chest.

Then it started to laugh and the others joined in as they detached from the wall. Sucking sounds mixed with giggles here, titters there.

Now he could see the demon auras infesting these once-human beings. He could smell the evil like a thick and heavy blanket over the room. Somehow this house had hid them from him. But he had no time to try and figure out why.

He raised the Weapon, and the demon in front of him screamed and charged. Its long arms caught him by surprise and its claws came within inches of his face before the blade found its mark to rip through the demon-infested human, tearing its human soul out.

Christopher could almost hear the Weapon singing in joy as it harvested a new soul. He didn't give it time to revel. Christopher reversed the blade, slicing through the next one that charged at him. He reached out to the Hell power that sat just beneath the surface, and it leapt to fill him up.

It burned through him and with it came the hunger, the need to harvest souls. The Weapon connected with the power inside him and the energy billowed out from him in an explosive flash of crackling energy and light.

The flesh demons around him stepped back and shielded their eyes as he unleashed some of his power, but they recovered quickly. He had not done any real damage to them. But the brief light gave him a good view of the room around him before they swarmed back in. It seemed as though the entire upper floor of the house was one large room—perhaps originally intended as a ballroom back when this was a promising neighborhood, before the area changed to the slum it was now. Just before bringing his sword to bare on another demon, he spotted a staircase leading down in the back of the room, now filled with the flesh demons. The walls were a sticky mess where they had been attached moments before.

A roar shook the house and, as though reading his thoughts, Hellcat shot out of the shadows and plunged into the group of demons between Christopher and the stairs. Christopher spun, blade cutting and cleaving in a circle. Souls dragged from the blade like strands of thick spider web, but the Weapon was insatiable and drew them all in.

The Lord of Damnation cut through the flesh demons like chaff, the Weapon wailing a joyous song. In front of him, Hellcat pounced from demon to demon, ripping them apart with tooth and claw.

As inexperienced as he was, Christopher was more than a match for any of these demons or even a smaller group. But the room was full of them, and more were coming out from the wall through some sort of perverse birthing process. Claws and teeth were getting through to him, even as the blade sung its deadly song.

Just like on the streets in front of the hotel, he was going to lose by sheer, overwhelming force. He had to get out of this room; the space was too confined, there were too many of them. He made a run for the stairs, following Hellcat.

Claws racked at his back and scored deep on his thigh and chest. He would never had made it if not for Hellcat. She cleared the way, using her own tooth and claw method. Her sheer size, which seemed to fluctuate depending on her anger and the amount of shadow she had to draw on, drove the flesh demons back. Here, though the darkness was not natural, she had found enough shadow to be at least twice the size of a normal panther, like a large tiger.

The horde tried to close in behind her, separating the two of them. The blade in Christopher's hand shifted, and intuitively he grasped it with both hands as it morphed into two axes. Now, weapon in each hand, he was able to chop his way through, hack and slash style. Blood splattered everywhere, souls ripped free. The hunger inside of him absorbed all the bloodshed, all the killing and soul-stealing, and wanted more. Always more.

Hatred and anger boiled over. He ignored the bites and claw slashes. He lost himself in the bloodshed, in the joy of killing. These were weak demons, no skill or tactics: simple violence was all they understood.

Before he knew it, he was standing at the top of the stairs. And there he hesitated.

His hunger wanted him to stay. He was shredded, severely injured and weakening, but there were still so many souls here. They were there for the taking. He could lose himself in this, the pleasure of damnation.

A roar from Hellcat brought him back to reality. He snapped out of it. What was he thinking? He needed to find and stop the Collector. Christopher had no idea if he was in this house of horrors, but he had to find out.

He jumped down the stairs to the large foyer below. This floor of the house was significantly different than above. The walls on this level were not the fleshy thick ones of the upstairs. They were a cold, dark gray like the outside, and discolored with mold and water damage. But the smell was better than the rotting stench above, though not by much. It had a familiar scent; to Christopher's heightened senses it smelled almost metallic.

His eyes also saw more down here. He did not see windows, but his night vision showed him everything.

The floor was bright red, shiny, the color of fresh blood. As he moved he saw that it indeed was blood. The entire floor was covered with a thin layer of the stuff. It filled every spot like a giant, shallow pool. As he stepped, the hollows left behind by his feet filled. It was like standing in the aftermath of a gruesome flood.

How many had been slaughtered to make this much blood? And why hadn't it dried yet? It should be coagulating, not a fresh, slick mess.

Hellcat stood at the edge of the stairs looking up. He could hear the demons above making their way down. They were surging down in one fleshy blur. Christopher looked for an exit. There was the front door, but retreating now sort of defeated the purpose. A hallway led away from the foyer. It seemed like his best bet. He needed to stay alive long enough to find the Collector. That hallway was his only choice. Of course, he considered, that was probably exactly where they wanted him to go.

He splashed through the room, sliding and limping down the hallway. Blood, kicked up from his running, splattered the gray stone walls making it look as though the walls bled black. He saw movement, a disturbance in the pool ahead.

At the other end of the hallway a form rose from the blood pool. Ripples spread from it as it broke the surface. It was humanoid and covered in blood—drenched in fact: the red coated him from head to toe as though it was made from the stuff rather than just covered in it. And maybe it was, Christopher would put nothing past this house of horrors. The figure seemed to sprout straight from the floor.

Muscle, striated and raw, showed through the blood and Christopher could see its black, rotting teeth grinning at him. The lack of skin didn't seem to bother it.

Behind it Christopher could see more blood demons popping up in a straight, smooth motion. A growl from Hellcat, paws drenched in red, made him turn his head. Behind him, in the room they had just left, more demons were rising.

Flesh above, blood below.

Once again, he was surrounded. The hunger raged in him to cut into these demons like he had upstairs, but that way led to madness. He could hack all day and eventually he would die.

There was a door to his left. He kicked it open and saw stairs beyond. A moan escaped the demons, a wet, gurgling sound that in unison sounded like the rapids of an angry river.

Christopher didn't hesitate, he plunged into the dark of the stairs. It occurred to him this house and now these stairs were confining. He was not a skilled fighter; that was more than obvious with just his few visits to the training books in the Library, but he was much more effective when he had more room. When he had space, he could use his quick movement and control of shadows to assist. Here his options were limited.

They were herding him.

As if responding to his thoughts, the Weapon became two large knife blades, one for each hand. The stairs doubled back, ending at a stone floor and a wall with a massive door. A door made of faces.

Red and brown, the door glistened like the blood flood upstairs. Only this wasn't liquid. Faces writhed and twisted in the door, each briefly rising to the surface before fading back and another took its place. It looked like something out of the Hellraiser movies Hamlin made him watch as "research". But these faces were not human: each was a demonic visage of anger and pain. There must have been hundreds.

Behind him blood was flowing down the stairs like a red waterfall display. The blood demons were coming. He had to go through the door.

As he reached for it, the handle morphed into a gaping mouth lined with needle teeth, like some sort of vicious worm. He wasn't grabbing that.

He looked down at the knives in his hand and even as he thought it, the Weapon shifted into a massive war hammer. For the first time it changed in response to his thoughts, not in anticipation of his need. It vibrated with hatred and anger, the souls it had drunk had excited it more than ever before. He didn't have time to contemplate what this new-found control meant. He could hear the wet, gurgling moans of the blood demons.

He released the power of Hell inside of him, channeling it though the Weapon. It almost hummed with glee as he brought the Weapon back over his shoulder and, with a war cry that would have made his Cossack trainer proud, he swung it straight at the door, feeling the power release as it smashed into the face coated barrier.

The door burst inward in a cacophony of screeches, screams, roars and moans. The concussion of the blast shook the entire house. Plaster from the ceiling rained down on them. That door had been held by something powerful, something he had released.

Behind him flesh demons were charging down the stairs. Where the blood had pooled by the steps more blood demons were popping up. They would be on him in seconds. Beyond the broken door was a short set of stairs, five or six steps, and then it opened up into a large room with a hole in the center.

The room was some sort of subbasement. There were no windows and the walls were gray brick, older looking than the rotting walls above, as though this room predated the house. It had an archaic feel to it, but it was also the cleanest smelling room he had encountered. Christopher welcomed the stale, musty scent over the rot and putrid above.

The hole was a perfectly round gaping circle, no lip or rail around it—just a shadowy hole in the ground. In this house Christopher wouldn't be surprised if it was an express route straight to Hell.

Balls of energy—demonic essences released from the door when he had smashed it—floated through the air like sickly colored bubbles. Most of the demonic energy floated away, quickly disappearing down the hole. But one large energy ball grew and twisted into a new shape. A new, horrific shape.

It was something out of a nightmare. It's what would have happened if Cthulhu had fucked a pile of Jell-O. Long tentacles stretched out from each side of the giant head. Huge oval eyes hovered above a vertical gash of a mouth. A mouth with several sideways jaws, each containing a layer of teeth. The mouth gaped wide, showing just how far its massive jaws could open, and bellowed out a roar.

Tentacles whipped about, throwing off great clumps of slick slime. The monstrous head sat atop a body that was more a sickly, gelatinous mess than a real body. The tentacles were long enough to reach the sides of the oversized room. He would not be able to run past it. If he assumed his prey was in the hole, he would have to go through it.

Behind him Christopher heard Hellcat roar as she attacked the flesh and blood demons trying to come through the door. She held the doorway, but he knew she couldn't hold it for long.

He charged at the demon. The Weapon shifted in his hands and then he was holding two large curved blades, heavy enough to chop into the tentacles, but light enough to be quick.

A tentacle unfurled at him and he chopped into the appendage. It was a clean slice and it fell to the ground; the remaining stump spurted a white, thick fluid that looked more like mucous than blood. The Weapon embraced the violence with relish despite the lack of a soul to damn in this demon incarnate.

A second tentacle darted at him, then a third, and a fourth. The Weapon sliced through the air, severing one appendage and wounding another. The fourth tentacle, slightly smaller than the others, whipped around his right arm, catching it up before he could strike. It was slick with slime but tightened so quickly he had no time to pull his arm away. It crushed his bone and muscle. The blade in his left came down on the tentacle, sending it writhing to the floor.

He darted back, his crushed arm hanging loosely at his side. He could still hold the other blade, but swinging it was another matter. Christopher felt a burning pain race down his back, and he turned to see a flesh demon, its clawed hand dripping with his blood. Christopher spun and danced out of the way of a striking tentacle, clumsily slicing into the flesh demon.

There were too many—too many tentacles, too many demons, just too many. Despite Hellcat's viciousness and deadly claws, flesh and blood demons were starting to get past her too. One on one he could have defeated any of these demons. But there were too many...

One on one.

He spun back to the tentacle demon. Too many tentacles. He had attacked the tentacles like each one was an enemy, each had to be defeated to get to the real goal of getting to the stairs. But the tentacles weren't really many. There was only one real target.

He struck at another blood demon, slicing its head off neatly. More were stepping into the room fighting their way past Hellcat. He only had moments. He put the two blades together and commanded the Weapon to become a pocket knife again, putting his new-found powers of control to the test.

It resisted. Perhaps it was the eminent battle and souls to claim, but he could physically feel it push back. Time for the real test. Christopher pulled on the Hell seed inside of him—the source of his power—and then picturing an almost comically large hammer made of power, mentally slammed it down on the Weapon.

Surprisingly it relented and became a simple pocket knife once again. He clasped it firmly in his one good hand and once more charged at the tentacle demon. This time he gathered his power about him and then he jumped, streaking through the air toward the head of the monster. He ignored the tentacles. They were not the target, they were a means.

The thick, sickly green appendages whipped through the air and caught him. One pythoned around his torso, another wrapped around his thigh. Two more joined the one around his chest and another snagged his half-healed arm. But he kept the hand holding the pocket knife free, held high above his head.

Then the tentacles constricted, squeezing him like giant snakes. Air rushed from his lungs before he could stop it. He felt muscle and bone compress and pain throbbed through his whole body. He drew upon his power, sent it radiating out through his body, reinforcing muscle and sinew to withstand the squeeze. Still he felt joints pop, his ribs crack, his head throbbed from the pressure. The tentacles themselves became sandpaper as they tightened, pulling off skin like the world's worst carpet burn.

Christopher resisted, but he didn't struggle. The demon pulled him quickly toward its mouth. The tentacles squeezed harder and he concentrated his Hellfire energy to hold off the pressure from crushing him. The pain was intense, he felt his ribs breaking. Still he held steady.

The demon opened a wide, gaping mouth spread sideways, its multi-jawed mouth chomping open and closed quickly, like a demented mulcher. It pulled him closer toward that mouth; if any part of him got caught in those jaws he would be shredded. But he had no intention of passing through those jaws.

Just a moment before his outstretched hand entered that mouth, Christopher commanded the Weapon to become a lance. He pictured it in his head, something from a movie, a thick, metal spear coming to a point, with a large metal cuff to protect his hand. He didn't know if that was what a real lance looked like. It didn't matter it was the Weapon he needed right now.

The Weapon needed no encouragement, it shifted in his hand. A large spear tip radiating power and energy sprang outward, while a cuff grew around his hand for protection. The lance crackled with energy, bands of power played across the shaft.

The demon had no time to react; it couldn't stop the momentum of pulling its prey to its mouth. Christopher was already too close. The lance shot out from his hand and even before it reached its full length, it was piercing through the demon's maw. Its dark oval eyes widened in surprise as the lance drove into the face of the demon.

It had been pulling him with all of its strength; Christopher used the momentum to drive the lance deeper into the demon head, through that teeth lined mouth. Even as its tentacles started weakening, Christopher drove the lance deeper. The teeth stopped chomping and the demon fell back. Christopher went with it until it hit the ground next to the hole. His lance was wedged inside its skull, the multiple rows of teeth clamped against the hand guard of the lance. Christopher crouched on its chest, hand still holding the lance.

The Weapon, as though anticipating his command, changed back into a simple pocket knife. No resistance this time. The demon body was already becoming incorporeal, fading into nothing. There was no ball of energy to return to the collector, or to hell for that matter. He hadn't just ended the demon host, he had ended the demon itself. Christopher stepped off of it just as it faded.

A glance over his shoulder showed Hellcat still standing, but she was injured and weakened. Flesh and blood demons were slipping around her, but she had held them back long enough.

"Come on, follow me," Christopher commanded. He turned to the hole.

It wasn't really a hole, it was the top of a wide spiral staircase that led down into darkness. He plunged down the stairs before the demon horde could reach him. A strangely unsettling yowl behind him told him Hellcat was just behind him. So, he suspected, was the demonic horde.

The stairs were stone and apparently went on forever. He ran down through several revolutions of the spiral and saw no bottom in sight. Perhaps this hole really did lead directly to hell. After several more revolutions, the stone floor changed. It had started as old, but still man-made brick, now it seemed to be made of natural stone. The walls, too, went from smooth brick to the uneven surface of carved rock. He was in an area built long before the dark house upstairs.

His body ached, broken and battered from the dark house above. He was healing, but his ribs screamed in pain with every step. He moved fast—he had to with the devils on his tail—but he wanted nothing more than to just sit down on the steps and take a breather.

He could hear the moans, screeching, and wet footfalls of the horde behind him. No matter how worn out he was that sound drove him on. If he stopped, even for a second, he and Hellcat would be overwhelmed. At least he could save one of them.

"Hellcat, fade," He commanded.

She growled as though offended at his request and ignored him.

So much for the authority of the Lord of Damnation.

He slipped several times, sending him sliding off down the hard, stone steps. Each time was a new test of pain as he skittered across the sharp stone edge of the stairs. Just as he decided the stairs were not a gateway to hell, but hell itself, they came abruptly to the bottom and faced a large doorway. Without thinking he charged through it.

Into a land of wonder.

It was a massive cavern. The largest he had ever seen. The floor of the cave was the size of a small valley, complete with a small river running down its length. The cave wall, easily hundreds of feet across, stretched off into a ceiling hidden by shadows. The river emerged from the wall, close to the doorway Christopher had just passed through. The cavern floor was littered with large, moss-covered stones covered. Large, tree-like plants grew from the wall and the ground near the river.

All this was as a blur as he ran headlong into the cave. The cavern was dark, but his enhanced vision cut though the blackness, so it took him a moment to realize there was light. He was a good fifty feet into the cave before he spotted its origin—high overhead from the top of a large stone pyramid that dominated the cave. It had taken Christopher a moment to understand what he was looking at.

The large, man-sized bricks that made up the pyramid were old and weathered with rounded edges and moss. More moss carpeted a wide swath of step-sized stones that cut through the middle, creating an obvious path to the top. From the base of the stairs behind him it had looked like a large natural stone formation. Up close, it was clearly a man-made pyramid.

He also realized the flesh and blood demons were no longer right behind him. He looked and saw them still coming out from the stairwell, but they were no longer running. They came out slowly, fanning out around the cavern.

They were no longer chasing him because he was right where they wanted him. The trap was sprung, now he just had to figure out exactly what it was. He slowed to a walk as he approached the pyramid.

He looked toward the top, where the lights were coming from. He could be at the top in seconds, but something told him to look before he leapt this time. The light came from several construction lights; heavy-duty powerlines ran down the side of the pyramid. The structure may have been ancient, but somebody had made a hasty attempt to modernize it.

But he took in all of this on the periphery. What caught his attention, what turned his stomach to the point where he didn't know if he would vomit or scream in anger, was what he saw in that pool of hastily erected light.

There was a big man, larger than any person Christopher had ever seen:—tall, but also impossibly wide—dressed in an expensive, perfectly-tailored suit. It was out of place, not the kind of outfit you'd wear for spelunking. Next to him a girl knelt, young, maybe early teens. She was also dressed a little formally for the location, in a long, flowing dress. Her head was bowed as she stared at something glowing in her hands.

Christopher felt a strangeness when he looked at her glowing hands, as if there was something there he should have been able to see. Something he should have known.

The Collector was there also, dressed in his archaic priestly clothes. The Collector grinned down at him with such a smug look Christopher wanted to punch him in the face.

But a moment later, none of this was important. To see enemies known and unknown standing before him, he barely even noticed. It was the last figure up there that took all of his attention.

At the top of the pyramid Eris hung limp from two short pillars like some sort of ancient sacrifice.

22

Dark Eris landed on the roof of the building. Her huge bat-like wings pulled into her back. She was in her demonic form, a gigantic skeleton creature with huge, leathery wings. She'd had no choice, flying was the fastest way to get here. She glanced at the cellphone in her over-sized claws. Yeah this was the spot.

She stood on top of a single-story building. The roof itself was cracked and peeling. She could feel it sagging beneath her large talon-like feet. It was rotting. She could smell it.

In fact, the whole area smelled...off...different than other areas of the slum. The rest of the slum had its stink of course, but it was the smell of life; dinner cooking, the scent of exhaust from an old car, even the smell of refuse was sign that someone lived there.

Here there was nothing. Not even a sound.

That was even odder than the lack of smells. Where were the sounds of music? The sounds of kids playing in the background, a fight between a husband and wife? Where was the barking of stray dogs or people laughing?

Nothing, just silence. It was eerie. She looked off the building.

Nothing walked in the streets. She couldn't even hear bugs in the distance. It was not natural, this silence. Something was wrong. Her eye was caught by a structure across the street. A large, dark gray house. It stood alone, the buildings on either side had rotted away, leaving piles of rubble.

It drew her attention, stood out like a black spot in her vision, but that house wasn't where the coordinates had led her. They had led her to the one she was standing on. A very plain, flat structure. She would check this one out if she found nothing then she would move on to the black house. Like knows like, and she could feel evil in that black structure.

She looked around once more at the streets. Christopher was nowhere to be seen. He might not have even arrived. She flew here direct; he was following his nose. He could be hours away.

Or he could be captured or killed in the building below her. She didn't know why this bothered her so much, but then again, she didn't know why anything he did bothered her. She was a demon: she delighted in torture and despair. But something or someone had a purpose when placing her in this body. It was a curse of some sort, the only explanation. If only she could remember more. But her memories of the time before she woke up in this body were fuzzy.

Regardless, Christopher was the ticket out, so she had better make sure he was still in one piece.

There was a trapdoor in the roof and she ripped the door up off its hinges. In her demonic form it was hard to reign in her strength; she wanted to break things and hurt people. It was her nature, to be destructive. The door was too small for her to pass through. More destruction was in order.

Grabbing both sides of the trap doorway she pushed. The wooden frame splintered and the surrounding plaster disintegrated into dust. Now it was wide enough to accommodate her large body. After a quick glance, she dropped down into the room below.

It was empty. Debris, trash, pieces of plaster, and old beer bottles lay scattered about. The interior wall of the room had been removed, clumsily as the exposed brick attested to. Portions of walls still stood in key spots, supporting the sagging roof. That was odd, Eris thought inside, it was as though someone was intentionally trying to make the place look like it was about to fall apart. Maybe to discourage trespassers?

The only exit out of the room besides the front door was a dark hallway. She stopped just before entering. There was no way she would be able to fit. Only hesitating a moment, she shifted back into her—or rather Eris'—human body. She would need a moment to change back if something surprised her, also assuming Eris doesn't take control—*I won't*—it was a risk she had to take.

The hallway was short, ending at a large, wooden door. It looked old and decayed but when she tried it, it was solid and much newer than it looked. She held the doorknob and cranked it with just a little of her demonic strength. The doorknob sheared off in her hand. Again, overt destruction felt so good.

The door slowly creaked open. Beyond was a short flight of stairs that ended in what was obviously an elevator door. Bingo.

The elevator had a card reader. She pushed the button just to be certain and nothing happened. That's when she spotted the security camera mounted just above the door.

"Dammit," she muttered to herself.

Why do you always have to charge ahead? Why can't you take a moment to think? Eris inside said.

"I'd beat the shit out of you if it wasn't for the fact that I'd be punching my own face," Dark Eris whispered. "Anyway, there's no point in hiding now."

She released the demon form and felt the snap and crackling

flashes of pain as her body once more became the giant demon of her true self. She grasped the edges of each sliding door with claws and wedged them in the small crack between them. Then with a heave, she bent them back. They ripped from their rails and clattered to the floor. Beyond, the elevator shaft dropped away into darkness.

She grabbed the cable with one hand and used her other to hold onto the side of the shaft. She was big enough to stretch across the opening with her legs and arms, so between the walls and cable she moved down quickly, hand over hand.

The shaft went fairly deep below the surface. Whatever had been built here was huge. Someone had managed to build an extensive underground facility without anybody on the surface knowing. That took lots and lots of money.

The elevator car was at the bottom. She landed on it with a thump. The reinforced steel box would be a pain to tear into, luckily there was a hatch with an emergency release on the outside. She became human again to get through the small opening. After confirming it was empty, she dropped down.

It was a service elevator, plain steel floor with a tread that prevented slipping. It smelled of oil and metal, and a small amount of BO. There were two buttons next to the door, only two floors and no call button or emergency stop. There was a door open button, however.

The metal doors opened and she immediately realized where the B. O. smell was coming from. The room beyond was a combination kitchen and living room. It looked like it had been built in the seventies and never been cleaned since. It smelled of old food, body odor, and death, which was easily explained by the body hanging from an exposed electrical pipe running along the ceiling. Below it a chair lay on its side.

The body was still swinging, so he must have kicked that chair moments ago. Perhaps while she had been up on the roof. The man seemed older, maybe in his forties, gray hair just starting to come in. He wore a tactical vest and belt; a hat on the floor next to the chair said security. She doubted it was her arrival that had caused him to take his life. Suicide didn't seem like a promising tactic when you had a trespasser approaching. No, something else had caused his despair.

She checked two of the doors. One was a bathroom in desperate need of cleaning. The other, a bunkhouse that smelled worse than the shitter. Nobody was in them, and she didn't bother searching. Not even Christopher was that important.

Beyond that final door, however, was the whole purpose of the complex. There were several desks, topped with dozens of monitors, and beyond them a glass wall separating this room from what looked like a giant computer room. A data center she thought she had heard Hamlin call this type of thing, a room with rack after rack of computers.

"And I thought the lair had an impressive set up. It's got nothing on this place," she said to herself. Above the desks two other bodies swung, almost imperceptibly. A coordinated suicide, and a recent one. Interesting, but this didn't get her any closer to Christopher.

The computer monitors each had various video streams playing out and social media windows open, messages and posts scrolling past. The videos were similar to what Hamlin had been watching at the lair: riots, destruction, violence. National news internet streams broadcasted that many were dead, vital infrastructure had collapsed, and unprecedented levels of unrest and chaos had engulfed the city.

The private streams were even worse. Many showed images of the death and destruction up close, images that would never have been shown on official news channels. Dead bodies—men, women, even children in some cases.

My god, Eris said inside. *How can people be so vicious*?

Of all creatures, supernatural or not, humans have the highest capacity for evil. When manipulated, twisted to dark desires, it can become a horrible weapon, Dark Eris thought back.

Then she heard a noise. A quiet, human noise. She looked around the desk closest to her, the one without a body hanging above it. A young man, perhaps a little younger than Chris, sat against the stone wall, face in his hands. Despite trying to be quiet it was obvious he was sobbing.

A crying kid. This was a job for Eris.

I can take over, Eris said inside.

Dark Eris looked around once more to confirm they were in no immediate danger. *Okay, but at the first hint of danger I take over again. Agreed*? She thought back.

"Yes," Eris said out loud as she took over control.

The kid looked up, face wet with tears and snot. He might have been surprised, but he looked through her, almost as if she didn't exist, like her presence may have been imaginary and he wasn't sure how to tell. Then the boy's eyes slid to the monitor on the desk. His face turned white at the images of death. Then he stared at the bodies hanging from the ceiling.

And Eris knew he was going to lose it. She moved fast, sinking down to his side. She grabbed a hold of his hand, wet from crying.

"Hey, Hey, look at me. Don't look at them, look at me," Eris said.

He didn't respond, he stared emptily at the gently swaying bodies.

"Hey." Eris grabbed his face and forced it away from the gruesome display. "Look at me."

His eyes focused on her. Then he said something in Spanish.

"I don't speak Spanish," Eris said.

"I did this," he said. He spoke clearly with a heavy accent. "I have done all this."

"No, no. This is not your fault."

Well we don't really know that, do we? He could be the mastermind behind all of this, thought Dark Eris from inside.

"This boy is no mastermind," Eris said.

The boy focused on her, he frowned. "Who are you talking to?"

"Never mind," she said. "I was just saying whatever you did, it was not all this." She gestured at the computer monitors. "No one person could do all this."

"Yes, I could. I disabled the power grid, I...I sabotaged the airport software. I took down fire and police systems." He paused and released a sob, then he clutched at her shirt. "I did all this, but I didn't know. I didn't know! They told me it was just for fear, nobody would really die. Just fear, just to make them stop and take notice. Take notice of us."

He let go and slumped back, crying freely now. She had to talk fast or she would lose him, his mental state was deteriorating.

"It wasn't you. You were a tool. Like these others, you were used by people with agendas far bigger than yours. But you are different, you're strong. You need to see that."

"I killed...people, children they say. I don't remember what I did exactly, but this is all my fault."

"You were manipulated."

He looked up once again at the hanging bodies. "That's what I must do. They had it right, we don't deserve to live."

He started to get up, struggling in his grief. Eris pushed him down firmly. "That won't solve anything."

"Yes, it will. It's the justice I deserve, no less."

"So, you're a monster?" Eris asked. She had to change tactics. She didn't know this kid, she had to go on instinct.

"What? No. I didn't want all this, that's why I need to end it." Once again, he started to rise.

She slammed him down again, harder this time.

"End what? I don't think you have any idea what *you* really did. I think you were used like a fucking wrench to do the bidding of some bad son of a bitch. But let's say you did do all of this. How's killing yourself gonna fix it? Who's gonna give a fuck about what a kid does in a bunker somewhere while their world is going to hell? It will fix nothing, and your 'justice' will be for nothing."

Nice one girl, Dark Eris thought inside.

He looked back at her, his mouth open. "Who are you?"

"I'm the one trying to help fix what's going on. I'm the one keeping a kid that might be able to help from committing suicide. My name is Eris, and my friends and I are trying to stop these Days of Chaos."

He winced at the name. "I didn't come up with that name, that was the man. The man in black sunglasses."

"What man? What was his name? Did he look like a priest by any chance?"

He looked back at her, suddenly confused. "I don't...there was a man. He was my friend. We were going to change the world." He looked around suddenly disgusted "But it was here that changed, it was me."

Christ, here come the waterworks again, Dark Eris thought inside.

The boy started to cry again. "I did change, I became the monster. I just wanted things to change, to be better. I don't...I didn't want this."

Once again, he stared at the hanging bodies, "I need to die. Everything will be better when I die."

Trust me, if he did what he said, everything will most certainly not be better when he dies. He would take the express bus straight to Hell,

Dark Eris thought inside. *We're wasting time. Cut him loose and let's try to find Christopher.*

"Hush," Eris said.

"I won't. I have to die," the boy said.

This time he resisted harder as she pushed him down. If she hadn't been there he would be dead by now. Like the rest of them. That was some coincidence, all four of them hanging themselves. Seemed odd that at least one of them wouldn't have balked at the idea of suicide, no matter their crimes.

It's still controlling them, thought Dark Eris from inside.

"What?" Eris asked out loud.

"I have to die," the boy said. He was pleading with her, but he was also reluctant. A part of him was looking for an excuse to not go through with it.

I'm guessing whatever force was controlling or manipulating these hackers, if that's what they are, gave them one last command. To kill themselves.

"I've got to get him out of here," Eris said. "What's your name?"

He focused on her again. "Who do you keep talking to, is there someone else here?"

"Sort of. Now tell me what your name is."

"Juan, Juan Flores. I think." He laughed, maybe a little too hysterically. "I'm not even sure of my name anymore. But yeah, Juan is as good as any."

"Juan, we need to get out of here," Eris said. She looked quickly around the room. There was another door besides the one she came through. "Where does that door go?"

Juan looked vaguely at the door and said something in Spanish.

"English," Eris said.

"I don't know. I never noticed it until now. This whole place is different. It was better, cleaner, not this pig sty. I think it was in a large building." He shook his head. "It's all gone now. Whatever it was, it was pretend. This is reality."

He looked at her once again. "I really didn't want this to happen. I didn't..."

He was stronger now, a little more in control.

Whoever is controlling him is losing it. Or letting him go, Dark Eris thought from the inside.

We have to take him with us, Eris thought back.

What? Take the mortal with us to fight demon hordes? That would be mean even for me. He wouldn't last a minute.

"We can't leave him here, he'll kill himself the minute I leave," she said, this time out loud. Juan looked at her with a mixture of curiosity and bemusement.

I don't think so, I think he's back in control. In shock. Probably psychologically damaged beyond all repair. But he is *gaining control back.*

Eris thought for a moment. "Is there a place you can hide?"

Juan looked at her blankly. She couldn't tell if he was still confused or trying to think of a place.

"You mean like a closet?" he said suddenly.

"Yeah, sure. That would work. A closet."

"I think we have large storage closets in the server room."

He nodded to the big glass door.

"Listen to me, Juan. I don't have time to explain, but I need to leave. I'm going to look for whoever made you do this and try to stop him."

"I can come with you," he said. "I need to make up for what I have done."

"You don't understand. These are really bad guys..."

"I get it, but no offense—I know guys and girls are equal—but how are you supposed to stop them? I don't think two of us will have a much better chance, but I got nothing to live for anyway."

"I can take care of myself. Some things are not always what they seem."

"No way. You're just one girl; if they were able to do all this," he gestured vaguely around them. "Then you don't stand a chance."

If you are really serious about saving this kid, then it's time to shift his world view. Out of the way, I'm taking over, Dark Eris thought.

"Wait I..." Eris couldn't finish before she was yanked back from control.

Her body shifted, twisting and turning as Dark Eris took control and transformed into her demon form. Juan's eyes shifted from melancholy detachment to wide open with fear as the gigantic skeletal body took shape in front of his eyes.

She grabbed the kid by the neck and lifted him off the ground.

"How ya like me now?" Dark Eris said.

Juan screamed and clawed at her huge bony hand.

Great! You just traumatized him for life, Eris thought.

"You ready to get in the closet?" Dark Eris asked the kid.

He yelled something in Spanish.

"I'll take that as a yes."

She dragged him into the server room. It was cold, far lower temperature than the other room. It smelled of electricity, metal and wires. The background hum of the working servers filled the room.

She spotted the storage closet, but then hesitated.

"If I were to destroy these machines, would it stop what's going on out there?"

Juan swallowed hard and tried to speak. She gave him a moment; it was hard to think straight when staring down a monster like her.

Eventually he shook his head. "No, it is too late, all the code is out there in the real world doing damage. Destroying these won't help..."

"What?" she said and shook him slightly. "I don't have time for this."

"I can use them to help," he said and she was surprised at the new strength she heard in his voice.

"You can fix this? Why didn't you say so?" she was angry and it showed ten times worse on her skull-like face.

He paled, but continued. "I can't fix it. It's too...complicated for that. But I might be able to at least help."

He's having a hard time looking at you, no offense; let me take over, Eris thought. *We got his attention.*

Her body shifted and twisted down into her mortal body. She dropped Juan to the ground as she became Eris once again.

"They think all of you have committed suicide. If they come through that room and see you still alive, you won't be for more than a moment."

Juan stared at her, shocked at the transformation. She could tell any trust she had earned with him had taken a hit. He looked at the rack upon rack of servers. "I don't need to be at my workstation. I can work in here, directly on one of the boxes. I just need a laptop, and we got a bunch back here. I can hide behind one of the racks."

Eris wasn't convinced.

"Look, I can't stop what I helped to start, but I might be able to slow it down, maybe save some lives. At least get some emergency services back online. I don't know what was happening to me, I don't know how much is my fault or how much is their fault, but I have to try even if it means dying. And no, I'm not suicidal anymore."

He's right, Dark Eris thought, *whatever was manipulating him has faded. He's lucky he's so strong.*

"Okay, but stay hidden. We'll come back for you when it's all over," Eris said. She had wasted enough time in here already. She needed to find Christopher. There was only one other door out of the other room. It was her only option.

"Why?"

That stopped her before she could get to the door and she turned back to Juan.

"Why? I'm just a nobody. Why do you care?"

That surprised her. *Yeah, why do we care*? Thought Dark Eris. It was a thought, but it wasn't full of the usual sarcasm, it was a genuine question. And Eris had an answer for them both.

"I have seen what happens when someone who needs to care the most stops caring. And I don't want to lose that strength."

She turned and went through the door, shutting it behind her. The hallway beyond was narrow with a low ceiling. She would have to stay in human form for the moment. It had plain concrete walls for about twenty feet before giving way to natural rock wall. The hallway quickly became a passage that twisted and turned, sloping downward.

She rounded a bend and came face to face with a large metal door. She came on it so fast it caught her by surprise. The wall around this door was man made, but ancient, with primitive yet intricate carvings covering them floor to ceiling. This place was old. Dark Eris inside could smell it. Ancient, yet a little familiar.

The door however, was all modern. Thick steel it looked like. There was no way she was getting through that thing without using her demonic form. The passage had opened up as it approached the door and she was able to shift her shape. This time, however, she felt more pangs of pain as she shifted and a wave of exhaustion rolled over her. It was taking a toll, this switching back and forth. The human body was not meant for such repeated trauma.

She seized the metal door and ripped it from the hinges. Beyond was a large open room, a small cavern really. Tall enough for her to easily stand at her full height. The ceiling was covered in stalactites, except for a large space in the center the floor was a forest of stalagmites, most covered in ancient writing or a type of pictograph. The floor was also covered with symbols, some she recognized as the first language, but the meaning eluded her. The floor writing was recent, done with modern paint.

As with the passage behind her, there was no light, but she could see. The dark holds no secrets from the children of Hell. There, just part way across the large room, stood the Demon Collector. He stood as though he had been waiting patiently since the beginning of time for her to open the door. He held an unlit torch with a shaft that touched the ground.

Reacting on instinct, she roared and charged forward toward her prey. The Collector didn't flinch. He tapped the torch on the ground and the top bloomed into flame. Then he dragged the end of the shaft through the rock in a straight line, connecting a circle.

Too late she realized the trap. She came to a sudden stop. At her feet appeared a circle covered in symbols, and she was at the center. She felt trapped, like there was some sort of invisible cage around her, pressing in, pushing her down. She was suddenly claustrophobic, she wanted to scream in panic. She spread her wings to try and fly, but she couldn't; they sprang out from her back, useless appendages.

The Demon Collector, dressed in his anachronistic priest regiments, glasses slightly askew on his nose, spoke some words. Quick, guttural sounds in a long-forgotten language. And then she was hit over the head by a giant sledgehammer. It slammed through her body, forcing it to change and shift back to its mortal form. Dark Eris fell away deep down inside, far away from the light of consciousness.

Only Eris was left, on her knees sobbing quietly. The pain was immense, to have her psyche physically dominated. Dark Eris was an invader in her mind and soul, but to have her ripped away like that. It left a hollow ache inside. Dark Eris was still there, somewhere, but not close anymore.

"Interesting. He said you would come," the Demon Collector spoke. "The little man with slicked back hair said you would come through those doors and here you are."

He knelt down so he was on the same level as Eris. He didn't break the circle, but he was close enough she could smell his breath. It smelled like he was rotting inside.

"Like a present, just for me. I thought him mortal, but maybe there is something more to that little man. He knows so much."

She could hear noises from behind the stalagmites, shuffling, sucking noises. Without Dark Eris she could not see far in the dark. In the shadows beyond the little pool of light of the torch she saw movement. Human shapes, but not entirely; she saw blood and swollen flesh. The shadows held monsters.

The Collector reached out a hand and gently touched Eris' cheek. It was cold and slick with sweat. He could break the circle now, there was nothing to fear from this simple girl.

"I want to see your insides. The searching is half the fun." He ran his hand down her jaw and brushed her lip. Her stomach turned, his touch revolting. She wanted to pull away, but all her energy was gone. She couldn't move. "It will be my pleasure to collect you."

23

Eris!

Christopher acted without thinking. He leapt toward the top of the pyramid. Power raged though him and billowed out, darker than the shadows around him, darker than the deepest night. The Weapon arced into a large blade, infused with all the power of damnation radiating along its length.

He felt the satisfaction of seeing the giant man and the Collector flinch back as he flew through the air. The girl however, didn't move, didn't flinch; the little girl that could have been easily crushed by the power he was bringing towards her did not seem to care.

She stared at the glow in her hand and then she poked at it.

Christopher felt something wrench sideways in his gut. But it wasn't in his gut, it was deeper, so much deeper. And it hurt.

He screamed and his flight was caught up short. The power wrapping around him suddenly faltered. He fell to the steps of the pyramid. He smashed into the stone adding more bruises and cuts to his already beaten body. The Weapon fell from his grasp and clattered down the side of the pyramid. More cracks were added to his ribs, and he could feel his left shoulder separate as soon as he made contact with the stone.

But none of that was as painful or crippling as the pain inside. He couldn't even say where it came from, just a deep ache. He could feel something growing underneath it, something twisted and cruel. He looked up at the girl.

She smiled down at him with a smile half mad, half smug. Whatever was happening to him was coming from her.

"I did it. I did it," she spoke almost too quietly to hear.

"You've done something my dear. The question is, what?" The large man said.

"I can control him. He is mine," she whispered.

She was the key. Christopher was doubled over in pain, but he thought he could fight it. He spotted the Weapon a few feet away, propped up against one of the larger stones. He needed that. Without the Weapon he was useless.

With a grunt he tried to straighten out and crawl gingerly to where it lay.

"Control him," The large man said louder.

Christopher felt a fresh jab at the spot inside she was so expertly torturing. He cried out again and curled back into the fetal position. He looked back at her, she still had the vicious grin across her face. He hated that grin.

With his own grimace, he was moving again toward the Weapon.

"I said stop him, girl!" The large man yelled this time. Clearly, he was losing patience.

"I am trying. Look! I can hurt him."

"Hurting is not good enough. Even I could do that. He is useless to me if I can't control him."

"I just need more time. I'm close, I understand so much more now. Look, look how much it affects him this close." the girl said.

Christopher could see her squeeze the glowing vial in her hand. The he felt it a horrible sensation of depression closing in on him. It was like the air around him had suddenly become thick with tangible melancholy. It pressed in on him from every side and flowed in with his breath. He fell once again to his knees.

He crawled a little closer to the Weapon, each step was like lifting a thousand pounds. But for every foot he moved forward, it became a little easier. He was resisting and winning, slowly. Maybe too slowly.

She squeezed again, at least it felt like she had. The pain and now sadness increased. She seemed to be able to attack him with emotional pain. It was more devastating than physical. A part of him didn't want to fight, a part of him just wanted to give in to what she did. But he fought on.

He fell to the stone again, but now he was close to the Weapon. If he could just grasp it, he would have something, something to work with. He reached for it. It was close, so close.

Then he saw a splash of red next to it, then another. Rain drops of red fell around it, splashed along its blade. Then, just as his fingers brushed the hilt, a shiny red hand grasped it. Liquid crimson, like polish, coated that hand. The hand of a blood demon.

The Weapon instantly transformed again, back into the unobtrusive, plain pocket knife. And the demon picked it up. It would not be the Weapon for him, but while the creature had it, it wouldn't work for Christopher either.

"Well, that's that," said the Demon Collector.

"I suppose so," said the large man. "Somewhat anti-climactic. I was hoping for something... well I don't know, he is just a mortal. Kill him."

"No!" the girl screamed. "I need him, I need to practice. I swear I will get better. I promise."

Christopher heard a loud slap. The large man had hit the girl. She lay sprawled on the stone.

"Hush girl, you know not to speak to me that way. You had your chance and I will admit, it was not bad for a first try. But you are a witch. You have so much potential; we will find you more to experiment with. But this subject, this subject is too dangerous. I was hoping that you would learn the control quickly and we could turn him to serve, but you have far to go and he is too unpredictable to keep around."

"But this is the soul I have, I know it so well."

It was the missing part of his soul she held in her hands, Christopher realized. It was obvious now. That was the weapon they used against him, his own soul. The way he had changed, it was the girl, just as Eris had said...

Eris!

She was still hanging there, but she had awakened at some point. She looked down at him, tears streaming down her face. She mouthed words: *I'm so sorry*.

Christopher stood, the weight on his soul could not hold him down and he started climbing the stairs. The girl's eyes widened in surprise.

"You see, he is weak of course, easily dispatched at this point, but not fully under your control," the large man said.

Christopher ignored what they were saying to each other. He didn't even know who these people were. He had to get to Eris.

"The Alliance has more use for you Grace, but this one must end," the large man said. "We have what we need from this place. We found what we needed for the gate and it is time to go. This place is a dead place now, a killing ground for one last time before being shut in the dark forever. It is time for us to leave.

The mention of the Alliance caught Christopher's attention. They were the group behind all this. Even though he was about twenty feet below them, the large man noticed Christopher's hesitation.

"Yes boy, great Hunter," the large man said. He was at the edge of the stone platform looking down. Christopher hated that he was on his knees crawling. "I don't know who tipped you off, but this is all of our making, these Days of Chaos. Poetic don't you think? As we speak, chaos ravages Mexico City, we have bent modern technology to our will. We control the digital lives of the mortals and we can take it away at a moment’s notice."

He moved down the steps a little way to get a better look at Christopher. His bulk was so huge, it looked at any moment like he would topple down the side, but he moved with the grace of a man many times smaller.

Keep him talking Christopher thought. Just like in the Bond movies. The bad guys always liked to talk. He had no idea what it would accomplish, but it always seemed to work out for James.

"Hacking can be stopped, back doors plugged, passwords reset. You'll do damage, but no lasting impact," Christopher said. It came out as a series of gasps as he fought against the crushing of his soul.

"But that is only half the picture. The mortals are the real weapon.” The large man gestured back at the Demon Collector. “My friend's army walks among them, killing, causing their own violent chaos. As the mortals respond with fear and anger, the city will burn."

He took a few more steps down. Christopher crawled closer, saving his strength. If only he could get his hands on the big guy. He was sure he was the leader here. If he could just lay a hand on him. He may not have the Weapon, but he still had the power, and if he could fight whatever it is that the girl was doing he might be able to catch him off guard.

"But why Mexico City? Why here?

"That's the best part. This is only the beginning, this is just the first city. It was sort of a trial run," a smile spread across the large face. "We needed something here in this pyramid, and it turned out to be a great place to set up temporary shop, kill two birds with one stone kind of a thing. And it worked beautifully. We were even able to trap the great Hunter of Lost Souls."

A step closer.

"Frankly I'm disappointed. I have no clue how you defeated Rath, let alone that monstrosity that Anabelle created..."

As if on cue a dark blur shot out of the darkness and slammed into the large man. It was Hellcat, jaws snapping, claws poised to shred. But the large man was quick, quicker than he should be for his size. His arm sliced through the air and smashed into Hellcat before she could make contact with either tooth or claw. It was like she was hit by a tree trunk, and she fell down the side of the pyramid, tumbling limply down the stone blocks.

Christopher didn't see if Hellcat was alive or conscious, now was his chance while the man was still recovering from Hellcat's attack. He surged upward through the dark physical and mental depression and sprang at the large man. His weapon was gone, but he still had the hell power inside and he could at least do some damage. He had no other option.

He pulled power from the shadows and tried to focus the energy into his fists. He felt the witch squeezing his soul again, but he fought through it.

Again, the man moved incredibly quickly, and he caught Christopher by the neck, abruptly stopping his flight. The hand was a steel clamp around his throat, stronger than anything he had felt before. His air was instantly cut off. In a moment of panic, he clawed at the man's sausage fingers, trying to pull them away. But it was like pulling at rock. Then he looked into the man's eyes.

His soul was suddenly laid out for Christopher. His aura was the darkest black. Darker and more twisted than even Rath's had been. This man's power was immense and so was his evil, it stretched back thousands of years. He had killed thousand and would gladly kill a thousand more, a million. Whatever it took to rule. He was the most twisted, most vile dark soul Christopher had ever seen.

And he had just plucked Christopher out of the air like he was nothing more than an insect.

"You're just a kid, a pitiful little kid," the man said. His breath smelled like the way Christopher imagined a mortuary would smell, harsh chemical scents covering a perpetual rot. The large man slammed him down on the ground like he was a scrap of cloth. The stone steps beneath him cracked from the concussion, and pain exploded across his back. His head slammed against the rock, bouncing. For a moment the world went black, then came back with blurry images and smudged colors.

The large man was moving away from him. "And here I thought you a threat."

Christopher couldn't move, his whole body felt broken. And it didn't matter. Without the Weapon, hell even with it, he doubted he would have been able to defeat this powerful dark soul. He had swatted both Hellcat and himself like they were nothing more than an irritation.

"Enough of this Golyat," said the Demon Collector said. "I want to collect my prize."

As the world found some semblance of focus, Christopher could see the large man looking back at the Demon Collector with something approaching disgust. But Christopher doubted the

Collector even noticed. He stared at Eris with a hunger that turned Christopher's stomach.

It looked like the big man—Golyat—was going to say something when his cellphone rang. Christopher wasn't too surprised. They had run power down here to do whatever it was they were doing. It made sense they'd run communication lines. Golyat paused and fished it out of his pocket.

"Yes," Golyat answered.

This might be another chance. Hellcat still lay on the ground, but she looked at Christopher with a fierceness that let him know she was ready to try again. For a cat she was one vicious bitch.

"What the hell do you mean systems are coming back online? That's impossible. Is Mr. Stone there?"

Golyat stepped back onto the top of the pyramid. "That son of a bitch. I knew he was a weak link. Socialist bastard. I'm on my way." He slipped the phone back into his pocket. To the Collector he said, "There are complications. Release the rest of your army on the city. We have to speed up the timeline. Kill the Hunter and bring me the Book and Weapon."

He glanced at Eris hanging limply, pretending to be unconscious. He waved vaguely in her direction. "Do what you want with the girl, do...whatever it is that you do. Just dispose of her. Then abandon this place. Our work here is done."

He turned to the witch, she had never stopped glaring at Christopher. "Come Grace. The experiment is over. We will find you a less dangerous subject for your practice."

Her face twisted in rage and she snarled at Christopher before she stamped her foot like a spoiled child. "You messed it all up, I hope you suffer." Then she squeezed.

Horror whipped around him and crushed in. The breath left him and he fell back down to the ground as the strength left his arms. Golyat grabbed her by the arm and dragged her out of

Christopher's view over the edge of the pyramid. There must have been some passage or stairs through the pyramid, some back-up escape route.

But Christopher didn't have time to think it through. As the pain and pressure lessened around him, he suspected it was because the witch was moving away from him, weakening the link.

Christopher finally was able to stand all the way up. He was still weak, dizzy and bruised, broken in many places, but he stood. The Collector looked down at him. Flesh and blood demons surrounded him, the rest just below Christopher on the pyramid. There were a lot of them, but not as many as before. But then again Golyat had said that most of his army was out in the city causing chaos.

"I expected more from the Lord of Hell," The Collector said and Christopher looked up sharply. "Kill h..."

"What did you say?" Christopher asked.

"I said, kill him," The Collector repeated.

"No, I meant before," Christopher said. But it was too late.

The closest demon, a Blood, clawed at him. He wasn't sure if it was the one that had taken his Weapon or not, they all looked the same. But it didn't matter. His fist was a blur as it smashed into the demon's face. It fell back against its brethren. Like a domino effect, others were knocked down, but it barely made a dent in their numbers.

The next one came and then the next, Flesh and Blood working together, attacking as one. They surged at him and he punched and kicked, fueled by the Hellpower inside. For each he knocked back, two more appeared in its place and his punches and kicks were not as effective as using the Weapon. Strikes slowed them, but they did not stop.

From the corner of his eye he could see the top of the pyramid. The Collector had turned from him. He tore open Eris' shirt and laid a wicked looking knife against her smooth, pale stomach. She stopped playing dead and tried to kick him, and although her legs were secured to the posts, she managed to knock the knife out of his hand in a clatter to the floor.

He slapped her with crack that cut through the wet moans of the demons.

"Eris!" Christopher screamed. She had saved him so many times, and here he was unable to do anything to help her. Fury raged in him. He struck again and again at the demons. But he could still feel it, the hollowness of something missing; now he knew it was the piece of his soul. Eris had figured that out early on.

A demon clutched his arm. He wrenched it away and punched it, but another claw soon followed trapping him again. Another sunk his teeth into his shoulder. Eris screamed and he could see the Collector sinking the blade into her stomach.

In a rage Christopher threw the demons from him. They fell back at his violent outburst, but even he knew it was only a matter of time before they took him down.

If only he were whole.

The Hellpower flared up inside and he thought of something. He had accepted this power inside of him as a partner, and they held an uneasy truce, a truce that had allowed him to defeat the were-hellhound. But a partnership was all it had ever been.

Then he knew what he had to do. Even if it meant destroying who he was. That seed of hell had always been separate, like the demons that possessed the bodies around him. They shared a body, but were not the same. He had channeled the power through him, giving it its freedom. But never was it truly part of him. But now he had a piece missing inside...a hole to fill.

The demons were on him now. He was still fighting them off, but he had more important work. They pulled at him, gouged his flesh as he pushed them off and struck at them. These might be low level demons, but there were enough to kill him. He was weakening fast.

Mentally he pictured the seed of Hell inside of him and pulled it into his own soul. He wrapped it up, knitting it into his very being. It hurt. It burned. But it also felt right. It spread throughout him seeping into all his secret places. And as it touched every part of him he knew things, he began to understand. But he also changed. With knowledge comes change, and this at its core was the darkest of knowledge, this then was a dark change.

He could feel a coldness growing inside, but he did not have time to consider it. He was on his knees by now, throwing off the demons when he could. But more and more teeth and claws got through. His clothing—his real clothing, not just his shadow clothes—and his flesh were in tatters. But he understood something now, he did not know yet exactly what it meant, but he was sure of something.

For all his confidence, for all his learning and seeking power, the Collector had gone too far. Demons were the domain of Hell.

And Hell was his.

A huge head bearing a wide mouth lined with shark-like teeth swooped toward Christopher's face.

"Stop," said Christopher. And his words carried ancient weight stretching back from the beginning of time. He put no real power behind it, just the force of will from his newly re-forged soul. He didn't argue with it, he didn't *allow* it to work through him. The power, the will, it *was* him.

As one the demons stopped. Looks shifting between confused and concern spread across the demoniacally twisted human faces.

"Go home," Christopher commanded in that same soft voice full of dark will.

The demon closest, the one who had almost bitten off his face, suddenly stiffened, its face went slack. A glowing started in its chest, slowly making its way up through its throat and into its jaw. As soon as the glow hit its head, it leaned its head back and opened its mouth like a silent scream to the heavens. The glowing orb burst out from its mouth, stretching the lips out like it was giving birth. The orb popped out and floated upwards. The body left behind went limp and fell, an empty and used husk.

The glowing orb floated above them all for a moment before fading into nothing. Around him other demons were going slack, their orbs floating up and fading in the same way. One by one the empty mortal bodies fell to the ground, starting with those closest to him.

A clanging sound caught Christopher's attention. The Weapon had clattered to the floor as the body that had held it fell. Christopher reached down and picked it up. The power surged in him as he once again held the Weapon. But it was different this time, he wasn't just an observer. He understood the Weapon a little better now.

The demons that had been further away had looked confused for a moment as their brethren slipped away from their bodies. Now, they surged forward, some howling in confusion. He realized they may not have heard his voice.

"GO," Christopher cried.

The group surged back as though slapped. Then more orbs of power could be seen floating from the demons.

"NO!" screamed the Collector. "What have you done to my collection? They are mine!"

"No, Fredrick Bailey. They were never yours. You were not collecting, you were stealing."

"No! My power! What have you done to my power?"

The Collector looked down at the corpses in dismay. Tears forming in his eyes, his lower lip trembled. His hands, holding what looked like a scalpel, dripped with blood. Behind the little man Eris still hung from the pillars, but now she had a large gash across her gut, deep enough that the shiny reflection of her organs could be seen.

He needed to help her, fast. But he didn't move. At some level he felt an urgency to run to her. But a coldness had settled in him. He hesitated to see what the Collector was going to do.

"It was never your power you little thief," Christopher said. "You learned a trick maybe, but you are still a common little thug from the slums."

The little man looked at him sharply, glaring through the tears.

"Yes Freddy, I know all about you. You and your sick little games. You thought they meant something, but they didn't, they never got you anywhere."

"No, they were my prize, my collection. I was the master."

"No Freddy, you were the babysitter."

The Collector screamed, face red with anger. It would have been funny if his body hadn't been growing, changing. His flesh started to boil, faces, only vaguely human slid across his skin.

His clothing ripped away and he quickly outgrew his priest's cassock. More faces had appeared and rose from his skin, trying to burst through. The expressions were of eternal torment. By the time he had stopped growing he had more than doubled in height. Bony protrusions pierced the skin at his joints.

The Collector's own face had swollen, lips, nose, and brow distended like he had been attacked by the world's most sadistic bee swarm. As Christopher watched, the fleshy face turned gray. His skin was hardening to a bony mass of some sort. He bellowed and all the faces sliding just under his skin let out silent screams.

It looks like I made it to the boss level, Christopher thought. *The faces, perhaps a dozen, must be the demons inside of him, the last of his collection.*

"Depart," Christopher commanded. The faces stirred, then stretched and twisted in the hardening skin as though trying to get out.

The Collector made a deep rumbling noise. It took a moment for Christopher to realize he was laughing.

"I can hold on to these. Your words will not work as I hold them tight. They are my favorites and they give me more than enough power."

The Collector leapt down, sailing over carved stone stairs. Christopher dodged to the side, jumping across the face of the pyramid. The Weapon, now a long sword, slashed the air and clanged a glancing blow against the Collector's new, armored protrusions. It didn't penetrate the tough bone, but it took a chunk out.

The Collector howled. He moved toward Christopher on the other face of the pyramid.

"I will kill you boy, you have changed nothing. The rest of my collection runs through the city above, killing and indulging other violent delights. Your words of command will never reach them. The chaos they caused will be multiplied a hundred times in the each of the cities to follow..."

He had reached the edge of his side of the pyramid and was about to round the corner when Hellcat, a black blur of fur and fang, came wailing out of the shadows and onto the Collector's back. Hellcat sunk her teeth into one of the only fleshy parts left on the Collector, his swollen neck, and tore at it. The Collector wailed and tried to get at the beast on his back. But his arms, swollen with the energy of the demons within, were too large; his own body was Hellcat's shield.

Christopher saw his chance. He darted forward, slicing at the demon collage of a man. The Collector, perhaps sensing a greater danger than the cat, dodged to the side. Christopher's blade missed the target, but he recovered quickly enough that even one of his new teachers might have been impressed. The blade missed flesh, but it changed instantly into a mace and struck bone again, this time in the Collector's knee. The bone shattered at the blunt impact. Once again, the Weapon had chosen the perfect form.

The Collector howled and fell. Hellcat sprung from his back as he teetered. He fell down the face of the pyramid, holding his knee and screaming the whole time. Christopher didn't give him time to recover. He was at the bottom in a single jump, tendrils of his dark power, now more like extensions of himself than ever before, swirled about him and propelled him to the base of the pyramid.

The Collector hit the ground with a crunch and tried to roll to his feet, but Christopher was there, with the Weapon. As the Collector rolled to his knees, he raised his arm to block Christopher's strike. The mace clanged against the bony ridge along the Collector's arm, splintering more bone. But the Collector was still fighting; one blow from that bony fist and Christopher would never be able to recover.

Then Christopher noticed the faces. They were swarming. And where they rippled over his body, the bony surface moved like water; it couldn't be solid where the faces were. Now they were all gathering at his chest, mouths opened wide like a dozen birds looking for food. But it wasn't food they wanted, they were looking to him to feed them.

He swung the mace one last time straight down at the crouching giant. The Collector raised both his arms to ward off the blow. Just before it connected however, Christopher pulled the strike, and with a command obeyed quicker than ever, the Weapon turned into a long sword. Christopher lunged forward and the blade sank into the weak spot of a demon's mouth gaping open on the Collector's torso.

It hooked the dark soul instantly and Christopher, pulled tearing the soul from it earthly shell. The Collector screeched and tried to hold onto the soul pulling away like wet glue. But he could not stop the Weapon from slurping up his essence. He looked up at Christopher.

"I'll return, with a larger collection. They will bring me back through the gate and I will start my collection again. I will return."

The light went out of the Collector's eyes as the last piece of his soul disappeared into the satiated Weapon.

24

Eris!

Christopher leapt to the top of the pyramid, propelled by his tendrils of power. He landed by her side and his blade flashed, slashing through the ropes binding her to the columns. She collapsed in his arms, barely conscious.

Her stomach was sliced open and blood soaked the front of her jeans and tattered remains of her shirt.

"Eris! Eris! Listen to me. Where is Dark Eris? She can help heal you, you need to let her take over."

"She's gone," Eris said. Her voice was barely above a whisper.

"Gone? But...how?" And then realization dawned. He had commanded the demons home, to Hell. "But I didn't mean for...I didn't want her to go." Christopher said and realized it was true. He didn't want Dark Eris to go, he didn't want Eris dying in his arms.

"No, she is here. Just deep down inside, he...he did something to her," Eris said. Her eyes fluttered closed, then opened again.

"I'll get you to a hospital. I can get you there, you need to hold on," Christopher said. He thought he might be crying.

"No, it is all chaos up there. I don't know if the hospitals are even working. It's too late." She paused to swallow hard. "You, you're different. You are worse, darker than before. It's not good. Promise me you will stop. I love the man you were, not the monster you are becoming."

Her eyes sank closed again.

"You must find Juan," she whispered, but her eyes remained closed.

Fuck this shit.

Christopher gathered her in his arms and jumped from the pyramid. Power flowed around him and carried him across the cavern. The rage and anger flowed through him pulling and pushing him along faster, faster. When he landed at the base of the stairs his power propelled him forward and up through the spiral staircase.

Tendrils snaked out, carrying him up like a cross between an octopus and Spiderman. He flew up the stairs cutting the turns so close his shoulder crashed through stone. He sheltered Eris' body with his own and when he checked she still breathed, slowly and weakly.

In moments he was at the top of the stairs and charging through the empty black house. He couldn't hear Hellcat following, he assumed that meant she had faded. He couldn't pause to check, he had only one thought.

Save Eris.

The streets outside the house were still deserted, but in the distance, he could hear the chaos. Screams and gunfire. Parts of the slums glowed red from fires. It wasn't limited to the slum area either; from the amount of light all around him he would bet the rest of the city burned as well.

He had no idea where the nearest hospital was and Eris was right. The city was in chaos. Even if he found one, who knows if there would be anyone to help.

He had only one option. He leapt to the rooftops and shot through the slums. He jumped from roof to roof, dark power swirling around him pulling him through the city as though he almost flew. He didn't care about being seen, he didn't care about his own safety. All that mattered was getting Eris help.

The streets were full of people and fire and death. People stood stunned, but most screamed and ran. Others looted, taking what they could and beating down those who tried to stop them. He saw the occasional body, some returning to mortal form as a demon left its husk. Damning the Collector had ended his power over them, and they were returning home.

He may have stopped the Collector, but a lot of damage was done. It would take years to rebuild the city, to recover from this crazy night of violence.

But he didn't care about that now. He went straight to the lair. The poor souls in the street outside the slum entrance to the lair scattered as he descended from the rooftops. Some probably knew him from the internet, others just ran because he was fury incarnate. Shadow power rolled out from him and knocked aside everyone in his path.

He passed through the secret door and with one well-placed blow he knocked the rusty steel door off its hinges. He shot down the tunnel and into the lair.

Hamlin jumped up from the computer.

"What the hell happened..." Hamlin's words trailed off as he saw Eris' blood soaked front. "Oh my god."

"There's a hospital a few blocks from the zoo," Christopher said to him as he headed straight for the cube room. To Eris he said, "Hold on, just a few more minutes. Just hold on."

But Christopher was scared. She didn't move, he wasn't sure she was even breathing. She was dead weight in his arms.

25

The lights flickered.

Juan looked up from the computer screen. It wasn't the first time they had flickered; in fact the intervals seemed to be speeding up. Juan took a bite from the Dorito and chewed slowly. He only had a couple of bags of chips left and a sketchy-looking frozen dinner.

The computer screen didn't flicker, they were on a battery backup. Eventually as the power went out down here they would fade to black too, but for now. It was his only contact with the outside world. He had watched as his city came to its senses the next day like a college kid nursing one hell of a hangover and trying to remember exactly what happened.

Juan had worked for two days straight. First, he took down the bodies and put them in the large storage cabinets in the cold server room. It wasn't ideal, but it kept the smell reasonable. Then he went to work fixing, tweaking, helping where he could. He fixed systems he had been manipulated into damaging. He got emergency services back online as fast as possible, as well as aircraft control. He even siphoned money from rich assholes and used it to purchase medical supplies to be sent to clinics.

But it would never be enough. Never enough to make up for what he had done. It wouldn't be much longer now anyway. The water was still running, but when the power went the pump would shut down. His food was almost gone. The last thing to go would be the servers, but they couldn't last forever.

He had looked at the elevator, but it was no use. There was no way he could get it working again. He didn't need the doors, but the motor was shot and it was getting no power anyway.

He thought he could send out a message via social media, send an email to the police. But then he realized two things. One, he had no idea where he was—although he could triangulate based on his network location, they wouldn't find him deep underground—and two, he was pretty sure he didn't deserve to live.

But he wanted to. He had stayed here to fix as much as possible, but it might be time to try that other door, see where it could take him. When he had glanced through, it looked like dark tunnels. But it must lead somewhere right?

He heard a thud from above. Distant, but echoing throughout the room. It sounded like it was coming from the elevator shaft. He stood up trying to decide if he should go to the door or not when he heard a loud crash followed by the sound of screeching metal. He decided it would be best if he didn't go see what was behind that door.

In the end it didn't matter. It came for him.

The door to the computer room slammed open and darkness spilled in. A figure stood in the doorway, a band of power arcing from him. Juan jumped and ran to the far wall of the room, his back pressed up against the glass wall of the server room.

The figure came through the door. The shadows seemed to bend around him as though he were the master of darkness itself. The figure was cloaked all in black, his coat shifting shades of dark as though sewn from shadows. A hood covered his head and the darkness under that hood was the worst yet. Juan could feel the menace, the sheer power from whoever or whatever lived under there.

It was like seeing the devil himself. As the man came through the door the power came with him. Such strength that Juan could feel it, could almost taste it.

It was the devil and he had come for Juan. It made sense. What he had done, the demon girl who had found him. At least she had seemed nice. He stood a little straighter. If this was the end, he deserved it. He would not go with fear. But as the figure got closer and closer he felt his resolve weakening.

"So, Satan, you have come to take me to Hell? I am ready, and I will go proudly," Juan said.

"You're Juan, right?" the man said.

"Yes, I am Juan Flor..." Juan let it trail off.

A large panther, although it was too big to be a true panther, padded around the side of the figure then sat and started grooming itself.

"You did most of this? All of this computer stuff? The hacking, the damage?" The man asked.

"Yes, I did. It was all my fault and I know I deserve..."

"And you know a lot about computers, setting this stuff up, maybe running large systems in disparate locations around the world?"

"Um, yes, I guess..." Juan was getting confused.

"Would you like a chance at redemption? Some way to make up for all that you have done?"

This time Juan nodded, he was too confused to speak.

"I am not going to damn you to Hell, Juan. I only damn those worthy of such punishment. Unfortunately, I am here to offer you something almost as bad. A job."

26

Mr. Stone walked down the long cement hallway. To one side was a balcony with evenly spaced columns. Bright light, generated from massive lamps hanging above the large warehouse, flooded in between the columns and left long shadows every few feet. Mr. Stone hated light, the shadows were more his speed.

And as he passed through, each shadow stretched out further on the hallway floor, a piece of Mr. Stone sloughed off into the shadows. It was as though each step through the shadows was a cleansing that purified the man a little more. Slowly Mr. Stone disappeared revealing the true man underneath.

He was tall, powerful. Hair black as ink and eyes of the bluest sapphire. When the pretend Mr. Stone was gone, Jax remained.

The phone in his pocket vibrated. He slipped it out of his jacket and answered.

"Hello Mr. Smith," Jax answered, Mr. Stone's voice was still there, even if he had cast the visual glamour aside, and Jax tried to make it appropriately fearful and concerned. "Yes Mr. Smith. I know, it did not go according to plans. We were betrayed from the inside. I admit one of my team, a young hacker, suddenly grew a conscience and tried to undo everything..."

He paused as Golyat screamed a string of words, only a handful of which were a language used in the last five hundred years. Jax understood them all, he just didn't care to listen. He stepped to the edge of the balcony, still hanging back in the shadows, however. It wouldn't do to spoil the surprise too early.

"Of course, Mr. Smith. It was a huge catastrophe, one I personally take responsibility for. But I do not think it was entirely my fault...what do I mean? Why your little hero friend from New York. I saw the news, I saw when he showed up, and I am certain he was there to foil your plans."

More screeching through the phone. Jax held it away from his ear. It was getting annoying.

"Of course, Mr. Smith. I recognize that my organization takes some of the blame for the mismanagement of the infrastructure failure, although you must admit it was quite spectacular. I will make sure this does not happen again." A pause. "Yes, of course I can meet face to face. Are you back in the U.S. or still in Mexico? I can be on a plane and meet you in a few days."

Golyat had calmed, but his words still dripped with violence. Jax wasn't worried, he was a challenge but ultimately controllable. Jax knew, he had seen it.

"Great I'll take the first flight I can...okay yes, I can charter a flight. I will be there in forty-eight hours."

Jax hit the end call button and slipped the phone back into his pocket. Then he gazed down at the warehouse floor far beneath him. The warehouse was bustling with people making preparations.

Carved into the concrete floor of the warehouse was a circle fifty-feet in diameter. Around it, also roughly carved into the concrete, were a series of symbols and letters. The first language. Jax shook his head. The effort it had taken to have Golyat "discover" the language so he could create his gate... Jax didn't even want think about it. Sometimes he felt like he was herding monkeys with nothing but a stick and a banana.

There was Golyat now, on the warehouse floor supervising the installation of the artifact they had retrieved from the pyramid. Golyat slipped his own phone back into his pocket, his face still flushed red in anger presumably from their discussion moments before.

Sometimes Jax worried about him, you can't just hold in all that emotion. At some point Golyat was going to explode. Jax hoped he was nearby when it happened.

A large crane was setting the carved block down at the edge of the circle. Delicate and faded symbols, worn down over thousands of years, sprawled across its surface. Carved by hands that were not quite human, it was an essential component of the gate Golyat was building. As were the other artifacts surrounding the circle. Each had its place, each its purpose.

Golyat thought he was building the gate for himself; he would use it to openly rule the world. But Golyat didn't understand, he would never even be able to comprehend what he was truly building, or what purpose it would serve. It was not for him. Whether he knew it or not, he built it for Jax.

There was no organization, just as there was no Mr. Stone. There was just Jax, the puppet master, the far seer, the one who knows all.

Jax stepped back from the balcony. He reached out and with a finger, hooked the fabric of reality, and wrenched open a door to the Currents. Then with one step he was in them, flowing away.

ALSO BY ERIK LYND

NOVELS

Asylum

The Collection

THE HAND OF PERDITION SERIES:

Book and Blade

Eater of Souls

The Demon Collector

SILAS ROBB SERIES:

Silas Robb: Of Saints and Sinners

Silas Robb: Hell Hath No Fury

SHORTER WORKS

The Hanging Tree

Dark on the Water

His Devil

Dreams

Siege of the Bone Children

In the Pit

ABOUT THE AUTHOR

Erik Lynd writes novels and short stories primarily in the horror, dark fantasy, and urban fantasy genres. Currently he is in the middle of two ongoing urban fantasy series; Silas Robb and The Hand of Perdition series. He also writes the occasional horror novel such as Asylum and The Collection. He lives in the Pacific Northwest where yes it does rain a lot and no he does not mind it.

For more information...
www.eriklynd.com
erik@eriklynd.com

94584765R00323

Made in the USA
Lexington, KY
31 July 2018